POSTER BOY

BOOK 6 IN THE DCI JONES SERIES

KERRY J DONOVAN

For film lovers everywhere!

Chapter One

Near Shipton Village, Shropshire, UK

DCI DAVID JONES drained the wine glass and contemplated returning to the kitchen for a second refill but said no to the call of the slippery slope. No heavy solitary drinking for him. A small glass or two with his meal would suffice. He settled back into his comfy chair to review the end of another case. Hopefully, Melanie Archer would be able to live the life she deserved, free of the fear she'd endured for more than a decade. He'd done a good thing and allowed a satisfied smile to work its way onto a face he usually kept dour.

Seconds later, or so it seemed, the burping rattle of the mobile vibrating on the side table woke Jones from a light doze. He groaned.

Give me strength.

He snatched up the mobile and hit the "accept" option after briefly considering the alternative.

"Jones here. This better be important."

"Evening, David. It's me, Phil."

"Yes, I know it's you. I can read a caller ID when I see it." He tried to make his voice gruff, but it wasn't working.

"Sorry, boss. This isn't a social call." Phil sounded tense.

Jones sat up straighter, his senses prickling. Passing up the third glass of wine turned out to be a good idea—it meant he didn't have to wait for a lift into the city.

"Okay, Inspector. What's wrong?"

"Suspicious death in Bordesley Green. The Orchard Towers Estate. By all accounts, the body's been there a few days."

"Are you on scene?"

"Not yet. On my way there now."

"Any identification?"

"Vic Dolan's there with one of his newbies. He didn't want to say anything on the radio, but he asked me to call you out right away. Sounds serious."

Jones shot to his feet. Sergeant Victor Dolan happened to be one of the most reliable uniformed officers in Birmingham. He'd never hit the panic button and have Phil call in a DCI without justification.

"Vic's there now?"

"Yep. He's holding the fort until I arrive. The FSIs are on their way in."

"You mean the SOCOs," Jones grumbled.

"They're called Forensic Scene Investigators these days, boss."

"Not by me they aren't. We've been calling them SOCOs for years, and I see no need for the change of title. Their role's still the same, isn't it?"

"It is."

"Good. Text me the address. I'm on my way."

Chapter Two

Bordesley Green, Birmingham, UK

THE SETTING SUN SLANTED LOW. Blinding shafts of light burst through the gaps between the houses. As they drove, Dr Robyn Spence, PhD—recently appointed as one of three Team Leaders in the Racer-Colby Crime Laboratory—silently took in another part of her new domain. She'd only visited Birmingham a few times since her mother's retirement to the West Midlands, and she didn't know the UK's second largest city particularly well. After a fortnight of unpacking and trying to settle a reluctant and largely uncommunicative Zach into his new school and his new routine, she'd had precious little time to familiarise herself with her newly acquired bailiwick.

Patrick Elliott, her tall but painfully thin driver, pulled their glacier blue Range Rover to a stop at a T-junction where Broad

Avenue joined Orchard Park Road. He flicked the indicator left and waited for a line of traffic to trundle by.

"Ah, will you look at that, now?" Patrick said, nodding to the street sign. "I'd call that there a misnomer, so. I mean, the street's narrow and there's not a tree within three miles. 'Broad Avenue', indeed."

In the back, behind the driver's seat, Bill Harrap shot back in his Australian twang, "You ever think they might have chopped down all the trees to build the houses, mate?"

"In that case they should have renamed the bloody thing 'Narrow-road-with-no-room-to-drive-through-and-no-trees-either'." He shot her an apologetic glance. "Sorry, Doc. Didn't meant to swear. Slip of the tongue, it was."

Robyn smiled. "Not a problem, Patrick. But if you two carry on like this, I'll be booking you both an open mike spot at the Comedy Store."

"Ah now, you're not the first to suggest that, is she, Bill?" Patrick asked, glancing in the rear-view mirror.

"Too true, mate. I apologise for me old China's sense of humour, ma'am."

Robyn twisted in her seat and grinned at the broad-faced Aussie. "How many times do I have to ask you not to call me 'ma'am'? It makes me feel so old."

"Ah now," Patrick interjected, "hit him over the head a couple o' times with a brick and he might just get the message, so."

The traffic finally cleared and Patrick pulled the Rover into Orchard Park Road. He drove slowly for half a mile, following the directions voiced by the satnav, although he seemed reasonably familiar with the area. They turned left into Orchard Park Lane and Patrick pointed ahead to where two police cars—blue lights flashing —formed a barrier across the road.

A uniformed sergeant stood next to a young constable who looked pale and a little the worse for wear. The sergeant held up his hand and signalled for them to stop where they were—in the middle of the road. Behind them, a pair of constables rolled out crime scene tape to hold back a smattering of curious neighbours.

Another constable stood guard at a broken gate in a dilapidated wooden fence.

Patrick killed the engine ."And here we are, safe and sound, so."

The cool, early-evening sun cast a deep shadow over the houses and gardens on the western side of the road, but bathed those to the east in its bright yellow glare.

"Better than last time, mate," Bill piped up from the back. "Letting Pat drive is like playing the Lotto, Doc. Didn't anyone warn you?"

Robyn smiled again.

"Sober faces, gentlemen. This is a crime scene, remember."

"Yes, Doc," they answered in unison.

So far, everyone she'd met, both from the lab and the police, referred to Patrick Elliott and Bill Harrap as the best FSIs in the business. The fact they'd maintained the respect of their colleagues, despite being weighed down by the reputation of their former boss, Reginald "Ghastly" Prendergast, spoke volumes for their professional skills. From what she'd seen of their work so far, their reputations had been well earned.

The sergeant and his young charge approached the driver's side, and Patrick lowered his window.

"You made good time," he said to Patrick, but looked at Robyn.

Patrick made the introductions. "Sergeant Victor Dolan, this here's Dr Robyn Spence. Fresh from the Met, she is."

Sergeant Dolan's smile lit up his eyes.

"Evening, Dr Spence. I've heard a lot about you from Phil Cryer. Shame we have to meet under these ... well, you know."

"I understand, Sergeant. Are we okay here?"

"Yes, Doc. This is a cul-de-sac and we're about to close off the rest of the road."

"Is it bad?" Patrick asked, glancing towards the house being cordoned off with crime scene tape.

Dolan's eyes narrowed and his expression pinched. "Never seen anything like it, mate."

"Ah, and you've seen it all, so."

"Nothing like this, Pat. I'll leave you to it. Young Porterhouse has had a bit of a shock. He's in need of some care and attention. Dr Spence, guys, good luck."

He touched the peak of his flat cap with his index finger and shepherded the young constable away.

"That was interesting," Robyn said to Patrick. "Is he always so solicitous?"

"Huh?" Patrick asked.

"The way he looks after his troops."

"Sure and Victor's in charge of all the fledgelings. The trainees. PC Porterhouse won't have seen a dead body before, I imagine. Ah dear, I remember my first." He shuddered.

"Okay," Robyn said. "Let's get cracking, shall we?"

They climbed out of the Rover, filed around to the rear of the SUV, and struggled into white cotton coveralls and overshoes, before pulling on blue nitrile gloves. They clipped their ID cards to the breast pockets of their suits and ran a buddy check for inconsistencies.

Robyn caught sight of her reflection in the Rover's wing mirror. As usual, the outfit made her look like the Michelin Woman. The so-called extra small coveralls hung on her like a quilted duvet. When would the specialist clothing manufacturers realise petite women worked crime scenes, too?

Still, she wasn't about to sashay along the catwalk of a fashion show. She was here to do a job.

Robyn turned to the driver who loomed over her, tall and stoop-shouldered. "Patrick, you can run the outside. Bill and I will take the house and the camcorder. Follow us inside when you're done."

The Irishman nodded. "Okay, Doc. But you watch out for Bill, now. He likes to go for the artistic shots. All moody, with loads of strange angles. Sure, and he fancies himself as Mussolini behind the camera lens, so."

"Dolt, you mean Fellini. Mussolini was a fascist dictator." Bill wasn't a whole lot taller than Robyn, but he growled at the tall Irishman as though spoiling for a fight.

Patrick showed a full set of gleaming white teeth. "As I said, Mussolini!"

Bill held up a hand to shade his eyes. "At least I haven't had my teeth whitened. Jeez, mate. Those chompers are blinding. Good job we wear facemasks at a crime scene, or I'd have to tone down the brightness on the camcorder."

Robyn shook her head at their antics—so much for a sober approach—and stepped aside as Patrick grasped the handle of a large metal case. He grunted, yanked it from its retaining clips, and carried it towards the constable standing guard in front of the broken gate.

The PC jotted Patrick's name on the form attached to his clipboard, lifted police tape strung between two rotting fence posts, and stood aside. Patrick ducked under the tape and shuffled past another uniformed officer who pointed to a bay window. He placed the case on the ground well away from the windowsill, removed a digital camera, and returned to the gate to take establishing shots of the path and the section of garden beneath the window. He followed up by removing a fingerprint kit from the case.

Robyn studied the tall man's progress and nodded her approval. Despite their inane banter, Patrick Elliott worked with an ease born of skill, practice, and experience. She had no reason to believe that Bill Harrap wouldn't do the same.

Floating in her oversized suit, Robyn carried her metal case— half the size of Patrick's—towards the house. Bill folded yet another stick of chewing gum into his mouth and followed in close attendance, capturing the scene with a professional-grade camcorder.

Robyn activated her voice recorder and started dictating.

"Dr Robyn Spence, Senior Forensic Scene Investigator. Time … nineteen fifteen hours. Address … Twenty-six Orchard Park Lane, Bordesley Green. Patrick Elliott is running externals, Bill Harrap and I are about to head inside.

"The crime scene is a semi-detached house in the middle of a long row. The houses either side are well-maintained, but this one is in a state of disrepair. It looks to have been unoccupied for some time. The front gate is rotten and the larch-lap fence is falling apart. … Garden overgrown … grass running to seed … tall hedges throwing deep shadows … detritus lying around the front garden … paint peeling on the doors and windows."

After being signed in, they followed a brick pathway, carpeted with dark-green moss, to the part-glazed front door. Large bay windows framed each side of the door. She studied the area close to where Patrick had opened his case.

"Muddy scuff marks evident on the outside windowsill of the left hand bay … broken lower pane … possible point of entry."

Robyn rapped on the part-open front door and smiled as the big, blond, and recently promoted Detective Inspector Phil Cryer strode towards her. He showed little signs of a limp, having overcome the career-threatening knee injury through top notch microsurgery, first rate physiotherapy, months of hard physical graft, and plain good luck.

In fact, he looked as trim as she'd seen him since his rugby-playing days when he'd first hooked up with her old friend, Manda.

Always on the powerful side, Phil's waistline had spread in the years since he'd given up the game—the result of Manda's cookery skills—but the rehab had transformed him into the athlete of his youth.

She switched off the voice recorder. "Hey, Phil. Please thank Manda for the welcome package. The biscuits were delish. Zach munched through the whole lot in one evening."

Phil dipped his head. "As expected. He's a growing boy."

He glanced towards Bill, who'd lowered the camcorder, pointed its integral light at the path, and stood behind Robyn, awaiting instructions.

Phil stayed in the doorway, giving her no room to pass.

"How's the knee?" she asked.

"Not bad, thanks. Can you wait here, please?"

Okay, no small talk required. Understood.

"Of course, but why?"

She'd never worked a crime scene with Phil before and his friendly face had changed to professional mode. Not to worry, she could do professional, too.

"The ME's still in there. He's only just arrived. Won't be long though."

"Who is it?"

"Professor Scobie. You ever met him?"

She shook her head. "Not yet, but I've seen him on a few news reports. And I've read some of his published work."

Phil's full lips stretched into a rueful smile. "The press often drag good ol' Tim out if they need a talking head who can explain an autopsy without the gore and without blinding the public with science."

"Good man in the field?"

"One of the best."

"Will he take long to give me the scene?"

Phil's blue eyes lost focus for a moment, as though he'd forgotten something—which would never happen. "Not this time." He leaned closer and lowered his voice. "You ready for this?"

"Of course. I'm always ready, Inspector Cryer."

"It's a bad one. Really bad."

"Phil," she said, trying to keep her voice even, "I've worked plenty of crime scenes. I'm used to seeing a little gore."

His frown deepened. She'd never seen him so serious. A darkness behind his eyes betrayed an emotion she couldn't identify. Sadness? Anger?

"What's wrong?"

"The victim ..." Again, he glanced at Bill. "He's one of ours."

Bill stiffened and edged closer. "Who?"

"Charlie," Phil answered the stocky Australian, his voice lowered.

"Charlie Pelham?" Bill coughed. "Jesus, Mary, and Joseph!" He crossed himself.

Phil raise a hand and patted it in the air for silence.

"Keep it down, Bill," he said, lowering his voice to a near whisper. "We can't broadcast this or we'll be inundated with press."

"Charlie's dead?" Bill said, this time hushed. "What happened?"

"Someone's taken a knife to him. He's been butchered."

Chapter Three

SUNDAY 14TH MAY – Robyn Spence

Bordesley Green, Birmingham, UK

CHARLIE PELHAM? Robyn had heard the name, but couldn't drag the memory into the light.

"Who's Charlie Pelham?" she asked, matching her volume to the others'.

Phil sighed. His wide shoulders slumped. "A former member of the SCU. Left us under a bit of a cloud."

"Ah, I remember now. *That* Charlie Pelham. A Detective Sergeant, yes?"

"That's right," Phil answered.

He held out his arms and escorted them further out into the darkening front garden. Small groups of locals, some wearing slippers and dressing gowns, had gathered to watch the proceedings. In such a deprived neighbourhood, flashing blue lights would hardly arouse much interest, but so many police vehicles and so many police uniforms still generated considerable attention. In the near distance, the six Orchard Towers cast long shadows over the area. Their west-facing windows reflected the dying embers of the sun and shone like rectangles of gold. The occupants would have a perfect view of the crime scene.

Robyn shivered at the thought of so many unknown eyes watching her. Unnerving.

"What's he doing here?" Bill asked, leaning in closer. "Charlie, I mean. I thought he'd been sent to the crypt."

"The crypt?"

"A desk job, Doc," Phil answered. "Charlie's been working in the archives. Digitising the open unsolved case files."

"Cold cases? You don't think—"

Phil's upraised hand stopped her midsentence. "It's too early to speculate."

Bill beckoned to his Irish mate, who stopped his fingerprinting task and hurried towards them. Bill met him halfway and muttered in the tall Irishman's ear. Patrick lowered his head. Although Robyn never imagined it possible, his rounded shoulders sloped even more. He raised his eyes to hers, his expression behind the mask sombre.

The two friends and colleagues approached Robyn and Phil, as sober as she'd ever seen them.

Patrick nodded to Phil. "We're here for you, Inspector Cryer. Anything you need, let us know. We'll work through the night if needs be." He met her eye. "Okay by you, Doc?"

"Of course, and why wouldn't it be?"

"Your lad, Zach—"

"My personal commitments are none of your concern, Mr Elliott."

Patrick stiffened. "Of course not, ma'am. My mistake, ma'am."

Bill stepped in front of his mate to spare the Irishman's blushes. "The DCI?" he asked.

"On his way in from home," Phil answered. He peeled back the cuff of his coverall to expose his watch. "Should be here soon."

Patrick nodded and glanced up and to the east. "Won't take him long at this time of day. Traffic's light, so it is."

"Hope not."

"DCI Jones?" Robyn asked and added, "Lives out in the sticks, doesn't he?" when Phil nodded.

"Yep," Phil answered, arching an eyebrow, "the other side of Much Wenlock."

"With your permission, ma'am," Patrick said, touching a finger to his forehead, "I'll carry on with my work."

Robyn wondered whether she'd reacted too harshly. She didn't relish the idea of snapping at her colleagues, but she didn't like them becoming overfamiliar, either. A delicate balance she'd had to learn in a male-dominated world.

"Yes please, Patrick," she said, softening her tone and smiling. "I apologise for snapping."

"My mistake for asking, Doc. Always did have a big mouth on me, so."

"Strewth," Bill said, "if that ain't the greatest understatement I've ever heard."

"Wait up there a minute, you little—"

"I don't need to tell you how serious this is," Phil said, cutting into what promised to be ongoing banter. "When the story breaks, the media is going to be all over us, but we can't let it get in the way. Charlie was one of us, and we won't let him down."

"Too right we won't," Bill said.

Patrick frowned and lowered his head, staying unusually quiet and returning to his spot near the bay window.

She edged a little closer to Phil but made sure to keep her heavy case well away from his knee. "Can't believe I'm finally going to meet the elusive DCI Jones."

Phil pursed his lips and gave her the serious expression Manda told Robyn he'd been working on since earning his latest promotion. "Elusive? Don't know about that, but you won't be seeing him at his best."

"I can imagine. Not with one of your own in there."

"Yeah, and he's been in Nottingham for the past week."

"Ah yes, the escaped prisoner. What's her name? ... Archer?"

"Melanie Archer," Phil confirmed, "and she didn't escape, she was rescued and … taken into witness protection."

"Yes, I watched her news conference. Seemed a little suspicious to me. I think there's more to her story than the police are saying."

"Oh dear, Robyn. Forever the sceptic." Phil's hard stare told her this wasn't the time to probe.

It also told her he was hiding something.

Phil and DCI Jones would have worked the Archer case together. Phil would know the whole story, which was a heck of a lot more than he was letting on. With any luck, he'd tell her the truth over one of Manda's delicious dinners.

A door inside the house creaked open. Robyn leaned to one side, trying to see around Phil.

A man of average height with a stiff-backed, military bearing stepped through a door in the hallway. He wore the dark blue boilersuit of the Birmingham and Solihull Coroner Service, marched along the hall, and emerged into the fading daylight. He tore off his facemask and pulled back the hood to reveal a shock of wavy grey hair and an impressive salt-and-pepper beard. Professor Timothy Scobie, Chief Medical Examiner for the whole of Birmingham and University lecturer of international renown. Robyn would have recognised the telegenic doctor anywhere.

"All yours, DI Cryer," he said, his voice low and his demeanour solemn. As befitted the occasion.

"Any surprises?" Phil asked, matching the professor's tone.

"None."

"Cause of death?"

"Unless I find something untoward in the post, it's as expected. Exsanguination."

"Time of death?"

Scobie tilted his head and threw him an old-fashioned look. "DI Cryer, you don't seriously expect me to—"

"The boss is going to be here soon. You know what he's like. Your best guesstimate will do. We won't hold you to it."

Scobie shot a sideways look at Robyn. He read her ID and nodded.

"Good evening, Dr Spence."

"Professor Scobie. Good to meet you at last. Please call me Robyn."

"Welcome to the Midlands, Robyn. Sorry we had to meet under these ...." He let the sentence trail off and waved a hand in the general direction he'd just come from. "It's not exactly the lowest profile crime scene you'll ever process, I'm afraid."

"I imagine not," she responded flatly, not knowing whether the ME was sympathising or questioning her skills. She'd lost count of the number of times a "colleague" had done the latter.

"Professor," Phil interrupted. "TOD?"

Scobie frowned and harrumphed. "Suffice it to say, rigour has passed."

"So, he's been dead at least thirty-six hours?"

"At least, but I refuse to speculate further."

"You've not taken the liver temperature?" Robyn asked.

"No, Dr Spence. I have not. As you can imagine, to take an accurate liver temperature, one needs an intact liver."

Good Lord.

What on earth would she find in the room Scobie had just left?

"What was that?" Phil demanded.

Scobie ignored the question.

"Now," he continued, "if you don't mind, I'll be on my way. My people will be here shortly to collect the ... ah ... remains. I am therefore handing the crime scene over to you at"—he shot out an arm to expose his watch—"twenty-two minutes past seven." He jotted the time in an old-fashioned, flip-top notebook he'd pulled from a pocket in his coverall.

"DI Cryer," he said, turning to face Phil again. "Rest assured, I understand the sensitivity of the case ... and its urgency. When he arrives, please give my regards to DCI Jones. Tell him I'll conduct the *post* tonight. He'll have my preliminary report the moment it's ready."

"Thanks, Professor Scobie. He'll appreciate that."

"The least I can do, Inspector. The very least." He nodded

goodbye to Phil and, before leaving, leaned close to Robyn and lowered his voice so much, she almost missed his whispered, "Professor Lackland speaks very highly of you, Dr Spence. Take it slow, be methodical, and you'll be fine. Good day to you, and the very best of luck."

He hurried away, his pace brisk.

"That was interesting," she muttered, half to Phil and half to herself.

"The bit about the liver?"

"Yes. And the advice."

And the part about Lackland.

Scobie had obviously taken the time to investigate her background. Bob Lackland, her former boss, appreciated the quality of her work well enough to beg her not to leave her post at the Met and disappear into "the dark hinterland of the Midlands". Dear old Bob would have given her a glowing—and honest—report. On the other hand, what right did Scobie have to check up on her? As for his advice to "be slow and methodical". Darn it. What else would she be?

"Am I permitted to carry on now, Inspector Cryer?" she asked, aware of how heavy her case had become since she'd hauled it from the Rover. Although she could have lowered it to the path, she'd have had to decontaminate the stud feet before lugging it into the crime scene. Not a chance of letting that happen.

Phil's warm smile returned and softened his face.

"Don't let the prof upset you, Robyn. He's one of the good guys."

"He's been checking up on me. Who does he think he is?"

"One of the most respected MEs in the UK. And he's just cleared his schedule to run an overnight autopsy for us. Shows the character of the man."

"The murder of a serving police officer trumps everything else, of course."

"Of course."

Phil stepped aside to let her and Bill pass.

"Charlie's—the body's in the front room, Robyn. Let me know

as soon as you're done. I'll be out here with Vic, organising the door-to-door."

"Thanks."

Robyn stood to one side to allow Bill and his camcorder to pass.

"Better crack on," she said. "Wouldn't want to delay DCI Jones any longer than I have to."

"Better not, or he'll be moody as all hell."

"Really? The way Manda describes him, Davy Jones is a teddy bear."

Phil's eyes widened. "Bloody hell, Robyn. Don't you dare call him 'Davy'. He'll never forgive you, and you wouldn't want to start off on the wrong foot. And as for 'teddy bear', he'd have kittens and the rest of the team would die laughing."

She touched his forearm with a bent elbow. "Just kidding. Manda's given me a full briefing. I'll let you know the moment we're done. You've not touched anything in the room?"

Phil threw a hand to his chest. "Dr Spence, you know better than to ask that of a seasoned detective."

She shook her head. "Don't play the old soldier with me, Detective Inspector Cryer. If I had a fiver for every time a so-called seasoned professional had contaminated one of my crimes scenes—"

"What? The Met's golden boys are screw-ups? Who'd have thought that? But to answer your question, none of my people have entered the room. And the prof knows his stuff. Take it from me, the only fresh trace you'll find in that room will be from the body or the suspect."

"Who discovered the body?"

"No idea." He shrugged. "HQ received an anonymous call."

"Okay, enough said. We'll take it from here, Phil."

Robyn raised her facemask and pinched the nose bar to improve the seal. She pulled up the coverall's hood and tucked in her ponytail. Finally, she sucked in a deep breath and entered what she expected to be a charnel house.

Here we go. Slow and methodical it is.

Chapter Four

Bordesley Green, Birmingham, UK

ROBYN REACTIVATED the voice recorder and studied the bare boards of the entrance hall where dust and junk mail had been disturbed when the police pushed open the front door.

"Dead flies on the floor … been there a while … a number have been crushed flat … scuff marks in the dust."

She spoke quietly to Federico Fellini. "Make sure you capture those marks near the front door, Bill. We'll have to confirm who made them. Use a still camera, too. Then film the whole ground floor and lounge before we enter. While you do that, I'll go fetch the footplates."

"Right you are, Doc." Bill nodded and powered up the camcorder's attached light source. He took a slow, arcing pan of the doorway and focused on the floorboards.

Leaving the director to his work, Robyn lowered her case to the porch floor and retraced her steps to the Range Rover. By the time she returned with the stack of footplates, Bill had finished taking his establishing shots. He signalled for her to continue.

The hallway contained three doors and a staircase. Flies buzzed inside the room Scobie had exited. Robyn drew closer to the open doorway and, despite the facemask, caught the nauseating stink of sweet-rot and decay. She couldn't prevent her nose from wrinkling. She closed her eyes for a moment and gave up a brief and silent prayer for the deceased. The day she became immune to the sights and smells of death would be the day she'd give up her job and become a landscape gardener.

Robyn placed the footplates and her case on the floor just inside the room, well away from the corpse, and squatted to key a combination into the number pad alongside the case's handle. Its locks clicked. She open the lid and removed a digital thermometer from its internal compartment. While waiting for it to work through its automated calibration process, she stood and studied the darkened room in contemplative silence.

The overgrown conifer bushes in the front garden restricted the view of the sky, threw a deep shadow into the room, and added to the gloom of the encroaching sunset. Very little light bled through the room's dirty windows. Net curtains—shredded and holed with age and wet rot—stirred as a light breeze wafted through the broken glass. Outside the grimy window, Patrick, head down, dispersed fingerprint dust with a feather-light brush.

A green-and-cream-tiled fireplace sprouted from the centre of the wall adjacent to the door. Over time, soot had fallen from the chimney and now lay in a conical pile in the grate. The killer had dumped DS Pelham in front of the fireplace. Overweight and naked —at least from the waist up—he lay on a worn and filthy rug, and was part-covered by a crumpled blanket which had been pulled back at one corner to reveal the damaged chest and abdominal wall.

And such damage.

The body lay face up, his head slightly turned to the right, facing away from the window and towards the door. A deep gash ran from above the left ear to the chin. A flap of grey skin and purple muscle flopped over his nose, fully revealing the zygomatic arch. His face had been destroyed almost beyond recognition.

If the face was bad, the abdominal cavity looked as though a bomb had exploded from the inside. Flaps of skin and viscera hung open, exposing ribs and vertebra. Little remained of the internal organs and tissue. No wonder Professor Scobie had been unable to take a liver temperature. Almost nothing remained of the organ. The thoracic and abdominal cavity had been eviscerated—totally destroyed.

Blood had seeped into the threadbare, mottled rug, but not much of it, and no blood splatter showed on the floors or walls. The rest of the body, at least the part visible above the blanket, seemed undamaged except for areas where wildlife, probably rats, had torn at the fleshy parts of the wrists and throat. The lack of blood spatter and the scarcity of organ tissue told a story. The actual crime scene lay elsewhere. Wherever DS Pelham met his end would have been an abattoir.

She restarted the recorder and continued her dictation.

"The floor, bare boards ... heavy film of dirt and dust ... cobwebs confirm that the house has been uninhabited for quite a while."

The thermometer bleeped.

Robyn set out a trail of the metal footplates from the door to the side of the body, and from the body to the window, balancing on one plate while laying the next. The first time she'd attempted the manoeuvre at college, she'd ended up flat on her backside—not the most professional thing to do had it been an actual crime scene. Luckily, she'd perfected the action since then, and it had become second nature.

Using the plates as stepping stones, she returned to the body and stood over it.

"Room temperature at ... 19:27 is ... 24.3 degrees Celsius ... maggots infesting the open wounds are immotile, possibly at the secondary instar stage ... suggests the victim's been dead more than one day but less than three. I will collect eggs and larvae for timing data. Evidence suggests this is a secondary crime scene—a dumping site. Not enough blood here and no splatter. The body may have been transported in the rug and covered in the blanket afterwards."

Bill's light footfalls returned from the rear of the house and the camcorder's light shone into the room, casting her shadow over the gutted corpse.

"God alive," Bill muttered. "What the hell did they do to you, Charlie? You ever see anything like this before, Doc?"

"No. You?"

"Never. What the hell kind of weapon could do that?"

Robyn pulled back her shoulders. "No idea. Let's leave cause of death and possible murder weapon to Professor Scobie and carry on with our work, eh?"

"Sure thing, Doc. I've done with filming on the ground floor. Want me to fetch the lights from the Rover before taking the walk-through footage upstairs?"

"Yes please. Need a hand?"

"Nah. I'll be right, but thanks anyway. Need to suck in a bit of fresh air before I get started. Charlie may have been a Grade A arsehole, but he didn't deserve to end up like that."

"No one does, Bill."

Amen to that.

FIFTEEN MINUTES LATER, battery-powered, high-intensity LED lamps stood on tripod stands in each corner of the front room. They illuminated the scene with intense light but did nothing to dispel the overriding gloom.

Robyn stooped to pull a 35mm, digital camera fitted with a 12x optical zoom lens from her meticulously packed case. She unclipped a leather retaining flap to expose the segmented container housing tweezers, sample bags, jars of fingerprint dust, and brushes. The inch-by-inch room examination could begin.

Next to each item of special interest, she placed yellow numbered tags, complete with indexed measures to scale the photos for future reference. Brilliant white flashes accompanied the sound of its motorised camera shutter. She sealed fluff, strands of hair, and screwed-up pieces of newspaper into transparent evidence bags, and covered whole areas with black fingerprint dust.

It took twenty minutes before she was ready to begin the next, most delicate stage. She slid on a pair of safety-glasses and started her work on the body.

Headlights raked the room as a car pulled up outside. Moments later, a man's voice called out, "Where's DI Cryer?"

"Over there by the bus with Sergeant Dolan, sir. They're organising the house-to-house."

"SOCOs been here long?"

"Less than an hour, sir."

"Where's the body?"

"No idea, sir. Nobody's saying nothing."

"Anything."

"Excuse me, sir?"

"Nobody's saying *anything*, Constable. It's a good job I don't read your daily reports."

Behind her mask, Robyn smiled at the constable's half-mumbled and fully chastened, "Yes, sir. Sorry, sir."

The teddy bear's arrived.

Chapter Five

SUNDAY 14TH MAY – Evening

Bordesley Green, Birmingham, UK

JONES FROWNED at the grammatically challenged constable—a youngster he couldn't name—and took a moment to study the area.

Number 26 Orchard Park Lane, a brick-built, tile-roofed, semi-detached house, stood in the middle of a long, curving row of similar tired houses. On the opposite side of the road, another curving row of matching semis faced them.

Six tower blocks, The Orchards, each ten storeys tall, loomed over them in a wide semi-circle, seemingly crowding in on all sides. Lights blinked on behind darkened windows. Alderman's Brewery squatted between two of the blocks, its brewing stacks reaching half as high as the towers.

Inquisitive neighbours clustered in small groups, hoping to see something of interest when they could—and probably should—have been inside, watching TV.

Move along, now. Nothing to see here.

Apart from Phil's unmarked car, a quartet of official vehicles blocked the road—a Ford Transit minibus, two patrol cars, and the SOCO's Range Rover. Blue lights still flashed on one of the patrol cars.

"No need for those blues, Constable," he said. "I'm sure the whole neighbourhood knows we're here by now."

The lad rushed past him to cancel the warning lights.

He waited for a second constable to sign him in as the SIO on scene, before heading towards the minibus. Before he'd reached the halfway point, Phil stepped out from around the back of the vehicle, closely followed by the stocky Vic Dolan, ever impressive in his shirt-sleeves, stab vest, peaked cap, and comms gear. Jones stopped at the gate of Number 26 and waited for them to reach him.

"Philip, Victor," he said, nodding to each in turn. "What was so serious you had to drag me out of my nice warm home so late in the day?"

Phil stepped closer and turned his back to the constable guarding the gate to Number 26.

"Sorry, sir," he said, keeping his voice low, conspiratorial. "Vic thought it best you were here from the outset, and I agreed with him."

"Why?" Jones asked, looking at the senior sergeant.

"The victim, sir," Vic said, hiding his mouth from the rubber-neckers behind a cupped hand. "It's Charlie. Charlie Pelham."

Dear God.

The breath caught in Jones' throat. The monstrous implications rattled around in his head. He clenched both fists and dug the nails into his palms.

"Charlie? You're certain?"

Vic nodded, his expression deadly serious. "Yes, sir. It's definitely him."

"Hell." Jones scanned the neighbourhood. Built up. So many houses. So many potential witnesses. So many potential suspects.

"Who called it in?"

"Anonymous call, boss," Phil said.

Jones nodded.

"We'll need a copy of the recording."

"I've already asked for it."

Taking his time to absorb the enormity of the situation, Jones started running on autopilot. "Any idea how long's he been there?"

"Difficult to say, sir. He's been dead a while. At least a few days. And … the body. God"—he winced—"it's a real mess. He's been hacked to pieces and stripped naked."

"But his face is intact?"

Vic shook his head. "I'm afraid not, sir. Not at all."

"How can you be so sure it's Charlie?"

Vic broke eye contact for a moment as though upset at reliving the memory. "I recognised the tattoo on his forearm. So proud of that bloody ugly piece of ink, he was."

Jones remembered it, too. Pelham—a lifelong Chelsea fan—never tired of flashing the tattoo that commemorated his team's Champion's League win back in 2012. Whenever the subject of football came up, Pelham would roll up his sleeve and bore his audience to tears with a blow-by-blow account of the final he'd travelled all the way to Munich to watch live. Once again, the details ran through Jones' mind. One goal each after extra time, "The Blues" won four-three on penalties. Jones had given up counting the times he'd heard how Didier Drogba had held his iron nerve to score the sudden death penalty to win them the trophy. Jones sighed. Thankfully, he'd never have to tune out that story again.

For God's sake, Jones. Where's your pity?

Eventually, the realisation hit. At some stage, he'd have to tell Charlie's wife, Lydia. It would be cowardly to leave it to a Family Liaison Officer.

Tempting, but cowardly.

He didn't relish giving Lydia the bad news. Not one bit of it. Still, that could wait until they needed a formal identification. The morning would do. Or the next day.

Or the next.

"Thanks, Victor. Did you enter the house?"

"Had to, sir. Needed to check for signs of life and … you know, secure the scene."

Jones knew. Protocol demanded it.

"Not that there was any chance of his being alive," Vic continued, glancing over Jones' shoulder in the direction of his officers. "There's a broken pane of glass in the front bay. Where the killer would have gained entry. We—that's PC Porterhouse and I—kept well clear of the window. Didn't want to contaminate any evidence. Patrick Elliott's working the area now." Unnecessarily, he pointed to the slim SOCO, who knelt at the window beside his open case. The Irishman's soft humming showed him as totally absorbed in his work.

Vic continued. "We could just about see the body through the window, but couldn't make out any details. I had to break open the front door. It wasn't difficult. The frame's rotten."

"Where was Porterhouse at the time?"

"I told him to guard the gate to keep the neighbours out of the garden. As you can imagine, the lad was a tad queasy. His first body." Again, he swallowed and shook his head sadly. "Damn, it's tough thinking of Charlie ending up like that."

"So, you entered the house?" Jones asked, keen to move the story along.

"Yes, sir. Kept to one side of the hall to minimise any disturbance. The lounge door was already open. I stayed in the doorway. The smell." He shook his head slowly at the memory. "And the flies," he added.

"Bad?" Jones asked, not really needing an answer. He could tell the state of the corpse from Victor's reaction to finding it.

"Over the years, I've seen my fair share of bodies but … God above, what a mess. Even though it was half-covered by a blanket."

"You didn't enter the room?"

"No, sir. Didn't need to. Death was obvious, and then I saw the tat on his forearm and called Phil as the senior detective on call. I also suggested he contact you. Thought you'd want to be the SIO on this one, since Charlie used to be one of your—"

"Good work, Sergeant."

"Thank you, sir."

"How's Porterhouse?"

"Fine, sir. Took it really well, considering. I've teamed him with PC Calder. She'll look after him."

"Porterhouse," Jones said, nodding thoughtfully, "I remember him. Handled himself well during that bomb hoax last year. How's he doing?"

"Progressing well, sir. Bright lad. He'll make a solid officer."

"Good. I'll have a quiet chat with him when things settle down a little."

Vic arched an eyebrow. "When's that likely to happen, sir?"

Not anytime soon.

Jones let the question go. "Have you and Phil organised the initial house-to-house?"

Vic and Phil nodded.

"Alex and Ben are already on it," Phil said. "They'll canvass the street first and see what we have. Vic's going to coordinate the troops when we're ready to spread the net wider."

"Don't hold your breath, though," Vic said. "The OTT isn't exactly home ground."

"Thanks for that, Victor. Maybe they'll surprise you."

Vic's cynical expression told Jones what the sergeant thought of that suggestion. "Maybe. Can I go, sir? My guys are looking a little restless."

The group of seven uniformed officers near the minibus stood in a huddle, looking expectantly at them.

"Pair them up and have them ask the ghouls a few question," Jones said, waving his arm at the disparate groups of locals.

Vic stretched his lips into a thin smile. "One way of emptying the streets, I suppose. At the very least, it'll keep the beggars back from the crime scene tape."

"You never know," Phil offered, "one of them might have seen the body being dropped."

"It was a body drop?" Jones asked, glancing at Vic.

"Ah yes, sir. Not much blood in there." Again, he nodded towards the house. "Didn't I tell you?"

"No, Sergeant. You did not."

Vic lifted a shoulder. "Sorry, sir. You'll see it for yourself soon enough. Mind if I toddle off? My people need me."

"Okay Victor. Off you toddle."

The sergeant dipped his head to Phil and hurried away to give his troops an aim in life.

Jones glanced over his shoulder, taking in the threatening shapes of the six towers. The sun had set fully and the pale grey windows reflected the colour of the darkening sky.

"Charlie ran a couple of confidential informants up there, didn't he?" he asked Phil.

"He did," Phil nodded, "but he's been on desk duty since you kicked him out of the Unit. There's no reason for him to have gone anywhere near them."

"Why else would he have ended his days here?" Jones said, looking at the house.

"No idea. Charlie's not the type to volunteer for anything he didn't absolutely have to do. Don't like speaking ill of the dead, but he was a right lazy sod." He lowered his voice even further.

"Keep that sort of talk to yourself, Inspector."

"Of course. But it had to be said."

"Don't suppose you know any of their names?"

"His CIs? Nope. Not offhand. I never asked, and Charlie wasn't one to tell. I'll look into his semi-literate scratchings when we're back at base."

"It's a priority. Can't you search the files on your tablet?"

"Not a chance, boss. Charlie was even worse than you when it came to updating the database."

"Hmm. Why do you think I invited you onto the team, Inspector Cryer? Why keep a dog and ... Well, enough of the chitchat. Since the SOCOs—sorry, the 'FSIs' are inside, I assume the ME has been and gone?"

"Yep. He didn't take long to pronounce. In and out, lickety-split."

"Who attended?"

"Given the sensitivity, I specifically asked for the prof."

"Good idea. Although I'm surprised you could get hold of him. Busy man."

Phil grimaced. "Sorry, boss. I've a little confession to make."

"Out with it, Philip."

"I used your name for the request. Didn't think you'd mind."

"Inspector Cryer," Jones said, dropping a hand on Phil's broad shoulder, "that sort of initiative will earn you plenty of Brownie points. Knowing Tim Scobie, he'll be putting a rush on the PM, yes?"

Phil up-nodded. "Yes indeedie. He promised to start the moment they delivered the body. The Coroner's men are on their way, so I'm told."

"Nothing to do but wait for the SOCOs to release the scene, then?"

"Not a lot. Shouldn't be long though. According to Mr Ntando, the next door neighbour, the house has been empty since the owner died. Best part of a year, he reckons. Nobody seems to know who owns it now. I sent Wash back to the office. He's setting up the case-file and fielding the phone calls. I've also asked him to identify the current owner, but it could take a while."

Jones nodded. "Ryan's good at that sort of thing. If there's a paper trail anywhere, he'll find it."

"So, while we wait, are you going to call Not-Bob?" Phil asked, one eyebrow arched and a mischievous twinkle in his eyes.

Jones frowned. "That's Superintendent Havers to you, Inspector Cryer."

"Yes, sir. I suppose it must be." Phil's reply couldn't have been any more deadpan.

"You didn't think to call him yourself?"

"Oh no. Thought I'd leave that utter delight to you, boss. SIO's prerogative, don't you know."

"Thanks."

"Thought you'd appreciate it."

"Sometimes, I'm not all that fond of you, Inspector Cryer. You know that?"

"Really, sir? I always think so highly of you."

Smart alec.

Jones dug a hand into his pocket for his mobile before remembering his intentional lapse.

"Darn it, I never did catch Not-Bob's mobile number. Do you mind?" He handed his phone across.

"Shouldn't that be 'Superintendent Havers', Chief Inspector?"

"Yes, I suppose it should be."

Phil grinned—hiding it behind a raised hand to keep any hint of amusement from the onlookers—and added the Super's name and numbers to the phone's contact list. He didn't need to look up the details. Phil only ever needed to read a phone number once before it remained locked in his spectacular memory forever.

Jones retrieved his mobile and snorted at the new entry, *Not-Bob, Never-Bob,* followed by both the Super's contact numbers—his direct office number and his police mobile.

"Droll, Philip. So droll."

Phil winked. "I thought so, boss. While you update the Super, I'll find out how Wash is getting on."

Jones sighed. "Yes, you do that."

Unable to delay any longer, he took the plunge and dialled. Havers answered on the third ring.

"Chief Inspector Jones?" Havers opened. "This must be serious."

The Super had updated his phone with Jones' number. Typical of a tech-savvy young thruster.

"I'm afraid it is, sir."

"Okay, David. I'm all ears."

Chapter Six

SUNDAY 14TH MAY – Evening

Bordesley Green, Birmingham, UK

"THANK YOU, SIR," Jones said, unable to end the conversation soon enough. "I'll brief you first thing in the morning."

"Sergeant Pelham was one of our own, Jones. Would you like me to contact the widow—er, I mean, Mrs Pelham?"

A lifeline.

Could he take it?

Havers continued. "I'd hate for her to hear about this from an outside source, and she will need to formally identify the remains."

"I was going to do the notification tomorrow. I'd rather hold off until after the autopsy. Lydia, I mean Mrs Pelham, can be a little … volatile. No telling how she'll react and we need to keep this under wraps for now."

"Of course. Heaven knows what the press is going to make of this. A public relations nightmare."

"Hardly a walk in the park for Lydia Pelham either, sir."

Havers harumphed. The man actually harumphed.

"Quite so, Jones. Quite so. A disaster for everyone. Are you sure you should be the one to break the news?"

"I'll have to, sir. We'll need Lydia's permission to search her home. Charlie might have left some notes. He wasn't averse to taking files home with him. We might find a list of his unofficial CIs."

"Unofficial CIs?" Havers said, raising his voice. "Are you telling me DS Pelham kept some of his Confidential Informants off book?"

"Yes, sir."

We all do.

"That's highly irregular."

No it isn't.

"Yes, sir. We might be able to find out where he was going and who he was meeting. I'll task one of my team DI Cryer or DS Olganski to go through his desk in the archives tomorrow morning. If you could arrange to have his workspace sealed until one or the other is free, I'd appreciate it, sir."

"Of course, Jones. Of course. Consider it done. But I'm still not sure you should be the one to break the news to Mrs Pelham. Given your recent history with the, ah, deceased, I imagine there's a little bad blood between you and the Pelhams."

No kidding.

"Possibly, sir."

"At this stage, I ought to inform you that DS Pelham made an official complaint about you via his Union Rep."

"He did?"

"Indeed. He accused you of having a personal grudge against him."

"Oh dear."

True enough. I did.

"Complete nonsense, of course. Wouldn't hold up at a tribunal. He actually claimed you deliberately damaged his career and held back a promotion ... I tried to dissuade him from making the complaint official, but he refused to listen to reason." Havers paused for breath before rushing on. "However, that's all moot now, of course."

Moot?

When did anyone Not-Bob's age ever use the word "moot"?

"Yes, sir. I'm afraid it is."

Jones ended the call after giving Not-Bob at least some credit for not raising any objections to Jones investigating the murder of a former colleague. Some senior officers he'd had the misfortune to work with in the past would have insisted he passed the case on to someone who didn't know Charlie Pelham personally. However, that would have meant drafting in an investigator from another force, since every senior officer in the West Midlands Police knew the man.

Not a chance.

Jones would have threatened to resign if Havers had tried to side-line him. Whoever killed Charlie Pelham would feel Jones' hand on his collar. And that was a promise he'd make to himself alone.

"That sounded interesting, boss," Phil said. He'd ended his call to Ryan and unashamedly eavesdropped on Jones' conversation with Havers. Jones had helped Phil hear both sides of the call by holding the mobile slightly away from his ear.

"Yep," Jones answered. "Interesting."

"Is Not-Bob for real?" Phil whispered.

"In what way?"

"Does he really think you didn't know Charlie was screaming blue murder and calling in the ankle-biters?"

"Seems that way."

"Bloody hell, Charlie never stopped banging on about it to anyone who'd listen. Unless that part about Not-Bob trying to 'dissuade' Charlie from making the complaint official was a load of bull and the Super wants to appear to be on your side. One of the troops."

"We'll never know. Anyway, let's get back to business, shall we? What did Ryan have to say?"

Phil dropped his phone into a pocket. "He's confirmed the identity of the previous owner—the one who died—as a Mrs Edith

Shipley. Hasn't found out who inherited the place yet. I've told him to keep working on it."

"Fair enough."

"Mr Jones?"

Bill Harrap appeared in the doorway to Charlie's current resting place, instantly recognisable—despite being fully encapsulated by his white boiler suit—by his squat shape and his gum chewing.

"Yes, Bill?"

"You can come in now, if you like, sir."

"Already?"

Bill stopped chewing and nodded. "We're done in the hall and the lounge, and there's not much to see in the rest of the house. Nothing's been in here for months but the local wildlife. Undisturbed dust and cobwebs all over the place. The doc thought you'd like to take a look at the bod—I mean, the scene, asap."

"Thanks, Bill."

"No worries, Mr Jones. We've got to get the bastard who did that to—"

Jones held up his hand and Bill stopped mid-sentence.

"Not one word of this until we're ready to make the announcement, please."

"Of course, Mr Jones. I wasn't going to name names. No chance of that. And, by the way, if there's anything we can to do help, just ask. We'll be pushing all the lab work to the top of the queue. The other cases can wait. This one"—he shook his head and pulled in a breath—"close to home, you know?"

"Thanks, Bill. I'd appreciate that."

The FSI who used to be a SOCO stepped past them, carrying a plastic box full of evidence bags to their Range Rover.

With Phil in tow, Jones pushed through the broken gate and strode along the moss-covered path. At the front door, he pulled a pair of booties over his shoes, tugged on a pair of blue nitrile gloves, and hooked a facemask over his ears.

Jones stepped through the opening, stopped in the open doorway to the lounge, and took in the full scene. Phil stood behind him, tall enough to look over his shoulder.

He soaked in the sad spectacle, curiously unmoved by the horror. Jones recognised the symptoms. The professional in him had switched into work mode. Despite the damage done to a former colleague, he could allow no room for emotions.

Jones had a killer to find. A vicious killer, too.

Charlie lay on a rug in the middle of the room. Naked, mutilated, filleted, but definitely their former teammate. Even without the unmistakeable and garish tattoo, he'd have been recognisable. Regardless of the swelling, the mutilation, and the blackened skin, enough remained of his face to make the identification.

Charlie, Charlie. What the hell did you do to deserve this?

He swallowed. Charlie's past sins were forgiven if not forgotten.

A tiny SOCO in a baggy white coverall knelt near Charlie's head.

The woman snagged something with a pair of tweezers and sealed it into a glass jar with a perforated lid. A maggot? She wrote on the jar's label.

So, this was the new team leader Phil had told him so much about. Dr Robyn Spence, Manda Cryer's close friend. Her fame and skillset had preceded her, and he could be certain of one thing. The latest addition to the Racer-Colby Crime Lab would be better than her unfortunate predecessor. Of that, there could be little doubt.

Nobody could be worse than poor old Ghastly. A bright-eyed novice straight out of forensics college would be an improvement on the medically retired former team leader.

Jones studied the corpse for a moment longer and cast his eyes around the rest of the room, locking it into his memory—sights, sounds, smells. He couldn't afford to miss a thing.

Dr Spence began packing away her kit.

"Okay to come closer?" he asked.

The petite woman looked up and checked him for protective overshoes and gloves. She nodded, pulled the mask away from her face. Full lips, slim and symmetrical face, no makeup. Bright green eyes.

"It's all yours."

She gathered her paraphernalia and stacked it neatly in a corner of the room.

Jones appreciated the new SOCO's desire to keep the crime scene free of clutter—it showed a neat and orderly approach to her work.

Good start.

He took his lead from her, removed his mask, and tucked it into a jacket pocket. He rubbed his chin, glad to be free of the cloth restriction.

Dr Spence smiled. "Nice to meet you at last, Chief Inspector." She pushed forwards her bent right arm and they bumped elbows. "I'll be back after taking a look around the rest of the house. Please restrict your movements to the lounge and hallway until I release the full scene."

Dr Spence's voice had a low, dusky pitch, at odds with her slight frame.

She left the room, allowing Jones and Phil space to approach the body. Phil stood while Jones squatted on his haunches. His aging knees creaked as they took the strain.

"I'd say the killer transported the body in this rug. Charlie"—Jones grimaced at the use of the first name—"may have been standing on it when he was killed. Might give us a clue to the location of the actual crime scene." He glanced up at Phil. "Reeks in here. Why did it take the neighbours so long to notice the smell?"

"I wondered that, too. Apparently, the family next door has been on holiday for the past week and with the garden so badly overgrown, it might have masked some of the stench."

"Hmm. Alderman's Brewery isn't far away. Can you get someone to find out when they last did a fermentation? The smell might have concealed the stink."

"I'll ask Wash to give them a bell."

Jones pointed to Charlie's glistening torso. "You ever seen anything like this in your research?"

Apart from having a failsafe eidetic memory, Phil's reading speed and his overall retention happened to be off-the-charts astonishing. On top of which, his appetite for knowledge seemed insatiable. The man read case files for fun—even case files from other jurisdictions.

"Afraid not, boss."

"Neither have I." Jones slowly shook his head.

"Looks like he swallowed a hand grenade after pulling the pin," Phil announced, showing all the sensitivity of a youngster brought up on a diet of video games and gore-fest movies.

Jones curled his upper lip. "Thanks very much for that, Philip."

"Sorry, boss. But it's true."

Outside, cameras flashed in the advancing gloom. Raised voices and shouted questions signalled the arrival of a local media.

"The vultures have landed," Phil growled.

"They're a bit slow tonight. More often than not they beat us to the scene." Jones returned his attention to the body. "The Super said he can't free up any more officers tonight. We're spread too thin, despite ..." He waved a hand over Charlie and let the statement hang in the air.

Phil jerked up his head. "Typical. Bet he still wants results by yesterday morning, though."

"Steady, Phil, you're talking about the new boss, remember." Jones squatted again, resting his elbows on his thighs for support. "We'll have to manage with the people we have 'til then. I doubt we'll have much luck with the door-to-door, but let's wait and see." He sniffed the air above the body. "Judging by the smell and his colour, and the maggots, he's been dead at least a day and a half, maybe two."

Phil's face glistened with sweat. He undid his top shirt button and loosened his tie. "The prof refused to speculate on a time of death—"

"Wouldn't expect him to."

"But rigor's passed."

"Yes, I see that."

"As I said, the prof's running the PM overnight and we should have the prelim report by first thing tomorrow morning."

"Thanks, Philip. Can you check on the progress of the door-to-door? Make sure Vic and his people have all they need."

Phil headed out of the room, leaving Jones alone with his thoughts and Charlie Pelham's last remains. He retrieved his notepad from his sagging jacket and began his own preliminary investigation. He hadn't noticed it before—the stink of decay had masked it—but on leaning closer to the body, he caught the faint smell of lemon-scented bleach. Not for the first time, he bemoaned the television crime scene programmes that taught even the thickest criminal how to confuse the forensics.

He turned as Dr Spence re-entered the room, hood down, pony-tail tucked into the back of the coverall. No frills at a crime scene.

"Any fresh dabs in this room?" Jones asked without much expectation.

"No. You did notice the victim's hands though?"

Jones nodded and, without looking at the body, said, "The right hand is clenched. The other is open, palm down. Why?"

Dr Spence smiled again—it reached all the way to her jade eyes. "They told me you don't miss much. Come and take a closer look."

Jones followed her and crouched next to the body again, resigned to the complaints his knees would make later. She lifted Charlie's clenched right hand. The wrist and forearm joints moved easily.

"Rigor's no longer present," he said.

She nodded. "Now look at his left palm. The hands were balled into fists when I arrived. I opened this one to take fingerprints, but look." She rotated the wrist to reveal the open palm and showed the fingertips. "The skin of each fingertip has been shredded. It's the same with the other hand. Definitely not surgical cuts, though. See how the skin is torn? Killer used a dull blade, maybe a blunt modeller's knife, or a box cutter." She paused for a second before adding, "I'd guess it was done after death."

"Hope so." Jones agreed. "Can't see any restraint marks on his wrists or arms, and nobody could sit still for that torture if they were conscious." He grimaced. "The ME will confirm whether it was done ante- or post-mortem."

"He will," she said, nodding. "Begs one question, though."

"Which is?"

"Why go to the trouble of damaging the fingertips but leave the tattoo untouched?"

"My thoughts exactly." Jones tilted his head. "He might have been disturbed. Were the fingers mutilated here or at the primary?"

She paused to think before answering. Another good sign.

"There are no pieces of skin tissue left on the rug, but he might have done it here and taken the bits with him." She looked up and their eyes met again. "And yes, I am calling the killer a man. I doubt a woman could move the victim any distance. At least not without help."

"That's a reasonable working hypothesis."

Jones leaned in to study the torn fingertips, but found himself close enough to the SOCO to smell her perfume above the stench of the body and the masking bleach. He couldn't put a name to the fragrance but, worried he'd encroached into her personal space, he stood and stepped back. Thankfully, this time his knees didn't creak in protest.

Dr Spence straightened, too. "There's some trace evidence under his remaining nails which might be of use, despite the bleach. And we might find something on the rug and the blanket. They're both old and worn. We'll take them back to the lab, of course." She broke off and shrugged her slender shoulders. "There's not an awful lot to work with here though, Chief Inspector. Sorry."

Jones crossed to the broken window. "Anything of value over here?"

"I have someone in the garden." She joined Jones in the bay, and leaned towards the break in the glass. "Patrick, are you still there?"

The tall and angular Patrick Elliott, his full, dark beard largely hidden by a facemask, appeared in the window and stared at Dr Spence and Jones from behind a pair of safety glasses. "Evening, Mr Jones. That's a shame, so." He said, his eyes flicking to the body before fixing on his team leader—an altogether more pleasant sight. "Yes, Doc?"

"What do you have for the Chief Inspector?"

"Well now, there might be something." Patrick held up a plastic vial containing a triangular shard of glass and pointed to a dark stain on one of its pointed edges. "This is probably blood, but I can't be sure. There's not enough to test here, but if it is blood, there'll be more than enough for DNA analysis. But we'll not have the results for a few days, I'm afraid."

"A few days?" Jones asked.

Patrick grimaced beneath his mask. "We'll put a rush on it, sir. But the court-accredited labs are backed up to overflowing, and PCR analysis takes a wee while, so. Can't rush the process, I'm afraid."

Jones sighed. "Fine. Thanks, Patrick. Please do what you can. Well spotted though. Is there anything else?"

"There are a few footprints below the sill. I'll be taking casts. And there's a partial palm print here, but it's smudged and probably useless." He pointed over his shoulder. "Over there near the hedge, I found a load of trample marks and a few broken branches. I'd hazards a guess that the local kids have been playing hide and seek in the undergrowth. I've collected and bagged dozens of drinks cans and sweet wrappers. There are a few other papers, you know. Advertising flyers and movie posters and the like. Nothing else that stands out, though. I'm not holding out much hope of finding anything useful, but I'll not stop 'til I've been through the lot. You can be sure of that, so." He glanced over his shoulder. "Ah, look there. Here come the body snatchers. Want me to have them wait until you're ready for them?"

"Yes please. We won't be long."

"Right oh, sir."

Jones nodded his thanks once more and turned back to the room but found it empty. Surprisingly disappointed that Dr Spence had left without saying goodbye, he lifted his notepad and turned to a fresh page. He didn't expect to find anything the SOCOs had missed, but he had his methods. They'd brought him success in the past, and he'd continue to use them in the future.

TWENTY MINUTES LATER, after learning nothing new, Jones stepped out of the lounge, leaving poor Charlie to his date with Tim Scobie's mortuary slab. He made cursory inspection of the other rooms and almost bumped into Dr Spence in the kitchen.

"The Coroner's people have arrived," he said. "They're waiting in the front garden. Can I send them in now?"

"By all means, Chief Inspector. We're just about finished in here. After they've removed the body, we'll run a final check before handing over the scene."

"Thank you, Doctor Spence."

"You're welcome," she said, giving him another pleasant smile. "All part of the Racer-Colby service." She brushed past him, heading for the lounge.

Jones exited the house, intending to check on the results of the canvass so far.

He rubbed tired and gritty eyes and took time to study the uniformed officers as they questioned the immediate neighbours. With so few troops, progress would be excruciatingly slow. The tower blocks would have to wait until morning.

"What's going on in there, Chief Inspector?" one of the gaggle of reporters called out.

"You found a body?" another added.

"Can you tell us anything?"

"How about a quote?"

"C'mon, Chief Inspector. Give us something," a woman Jones recognised from the local TV news called.

They shouted their questions from the far side of the road, behind the barrier tape. Cameras flashed repeatedly from within the group.

Jones ignored their entreaties and turned away.

Two men in dark blue coveralls stood in the garden, staying close to the gate, well out of the way. The Coroner's logo on each man's chest showed their origin and purpose. He signalled to them.

"The body's ready to be moved now. Be careful with it."

One of the men gathered up a collapsible stretcher, the other had a folded, black plastic body bag stuffed under his arm. They nodded to him and entered the house.

Jones surveyed the outside area in the gathering twilight.

Nothing he'd seen so far had suggested Number 26 to be anything other than the secondary.

So where's the primary?

The sun had dipped well below the rooftops since he'd entered the crime scene, and the evening gloom matched his mood. So much for maintaining a professional detachment. As if that could ever happen in such a situation.

Poor Charlie. Poor useless, argumentative Charlie.

A call from the house made him turn to see Dr Spence beckoning to him from the front door. Excitement flashed in her eyes.

Heart rate quickening, he hurried towards her.

"Dr Spence?"

"We've found something underneath the body!"

Chapter Seven

SUNDAY 14TH MAY – Evening

Bordesley Green, Birmingham, UK

BEHIND DR SPENCE, the coroner's men emerged from the darkened hallway with their heavily laden stretcher. Jones raised his hand to halt their progress.

"Sorry, gentlemen. Could you wait a moment while the doctor and I take another look at the room?"

The lead man, a chunky fifty-something with slicked back, shoulder-length hair, allowed his shoulders to slump a fraction. He turned his head slightly and spoke to his mate. "Okay, Rog, lower it and drop 'em."

"Right you are, Si," the tail-gunner, Rog, said. "Back up three first. We don't need an audience.

In a nicely synchronised movement, they backed three paces into the hall, bent at the knees, and lowered the stretcher to the floor. Once down, Rog released a lever and said, "Okay." When they stood again the wheeled legs dropped to the floorboards with a wooden thump and locked into place, leaving the stretcher's bed at table height.

"Quick as you can, sir, if you don't mind," Si said. "We've got a double collection on the other side of town, but the prof wants this body back at the mortuary first. Gonna be long night."

Jones breathed in through his nose.

"It'll take as long as necessary. I'll call you when we're done."

Si checked his watch and exchanged resigned looks with his mate.

"If you insist, Chief Inspector," he grumbled, fishing a packet of cigarettes from a pocket of his coveralls. "We'll wait in the front garden. Again."

Jones let them pass, sidestepped around the stretcher, and re-entered the lounge. The rug, now free of its unfortunate passenger, proved to be as ancient and worn as they'd anticipated. Its red and blue pattern had faded over time and the threadbare patches of pale brown fibres showed a history of heavy wear. Dark red splashes of blood and tissue, where Charlie's remains had rested, stood out sharply against the faded dyes. The blanket that had partially covered him lay in a folded square alongside, ready for packing into a large evidence bag.

Dr Spence had already removed and bagged the pieces of loose tissue from the rug before allowing the coroner's men to move the body, but the dark patch in the middle was still a slick and gory mess.

The shiny silver object sitting roughly where the small of Charlie's back had been sparked Jones' keen interest.

An oval St Christopher medallion lay face-up, its decorated surface worn almost smooth. Jones doubted it could have been Charlie's since the Detective Sergeant hadn't been the least bit religious. His heart rate rose. The medal might have fallen from the killer when he moved the body.

Dr Spence lifted the object with a pair of plastic tweezers and sealed it into a transparent evidence bag before handing it to Jones. He held the bag up at an angle to one of the LED lights. The heavily worn front sported an embossed outline of the Patron Saint of Travellers carrying a baby. Nothing unusual about the front, but faint scratches on the reverse side suggested the faded remnants of an engraving. Unable to make out the letters, he handed the package back. "Can you read the inscription?"

She held the package up to the light as Jones had done and shook her head.

"Just a tick."

She turned to her case, retrieved a jeweller's loupe, and returned to the light where she studied the medal closely. "No, sorry. It's too badly worn. I might be able to do something with it in the lab, but" —she squinted beneath a fresh mask—"silver's the devil to work with. It's really soft and the acid test can be somewhat aggressive."

"No sign of a chain on the rug or anywhere else in the room?" he asked, although he already knew the answer.

Dr Spence shook her head. "Afraid not."

"Hang on, I've had an idea." He stepped out into the hall and across to the stretcher. "Do you mind, Dr Spence? I'm not really dressed for this." He beckoned for her to join him.

"You want me to check for marks on his neck?"

He and the slightly-built SOCO, no FSI, were definitely on the same wavelength.

"Yes please. Just to be sure. If the medal was Charlie—er, the victim's, it'll save us some time."

She moved to the other side of the stretcher and unzipped the body bag. "If you'll hold back the flap, I'll examine the body."

She placed a hand on Charlie's left shoulder and gently moved his head to stretch the neck tissue. Nothing. She repeated the process for the other side with the same result. "Now for the tricky part," she said and raised both shoulders off the stretcher, grunting from the effort. "You'll have to help me here, Chief Inspector. Can you check the back of the neck?"

Jones held his breath and tried not to shudder, unwilling to show the forensics specialist any weakness. When he lifted Charlie's heavy head, tissue squelched as the flaps of flayed skin moved and settled. The matted blood in the hair smeared his nitrile gloves, making the head slippery. Jones tried to ignore the smell of rotting offal and the metallic tang of blood. It took more strength than he expected to hold up the head and overcome the gag reflex.

Together, they scrutinised the back of a neck stained blue-green with post-mortem lividity but otherwise unmarked.

"Nothing there," he managed to say before lowering the head and stepping as far from the body as he could without seeming like a wimp.

"Thanks for the help, Dr Spence," he said, peeling off the claggy gloves and dropping them into the evidence bag she held out for him.

"No problem. But if we're going to be working so closely together, I think you should start calling me Robyn."

Jones paused for a moment before showing her a smile.

"Thanks for the help … Robyn."

"Better. But I suppose I should continue to call you Chief Inspector, for appearances' sake?"

"David will do … in private."

Hell. Why say that?

"Right, David," Robyn said, then got straight back to business. "We'll examine the rug properly in the lab, but I'd like to take a good look at it here, if you don't mind. Just a sec."

She hurried from the house and reappeared a few moments later with an empty body bag. "We keep a few of these in the Rover for large items like this." She laid the plastic bag on the floor.

Jones stood back while she took a dozen close-up reference photos. After five minutes searching the material on her knees with a magnifying glass and a black light, she turned to him. "Nothing stands out in particular. There's an awful lot of trace evidence here, though. Fibres, insect remains, food, and other household grime." She sat back on her haunches, rolled her shoulders, and stretched her neck.

"There's a stain over there," she said, pointing to a spot a few inches below where they'd found the medal, "that looks suspiciously like semen, but I'll confirm that later. I don't want to degrade it by running any rushed tests here. Might provide some DNA."

Patrick Elliott appeared in the doorway. "I'm done with the outside, Doc. Will you be needing me for anything in here, or shall I go help Bill upstairs?"

"He's nearly done up there. Nothing much in the rest of the house. You could help me bag this rug, though."

"Happy to."

He unzipped the spare body bag and they carefully folded the rug, lengthways, in half, and in half again. A smaller bag took care of the blanket.

"Now then, will you look at that." Elliott pointed to a dark patch on the floorboards which had been covered by the rug. "What do we have here?"

Robyn stepped alongside Elliott and frowned. Jones moved closer and tried to see what they'd uncovered, but Robyn's shoulder blocked his view. She shuffled aside to let him approach.

"What is it?"

She smiled up at him and her eyes glistened under the bright lights. Jones heartbeat quickened. No doubt the effect of finding another clue.

"Looks like garden soil or compost mixed with flakes of rusty paint. But see this?" She pointed to a triangle of blue paper, each side around five centimetres long, the hypotenuse jagged and torn.

Jones squatted and focused on the blue scrap. "Looks like the corner torn from a much larger piece. That black smudge, might it be printer's ink?"

"Could be, but it's probably too far gone for restoration. It's thick though, closer to card than paper, so we might get lucky and identify its origin."

She placed the paper or card in a plastic evidence bag and sealed it carefully. "We'll put this in the Range Rover's chill box until we can work it. Best way to preserve damp fibres. Patrick would you mind?"

The tall SOCO nodded. He initialled and dated the bag before shuffling from the room.

"Now for the dirt," Robyn said and removed a battery-operated miniature vacuum cleaner from her capacious metal case.

Jones left her to it and allowed Si and Rog to take the body. Neither man offered him their thanks for so speedy a release.

Outside, Jones breathed in the fresh, clean air, clearing his sinuses of the taint of death.

Jones spent the following thirty minutes prowling the house and gardens. He switched his brain to automatic, soaking in the atmosphere and keeping out of Robyn's way.

At 21:58, Robyn finally handed over the scene, and the FSI team packed up and left. Jones stayed in and around the house. This was the only way he knew how to work. Immerse himself in the victim's final resting place and, by some sort of osmosis, gain a "feel" for the case. This time though, he already knew the victim.

Apart from all that, he needed to hide in the house until the canvass finished for the night. He hated door-stepping. Always had and always would. Detested the smells and detritus of other people's lives. He'd done enough of that as a junior officer, and now he had his team and the uniforms to do it for him.

Rank had certain privileges, and delegation happened to be foremost of them.

At 22:30, he called off the canvass and sent the uniforms home —they'd long overstayed the end of their shift. More to the point, no householder wanted a police officer calling later than that—if at all.

He gathered his team outside the house.

"Anything?" he asked Phil.

Phil held up a thick sheaf of template questionnaires. "As we thought, nobody saw or heard anything unusual."

"Wouldn't expect anything else in a place like this," Ben said, glancing around and being unusually negative.

"We need to expand the search to the towers," Jones said, "but that can wait until morning."

"Find anything interesting in the house?" Phil asked.

"Nothing that points us anywhere specific. The SOCO—sorry, the FSIs will work through the evidence and get back to us when they have something. Meanwhile"—he checked his watch—"there's nothing more we can do here tonight. Go home and get what rest you can. I've a feeling this is going to be a long one."

"What time do you want us in tomorrow, boss?" Alex asked, stifling a yawn with the back of her hand.

"Arrive as early as you need to update the system, but I'll see you in the briefing room at oh-nine-hundred hours, bright-eyed and ... whatever. Off you go."

Ben and Alex nodded their goodbyes and headed off, leaving Jones and Phil alone, apart from the solitary constable guarding the house.

"I've called in a local handyman to board up the window and secure the front door," Phil said, checking his watch. "Promised to be here in fifteen. Any point leaving the uniform in place after they've done their stuff?"

Jones pinched his lips together. "Not really. I'm satisfied it's just the dump site, and we've learned all we're going to from the place. I'll make sure the duty officer sends regular patrol cars through the night to ward off the ghouls. After that, we can turn the place over to the owners, assuming Ryan can find out who they are."

"By the way," Phil said, smiling wide. "I never had the chance to congratulate you on the Melanie Archer case. Bloody good job, boss."

"Thanks, but I didn't do much."

"Oh no, not much. Let's see." He held up a hand and counted off the points on his fingers. "You solved two separate but linked murder cases, one of them a triple-header, and by doing so, you exonerated a remand prisoner. On top of that, you exposed a corrupt senior police officer. And all in less than a week. Must be some sort of record even for you."

"I had plenty of support. Yours included—which is amply covered in my report."

"Just saying good work, boss. It's a privilege working with you."

"Get out of it, Philip." Jones swatted a dismissive hand at him. "We're only as good as our last case. The brass will soon forget about Nottingham if we don't find Charlie's killer quickly."

Phil sighed. "True enough. Any ideas?"

"Not a sausage. And I'm too tired to think straight right now."

"Why don't you head off home? It'll be gone midnight before you turn in. I can hang around here for the builder."

"Are you sure? Doesn't seem right to leave you here and slope off to my pit."

Phil sighed. "I'm the one on call, boss. And you're supposed to be on leave until tomorrow. When was the last time you took a whole weekend off?"

Jones tried to think, but the answer eluded him.

"Ask me an easier one."

Like who killed Charlie Pelham.

"Nope," Jones continued, "I'll wait here for the builder. You pop off home before Manda turns in, and don't forget to give her my best."

"Talking of Manda," Phil said, edging closer and lowering his voice to a whisper, "she's bound to ask me what you make of Robyn."

Oh for goodness' sake.

"Okay, Detective Inspector Cryer," Jones said, scowling, "you've made your point. I'm off. See you in the morning."

"Aw c'mon, David," Phil pleaded, hands open. "Give me something to placate Manda. She'll be bending my ear all night."

Jones sighed heavily and shook his head.

"Goodnight, Philip. See you in the morning."

He turned and headed for his leased Škoda, inwardly smiling the whole way, until he was alone in his car when a small part of him wondered why he'd let Robyn call him David so readily.

Chapter Eight

MONDAY 15TH MAY – Morning

Police HQ, Holton, Birmingham, UK

THE SUN HAD BARELY RISEN above the rooftops by the time Jones pulled to a stop in his designated parking spot at HQ. He slipped out of the Škoda and pressed the button on his key fob. The central locking system fizz-clicked and the indicators flashed twice in response. After tugging on the handle twice to confirm the lock, he straightened, rotated his shoulders, and twisted his back to release the cricks—an operation that seemed to take longer each morning.

The rattling, rumbling burble of a leaking exhaust system caught his attention. Jones turned towards the discordant noise and waited for Phil to reverse Manda's little Renault Clio into the parking space beside his. Phil extricated his shoulder from a tangled seatbelt, climbed out, and slammed the door. It didn't catch first time. He grumbled, slammed the door again, and turned the key.

"Got a match, boss? I'm gonna torch this bloody thing."

"Morning, Philip. In a great mood I see."

Phil cast a disgusted sideways glance at the Renault and sneered. "Bloody sardine can. I need a better second car. Driving that chuffing thing's gonna cripple my back." He took a breath and added, "Sleep well?"

"Very well, thanks," Jones lied.

He couldn't remember the last time he slept through the whole night, and having the image of Charlie's destroyed body bouncing around inside his head didn't help one little bit.

"Yeah," Phil said, knowingly, "me too."

"What's wrong with your car?" Jones asked as they crossed the near-empty car park, heading for the main entrance.

"Manda's taking Paul and a girlfriend out of town for the day. They're visiting a mate in the country, so I'm lumbered with that heap of junk. It's her punishment for my inability to prise any information out of you about Rob—"

"That again? For pity's sake, give it a rest, will you?"

"Well, you did ask, boss."

Phil grinned and they continued towards a pair of fully glazed steel doors. Jones bounded up three steps to an open atrium protected by a sloping glass roof. Phil took a little longer and Jones had to wait while his oppo keyed the new number into the keypad entry system. They stopped at the front desk to say hello to the grey-haired Sergeant Featherstone, who sat behind a security screen bolted onto an oak-panelled counter, his shoulders slumped.

"Terrible news about Charlie," Feathers said, just above a whisper.

Jones and Phil nodded.

"Any idea what he was doing on the OTT?"

"Not yet," Jones said. "We're working on it."

"You'll get there," Feathers announced, showing more faith in Jones' abilities than he did himself.

"We'll do our best," Phil answered.

"Anything I can do to help, you only have to ask."

"Thanks, Feathers. We will," Jones said.

Together, Jones and Phil strode along the corridor. He left Phil at the bank of lifts and headed for the stairwell, but stopped halfway and retraced his steps.

"Forgot something, boss?"

"Do you mind rummaging through Charlie's desk in Archives first off? You never know, he might have put something in his diary for Thursday or Friday."

"Fat chance. That would be too easy. Where are you headed? The office?"

"Nope, Not-Bob wants a review before I give the briefing."

Phil lifted his chin and smiled. "Good luck with that, sir. I'd rather sift through Charlie's desk. You start climbing and I'll wait ten minutes for the lift."

"You could always join me. The exercise would do you good."

Phil patted a taut stomach that showed the result of months of rehab and an improved diet. "You climb all the way up to the seventh floor if you like. I get all the exercise I need in the gym and looking after two livewire kiddies."

Jones turned and pushed through the emergency doors to the rear stairwell.

The day he volunteered to enter a cramped metal box—one that hadn't been properly sanitised since its installation—would be the day he'd accept the early retirement HR kept threatening him with.

THE WALL MOUNTED clock outside the seventh floor briefing room read 08:59.

Jones rubbed the sleep from his eyes, but it didn't help remove any of the grit.

He entered to a pleasant surprise—the team had actually kept the place relatively tidy during his brief secondment to Nottingham. Strangely, the lack of crumpled papers, discarded files, and empty coffee mugs littering the conference table's surface brought Charlie Pelham's demise into sharper focus—Charlie being the chief culprit in the SCU's Litter Stakes.

Even in death, Charlie Pelham left his mark.

Apart from Phil, all were present and accounted for.

Closest to Jones, Alex sat, eyes down, tapping away at her laptop. Ryan, hunched over his computer tablet, frowned in concentration. Ben, the team's most recent addition, sat beside Ryan, devouring what looked like a printout of Tim Scobie's interim autopsy report.

Movement in the far corner drew Jones' attention. A redheaded, bespectacled youth poked his head around the side of a large computer monitor, eyes open wide. On seeing Jones, he ducked back behind the screen, as though in hiding.

Jones stared at the corner, waiting for the youngster to reappear, but the redhead remained hidden behind the screen at a desk cluttered with electronic equipment.

"Alex?"

She raised her head and smiled. "Yes, boss?"

Ben and Ryan looked up, too.

"Morning, sir," they said.

He pointed to the corner.

"Anyone care to make the introductions?"

"Sorry, boss?" she said.

"Who's the young man sitting in the corner? Has he done something wrong? Is he being punished?"

Her grin widened. "No, boss. Holden is a civilian technical support officer."

"Holden?"

She nodded. "Holden Bigglesworth, boss. He joined us last week."

Jones turned to face the corner.

"Mr Bigglesworth?" he said and waited.

Slowly, the young man appeared from behind his barricade as he stood. Six feet tall, slim build, pale blue eyes, he smiled nervously and held his narrow shoulders tense.

"Y-Yes, sir?"

"*Holden* Bigglesworth?"

The youngster nodded. "Yes, sir."

"I imagine at least one of your parents was an English teacher?"

The youngster's brows knitted together for a moment then his shoulders relaxed. "Ah, my name. Yes, in fact they both were, Chief Inspector."

"I'm guessing they preferred JD Salinger over WE Johns?"

"My mother did, sir. And she got her way. She usually does. Although, to be honest, I'd have preferred to be called James. It would have made my life so much easier."

Alex and Ryan listened to the exchange, in obvious confusion, until Ben muttered, *"Catcher in the Rye,"* which appeared to explain everything, although Ryan took a little longer to catch the link than Alex.

"What exactly is your role here, Mr Bigglesworth?" Jones asked.

The lad swallowed. "Superintendent Havers assigned me to the Serious Crime Unit temporarily, sir. I'm supposed to help familiarise you—er, everyone, with the new equipment."

Alex's smile dropped. "The Super thinks we will be unable to cope with such advanced technology, boss."

"What advanced technology?"

Ryan pointed to the wall behind the conference table. "That advanced tech, boss."

Jones turned to face the front and frowned at the shiny new addition to the briefing boom.

"A whiteboard?"

Bigglesworth coughed to catch Jones' attention.

"Actually, Chief Inspector, it's a state-of-the-art *Prometheus 2050*. A digital interactive SmartScreen." He stood taller during the announcement, on firmer ground.

Jones nodded. "A *Prometheus 2050*, eh?"

"Yes, Chief Inspector. Best in its class, sir."

"What does it do?"

Bigglesworth opened his mouth and drew in a breath, clearly preparing to explain the device's technical mastery in great detail.

"No, don't bother," Jones said, raising his hand to forestall said explanation. "I'm sure we'll discover how it's going to make our jobs ever so much easier. I imagine, given time, it will eventually make detectives redundant."

Bigglesworth flushed bright red and sat back down.

Jones stood in front of the *Prometheus 2050* and pursed his lips The four-by-two-metre whiteboard covered a large portion of the rear wall. Above it a sign warned:

Serious Crime Unit – Briefing Room
Do Not Remove!

BELOW IT, a comedian had stuck a yellow note to the screen:

SCU – Do not stick papers on this screen!

JONES SHOOK HIS HEAD. He removed the note, crumpled it into a ball, and dropped it into an empty bin. Still shaking his head, he crossed to the large picture window, and lowered the venetian blinds to diffuse the bright, early-morning sunshine. He filled a plastic cup with water from the cooler, returned to his preferred position at the head of the table, and set the cup down on the stained wooden surface. Once again, he wondered where the beermat coasters kept disappearing to.

He paused to take in the whole team, including the redheaded newcomer, Bigglesworth.

"Before we begin, I assume you've had a chance to read the case file and input all your notes?"

All three nodded. Bigglesworth ducked back behind his screen

After a late night and an early morning, they already looked exhausted. Investigating the murder of a former colleague, no matter how widely disliked, would cause emotional and physical stress in the most experienced officers.

"Where is everyone, boss?" Ryan asked, looking around and taking in all the empty seats. "We're not working this case alone, are we?"

"I've asked for some uniforms to help with the rest of the canvassing and the office work. However, since we're dealing with the murder of a fellow officer, I don't want to broadcast the more ... sensitive details. I'll call them in later."

"The prof's interim report doesn't make good reading," Ben said, holding up the printout he'd been studying. "Wouldn't be a good idea for the details to get out."

"Nah," Ryan said. "They're grizzly enough to turn even my stomach. 'Scuse the pun."

Jones scowled at his subordinate.

"DC Washington, that's unacceptable."

Ryan winced and held up a hand.

"Sorry, boss. My bad."

"Don't let your dislike for Charlie affect your work."

He straightened. "Never."

"Okay, moving on." Jones hooked a thumb over his shoulder at the whiteboard. "Mr Bigglesworth?"

A hand in the corner shot up.

"Yes, Chief Inspector?"

"No need for that, lad. We're not in school."

Bigglesworth dropped his hand to its preferred position—heel resting on table, fingers hovering over the keyboard.

"Sorry, sir."

"I assume DS Olganski has been through the running order with you?"

"Yes, sir. She has."

"Okay, would you mind demonstrating the wonders of the *Prometheus 2050?*"

Bigglesworth smiled awkwardly, pushed the metal-framed glasses further up his shiny nose with an index finger, and tapped at the keys. The whiteboard flickered into life and then turned blank again.

Ryan snorted and shook his head.

"C'mon, Biggles," he said. "Get it together, son."

Alex and Ben exchanged glances and turned to study the flickering screen.

Jones shook his head. "Ryan, that'll do. I'm sure Mr Bigglesworth is nervous enough without your heckling. I won't tell you again. When you're ready, Mr Bigglesworth."

"Sorry, sir, just a sec." The young man's face reddened even more and his fingers hit another pattern of keystrokes.

A close-up image of Charlie's naked corpse appeared in the top left corner of the board—clear, crisp, and in vivid colour. A black rectangle obscured his face and another covered his groin, but the exposed midsection showed where most of the damage had been done. A hush descended on the room.

Another photo appeared beside the first, this one depicting the whole of the front room of Number 26, Orchard Park Lane, an address now officially designated as a *secondary* crime scene. In the new photo, Charlie's body was a small shape in the centre of the room, head close to the fireplace. The case number, date, and other technical details appeared above both images.

Jones consulted his notes and made ready to address the team when the door opened, and Phil strolled in. He took a seat, pride of place, next to Jones.

"Any luck downstairs?" Jones asked.

"Yep. You'd never believe it, but Charlie completed all his dailies, filled in his diary, and left a note to tell us who he planned to meet on Thursday night. Case closed."

You're right. I don't believe it.

"Now pull the other one," Ryan said, sniping away from his chair. "I'll give you ten-to-one against him bothering to phone in sick on Thursday or tell his team leader he was taking leave. Right?"

"No takers on that one," Phil answered, looking glum.

"How the hell did he keep his job, boss?" Ryan asked.

No idea.

"What did you find?" Jones asked.

Phil shook his head. "Didn't have time to do anything but collect Charlie's personal papers and drop them on Wash's desk." He turned to Ryan and dipped his head. "Good luck, Detective Constable Washington. It's a real mess."

"Thank you, sir," Ryan said, his voice a dry monotone.

Jones fiddled with the knot in his tie for a second and began. "Right, moving on. Ryan, have you found out who owns the house?"

"Ah, yes. The place was left abandoned when"—he glanced at his tablet—"Mrs Edith Shipley, died last year, on 5th September. Her only living relative, a nephew, Eric Bowden, inherited the place. I found his details on the Land Registry's website. Bowden lives in London—Kensington, no less. Bloke's done pretty well for himself, by all accounts. I have the address if you need it." He held up the tablet.

"Not really. Make sure it's in the case file. Any details on him?"

"Yep. I found him on the Companies House website. He's the Owner and Managing Director of *Bowden Associates PLC*, an asset management company. His wife is down as Company Secretary, and the registered address is the same as Bowden's home address. And by the way"—he paused long enough to eye each of them in turn before returning his focus to Jones—"they reported annual pre-tax profits of a little over five million pounds for the past three years. Like I said, he's done pretty well for himself. No wonder he doesn't care about a semi-detached hovel in Bordesley Green."

"Where was he during our timeline?"

"No idea, boss. Bowden isn't answering his phone and hasn't responded to my voicemail message." He yawned. "Sorry, sir. Late night."

"For us all, Ryan," Ben said, his deep voice rumbling.

"Anyhow," Ryan continued, "it's still early for some people. I'll try calling him again after the briefing. If I don't get any luck by lunchtime, I'll ask the locals in the Met to take a sniff around his gaff."

"Thanks, Ryan. Alex, what do you have from Professor Scobie's prelim. Any idea as to the murder weapon?"

Alex tapped the screen of her laptop. "Items twenty-three to twenty-nine please, Mr Bigglesworth. Folder one."

"It's okay to call me Biggles," the lad announced, gaining confidence in his role. "I'm used to it."

She nodded. "Okay, Biggles. If you please."

Seven images appeared below the others—an array of five x-ray images, and below them, two scanned documents.

Alex looked up from her laptop. "The professor said it was the worst damage he had seen outside of a bomb blast. The abdominal cavity is so badly destroyed that he cannot identify a single intact organ. If not for the tattoo, the body would only be identifiable through dental records and DNA. But the trauma has helped us in one way."

"Which was?" Jones prompted.

"That is what the first document relates to, boss," she replied.

Jones squinted and tried to bring the text into focus. "Mr Bigglesworth, can you make it any bigger?"

"I can, but it's a touch-screen, sir," the lad replied.

"So?"

Phil jumped up and approached the board. "It's new, boss. Installed last week, while you were off gallivanting in Nottingham." He winked.

"Yes, Inspector, it's the *Prometheus 2050*. One of Superintendent Havers' new initiatives. We've been through this already. Show me."

Phil placed his index fingertips on the screen, expanded the first document, and dragged it closer to Jones.

"Wonderful," Jones announced, making his voice chalk dry.

Behave yourself, Jones.

"We know how much you love new gizmos, boss," Phil continued, smiling wide. "I'm surprised you haven't requested one of these beauties before now."

"Sarcasm is the lowest form of wit, Inspector."

"Is it, boss?"

Jones joined Phil at the board and tapped the screen with a hesitant finger. The image disappeared. "Oh for pity's sake. Get that back, Mr Bigglesworth."

"Yes, sir," the techie called from his corner.

"And what's wrong with Polaroids, anyway?"

Phil snorted. Alex smiled and shook her head.

The image returned and Jones tried again, this time with more success.

"Yes, I see. As I said, absolutely wonderful."

He performed the same action—successfully—to the second image, returned to his chair, and studied the documents in comfort. Both were now large enough for him to read easily. The first was a management summary of the interim autopsy report, the full version of which Jones had read at home on his laptop, while eating breakfast. The second was the abstract of a research report, published in *The Lancet* by a string of academics in 2015, the lead author being Professor Timothy Scobie, MB ChB, B Med Sci (Hons), MRCP, FCEM. Jones scan-read the first few lines before giving up.

The effects of flash freezing on human tissue.

During the thawing process, the 36S rRNA V8 gene region suffered significant degradation. DNA sequencing showed advanced protein denaturation. Furthermore, there was a significant shift in microbial community morphology in the remaining tissue. This shows that structural changes during the thawing process have important forensic implications when body tissue has been frozen antemortem.

JONES UNDERSTOOD about one word in three, but the gist was clear and gave credence to the conclusions drawn in Tim Scobie's preliminary report. Something had frozen Charlie from the inside while he was still alive. Jones shuddered.

What a hideous way to die.

"Okay, Alex. You were saying?"

Alex ignored the whiteboard and read directly from her laptop.

"The professor found that the superficial wounds were produced by a knife, the blade of which is most likely between eight and ten centimetres long."

"A knife?" Ryan asked. "A knife did all that?"

Again, Alex dipped her head and continued. "The wounds on the face, arms, and upper body, certainly."

"What about the abdominal injury?" Ben asked, his deep voice carrying well without the need to add much volume.

"Professor Scobie refused to speculate—"

"Of course he did," Phil interrupted.

"But," Alex carried on, "he did say the trauma was extensive and death would have been … rapid."

"So, Charlie didn't suffer?" Ryan asked.

"Not for long," she answered.

Charlie's former and much put-upon partner took in a breath and opened his mouth, but Jones silenced him with a glower and a headshake.

"Alex, are you done?"

"No, boss. There is much more."

"Carry on."

"Image thirty-eight please, Biggles."

Another document appeared on the screen, superimposed over the existing ones, but again, too small to read.

"Professor Scobie couriered a number of tissue samples to the laboratory overnight." Alex looked up from her screen and glanced at the image on the whiteboard. "This document is from the laboratory which suggests a methodology of death."

"Which is?" Ben asked.

"Image thirty-nine, Biggles," she ordered. "The laboratory has identified this as the most likely murder weapon."

The photo of an ordinary-looking hunting dagger flicked onto the screen. The index scale above the knife measured the blade at fifteen centimetres, its lower edge honed and curved to a sharp point, the front third of the upper edge serrated. The handle appeared rubberised. A small hole behind the serration and a steel button on the top of the hilt were the only things marking it as different from a standard hunting knife.

"A Hornet!" Phil gasped, clenching his right hand into a fist. "Damn it. I should have realised sooner. I watched a programme about these things a couple of years ago on National Geographic. Evil bit of kit."

"Explain yourself, Inspector," Jones said. "How could that knife have caused so much damage?"

"It is an injector knife, boss. The handle contains a cylinder of CO2. Once the blade's inside the victim, the attacker presses that button on the handle, and it injects around 800 psi of gas into the body." He winced before hurrying on. "It creates a football-sized gas pocket inside the body. Freezes all the surrounding organs. God, what a way to go."

"Who on earth makes something like that, and for what reason?" Jones demanded.

"An American company, *Florida Hardware Inc*, sells them over the internet. Officially, the knife was designed for divers. To protect them against shark attacks, would you believe?"

"Killing sharks? And one of these things might be doing the rounds in Brum?"

Phil scratched his chin. "Looks like it, boss."

"God alive. What's wrong with people these days?"

"How long you got, boss?" Ryan asked through a wry smile.

Jones moved to the document and manipulated it in the same way Phil had done with the others. He speed-read to the bottom. The print below the signature line read, Dr R Spence.

So, Robyn had worked through the night to identify the murder weapon. Jones made a mental note to thank her for her efforts.

"What about the blood found on the broken glass from the window?" Jones asked.

Alex shook her head again. "I am afraid that it is the same type as Charlie. Dr Spence suspects it is secondary transfer from the clothes of the killer, who would have been covered in blood from the attack. Perhaps he didn't take time to change his own clothes before discarding the … body?"

Jones strode across the room and refilled his cup from the water cooler.

"Did we find anything from last night's canvass?" he asked, desperate for something to latch onto.

Ryan answered. "Nobody saw anything unusual around the time we think the body was dumped." He checked his notes. "Professor Scobie confirmed time of death as between late Thursday evening and early Friday morning. He can't be more specific due to the condition of the body. We're not finished yet, though. Still loads of doors to knock, and we haven't even started on the Towers yet."

Jones returned to his chair and took a long drink before replacing the cup carefully on top of the ring it had already created.

"Let's have a quick review," he said. "Phil, do you mind?"

"Okay, where are we?" Phil breathed deep and faced the table. "One, the initial attack was frenzied. Two, according to the prof, post mortem lividity shows that Charlie lay in the same place—on his back—for as long as five hours before being moved. Three, the killer stripped and cleaned the body carefully, but not until a significant time after death. And four, an anonymous caller tipped us to the body's location."

"Do we have a recording of the emergency call?" Jones asked.

"Still waiting, boss," Ryan answered. "Technical issues in the Comms Room."

"Chase them up when the briefing's over."

"Yes, boss."

Jones turned to his second-in-command. "Carry on, Philip," he said, rolling his hand forwards.

Phil leaned forwards and rested a hand on the table. "Okay, well, I got to wondering about the five-hour delay. I think it's safe to assume that wherever the attack occurred, it would have been indoors, out of sight of onlookers. And, no matter how quickly he died, Charlie was bound to have cried out. There'd have been a hell of a lot of noise and a bucketload of blood. So, he was killed indoors, agreed?"

Phil scanned the room.

Jones followed Phil's gaze to make sure the team were giving him their full attention. Bigglesworth even popped his head out from behind his fortifications.

Phil continued. "So what was the murderer doing in those five hours?" He pointed at the images on the screen. "No one but a ghoul would have wanted to stare at that for five hours." He paused to let the photos emphasise his point.

Ryan broke the brief silence.

"Has to be a local," he said. "Someone familiar with the area."

"And a non-local would have needed a vehicle," Ben agreed, "but none of the neighbours noted a strange car parked outside the house on Friday night."

"If he didn't do it by car, how did the killer transport the body to the dump site?" Ben asked.

"God knows. I wouldn't want to carry a dripping body any distance on my own," Ryan said. "Charlie would have weighed a tonne, even with half his innards missing." He shot Jones an apologetic glance.

"Do you reckon the killer had help?" Ben asked.

"An accomplice?" Jones said. "More than one person wielding an injector knife? God help us."

"According to Professor Scobie, the wounds indicate a single attacker," Alex said.

"But we can't totally rule out an accessory after the fact," Phil countered.

They kicked the discussion around for another fifteen minutes without making much progress before Jones held up a hand.

"Okay, I think it's time to bring in the support team. Phil, do you mind calling Vic Dolan for me?"

Phil reached for the mobile he'd placed on the table and started dialling.

"Mr Bigglesworth," Jones said, "clear the whiteboard, if you please."

Chapter Nine

Police HQ, Holton, Birmingham, UK

MINUTES LATER, the door opened and Sergeant Victor Dolan entered, leading his troop. He nodded at Jones and the others, and held the door open, chivvying his people along.

"Come on, come on. Take your seats. The Chief Inspector doesn't have all morning."

The uniformed officers hurried in—nine constables and two more sergeants.

Jones waited for the shuffling and chair-scraping to stop before standing and facing his expanded audience.

"Is this all we have, Sergeant?" Jones asked. "There are a fair few more doors on the OTT to knock."

"Inspector Macklin sends his apologies, sir," Vic answered, shrugging. "We're all he can spare. Don't worry, though. They're all keen as mustard. Aren't you?"

The comment raised a few smiles, but the tension in the room couldn't have been much more tangible.

Jones breathed deep. "Okay, this will have to do." He cast his gaze over the group, recognising the dark-haired youth sitting in the middle of the front row. "Morning Porterhouse. Fully recovered from last night's shock, I hope?"

The young constable swallowed hard and the faces on either side turned to stare at him.

"Yes, sir. Thank you, sir," PC Porterhouse answered, his Swansea accent as strong as ever.

"Opened any suspicious packages lately?" Jones asked, taking the opportunity to try and ease the room's tension.

"No, sir. Once was more than enough." His sheepish grin made him appear even younger than his nineteen years.

Jones smiled down at the lad. At the same age, if Jones had been involved in a bomb hoax, he might not have acquitted himself quite as well as Porterhouse.

"Right, now. Listen carefully, take notes, and remember this." He ran his eyes around the room. "If you think of something important we've missed, ask away. Otherwise, save any questions until the end. And never forget, we're dealing with the murder of a fellow officer here. Keep all the details to yourselves. Nothing is to reach the ears of the great unwashed. And by that, I mean the press. Do I make myself clear?"

Nods accompanied a muttered and ragged chorus of, "Yes, sir."

"Okay then." He turned to Ryan. "First things first, any sign of DS Pelham's car?"

Ryan shook his head. "None, sir."

"Doesn't it have a tracker?"

The DC wrinkled his nose as though reacting to a bad smell. "Not a chance. It's a ten-year-old Ford Fiesta. No tracker, no info-tainment system, nothing. Wouldn't surprise me if the bloody thing had a cassette player."

A couple of the new arrivals snickered.

"Any ANPR hits?"

Jones referred to one of the few technical innovations he could actually support. One of the few that actually helped the police—the thousands of Automatic Number Plate Recognition cameras dotted around the UK.

"The most recent sighting of Charlie's Ford was last Wednesday," Ryan announced. "The day before he died. He tripped a city centre camera at 18:57, but since then, nothing."

"Where exactly in the city?"

Ryan slid a finger up the screen of his tablet until he found the note. "The corner of Hoxton Street and Eaves Road, boss. And you know what that means."

"The Bold Dragoon," Phil answered for Jones. "Charlie's favourite watering hole."

At that moment, Jones' mobile vibrated. He fished it out of his pocket, read the caller ID, and held up his hand. "It's Dr Spence from the crime lab. I'd better take this. Keep your voices down."

He accepted the call.

"Jones here, Dr Spence."

"'Dr Spence', David?" she said. "Why so formal?" A lightness in her tone showed her amusement.

"I'm in the briefing room."

"Ah, I see. In that case, I'll be, er, … brief."

Despite the situation, he smiled at her deliberate pun.

"Thank you, Doctor."

"We've just completed the second confirmatory analysis of DS Pelham's blood sample. I thought you should know right away."

Jones sighed. "Don't tell me. You found high levels of alcohol."

"I'm afraid so. How did you know?"

"I'm a detective," he said, smiling, "and I knew Charlie Pelham. How high?"

"One hundred and ninety-three milligrams per millilitre of blood. Which is—"

"Well over twice the legal driving limit."

"Precisely. At least it shows DS Pelham didn't drive to his killer."

Wanna bet?

"Perhaps he took a taxi?" she suggested.

"Perhaps. Thanks for letting me know, Dr Spence."

"No problem, David. I'll send you the other findings as soon as we have them."

"No results on the medal yet, I suppose? Or the trace under his fingernails?"

"Give us a chance, Chief Inspector," she answered, sounding tired. "One thing at a time."

"Sorry, but you know what we're up against here. Anyway, thanks for the information. And thanks for working through the night. You must be exhausted."

"I am, and you're welcome. Bye, David."

"Bye, Robyn."

Phil's eyes widened at Jones' use of her first name, but the others didn't seem to notice. When Jones relayed the information to the room, a hand shot up. It belonged to one of the young constables.

"Yes, lad?"

"Can we assume DS Pelham took a taxi the night he died?"

Ryan snorted and waved yet another apology in response to Jones' glower.

"That's what Dr Spence suggested, but I'm afraid neither of you knew Charlie Pelham. But let's not assume the worst. Who's been assigned camera duty?"

At the back of the room, Sergeant Williams raised her hand. "I have, sir."

"Morning, Bethany. Any sign of DS Pelham or his car in or around the OTT the evening he died?"

"None so far, sir. But we've loads more footage to wade through. PCs Akhter and Rahman are working the screens at the moment. I've also sent a team out to chase up the footage from private cameras. There are a few businesses in the area that might have useful CCTV images."

"Thank you. How long have you been on duty?"

"Since midnight, sir. We're happy to stay a little longer, though."

"Good for you, but don't overdo it … and make sure you keep a note for your overtime claim."

"Yes, sir." She smiled.

Ah, the energy of youth.

A hand shot up from IT corner.

"Yes, Mr Bigglesworth?"

The redhead leaned to one side to make himself more visible.

"Sorry for asking, sir, but where exactly is the OTT? I thought we were talking about the Orchard Towers Estate. Shouldn't it be the OTE?"

Heads turned and a low murmur rippled around the room.

"It's a police joke, Biggles," Ryan answered. "The place is a war zone. Drugs, violence, knife crime, gangs. Any uniforms venturing onto the Orchard Towers Estate are taking their life in their hands. It's a bit like going over the top in the trenches. Over the top, OTT. Get it?"

"Too right," an older constable announced to a chorus of agreement. A few quiet titters broke the tension.

"Ah," Bigglesworth said, blushing again, "I see."

"Okay, that's enough," Jones said. "Let's move onto the search. Inspector Cryer?"

Phil stood and addressed the room.

"Since we're making the assumption the killer's a local, we're concentrating all our efforts on the OTT and the immediate suroundings."

"Sir?" a voice rang out. It came from a dark-haired twenty-something in the front row.

"Yes, PC Halle?" Phil asked.

"How can we be so sure he's a local?"

"Because of the location of the body drop. Number 26 is the only derelict house in the row."

"But why that particular house? You don't think he passed by in his car, saw the place was abandoned, and took the opportunity to dump the body there and then?"

"No. It's obvious the place is derelict when you see the state of the garden, but Orchard Park Lane is a cul-de-sac. Only a local would know the house was a potential drop site."

PC Halle frowned. He seemed about to ask another question but shook his head and remained silent.

"So," Phil continued, "we need to ask ourselves who could have known Number 26 was empty."

Another constable, Peter Haldane, threw up his hand. "The Towers, sir?" he said in response to Phil's nod.

"What about them, Pete?" Phil asked.

"I know the OTT pretty well. It's been on my patrol for years. The way I reckon, anyone living in the top few storeys would be able to see right into Number 26's front garden. They'd know it was a derelict."

"You make a good point, Constable," Jones said, joining Phil in front of the whiteboard, "which is why our next move is to knock on every door on the OTT."

"But," Haldane said, "why did he bother?"

"What do you mean?" Phil asked.

Jones knew the root of Haldane's question but wanted the conversation to play out in case his own overnight revelation didn't hold water.

"Well," Haldane said, looking a little uneasy, "the Towers are due for demolition soon, right?"

Jones and Phil nodded.

"So," Haldane continued, "the Council's been trying to empty the place for years. It's left the blocks to rot. Some of the flats have been empty for ages. A few have been turned into squats and others are shooting galleries—I mean, drug dens."

"And," Phil said, "your point is?"

"Why take the risk of lugging Charlie—er, DS Pelham's body all the way down to Orchard Park Lane? Why not just dump him in one of the empty flats? They already stink to high heaven. We wouldn't have found him for ages. Months even."

Maybe that was the point.

The mobile phone on the table in front of Ryan rattled. He snatched it up, glanced at the screen, and stood. "Sorry, sir. It's Eric Bowden. I'll take it outside." He accepted the call and hurried towards the door. "Mr Bowden, thanks for returning my —" The door closed behind him, cutting off the rest of the conversation.

"Constable Haldane, you were saying?" Jones said, nodding his encouragement.

"Well, it seems to me," Haldane said, growing in confidence and making a bid to be considered next in line for a vacant detective slot, "that dumping Charlie in the lane wasn't very bright."

"Perhaps he wanted to draw our attention away from the Towers," Jones suggested, playing Devil's Advocate.

"Didn't work though, did it," Haldane shot back.

Good lad.

"No, Pete," Phil said, thoughtfully. "It didn't."

"So, why did he bother?"

"When we find him," Phil said, "that's one of the questions we'll be sure to ask."

"My money says he's gonna spout 'No comment' all the way through the interviews."

"We'll see, Constable."

"Sir?" PC Porterhouse said, pushing up a tentative hand.

"Yes, Gareth?" Jones said.

"Do you think he *wanted* us to find the body?"

Yes, I do.

"That's another question we'll be asking," Phil answered.

"And don't forget the anonymous tipster," Porterhouse added.

"We haven't," Phil responded.

"Right," Jones said, drawing a line under the speculation, "top priority now is the door-to-door. I want every one of those flats knocked by the end of the day. Mr Bigglesworth? Can you pull up a map of the estate?"

Everybody except the redheaded lad in the corner, turned to face the screen.

An ordnance survey map of the area expanded onto the Smart-Screen, showing the six high-rise blocks grouped in a wide semi-circle around Orchard Park Road and Orchard Park Lane. Jones move closer to the screen and expanded the map by stretching his fingers across its surface.

That was easy. Must be getting the hang of it.

An aerial photograph of the area of interest materialised in the top right-hand corner of the screen. "Nice one, Mr Bigglesworth," Jones said. "That type of initiative will push you towards the top of my Christmas card list."

The civilian's boyish face broke into a wide smile, revealing an upper row of teeth in tramline braces.

The aerial photo reminded Jones about something and he pointed to an area on the picture. "Anybody find out whether they were brewing last week?"

"Yes, boss," Alex responded, "from Wednesday through until Saturday evening."

"Right, thanks. It would have masked the smell coming from poor Charlie."

Phil lowered himself into his chair and massaged his knee as though out of habit. "I've been through the questionnaires from last night's initial sweep. As Ryan said, there's nothing of any use. Either nobody answered, or we drew a blank."

"Doesn't matter, I want all the doors knocked again. Orchard Park Road and Lane, and all the towers. But let's try to narrow our search first."

After a few seconds' scrutiny, Jones identified two towers with potentially the best views of the house—the middle two, Towers 3 and 4.

He reached out and tapped two fingers on the whiteboard. The map expanded to cover the entire screen. "DI Cryer will organise the search teams. Target these two as the 'hot' blocks first, and spread out from there. Right, then. Gather in the car park in thirty minutes. I've already sanctioned a catering wagon for drinks and sandwiches. You'll be working through lunch again."

Vic ushered his people away. One of the older constables ruffled Gareth Porterhouse's hair and called him a "teacher's pet". The young constable reddened, but took the gentle ribbing in good spirit.

Jones' team stayed behind for final instructions, but before he could say anything, Ryan returned, a look of disappointment showing on his moon face.

"What did Eric Bowden have to say for himself?" Phil asked, jumping in before Jones could.

"He's out of the frame, boss. Bowden and his wife have been on a cruise in the West Indies for the past three weeks. They flew from Heathrow to Kingston, Jamaica, and sailed on the *Ocean Cloud*. Okay for some, eh?"

"Three weeks on a boat with a load of drunken toffs?" Ben said. "Not my idea of a holiday."

"Sour grapes?" Ryan asked, grinning. "Anyway, they only got back home this morning, which is why he didn't answer my calls last night."

"Have you confirmed any of it?"

"Not yet, boss. I asked Bowden to send me copies of their electronic booking slips." His mobile buzzed again, and he tapped the screen. "Yep, this is it." He scrolled through the email for a few moments. "Looks kosher to me, boss."

"What did he say about the house?"

"Not a lot. Claims not to have any interest in the place. He plans to sell it at some stage, but he hasn't instructed an estate agent yet. If you ask me, he spent more on his bloody cruise than he'll ever get for Number 26."

"Okay, Ryan," Jones said. "Confirm they were aboard for the whole cruise, but there's no need to rush."

Phil held out a hand. "Can I have a quick word, boss?"

"Fire away."

"In private?"

He arched an eyebrow. "If you like. Okay guys, go powder your noses. Meet downstairs in twenty-five. Alex, see you in five."

Alex nodded. She, Ben, and Ryan gathered their belongings and filed out of the room, closely followed by Holden Bigglesworth.

"Okay, Philip. Spit it out."

"When you dismissed the uniforms, you said, '*You'll* be working through lunch again.' Not, 'we'."

"I did indeed." He dropped the smile.

Out with it, Phil.

"You and Alex aren't coming with us?"

"Believe me, I'd like to, Philip. I really would. But I have a much more onerous task to perform."

73

"More onerous than standing in the hot sun, supervising a load of sweaty cops hammering on doors and talking to even sweatier members of the public?"

Jones nodded. "Much worse." He paused. "I have to break the news to Lydia Pelham."

"Ah, I see. I was going to offer you a swap, but I've changed my mind. And you're taking Alex with you?" His grin bordered on nasty.

"Yes, for my protection, not Lydia's."

"Don't blame you." He grabbed his phone from the table and slipped it into his pocket. "Oh, one more thing. Haldane made sense, didn't he?"

"He did. As did young Porterhouse."

"You think the killer wanted us to find Charlie sooner rather than later?"

Jones winced. "Yes, I do."

"Bloody hell. Why would he do that?"

"No idea, but I've got a bad feeling about this case."

"Yeah, me too."

Jones suppressed a shudder. The dark cloud hanging over his head hadn't felt so heavy since the Hollie Jardine case.

Chapter Ten

MONDAY 15TH MAY – Afternoon

Edgbaston, Birmingham, UK

JONES INDICATED LEFT and pulled into Church Street, Edgbaston, a leafy and treelined part of the city. Cottonwool clouds cast small shadows, and the trees threw stippled images across the road. He lowered his sun visor and eased up on the throttle, squinting through the Škoda's dust-and-insect-smeared windscreen. He worked the washer, but it struggled to clear the grime. The car needed a full valet. He'd been too busy to run it though the carwash since his return from Nottingham. Another chore to add to his to-do list.

"This is rather impressive," Alex said, glancing around the neighbourhood. "I expected something different for Charlie."

"A flat on the OTT?"

She showed him a gentle smile. "Something of the kind."

"Lydia Pelham owns a string of beauty salons. She's doing well, by the looks of things."

"Ah, I see. Have you visited here before?"

He shook his head. "No reason to."

No desire, either.

"We're looking for Number 118."

"Even numbers on your side, boss." She pointed to a bay-fronted, detached house on the right. "There is Number 56. Keep going."

Jones added a little more pressure to the throttle.

"You are certain she is home?"

He slowed the car even further and dipped his head. "I called her flagship salon before we left. She's working from home today."

"She knows we are coming?"

"No. I told them I wanted to book a facial for my wife and only Lydia would do."

Alex tutted. "You are a bad man."

"Needs must, Alex. I wanted to gauge Lydia's reaction to the news face-to-face."

"You think she might have something to do with what happened to Charlie?"

"Not really, but who knows? Would you want to share all this with someone like Charlie?" He pointed through the windscreen at the expensive houses lining the street.

"Not I, boss. But it takes all sorts."

Thirty-two houses later—each more expensive-looking and impressive than the last—Jones spotted their destination. A two-metre-high wall and a pair of wrought iron gates protected a large bungalow in a massive plot. He almost whistled. The place wouldn't have given much change, if any, from two million pounds.

Lydia *had* been doing well. Very well. What on earth did she see in a useless lump like Charlie?

"Ready?" Jones asked.

"As I will ever be, boss."

"It's always been the worst part of the job."

"You've done this a few times in your career, I imagine?"

Jones sighed. "Once or twice, but it never gets any easier. Sorry to put you through this Alex, but I needed a chaperone and you're a better option than an FLO."

"Not a problem, boss. Lydia Pelham and I have met before."

"Really?"

"At the last three Christmas parties. She is great fun. The life and soul."

"Ah, yes. I see." He screwed up his face. "I don't do Christmas."

Too many painful memories.

"I know, boss."

Her sad smile told him how keenly she still felt the loss of her wife, Julie. He and Alex had the death of a spouse in common, not that anyone in the team knew it, except Phil.

"Okay, let's get this over with." He pulled into the short drive and stopped close enough to press the call button on the video intercom system built into the curved wall. A green light above the camera lens powered up. He looked into the lens, but kept his face serious.

"*Jones? That you?*" Lydia's smoker's voice sounded surprised.

"Morning, Lydia. Can we come in, please?"

"*No you … can't. Bugger off!*"

The green light deactivated.

"Charming," Alex said.

"She's always had a wonderful way with words."

He reached out and pressed the button again.

Green light on.

"*I told you to bug—*"

"Lydia, let us in. It's about Charlie."

"*If you've come to try and convince me to sweet talk him into droppin' the complaint, you can do one!*"

"It's nothing to do with the complaint, Lydia. Please let us in."

"*Who's that with you?*"

"Alex. Alex Olganski. My DS."

"*Charlie's replacement? Oh fuck, this is official, innit. What's he done now? Wrapped his car around another lamppost? Has the idiot hurt himself?*"

Before Jones could respond, the green light dimmed, electric motors hummed, and the double gates rolled apart. In case Lydia changed her mind, Jones waited for the gap to widen enough to allow access before stamping on the throttle and darting through.

The Škoda's tyres crunched on the short gravel drive, and Jones parked in front of a fully glazed front door. Before he could release his seatbelt, the door pulled open and Lydia appeared, wearing a thin dressing gown and no makeup. She'd piled her long, bleached hair on top of her head and held it in place with a black plastic hair-grip. In her right hand, she carried a tall glass, half full of a thick red liquid that could have been a tomato juice—or a Bloody Mary.

"Come on," Lydia snapped, "what's happened? What's my Charlie done now?"

Jones extricated himself from the seat belt, climbed out of the Škoda, and headed straight for the house. Alex followed. They stopped at the door, but Lydia stood in the gap and showed no signs of letting them past.

"Lydia, can we come in, please?" Alex said, her voice low and soothing.

"I-I'm not dressed," Charlie's widow said, pulling the panels of her dressing gown together at her throat.

Jones averted his eyes, hoping she wore something underneath. The last thing he needed was to catch a glimpse of a naked Lydia Pelham.

The very last thing.

"It's important, Lydia."

"Fine. C'mon in, then, if you're comin'."

Lydia backed away and leaned against the inner wall. She raised the glass to her filler-plumped lips and took a healthy swig.

"No," she said. "Case you're wonderin'. It ain't a Bloody Mary. Straight up tomato juice. Didn't even add any Worcestershire sauce. And definitely no vodka." She drained the glass and held it close to her chest, gripping it in both hands.

"What's happened to my Charlie?"

Tears formed in Lydia's big brown eyes. She tried to match Jones' frown but the Botox caused her to lose the struggle.

"You need to sit down for this. Can we go through to the lounge?"

Her lower lip trembled and the tears rolled down puffy cheeks.

"Oh God. He's dead! My Charlie's dead, ain't he!"

She collapsed, wailing, to the parquet floor. The glass fell from her hands and rolled in a semicircle around her knees.

"Alex?"

Jones stood back as Alex swooped in to offer comfort.

IT TOOK Alex fifteen minutes to help Lydia into the master bedroom to wash her face and dress, fending off desperate and raised questions the whole time. In the meantime, Jones found the kitchen—beautifully designed in blacks, greys, and dark blues, with acres of pure white quartz surfaces. Thousands of pounds had been sunk into such a kitchen. It made Jones' own hand-built oak and woodblock galley pale by comparison.

After taking a minute to work out how to programme the instant kettle, he made a pot of tea, delighted to find a caddy of leaves in one of the cupboards—large leaf Darjeeling—when he'd expected to suffer teabags.

When he thought of the mess Charlie created everywhere he went, Jones wondered how *Chez* Pelham could look so pristine. Lydia either spent long hours cleaning up after him or, more likely, employed people to do it for her.

Alex popped her head around the kitchen door.

"Boss, she is ready. We are in the front room." She pointed over her left shoulder.

"On my way."

He loaded the tray with the necessary items and carried it through. Lydia, fully dressed in tight jeans and a loose-fitting top—thankfully buttoned up to the throat—refused the tea, and Jones set it down.

Pity to waste a nice cuppa, but such is life.

"There's no easy way to say this, Lydia, but I'm afraid Charlie was murdered."

Her mouth formed an "O", but no words came out. Tears fell again, this time silent. She dabbed her eyes with a fresh tissue taken from a box on the glass-topped coffee table and blew her nose.

Jones gave her time to settle before asking his first question.

"When did you see him last?"

Lydia shuddered and closed her eyes. She wiped them with the same dirty tissue. Jones looked away.

Alex, sitting close beside Lydia on the triple sofa, placed a hand on her shoulder and squeezed.

"H-How did he ... did he die?"

"A stabbing." Jones spared her the details.

She'd learn more at the Coroner's Inquest, but she'd probably be stronger by then.

"D-Do you know who?"

"Not yet, but we will."

She blinked away some more tears. "Will you?"

"We'll do our very best. I promise."

"They're letting you head the investigation, despite—"

"Yes."

Jones stiffened, expecting an outburst, but she nodded and said, "Good. Charlie always said you were the best detective he'd ever worked with."

Jones couldn't have been more stunned.

"He did?"

She nodded and wiped her eyes again, this time with a clean tissue.

"Just because you and him fell out, don't change things, does it? My Charlie deserves the best, doesn't he?"

"He does," Alex answered for him.

"Lydia?" Jones said.

"Huh?"

"Will you help me find Charlie's killer?"

She looked into his eyes for the first time in a while and blinked away the latest flood.

"I-If I can."

"When did you last see him?"

"Um, Thursday morning. At breakfast."

Thursday? Excellent.

They were making progress at last. Placing Charlie at home on Thursday morning narrowed the timeline.

"What time did he leave?"

"We had a stinking row," she said, speaking to the crushed tissue and answering the question before Jones had time to ask it. "He'd come home in the middle of the night, roaring drunk as usual. Parked his old car across the drive, blocking me in again. We screamed at each other for a bit, and I threw him out, again."

"This was Thursday morning?"

She nodded. "Are you going to ask why I didn't raise the alarm when he didn't come back?"

"Why didn't you?"

"It's happened before. Loads of times. Charlie and I have a flaming row. I throw him out. Charlie disappears for a couple of days in one of his drinking holes. Then he crawls back, tail between his legs, and I forgive him. Only this time, he isn't coming back. Is he?"

Her lower lip started trembling again.

To stave off another outburst of tears Jones jumped in with another question.

"When he left on Thursday morning, did he take his car?"

She looked up and her eyes snapped into focus.

"What?"

"Did he take his car?" Jones repeated.

She sniffled into the new tissue, which looked ready to disintegrate in her hands. He grabbed the box and offered her a fresh one, which she took and rolled up into the first.

"I screamed at him and he left." Tears fell again. She let them fall. "That's the last time I'll ever see him, right? The last thing he heard me say was, 'Get out!'. Oh my God. What have I done?"

"Lydia, did he take his Ford?"

Finally, she wiped away the latest stream of tears.

"Huh? N-No. He took the Citroën. The Ford's in the garage with a damaged nearside front wing and a flat tyre."

"Citroën?"

No wonder they hadn't found Charlie's Ford.

"The housekeeper's car. She's away for the week, and I wouldn't let him take my Audi." She gulped. "I told him to call for a taxi, 'cause he still reeked of booze. Then he just stormed out after telling me to sod off."

"Lydia, do you have the registration number?"

She took a deep, settling breath and nodded.

"Just a sec."

She picked up her mobile from the coffee table and worked the screen.

"All our cars are leased through the company. It saves on the VAT. I keep a list. Here you are."

She turned the mobile towards him. Jones flashed a look at Alex, who picked up on his meaning. Alex held out her hand and Lydia dropped the phone into it. She excused herself and left the room, but stood in the open doorway—for Jones' protection rather than Lydia's. Protocol demanded a witness-cum-suspect should never be left alone with an officer of the opposite sex.

"Lydia," Jones said, keeping his voice down, "did Charlie have an office here?"

She nodded.

"Mind if I take a look?"

"What for?"

"Did he keep a diary?"

"Charlie? A diary? Fat chance. A few notes on scraps of paper, maybe."

"Can I check it out anyway?"

Another sniff.

"If you have to." She waved a hand towards Alex. "The office is the third door along from the kitchen. I stuff all Charlie's papers in the bottom drawer of the filing cabinet. It's a real mess. Don't know what you hope to find."

Nor do I.

82

As he stood, Alex ended her call and stepped back into the room.

"Sergeant Williams has the details. She will contact NADC right away."

"Thanks, Alex. Take over for me, will you?"

"David?" Lydia called.

She'd never used his given name before. He had no idea she even knew it.

"Yes, Lydia."

"Where did you find him?"

He hesitated a moment, not certain she really needed to know. On the other hand, the local TV news would be on soon and she'd be bound to find out from someone.

"The Orchard Towers Estate," he said.

"The OTT?"

"Yes. Any idea why he'd be there?"

"None." She lowered her eyes to her lap. "Absolutely none," she added, jaw clenched.

Jones recognised a lie when he heard one. The first she'd told since opening the door to them.

———

IT DIDN'T TAKE LONG to search the Pelhams' home office. He found Charlie's papers where Lydia said they'd be.

Like Charlie himself, the notes were an unholy mess. Hastily scribbled, scratched onto scraps of paper torn from notebooks, they were stuffed into three lever arch box files. He flipped through the contents of the first box and soon gave up. If this wasn't a job for Phil Cryer's keen eye, or for Ryan Washington's experience of working with Charlie, nothing ever would be.

Seeing Charlie's erratic penmanship and reading his semi-literate scribblings brought to mind the last time he'd had any offi-cial contact with the man as a direct subordinate. The meeting had taken place in Jones' office upon his return from France during the Hollie Jardine investigation. He remembered the scene clearly.

"What the hell's wrong with you, man?" Jones had said.

He stood less than a foot from Charlie, close enough to make out individual beads of sweat on the foul-smelling man's shiny forehead. Jones kept his voice low, but allowed rage to colour his tone.

"Don't know what you mean, boss." Charlie's words oozed innocence, but his voice faltered. His eyes remained fixed on a spot above Jones' head, but his Adam's apple bobbed beneath the triple chin.

"Why did you make that announcement to the press? You practically sent the kidnapper an open invitation."

"Hang on a minute, boss. I ain't taking the blame for Hollie Jardine going missing again. That ain't right."

"You bloody well *are* to blame! What were you trying to do, grab some of the limelight?"

"That's offensive, that is. I'm offended by that." Pelham lowered his eyes to meet Jones' fierce glare. "The media had a right to know what were happ—"

"Moron!" Jones shouted.

Charlie flinched under the force of the word. "I heard all about it from more than one source. You stood there smirking, lapping up the attention. You supercilious bastard." Jones had never sworn in the station before, rarely even raised his voice, and the startled look on Charlie's face showed the impact.

"I-I … er …" Charlie backed away, head shaking and jowls quivering. "It happened so fast, boss." He threw both hands out in front of his chest, as though trying to ward off an impending attack. "I … were just … just—"

"You did nothing to help find her. Your timekeeping's appalling. You're paperwork's a joke, and you always take the easy way, the lazy option. You're nothing but a useless lump." Jones whispered the accusation and backed away from the trembling man. "You're finished in the SCU. Pack your bags and take a week's leave. I'm having you transferred to Records. By the time I'm finished, you'll be lucky to find yourself writing parking tickets on the OTT. You are dismissed."

"You can't do that. It's … unfair." Charlie advanced half a step but stopped when Jones bunched both his hands into fists.

"Watch me. The transfer papers will be with HR within the hour."

Charlie crumpled in front of Jones' eyes.

Jones twisted the dagger. "And if I can find anything criminal in your background, taking backhanders from the press, dereliction of duty, *fraudulent overtime claims*"—Charlie grimaced—"or a faulty bloody brake light, you can bet your useless life I'll nail you for it. Now get out of my sight!"

After his outburst, Jones had dropped into his chair and turned his back. The office door slammed shut. He thought he heard the disappearing Charlie say something hackneyed and uninspired like, "You've not seen the last of me, Jones," but that might have been in his imagination.

As Jones sat in the chair in the Pelhams' home office, the weight of the case bore down on him. Kicking Charlie off the team had been justified, of course it had, but he couldn't let his negative feelings for the man cloud his judgement or cast a shadow over the investigation.

HE FOUND Alex and Lydia where he'd left them, in the lounge. The moment he stepped through the door, they stopped talking and looked up.

"Find them okay?" Lydia asked.

"Yes, thanks. I left them on the chair in the hall. Alex, can you give Lydia a receipt for three box files filled with assorted papers?"

"Don't bother," Lydia said. "I never want to see them again."

"Nonetheless, the law requires us to give you a receipt. Alex?"

He stood in the doorway while Alex did the business. The whole time, Lydia Pelham refused to meet his gaze. She simply stared at the tissue crushed in her hands.

"Lydia?"

"Yes?" she answered, without looking up.

"The Orchard Towers Estate?"

"What about it?"

She still refused to make eye contact.

"Come on, Lydia. Why did we find Charlie on the OTT?"

"No idea." She swiped her eyes with the tissue but they didn't look wet, more angry. "Will I need to identify Charlie's … body?"

"I'm afraid so, but there's no rush. Tomorrow will do. I'll have someone contact the Coroner's Office to arrange a time. A Family Liaison Officer will be in touch. She'll go with you."

"Okay." She stood. "Now, please go."

Alex stood, too.

"Do you have anyone you can contact? Someone to stay with you?" she asked.

Alex rested a hand on Lydia's forearm, but she snatched it away.

"Yes. I'll call my sister. Thank you. I'll show you to the door."

"That's okay, Lydia," Jones said, "we can see ourselves out. What about the gates?"

"They'll open automatically."

Jones collected the box files and they quickly made their way back to the Škoda. Before he fired up the engine, Alex turned to him.

"That was interesting," she said.

"What was?"

"The way she changed after you mentioned the OTT."

"Yes, that's what I thought."

"What is she hiding?"

What indeed.

Jones had no idea, but he knew a man who might.

Chapter Eleven

Edgbaston, Birmingham, UK

JONES PULLED through the gates and turned left onto Church Street, heading back into town.

"Where are we going to now, boss?"

"We're heading out to the OTT to help with the canvass, but Holton's on our way. We can drop the box files in Phil's office, grab some lunch, and then head out."

"That is a good idea. I missed breakfast. Could not face anything substantial this morning."

Me neither.

He shot her a sideways glance. Alex had been losing weight recently—ever since Julie's murder. She looked a little drawn.

"How's it going with the grief counsellor?"

Alex turned her face away, seemingly watching the buildings flying past the window.

"It is going well."

"Anything I can do?"

"No, boss. But thank you."

"If you need more time off—"

"No, sir." She tore her gaze away from the lacklustre view and stared eyes-front. "That is the last thing I need."

"Understood."

He pursed his lips, swallowed, and focused his concentration on filtering onto the ever-busy ring road.

"I'm always here if you need to talk."

"Thank you, boss. I appreciate that."

"You're important to me … and to the team."

"Thank you."

After five minutes of silence, Jones' mobile buzzed. Without taking his eyes from the road, he hit a button on the steering wheel and the call connected.

"Jones here," he said to the car's built-in mic.

Alex stared at him wide-eyed.

"What," he whispered, "you think I don't know how to work Bluetooth?"

He winked and she smiled, a little like her old self.

"It's Ron Macklin, Chief Inspector. In the ops room."

"Afternoon, Ron. What's up?"

Without indicating, a red panel van in the outside lane cut in front of them, causing Jones to dab a foot on the brakes and sound the horn.

"Moron!" he growled.

The driver stuck his hand out the window and gave Jones the finger. On a quieter day, Jones would have worked the blue lights, pulled the man over, and read him the riot act.

"Excuse me, sir?"

"Sorry, Ron. I'm on the ring road and the standard of driving is as high as ever. What can I do for you?"

"We've found a body."

Another one?

"Where?"

"Sandwell Valley Country Park, West Bromwich."

Jones eased his foot off the throttle a little and slowed the Škoda to a sedate fifty-five. The driver in the Volvo behind began tailgating and flashing his headlights. Jones ignored the angry hurry-up.

"You know what we're dealing with right now, Ron. Can anyone else take it? What about DI Jordan? He's local to West Brom."

"Sorry, sir. His team's down one detective—broke his leg playing footie—and they're working that triple stabbing in Handsworth. Gangs are involved. And before you ask, DI Scranton's in court all day. His DS, Paul De Villiers, is on scene, but it's his first solo run as lead investigator, and ... well, I think he could do with some support. Normally I wouldn't ask, what with Charlie's ... you know, but there's no one else I can call."

"Okay, Ron. Send the details to Alex's mobile. She's with me in the car."

"Thanks, Chief Inspector," Macklin said, sounding relieved. "I'll call De Villiers and let him know you're on your way."

I bet he'll be delighted.

"Okay, Ron."

Jones indicated left at the next slip road. They'd have to double back on themselves.

Two minutes after he'd ended the call with Macklin, Alex's mobile bleeped in her hand. She opened the email and started reading.

"What do we have, Alex?"

"Earlier this morning, an elderly couple walking their dog spotted what looked like the body of a man in bushes near Swan Pool. You know it?"

"Yep. It's just off Park Lane. Near the mountain bike trails."

Jones picked up the A41 north and flicked on the blue lights. As usual, the other drivers ignored him until he activated the two-tone sirens.

THREE PATROL CARS formed an L-shaped barrier in the far corner of the Swan Pool car park. They blocked off the exit leading to the MBTs. Two other official vehicles completed the gathering—a SOCO Range Rover and a fire engine. A few civilians interrupted their strolls to take a gander, but most carried on with their walks. According to the notice boards at the entrance to the car park, the hiking trails around Swan Pool offered a choice of both gentle and strenuous exercise suitable for the whole family.

"DCI Jones and DS Olganski," Jones said, showing his warrant card to a strangely familiar constable guarding the entrance.

He noted their names on his clipboard.

"Where's the body?"

"Follow the left-hand trail for half a mile, sir. Trail number three. It's one of the tougher ones. A bit of climbing involved."

He glanced at Jones' feet and nodded, seemingly happy with Jones' choice of footwear—walking shoes with thick soles.

"Thanks for the warning, Constable ...?"

"Parkin, sir. We met on the Raymond Collins case."

"Aha. Thought I recognised you, lad. How's the rugby training going?"

Parkin's flying tackle to take down the fleeing murderer would live long in Jones' memory. At the time, he considered it worthy of gracing the hallowed turf at Twickenham.

The young constable offered a sheepish smile. "It isn't, sir. I prefer footie."

Jones sniffed. "Takes all sorts, I suppose. You weren't first on the scene, were you?"

Parkin shook his head. "No, sir. I've only just arrived. As have the SOCOs and the fire service." He nodded towards the Range Rover. "If you hurry, you might catch them up. They had quite a bit of gear to carry."

Jones heartrate kicked up a notch, as he thought of the diminutive Robyn Spence. But it was ridiculous to assume she'd be attending this scene. She'd been up most of the night and still had plenty of work to occupy her on the Pelham case.

"Thank you, constable. Keep an eye on the cars, eh? Loads of nasty people about. Wouldn't want any of them going missing." He winked.

"Will do, sir."

Jones turned away from the smiling Parkin.

"Alex, are you ready for a hike?"

"Always, boss."

TEN MINUTES IN, they reached the top of another steep rise. Jones paused for a breath and to remove his jacket. The afternoon sun warmed his back, and sweat formed on his brow and under his armpits. He wiped his face with a handkerchief and marched on. At his side, Alex's heavy breathing confirmed the trail's difficulty was causing his breathlessness, not so much his advancing age.

"Beautiful place, boss," Alex said, gazing around at the scenery. "I haven't been here before."

Trees and bushes stretched up and out around them. The sweet smell of the country filled his lungs. Such city green spaces were invaluable to the nation's health and wellbeing. To the south, the dark waters of Swan Pool seemed to absorb the sunlight rather than reflect it back at him.

Only slightly unnerving.

They took a sharp turn at the bottom of a steep-sided valley where two trails crossed and he almost stumbled into the back of a lone civilian who stood, staring uphill, forearms tight to her chest, hands clasped as though in prayer.

"Excuse me, miss."

The woman jumped and spun around so fast, she almost toppled over.

Jones reached out a steadying hand, but she brushed it away.

Makeup free, angular features, grey eyes, short-cropped dark hair plastered to her head with sweat, she stood as tall as Jones— and about as slim. She wore loose-fitting clothes, jacket and trousers, and hiking boots. A small backpack hung off one shoulder. It looked light.

Jones smiled. "Sorry, miss. Are you okay?"

"You startled me," she gasped, her voice husky, breathless. "I'm fine now, thank you."

"Good, good. Out for a walk, I see?"

Idiot. Of course, she's out for a walk.

What else would she be doing in the park?

The woman nodded. "It's so peaceful here. Apart from the mountain bikes, which can be a nightmare. Dangerous, too. Never keep to the right. What's happening?" She pointed to the crime scene tape stretched across the narrow path that led uphill and straight ahead.

"As the tape says, miss, this is a crime scene." Jones flashed her his warrant card. "I'm DCI Jones. This is my colleague, DS Olganski."

"A crime scene?" She read Jones' ID and shot Alex an appraising glance. "Out here? Really?"

"I'm afraid so. Hikers found a body this morning."

"A body?" She raised a hand to her mouth. "Oh my goodness."

She kept her fingernails short, unvarnished. Long fingers, strong hands.

"You walk here often?"

"As often as I can, but I avoid the weekends. As I said, the bikers can be dangerous, but …" Again, she glanced at Alex before sighing and shaking her head slowly.

"When were you last here?"

She glanced at the sky before speaking. "Um … last Thursday afternoon. Around two o'clock. But I didn't take this track. I walked, er … trail one. Or was it trail two? No, trail one. Definitely. The last time I walked this particular route was Tuesday."

"Did you see anything unusual at the time?"

Another pause for thought. Another glance to the sky.

"Not a thing, I'm afraid."

"No disturbed undergrowth, no strange smells? No strangers loitering around the park?"

She lowered her hand to her throat. "There are always plenty of strangers loitering around the place, Chief Inspector. After all, that's the whole point of being here. Not loitering, but hiking, I mean. Strolling. But, no, I didn't see anything out of the ordinary. And I'm sure I would have noticed a strange odour. I have an acute sense of smell."

He studied the striking woman for a moment and nodded.

"Thank you, Ms …?"

"Lean. Annette Lean. And it's 'Mrs', not Ms."

Jones smiled. The name suited her—not that he'd ever say so aloud.

"Thank you, Mrs Lean. If you do happen to remember anything, please contact your local police station."

Hand still at her throat, she nodded. "Of course."

"Would you mind giving my colleague your contact details?"

"I'd be happy to," she said, turning to Alex.

"You have this, Alex?"

"Yes, sir," Alex said, stepping closer.

He left her to it and headed off, ducking under the tape. Hopefully, Alex wouldn't take too long to follow him up the next hill.

When he reached the top of the rise, he glanced back. Alex and Mrs Lean were still chatting. Alex tapped something into her mobile phone and smiled. Mrs Lean smiled, too.

Seeing Alex smile again lifted Jones' spirits. They lifted even more when he spotted the small woman in the baggy white coverall directing operations at the crime scene below.

Chapter Twelve

MONDAY 15TH MAY – Afternoon

Sandwell Valley Country Park, West Bromwich, UK

JONES HURRIED to the bottom of the short slope. Robyn crouched on her haunches, peering over the edge of what looked to be a deep ditch, talking into her voice recorder. Five uniformed police officers stood in a circle behind another line of crime scene tape, watching the proceedings but doing little else.

Jones stopped ten metres up the trail, singled out the sergeant— a tall, square-shouldered man in shirtsleeves and stab vest—and beckoned him with a short wave. The sergeant scowled and stomped towards him.

"And you are?" the man asked, eyes narrowing. "Didn't you see the tape?"

"Detective Chief Inspector Jones," he snapped, showing his warrant card for the third time that day. "Your name, Sergeant?"

The sergeant straightened and pulled back his shoulders.

Behind him, smiles dropped from faces and the constables stood taller.

"Smallbone, sir."

How ironic.

"Well, Sergeant Smallbone," Jones said, stepping to one side of the man and leaning closer. "Yes, I did see the tape. Why didn't you station a constable to stop people wandering onto the crime scene?"

Smallbone's eyes flicked towards a large chestnut tree with a wide root bowl and returned them to focus on a point over Jones' right shoulder. "I ... was just about to, sir."

"Were you indeed? Carry on then, Sergeant. Don't let me keep you."

"Yes, sir." Smallbone spun around. "Johnson, Peters, guard the entry points. In and out." He pointed up and down the single trail.

Two constables peeled away from the group. One hurried up the path Jones had just descended. The other headed to the far side of the trail, where another line of tape cut off incoming hikers from the north.

"Very good, Sergeant. Where's DS De Villiers?"

Again, Smallbone's eyes turned towards the chestnut tree. He sniffed and his upper lip curled slightly.

"He's, er, indisposed, sir."

Jones remembered the first time he'd seen a dead body as a teenage police cadet. On that occasion, he'd been "indisposed", too —and ended up puking over his own shoes. It had taken him years to live down the embarrassment.

"When he's recovered, send him to me."

"Yes, sir. Certainly, sir."

"In the meantime, have your people search the outer perimeter of the scene. If they find anything, tell them not to touch it, just to point it out. Make sure they stay away from the area of interest and for pity's sake, tell them to take care. I don't want any accidents. Hi-vis vests on. Don't want anyone getting lost, either."

Smallbone's pinched expression told a tale.

"What is it?"

"Er, we left the hi-vis in the cars, sir. It being so hot and all."

Jones clenched his teeth.

"You'd better send someone back to the car park then, hadn't you," he said, working hard to keep his voice in check.

"Yes, sir. Right away." Smallbone turned again. "Collier!"

Jones left the lazy fool to issue his instructions and headed towards the action. The two remaining constables peeled away to start what would probably be an ineffectual and superficial search. They needed a whole load more people to search the wooded and brush-filled area around the body.

Moving on.

To Robyn's left, a firefighter wearing the white helmet of a station officer supervised a colleague in a yellow helmet. The second firefighter secured a length of rope around a tree and lowered the free end to one of her colleagues. Two firefighters and two SOCOs in baggy white coveralls stood, shoulder deep in brambles, partially hidden by the ditch.

"Dr Spence, what are you doing here?" Jones said, as he approached a scene of restrained order.

Robyn twisted at the waist, turned off the voice recorder, and looked up at him.

"Afternoon, Chief Inspector. I'm doing my job. What's your excuse?" Behind the clear safety glasses, her green eyes shone with amusement. The facemask hid what he expected to be a genuine, warm smile.

He stopped five metres away at the boundary of the second taped off area and plucked a pair of plastic booties from a box sitting on a small portable table. He leaned on the table for balance and stood on one foot to slip a bootie over his shoe.

"I meant," he said, "why are you still on shift? You can't have been home yet."

She stood, joined him by the table, and waited for him to tug on the second bootie before answering.

"Why, do I look tired to you?"

He held up both hands.

"Not a bit of it. And anyway, I can hardly see you beneath all that PPE."

"Thanks for being so concerned, David," she said quietly, "but I called you from home this morning. Managed a full four hours' sleep before heading back into work. Fresh as a daisy, me." She removed the safety glasses and rubbed her eyes with the wrist of a gloved hand.

"Ah, I see."

"And what about you? Are you the only senior detective in the whole of the West Midlands?"

"Seems that way. And I could say the same for you. Don't you have any cover?"

"The lab's spread even thinner than the police. I was on my way into work and received the call that sent me here. Don't worry though, Patrick and Bill are still working the evidence in the *other* case." Her eyes widened and she whispered the word "other" as though it were a secret they shared. "Besides, I'd only be getting in their way."

"Dr Spence," he said, pulling on his jacket, acutely aware of the sweat patches darkening his white shirt, "I doubt that would be possible. Now, what do you have for me?"

"Dead male, thirty to forty years of age, lean and well-muscled."

Unlike Charlie.

"We found him lying face down, and half-submerged in water. You can't really see it from here due to the undergrowth, but there's a small stream running down there." She pointed over the edge.

Although he couldn't see the water, he could certainly hear it babbling over rocks.

"The back of his head's caved in," Robyn continued. "He's wearing cycling gear, but no helmet. The paramedics pronounced death as soon as they saw him. Judging by the state of decomposition, the body's been here at least a week. No need to bother the likes of Professor Scobie on this one, not until the autopsy."

"Clothed this time," Jones said, almost to himself.

Her eyes creased into another smile that could have been a wince. "This time, yes. No backpack or identification on him, though. No tattoos visible either. Not so far."

"Fall off his bike after missing that corner, you think?" he asked, pointing to the sharp bend in the trail and the rocks on either side.

"Possibly. No obvious indication of impact on the rocks or trees, though. No blood or tissue trace anywhere, but it rained a few days ago and there's usually heavy traffic on this route, or so I'm told. We'll know more when we lift him out of the gully."

"Any sign of his bike?"

"Not yet, but it's pretty overgrown down there. Loads of nettles and brambles and such. We'll need help to search the area."

Jones nodded. "I'll call Smethwick, see if they can't release a few bodies for you. Live ones."

"That would make a change."

"I see you don't need any help with the lift."

"No thanks, David. We've strapped the victim into a stretcher, still face down. It's precarious down there, and I'm happy to let the fire service handle the rest. Station Officer Allam's people know what they're doing."

They certainly seem to.

Jones had been studying the preparations for the lift and had nothing to add to Robyn's analysis.

"Excellent. I'll leave you to it. Let me know if you need my help."

"Will do. Are you taking over here?" She shot a sideways glance in the direction of Sergeant Smallbone.

Looks like I'll have to.

He nodded. "For the moment."

"Good. We can chat later. When we've recovered the stretcher."

"Looking forward to it."

"DCI Jones?"

Jones turned towards the voice to find a shamefaced young man in a creased suit. Fortunately for him, his shoes carried nothing but scratches and mud—no signs of vomit.

"DS De Villiers, I assume?" Jones said, speaking quietly.

Smallbone watched them from the far side of the clearing, his eyes narrowed.

"Yes, sir," De Villiers answered, face pale. "Thanks for coming, sir."

"Not a problem, Paul."

De Villiers looked up, evidently surprised that Jones would use his first name.

"That's DS Olganski," Jones said, pointing to Alex, who'd arrived and taken charge of the search. "Go introduce yourself. She won't bite and she knows the drill."

"Yes, sir," he said, turning away.

"Oh, and Paul?"

"Yes, sir?"

"We're only here to help. This is your case. Yours and DI Scranton's."

De Villiers' taut face relaxed.

"Thank you, sir."

He turned and hurried away.

IT TOOK the firefighters fifteen minutes to extricate the stretcher and the body it contained from the steep-sided ditch and find a place on the trail wide enough and level enough to rest it. Halfway up, one of the stretcher's straps slipped, threatening to spill its load. Robyn called a temporary halt, waved away the help of her team-mates, fixed a safety line around her waist, and scrambled into the trench to refasten the strap. Once happy, she signalled for the lift to continue, and escorted the stretcher the rest of the way to the track.

Jones stood and watched the procedure, impressed with the way Robyn led her temporary team by example—the only way to lead with any success.

Once the stretcher was secure, Robyn unhooked her safety line. She tore off her filthy, heavy-duty gauntlets and replaced them with a pair of fresh nitrile crime scene gloves from a box on the picnic table.

"Thank you, Mr Allam," she said to the station officer. "I appreciate all the help, but we can take it from here. No need for your men to stay any longer."

The heavily built firefighter craned his neck to inspect the small ravine. "Are you sure, Dr Spence? I imagine you'll be wanting to search that wee ditch for evidence. It's slippery down there. Wouldn't want you to have to call us out again."

"Good point, but it's getting late. We won't be starting the search today and there's plenty of people to help carry the body."

Jones stepped forwards to interject himself into the discussion.

"I'll organise a rope team for tomorrow," he told Allam. "They'll make sure everyone's safe."

The station officer pursed his lips and nodded. "In that case, we'll leave you to it."

"Thanks for everything, Mr Allam," Jones said, waving to the rest of the man's team. "Much appreciated."

He left the firefighters to furl their ropes and pack up their gear, which they would do with near-silent efficiency, and turned towards the stretcher.

Robyn had already unsnapped the retaining belts and peeled off the waterproof sheet that covered and protected the body.

She knelt beside the stretcher and clicked the voice recorder into life.

"Male … possibly thirty to forty years old …"

Jones stepped closer and inspected the mess. It couldn't be described any other way.

The body lay face down on the stretcher, the back of his head a misshapen, mushy jumble of crushed tissue. Shards of white skull hung from flaps of darkened skin. Maggots infested the open wounds, gorging on the meaty tissue. The rest of the body looked intact, washed clean and white by the stream's swift-running water. No scratches evident on the exposed arms or legs.

As Robyn had said, the dead man's clothing had come straight out of the cyclists catalogue—bright yellow, tight-fitting top, knee length black shorts, shoes with quick-release cleats. Muscular thighs and prominent calves showed an experienced cyclist. So, why no helmet on such dangerous terrain?

Bravado? Idiocy?

"Are you going to turn the body?" he asked Robyn during a pause in her dictation.

She clicked off the recorder.

"Just about to. Mr Quinton, a tarp if you please."

"Right with you, Doc."

The shorter FSI grabbed a rectangle of folded heavy-duty plastic from a small pile of equipment and, with the help of his mate, spread it out alongside the stretcher.

"We need to turn him," Robyn said. "Careful, though. He's been through enough, and we don't need to add any damage."

Working together, they lifted the body from the stretcher and placed it face down on the tarpaulin. On Robyn's count, they rolled him over.

Quinton gasped.

His slightly taller colleague jerked away from the body.

Robyn stood and said, "Darn."

Jones stepped to one side to earn himself a better view of the corpse. Not a pretty sight.

The body had a blackened, pulpy mash instead of a face. The last time Jones had seen as much damage to a face, had been at an RTI, where the victim's head had been crushed under the wheels of an articulated truck on the M6 motorway. He'd hoped never to see as much damage again, but to see it here, in the beautiful country park?

Nothing remained intact.

Jones tried to make sense of the flaps of blackened skin attached to the skull, but an ear, parts of a cheek, and shattered teeth made no sense as a complete face. Half the lower jaw, the mandible, was missing, and he couldn't identify anything that looked like a nose.

Fallen off his bike, be damned.

Someone had deliberately and repeatedly smashed the cyclist's head, turning it into a distorted lump of blood, bone, and gristle.

"You see that?" Robyn asked, pointing to an area that might have once been the upper jaw. Some teeth remained, but none were intact.

"The smashed teeth?"

"No," she said, holding up an index finger. "Mr Selby, mind passing me my case, please?"

The taller SOCO duly obliged and placed the familiar metal case beside her on the dusty track.

Robyn dialled in the numbers to unlock the clasps and pulled open the lid. She removed a pair of plastic tweezers and lowered them towards the pulverised face. Moments later, after some careful tugging, she held them up towards Jones. She'd trapped something small between the pincers. Something Jones couldn't make out from a distance.

"What's that?"

"A splinter."

"From a tree?"

"Just a sec."

Jones case his eyes around the idyllic scene, looking for damaged bark and exposed wood. Apart from bruising to the larch tree where the firefighters had tied their rope, he found none.

Robyn dipped a hand into her case again, pulled out the same jeweller's loupe she'd used for the St Christopher medal, and fixed it to her right eye. She held the tweezers up to the sunlight and studied the splinter carefully. Seconds later, she lowered the tweezers and removed the loupe. After securing the splinter into an evidence vial and handing it to Selby for signing and dating, she fixed her green eyes on Jones.

"Not a tree, Chief Inspector. Unless they apply varnish to the trees around here. One edge has been worked on a lathe. I can make out fine lines running across the grain. Unless I'm mistaken, the splinter comes from a bat."

"A baseball bat, then," Jones said. "They don't turn cricket bats on lathes."

"Probably. I'll let you know for certain when I've put it under a 'scope."

"Murder," Jones said, stating the blindingly obvious. "Jerry Scranton's going to be pleased."

"Who's he, and why's he going to be pleased?" Robyn asked.

"Between the two of us," he dropped his voice to say. Robyn stood and stepped closer.

"Yes?"

"Jerry Scranton's the local DI. He's been looking for a juicy murder for months, and he's welcome to this one. I have more than enough on my plate."

"You're handing the case over?"

Jones nodded. "I'm only here because Jerry's in court today. He'd be upset if I muscled in on his action. Besides, Charlie's murder takes precedence, and the SCU has enough work to do. I'll have a supervisory role, but Jerry can run as SIO with this one."

Robyn nodded and turn her attention back to the body.

"The fingertips have been nibbled away, and without a face, I'm not sure how he's going to make the identification."

Jones avoided looking at the damaged corpse, preferring to focus on what little he could see of Robyn's face.

"He's been here a while. Someone will have missed him. I expect there'll be an entry on the MisPer database."

"Sir?" De Villiers shouted from the far side of the trail, some fifty metres distant. "We found a bike."

"Excellent," he called. "Leave it where it is."

Alex joined De Villiers, making sure he didn't get carried away and lift the thing out of the bushes in his excitement.

"Well now," Jones said, winking at Robyn, "that's a stroke of luck. Jerry's team should be able to trace it back to its owner. It'll help the case no end."

It would help all right—assuming the killer and the victim knew each other, and it wasn't a random attack by a baseball-bat-carrying nutter with a hatred of Lycra-clad cyclists thundering along the MBT trails without a care for the hikers.

Jones kept the dark thoughts to himself.

Chapter Thirteen

TUESDAY 16TH MAY – Morning

Police HQ, Holton, Birmingham, UK

JONES TORE a paper towel from the dispenser, wiped his hands, and used it to turn off the tap. He rolled it into a tight ball and tried to throw the soggy wad away but the swing-bin was full to overflowing.

Damn it.

Taking a rubber glove from his inner jacket pocket, he stretched it over his left hand before crushing the used towels down into the bin. Not for the first time, he wondered what the cleaners were paid to do. He tore off the glove, deposited it on top of the rubbish, exited the toilet, and all but bumped into Phil.

"Morning, boss."

"Philip."

"Enjoy your stroll through the woods with Robyn yesterday?"

Phil smirked, and Jones glowered at his DI's annoying double eyebrow hitch.

"Oh yes, Philip. Trudging along a bicycle trail to view a body with his head caved into a gory pulp ranks right up there with digging through landfills for human remains and dealing with the results of firework accidents on Bonfire Night. A total delight."

Phil dropped his grin.

"Yeah, apologies for being so flippant. It was hardly the ideal scenario for a romantic tryst."

"Philip!"

"Sorry, boss. Any news on the identification?"

Jones shook his head. "Nothing so far. No MisPer hits and the bike we found had been there for years. Rusted solid."

"Pity. I've not worked with Jerry Scranton. He any good?"

"Jerry's a decent detective. In fact, I was considering him for your job if you'd been forced to hang up your spurs." Jones stared pointedly at Phil's left knee.

"Oh, charming."

"Serves you right for winding me up about Dr Spence."

"Alright, David. You've made your point."

"And don't you forget it. Anyway, back to Jerry Scranton. He's a solid detective. If there's anything to find, he'll find it."

"And we're only a phone call away if he needs us, right?"

"We are indeed."

"Have you had a chance to go through the new door-to-door questionnaires yet?" Phil asked, glancing at the door to the loo.

"Not yet, I've been on the phone with Jerry since I arrived, talking him through what we know so far. Which is precious little. Alex handed her notes over to Jerry's oppo, DS De Villiers."

"Paul De Villiers?"

"Yes. You know him?"

"Yep. A damn good winger. Rapid quick, with good hands. He made the team the season I gave up playing. Showed loads of promise."

Jones raised an eyebrow. The timid DS he'd met the previous afternoon didn't seem the type to excel at a rough and tumble game like rugby. The Paul De Villiers he saw would have been more suited to football.

Stop it, Jones. No need to be so snippy.

"Not bumped into him at work, then?"

"Not so far. Where've you left it with them?" Phil asked, staring with longing at the toilet again.

Jones blocked the entrance, taking a perverse pleasure in making him wait.

"They were on their way to the country park. They'll be scouring the area for evidence at least for the rest of the day."

"Good luck to them. It's a pocket wilderness over there."

"I've ordered a rope team. They'll be safe enough. So, anything interesting from yesterday's door-to-door?" he asked, deliberately changing the subject.

Phil answered from memory. "Six towers. Six hundred flats in total, and we knocked every single door but more than a few were no-answers." He winced and pointed to the toilet. "Sorry, boss, I'm bursting."

"Yes I know. Did you have any luck with the PNC search for crimes committed with an injector knife?"

Phil groaned and all but crossed his legs.

"Not had long enough, boss. So far, I've searched for unsolved cases where a Hornet might have been used. I've gone back as far as 2013. Found none that fit the bill. I'll carry on after we've finished the house-to-house. Now, please?" Again, he pointed to the toilet.

"Have you quite finished quizzing me about Dr Spence at every possible opportunity?"

"Yes, David. All done. I promise."

"Okay, do your business and pop into my office when you're finished."

Jones stepped aside. Phil darted past and the door closed quietly behind him.

BACK IN HIS OFFICE, Jones removed his jacket, slipped it over a hanger and hung it on a hook on the back of the door. He threw the switch on the desk fan, hoping for relief from the rising temperature and humidity.

The fan oscillated noisily and threw warm air into his face.

Useless thing.

He picked up Phil's memo sticker. Someone had moved a pile of papers on his desk off-square. He nudged them straight. Why couldn't people leave things as they bloody well found them?

As usual, he found Phil's semi-legible scrawl difficult to read.

He wheeled his chair across the room to the IT station. The West Midlands Police logo screensaver disappeared as soon as he jogged the mouse, and he flexed his fingers before commencing. At least he'd improved on his infamous two-fingered pecking in recent months.

The yellow search menu appeared. Jones entered the ID for the Pelham case and started reading.

Fifteen minutes later, Phil entered carrying two takeout cups from the canteen and handed one across.

"Ah thanks, Philip. I knew there was a reason to keep you on the team." He winked.

"You're welcome." Phil pointed to the screen. "Anything strike you as interesting since our review?"

"Nope. You?"

"Nothing."

Jones sipped his drink. Hot and strong, it almost tasted like real leaf tea. Almost, but not quite.

"Find anything of value in the stuff I collected from Charlie's home office?"

"Not yet, but I'm still trawling through it."

Phil lowered his cup to the coaster on his side of the desk.

Jones checked the wall clock and decided against turning on the radio for the local news. It was bound to lead with Charlie's murder. These days, the death of a police officer still had the power to make the news organisations salivate. Since the press office's bland statement the previous evening, the media had learned nothing new, and their bulletins simply regurgitated the same second-hand facts with added speculation as fillers. He didn't need to torture himself with yet another replay of the doorstep interview with Lydia Pelham, where she pleaded for members of the public to come forwards with information to help the police find her "heroic husband's vicious killer".

"Six hundred flats and you knocked every door?" Jones asked.

"Every single one."

"How many answers?"

"Four-thirty-seven. None of whom had anything of value to impart—as expected. Of the one-sixty-three others, ninety-four seemed occupied, but no one answered. Uniforms will call on them again today."

"Which leaves, how many?"

"Sixty-nine unoccupied and likely derelict. Mostly of them are on the top few floors."

"That's a whole load of front doors to break down. Where've you left it?"

"I asked Wash to contact the council for a list of current and past tenants, but you know what they're li—"

"Ryan! Of course," Jones said, holding up a hand in apology for the interruption. "Knew I'd forgotten something. My visit to Sandwell Valley pushed it out of my head."

"Sorry?"

"Something Lydia Pelham was being evasive about during my visit."

"And you think Ryan might know?"

"He was Charlie's most recent partner." Jones reached for his desk phone and dialled the SCU office number. "If anyone knows anything, it'll be Ryan."

Alex answered his call. "Yes, boss?"

"Hi Alex, can you ask Ryan to pop into my office when he has a moment. And by that, I mean right away, please." He returned the phone to its cradle.

"You didn't fancy a short stroll along the corridor?" Phil asked.

"Nope. This particular conversation needs privacy."

Phil planted his hands on the arms of his chair and leaned forwards as if to stand.

"No, no. You can stay for this, Philip. Call it part of your personnel management training."

Phil shot him a quizzical look and dropped back into his chair.

"So," Jones said, "while we wait, let's discuss next steps—"

A sharp rap on the door interrupted Jones' thought. The door opened and Ryan rushed in.

"I found something, boss," he said, smiling and waving a clear plastic envelope. It contained a rectangle of yellow paper—a message note.

"That was quick," Jones said, beckoning him inside.

"I got lucky, boss," Ryan answered, his smile broadening. "It was close to the top."

"What?"

"Close to the top of the pile. I didn't have to search far."

"I think we're talking cross purposes," Jones said. "Come in. Close the door behind you."

Ryan's smile fell and a questioning frown replaced it. His gaze shifted from Jones to Phil and back again.

"Sorry, boss?"

"I just called the office and asked Alex to send you in."

"You did? I was already on my way here. Had to pop into the loo first though. Anything wrong?"

He pushed the door closed and headed for the spare seat beside Phil.

"Please remain standing, DC Washington. And stand up straight."

Ryan flinched, and the colour drained from his face. He blinked rapidly and stood to attention—or at least his best facsimile of one given his rounded shoulders—before focusing his gaze on a point above Jones' head.

"Well?" Jones asked.

"Excuse me, boss?"

"Are you going to tell me now, or do I have to drag out the thumbscrews?"

Ryan's frown deepened. He shook his head and shot a searching look at Phil as though wondering whether Jones might be playing a game.

"I'm sorry, boss. Tell you what?"

"Yesterday afternoon, Alex and I broke the news to Lydia Pelham. We also told her where we found Charlie."

Ryan's shoulders stiffened. He closed his eyes for an extended moment before opening them again. Understanding had emerged.

"Well?" Jones said.

"I was trying to protect her, boss."

"Trying to protect Lydia Pelham?"

"Yes, boss. I didn't want it getting out unless it was absolutely necessary."

Jones growled in annoyance.

"You didn't want what getting out?" Phil asked.

"Charlie's secret."

"We're trying to find a killer here, Detective Constable Washington," Jones snapped. "Charlie's extramarital shenanigans might have a direct bearing on the case."

"It doesn't, boss. I promise you. I checked the flat myself. She moved out last year."

"Who did?"

"Dolly Parton, boss."

"The singer?" Phil asked, confusion written large on his lean face.

"No, sir. Dolly Ambrose. Dolly Parton's her, er ... 'professional' name, if you know what I mean." An embarrassed smile stretched out on Ryan's moon face.

"A prostitute?" Jones asked.

No wonder Charlie wanted the relationship kept quiet.

"That's right, sir. Her professional name's Dolly Parton on account of her large ... assets, sir." The damn broken, he rushed on. "I didn't want Lydia finding out about it if it could be avoided. Reckoned she's already suffered enough. Deserved much better'n Charlie."

"Do you fancy her?" Phil asked.

Ryan's eyes widened. "No, it's nothing like that. Lydia's in her forties, y'know. Way too old for me. Like I said, I just wanted to protect her feelings. Anyway, when we found Charlie's body near the OTT, the first person I thought about was Dolly. I thought she might know what Charlie was doing there. He was forever 'popping in to see her'. Tried to make out she was an unofficial CI, but I knew better. After I finished here on Sunday night, I took a quick detour on my way home and knocked on Dolly's door."

"You did what!" Jones roared.

Ryan jumped.

"Yes, sir. Only she wasn't there. No one answered. Then I came into the office this morning and searched her records on the PNC. Turns out she now lives in a high-rise in Handsworth. Has done for the best part of a year. I haven't been able to find out who—if anyone—took over her flat on the OTT. I'm waiting for someone from the council to get back to me, but you know what they're like."

Yes, indeed.

"What number flat are we talking about?" Phil asked.

"Number 502, in Tower 3."

"That's one of the ninety-four, boss. No answer during the canvass," Phil said, utilising his wondrous memory.

He'd read all the questionnaires once and memorised the details. Once again, Jones sat in awe of his abilities. What must it be like to possess such incredible power?

"The occupant of Number 503, a Mr D Jarman, was asked about his neighbour. He told Constable Harkness that Number 502 had been empty for as long as he'd been living in the block."

Ryan looked at Jones again. "If Dolly had been there when I knocked, I'd have told you, boss. Honest. I just wanted to check her out first. See whether Charlie had been to see her. Since she'd moved out months ago, I thought it best to keep schtum. I'm sorry, boss."

"Can't say I'm not disappointed in you, Ryan."

Ryan lowered his eyes. "I know, boss. Like I said I *am* sorry."

"Do you know the worst thing?"

"No, sir."

"Lydia already knew."

"She did?" Ryan said, meeting Jones' steady gaze again.

"I'm certain of it. You risked your career, and maybe your life, for nothing."

Ryan swallowed hard.

"My life?"

"What if this Dolly Parton or her pimp *had* been responsible for Charlie's death? What might have happened to you going there alone and at night?"

Ryan shook his head. "Not Dolly, sir. I met her a couple of times. She's not that sort of pro. Doesn't have a pimp, either. I was perfectly safe."

Jones let Ryan's naïvety pass—for the moment.

"Make sure to write this up in your notes, Ryan. We'll discuss this again—during your annual appraisal. After I've had a chance to cool down a little."

"Yes, boss."

Jones held his gaze long enough to hammer home the point and then relented. "Okay, enough said. What were you so excited about when you burst in just now?"

Ryan swallowed and held up the now-creased plastic envelope he'd brought with him. Since his arrival, he'd crushed it in a sweaty fist.

"I found this when searching through the stuff Phil recovered from Charlie's desk in the archives. I reckon it tells us who Charlie planned to visit last Thursday." He hesitated.

"Well? Don't keep us waiting, Detective Constable Washington."

"Oh yes, right." He held up the envelope and pointed to the yellow note inside. "It's definitely Charlie's writing. I'd recognise his scribble anywhere."

Ryan stepped forwards, lowered the envelope to the desk, and smoothed it out. He spun it so Jones could read Charlie's spidery writing.

Lenny, #110. 21:30.

. . .

"I RECKON THAT 'LENNY' refers to Leonard Chiltern," Ryan said. "He's a heavy user and sometime pusher. Charlie used to squeeze him for information about drug movements on the OTT."

"Another of his unofficial CIs?" Phil asked, wrinkling his nose in distaste.

Ryan nodded.

"Said he kept Lenny off the CI list for his own protection. Never used to meet him on the OTT. Anyway, Lenny lives in Tower 3, the same one as Dolly."

"Phil?" Jones asked. "Number 110?"

Phil shook his head. "Another 'no answer', boss."

"But you know what this means?"

"Yep," Phil said, speaking directly to Jones and ignoring Ryan. "We now have two hot targets on the OTT."

"Two?" Ryan asked, looking from one to the other.

"Yes, Ryan," Phil answered. "Flat Numbers 110 and 502,"

"Why Number 502? I've already cleared it. Dolly doesn't live there anymore."

"But you didn't know that before you knocked on her door and searched the database, did you?" Jones asked.

"No, boss." Again, Ryan lowered his head.

"So how can we be certain Charlie knew she'd moved, too?"

Ryan paused for a moment before bursting out with, "Bloody hell!"

"Yes," Jones said. "Exactly. Philip, raise two warrants for a dawn raid on Numbers 502 and 110, please. I'm sure you'll be able to come up with enough probable cause. Alex can walk them round to the Magistrate's Court as soon as they're ready. I want to be breaking down doors first thing tomorrow morning."

"Yes, boss. And while I'm doing that, what are you going to be doing?"

Jones glowered at his subordinate, not caring that Ryan saw it.

"First, I'm going to contact Section 14 and arrange a full obbo on our targets. After that, I'm heading upstairs. Superintendent

Havers asked to know as soon as we made any progress on the case. Don't know about you two, but I imagine raising two search warrants, running an obbo, and setting up simultaneous dawn raids counts as progress, don't you?"

Phil smiled. Ryan didn't—he still looked chastened.

"Of you go, now," Jones said, waving them away.

As he reached for his desk phone, it rang with an internal call.

"Jones here."

"Morning, Chief Inspector, I'm just about to make you day."

Jones would have recognised Barney Featherstone's rumbling voice anywhere. "Hold on a moment, Feathers." He covered the mouthpiece. "Phil, just a sec."

Phil stopped, but Ryan rushed out, clearly delighted to leave them to it.

Jones hit the speaker button for Phil's benefit.

"Feathers," Jones said. "Don't tell me you found the car Charlie was using?"

"We have, sir. It helps to be looking for the right vehicle."

"I'm sure it does," Jones shot back. "Go on."

"A couple of ANPR hits pointed us to some traffic cam footage. You'll never guess where we found it."

"It's way too early in the morning for guessing games, Sergeant. But if you forced my hand, I'd say in one of the carparks near the OTT Estate, torched and unrecognisable?"

"Nearly, David. Nearly. It's in the carpark of the Alderman's Brewery Pub. And it's actually intact. The patrol I sent found it parked behind a couple of wheelie bins."

"Intact, you say?"

"Pristine. Weird, eh?"

"Weird enough."

"I've told the patrol officers to stand guard over it until the FSIs arrive. I take it that's okay?"

"Couldn't be better, Feathers. Thanks." Jones ended the call and replaced the handset.

"Intact?" Phil said, drawing closer to Jones' desk.

"Makes sense."

"In what way?"

"Not even Charlie would be stupid enough to park on the OTT itself. How many cars have been torched there so far this month?"

"Four. A Volvo, two Fords, and a—"

"Okay, okay. Enough."

Phil grinned. "Want to go check it out?"

"No need. We won't find anything the SOCOs don't. And I'll put a tenner into the Christmas party fund if they find anything worthwhile. Our man's too cute to have left any evidence in the car."

Phil tilted his head, his expression thoughtful. "We don't have a Christmas party fund."

"My tenner's safe then, isn't it. Off you go. I still have to call Section 14 and you have a couple of search warrants to write."

"I'd have been halfway through them if you hadn't called me back," Phil said, turning away before Jones could think up a witty response.

Earlier

The OTT Estate, Bordesley Green

Birmingham

Chapter Fourteen

THURSDAY 11TH MAY – Charlie Pelham

Bordesley Green, Birmingham, UK

Wheezing hard, Charlie breathed through his mouth, to help catch his breath as much as to avoid the rancid stink of wet rot, stale urine, and dog turds. At least they *looked* like *dog* turds, but in this place, who could tell? Could have come from any of the lowlife arseholes inhabiting the place.

He paused, took another pull from his hip flask—a taster only, to fortify himself for the climb—and trudged upwards.

"Why don't the fucking lifts ever work in this shithole?" he asked the graffiti-daubed walls.

It would have helped if he could use the handrail to pull himself up, but he'd forgotten his crime scene gloves, and he'd be buggered if he'd touch the plastic-coated grip. Christ alone knew what he'd catch.

Another flight of stairs completed and another fortifying sip taken. The whisky's warmth surged down his throat and into his belly, making him glow. His head swam pleasantly.

Nice.

Let them say Charlie was finished. He'd show the buggers. They'd written him off, but Charlie weren't ready for the knackers yard. Oh no. He still had contacts on the OTT, and he were going use them. Yeah, he'd use them right enough. Should have done it months ago, but never got around to it. The call came from out of the blue. One of his old CIs. A snot-nosed user whose info had come in handy in the past and would come in handy again.

He raised the flask to his lips and tilted it up. Empty. Not so much as a dribble.

Shit.

Why did he leave the half-bottle in the car? No fucking use down there. Still, a quick visit to Lenny for the info, and a trip down to the fifth floor for a knee trembler with Dolly afterwards. She always had a bottle on the go. Happy to share her booze and her favours with her old mate, Charlie, she were. Lovely tits on her, too. Huge big things.

He smiled at the familiar stirrings in his groin. It had been a while since he'd paid a visit to Delicious Dolly. Too long.

Months.

Yeah, a quick shag with Dolly for old times' sake. Just the ticket. The right way to end the night and start him on the comeback trail. He screwed the lid on tight, returned the flask to his hip pocket where it belonged, and continued climbing.

He belched long, hard, and open-mouthed, relishing the sensation. A satisfying rumble echoed though the stairwell, bouncing off the graffitied walls.

No multimillion-pound Banksy artworks in here. Just a bunch of illegible tags and misspelled curses.

Illiterate arseholes can't even spell "whores"!

He climbed. Upwards. Ever upwards, the thoughts of what was to come sloshing around in his head.

A couple of minutes' hard climbing later, he reached the fifth floor. He paused, considered passing on the visit to Larry and heading straight for the pudding stage of the evening, but that wouldn't do. Five minutes with Larry would set him up with the info, then he could have his fun.

He'd show the boss Charlie weren't finished. Weren't no has-been.

Damn it.

Jones, the little bastard, weren't Charlie's boss no more. Hadn't been for months. So why did he still think of him as "the boss"? Well, maybe after tonight, when Charlie'd gathered enough intel to land a big score … maybe then he'd regain some of his lost respect. Maybe then, he'd be invited back on the team. Maybe then they'd beg Charlie to come back.

Yeah, right.

Well, fuck that. Fuck them all. He'd show them what sort of cop Charlie Pelham was. A damn good cop, that's what. Once he'd landed the big fish, he'd be back on top. Too right. After he'd taken down the kingpin, Charlie'd be able to set up his own fucking unit. Let them come begging to him. He'd show them. He'd show the fuckin' lot of 'em!

Upwards, Charlie. Keep climbing, mate.

Upwards in both senses of the word.

———

HEAD SWIMMING, taking care where to place his feet, Charlie paused long enough at the interim landing to pull in half a dozen deep recovery breaths. A wave of nausea threatened to explode and he swallowed hard, forcing it back into the depths.

"C'mon, son. You can do this."

He swallowed again and trudged up the twentieth and final staircase. This high up, he half-expected to find Sherpa Tensing doing his altitude training.

Inwardly, Charlie chuckled at the age old joke.

After recovering his breath, he carried on. When had climbing a few staircases become so bloody difficult? He glanced down at his ever-expanding waistline and sighed. When standing upright, he couldn't see his feet no more.

"Fuckin' hell, Charlie-boy. When d'you get so goddamn fat, you old tub 'o lard?"

Breathing even harder, he reached the top landing. A gust of wind blew rubbish in eddies around his feet. He sneezed, shivered, and turned up the collar on his jacket.

Out in front, the balcony opened to the air, the spaces between the floors supported by crumbling concrete pillars. Rusted metal railings spanned the gaps between the pillars but offered dubious protection against a headlong plummet to the rubbish-strewn court-yard below. On either side of the stairwell, decrepit flats curved away to a point in the distance.

Which way, left or right? Five flats stretched out on each side.

The wind whipped in through the opening and cooled the sweat on his face. He paused again. Which one did Larry call home? What fucking number?

He'd visited the user loads of times before. Which one?

End of the row that's for sure.

The wind blew again. Caused him to sway and lean against the wall.

Fucking wind.

"Number 110," he said. "That's right."

He read the faded sign stuck to the inner wall of the stairwell. Two arrows. The left arrow pointed to Numbers 100-105, and the right to Numbers 106-110.

Yeah, that was it. Right. Which meant his left. Confusing, or what?

He sniffed the fresher air wafting in on the stiff breeze, cleared his sinuses of the foul stench of the stairwell, and cast another glance down at his spreading belly.

Ought to be ashamed of yourself, you fat git.

Maybe it was time to shape up a little. Perhaps he *should* give up the fags and the greasy food like everyone kept telling him. And the booze, too? Nah, not the booze. Whiskey were the only thing as made life tolerable. Whiskey and women.

Yeah, tots and totty.

Charlie smiled again. Life were good, and it were about to get even better. He'd shape up. Yeah, course he would.

The missus would appreciate it better if he were more like the slim bloke she'd married all them years ago. The tarts would appreciate it, too. Not that Charlie ever had no trouble finding a bit of slap and tickle on the side. Never had and never would.

One of the joys of being a cop. The tarts was ever so grateful when he turned a blind eye to the tricks they turned. An' more to the point, they never charged him nothing for their services, neither.

He sucked in another deep lungful of the fresh air, shuffled out into the open-sided balcony, and turned left. Four houses separated him from his target, but precious few of the part-glazed front doors or kitchen windows showed any lights. The tower seemed deserted, but who knew how many lowlife scum infested the rooms hidden behind the closed doors and the cracked and darkened windows?

A woman's cackled laughter echoed up from the courtyard below, carried on the growing breeze. Further away, a bottle shattered and a man cursed. Thumping, crashing music boomed out from open windows in the block opposite. Block parties fighting to outdo each other for noise and annoyance.

Charlie sneered.

All life spread out around him.

Lowlife. Lowlifes.

He sucked in his gut, tugged his trousers to a more comfortable position on his waist, and tucked in his shirttails. Finally, he straightened his tie and fastened the middle button of his jacket. Even if the place weren't nothing but a shithole, didn't mean Charlie couldn't look the part. If things worked out as he hoped, Larry would give him all the intel he needed for redemption.

He'd show DCI Bloody Jones he weren't useless. Weren't past it. Yeah, he'd show the lot of them. He'd get his own back for being put on fucking desk duty. Shuffling papers in the archives weren't a job for a thief-taker like Charlie Pelham.

Only question was—how to extract the intel from the miserable little shit without having to fork out no shekels. Things might need to get a bit physical. No matter. Charlie could do physical. Always had been able to handle himself, old Charlie P.

He dug his right hand into his jacket pocket and removed the telescopic baton he hadn't used in anger for years. Sure enough, the knurled metal grip slipped into his fist—comfortable as an old friend. He sniffed again, clearing the last of the stench from his nose.

"Okay, Charlie-boy. You can do this. Just like the old days."

He strode forwards, keeping well clear of the rusted railings to his right, hugging close to the relative safety of the flats. He hurried past four darkened homes, counting the number of cracked windowpanes and kicked-in door panels along the way.

Number 110.

Here we go.

The half-glazed wooden door sported multiple layers of peeling paint. A faded gloss topcoat—in red—flaked away to reveal layers of midnight blue, moss green, muddy brown, and finally, a pale pink undercoat. A busted bellpush, a broken knocker, and a rust-pitted letterbox decorated the rotting woodwork.

Charlie swapped the baton to his left hand, hammered three times on the doorframe with the side of his right fist, and stepped back, edging as close as he dared to the creaking railings. He counted to ten before repeating the process.

He took two paces away again and his arse brushed against the railings. They creaked and groaned. He glanced over his shoulder. Ten floors below, the poorly lit courtyard stared back. Dark and ominous, it drew him out and down.

Out and down.

Shit.

Charlie blinked away the swimming lights and the nausea.

He'd never been scared of heights, but the groaning railings didn't offer much protection against a push, a shove, or a totter. The image of him falling out and into the void made his knees weaken.

Pushing away from the edge—the magnetic void—Charlie's knees stopped trembling.

A heavy gust caught his overlong hair and blew it around his head. Leaning further away from the mesmeric space, he reached up and raked the hair out of his eyes.

Think of something else. Anything else.

A haircut. Long overdue for a trim. He'd book an appointment with Juicy Lucy, the hairdresser with the biggest arse he'd ever had the pleasure to slap. After a different sort of knee trembler, she'd cut his hair.

Ha!

Good old Charlie, always up for playing offside.

Behind him, the multi-coloured door creaked open on rusted hinges. Charlie spun.

The house remained dark, black. A shadowy shape stood framed in the part-open doorway, eyes glinting.

Charlie sneered.

"Took you long enough," he snapped.

"That you, Sarge?" Larry whispered, his rasping voice barely carrying the short distance between them.

Charlie puffed out his chest. "You called the meeting, shithead. Open up 'fore I ram this truncheon up your fuckin' arse."

Charlie swapped the baton to his right hand and flicked it open to its full fifty-centimetre length. The lightweight, tempered steel rod could pack one hell of a punch, especially when used by an expert. Although not exactly a ninja these days, Charlie considered himself skilled enough to make good on his threat to an emaciated junkie.

The door creaked again, opening a little further. A slightly paler outline cut into the black hole of the doorway. The figure cowered away, moving further into the darkened hall.

"There ain't no call to threaten me, Sarge. I thought we was mates."

Charlie trundled closer but stayed in the doorway. He couldn't see nothing past the threshold, and he weren't a fool. No telling how many people lived in the dive.

"Switch the lights on, Lenny."

"Ain't got no electric," Lenny whimpered. "Bastards cut me off a week ago last Friday."

"That's what happens when you don't pay your bills, dickwad."

"Got into a spot of bother, Sarge. Weren't my fault." The bent silhouette backed away from the fully opened door. "Got me a battery lamp in the parlour."

The silhouette turned, hobbled away and ducked through an open door halfway along the inner hall. A dim light flicked on, showing Charlie the way.

Wary, keeping his eyes and ears open and letting the baton take the lead, he stepped over the threshold but stayed close to the opening, waiting for his eyes to adjust to the gloom.

"C'mon, Sarge," Lenny rasped. "If you're … comin' in, shut the door … behind you. That wind's fucking arctic, and I … don't got no heating."

Charlie sniffed the hallway's foul air. Rich with the stench of stale sweat and blocked drains, the flat stank worse than the stairwell. How could anyone live in such filth?

"You sound bad, Lenny."

"Got me a … chest cold. Can't … shift the fucker. Come in if you're comin'."

After a few moments, Charlie's vision cleared a little.

Black bin bags, full to overflowing, lined one side of the hallway, barely leaving enough room for anyone to slip past. He kicked the front door closed with the heel of his boot and sidestepped towards the dim light.

He considered dipping his hand into his pocket for his mobile. The torch facility would help, but it would also leave him without a free hand to batter the intel out of the snot-nose, bug-ridden junkie. He'd have to do without.

Charlie shouldered his way through the internal door, expecting to find a room as shitty and rubbish-strewn as the hall, but he couldn't have been more wrong. In comparison to the rest of the place, the room might even have been described as tidy.

Lenny stood in the far corner of the "parlour", dimly lit by the battery-powered lamp that stood on a scratched and stained coffee table in the middle of the room. Surrounded on three sides by a sofa and two reclining chairs, the open side faced a TV large enough to rival the screen of a multiplex cinema.

"So, Lenny. Whatcha got for me?"

Lenny smiled, showing a set of brown teeth, one missing from the front. "Gold, Charlie. Pure fucking gold."

Charlie stood in the open doorway, keeping his distance.

The junkie straightened.

"What's it worth to ya?"

"Depends on what you got."

"How does twenty keys of smack sound?"

The breath caught in Charlie throat. "Twenty kilos?"

Lenny were talking a street value of over two million quid.

The junkie's gap-tooth smile widened. "Thought that would interest you, Sarge."

"When and where?"

"Tomorrow night. It's coming in by truck—part of a consignment of fags and booze."

Charlie's heart started racing.

"Where?" he repeated.

"Ain't tellin' you that 'til I sees the colour of your money."

"What's up, Lenny. Don't you trust your old mate, Charlie?"

"Don't trust no one when it comes to cash."

"I ain't let you down afore, son. An' I won't let you down this time. Cash on delivery, Lenny. You know that. I need proof you ain't pulling my todger."

Lenny shuffled forwards, hand outstretched and shaking.

"Can't you give me something on account?"

Charlie snorted. "Do me a favour, Lenny."

"I'm hurting, Sarge," he whined. "Just need enough for a little taste. That's all."

Charlie tightened his grip on the truncheon and moved further into the room. "Who's bringing the stuff in, Lenny?"

The junkie caught sight of the shiny metal bar in Charlie's right fist.

"The S-Slob," Lenny stuttered, raising his hands to ward off an attack.

Charlie stopped moving and dropped his shoulders.

Fuck, fuck, fuck.

What a waste of shitting time.

All them stairs.

"Slobodan Savić?"

"Y-Yeah, the Slob. That's the geezer. He's trying to muscle in on the Possie's turf. He wants to be the new big man on the estate."

"You lying piece of shit!"

For a moment, Charlie wanted to slam the truncheon into the junkie's rotten teeth, but it weren't worth the effort—or the risk. People might have seen him entering the estate.

Fuck!

"What's wrong, Sarge? D-Don't you believe me?"

"'Course I don't you worthless bag of dogshit! Slobodan Savić were extradited back to Serbia last month on account of him being wanted back home for drug trafficking and murder!"

The scraggy junkie crumpled in on himself. "R-Really?"

"Yeah, that's right. He were. Sod you, Lenny. I should throw you off that fucking balcony for wasting my time."

"B-But ... but—"

"But what, Lennie?"

"How about a taste, for old time's sake?" Lenny pleaded, folding his arms tight to his belly. "I've been good for you in the past, ain't I?"

"Past is past, Lenny. It don't get you no credit. I need knowledge. Give me some info I can use, and I'll see you right."

Lenny collapsed onto a sofa and curled into a ball. "Please, Charlie. A taste. All I need is enough for a taste. T-To see me right."

Charlie turned his back on the pitiful excuse for a human being and hurried from the flat and out onto the balcony. Out in the cool evening, he snarled and slammed the tip of the truncheon into the brickwork surrounding the front door. The tubular segments collapsed into one another and locked into place with a satisfying click. He dropped it into his jacket pocket and turned to face the railings and the near darkness.

The wind hadn't died. If anything, it had gathered strength. He shivered and pulled the lapels of his jacket tighter together.

What a waste of a piggin' evening.

Pinning all his hopes on a useless article like Lenny Chiltern were such a stupid thing to do. Typical of the decisions he'd made over the past few months. No wonder his life had run so far down the toilet, and now he had to face all them stairs again. He sighed. At least he were going down, not up.

And talking about "going down", there were always Dolly.

He smiled. Perhaps the night weren't going to be a complete bust after all.

Charlie turned right and hurried along the balcony to the stairwell.

IT DIDN'T TAKE him long to reach the fifth floor. He even managed to avoid tumbling headlong down the stairs in his haste, although he did slip on a dog turd halfway down the sixth flight and had to grab the sticky handrail to stop his fall. Fuck knew what he'd caught hold of. He'd scrub his hands clean in Dolly's place.

He stepped out from the stairwell. This time, he turned right. No need to think. He knew where Dolly lived. Visited her often enough in the past.

Number 504, brown door, cracked kitchen window, same as the last time he'd visited. When would the Council get around to fixing it?

Number 503, red door with a shiny lock. That were new. Interesting.

Here we go.

Number 502, blue door. Another shiny lock. What the fuck were going on here? Dolly must have had a break in. One of her tricks might have turned nasty.

He raised his hand to knock on the door, but held back. What if Dolly were in the middle of "entertaining"? If so, he'd give her and her punter a rude hurry-up.

Grinning, he grabbed the truncheon and used its base to hammer on the door.

"Open up! This is the police!"

In a blur, the door flew open and a shadowy figure shot towards him, arm outstretched, moving with the speed of an athlete.

The arm jabbed forwards. Metal glinted. Pain, sharp and electric, exploded through the back of Charlie's right hand. He screamed.

All strength in his fingers failed. The truncheon slipped from lifeless fingers. Clattered to the bare concrete.

A red line appeared on the back of his hand. Blood oozed from the wound. Skin separated, exposing the white of finger bones. Tendons and nerves dangled, but the pain.

Jesus, the pain.

A second slash. This one to the side of his face. Another slicing, stinging pain. His cheek. More movement. Another slice that turned into an electric arc of agony. His chest burned.

Run, Charlie! Fucking run!

Guts churning, he staggered away. Vomit roiled up from his stomach, leapt into his throat. Something tugged at his hair, dragging him backwards, into the flat. His heel caught on the threshold. He tripped, fell.

Blood splashed into his eyes, hot, blinding. Another wave of nausea hit. He rolled onto his side. Puked on the floor. Tried to swallow. Tried to push up but had no strength in his hand and flopped to the floor. Acid burned his throat. He gagged. Darkness blanketed his fading vision.

"Come to fuck me over have you, little piggie?" Dolly hissed.

Only it weren't Dolly standing over him, waving a huge, wicked-looking blade. It weren't no one Charlie had ever met before.

Straight, white teeth glinted. The slim figure bent low, grabbed Charlie by the hand, and dragged him deep inside the flat. Dragged him easy like he didn't weigh nothing. Charlie tried fighting. Tried kicking out, but the strength ebbed out of him. With every heartbeat, blood pumped from the wounds. The cold from the floor soaked into his back.

So cold.

The figure dropped Charlie's arm and straightened. He stood on Charlie's hand and leaned harder.

Charlie didn't have the strength to pull the hand away. He tried to scream but couldn't open his mouth. The pain wouldn't allow it.

"You shouldn't have come alone, little piggie," the man said, the smooth voice oozing disappointment, sadness. "You might have survived if you'd come with your mates. I might have let you live. Mind you, people as fat as you don't make old bones, do they? Never mind, though. I'm sure your buddies will give you a good send off. Died in the 'line of duty'. At least your wife will get a good payoff. Assuming you are married. Although who'd have an ugly fat pig like you?"

He raised the wicked knife and waved it in front of Charlie's eyes. "Let's see who you are, shall we?"

A hand lowered, patted Charlie down with the expertise of a pro. The hand came up, clutching Charlie's warrant card.

"Well, well," the man said, smiling even wider, dark eyes twinkling. "Aren't I the lucky one? My first police officer's going to be a Detective Sergeant."

Your first?

"I didn't intend involving the police for a while, but …" He shrugged. "Now's as good a time to start as any, I suppose."

Charlie held up his good hand. "Don't … please don't."

"If you believe in a god, now's the time to start praying, Detective Sergeant Pelham."

Thin lips peeled back. The white teeth shone, almost eclipsing the brightness of the descending blade.

Something pressed on Charlie's belly. The terrifying blade. At first, he barely felt it as the existing pains overwhelmed the new one. But the knife dug deeper into his flesh, ripping, tearing.

The man's smile widened as did his eyes. The mouth opened and a high-pitched laugh erupted from the dark maw.

Oh dear God. Help me.

A click.

A hiss.

Charlie's skin rippled, fluttered. Pressure built. His belly chilled, expanded. He couldn't move.

The man straightened again, waved goodbye. Stepped back.

Cold waves spread through Charlie's guts. They flowed, hardened.

His insides exploded. A red mist sprayed the room.

Blackness filled his vision.

Then, nothing.

Present day

Police HQ, Holton

Birmingham

Chapter Fifteen

TUESDAY 16TH MAY – Afternoon

Police HQ, Holton, Birmingham, England

JONES KNOCKED ON HAVERS' office door and entered without waiting for a response.

"Come in."

Havers looked up from behind his large desk. "Oh, there you are, Jones. You have an update for me, I understand."

"I have, sir."

"Come in, come in. Sit."

The gold tooling on the edge of the desk's burgundy-leather insert glowed in the bright afternoon sun. As during his first visit to the lofty heights of Havers' office, the desk's surface stood empty save for a desk phone, a pile of buff-coloured folders, and a mahogany desk tidy, which housed his Montblanc fountain pen. From the same earlier visit, Jones knew Havers' computer lay hidden in a dropdown compartment inside his desk.

Jones lowered himself into the visitor's chair. It wasn't any more comfortable this time.

"You've made progress in the case, I understand?"

Havers straightened in his seat and extended his neck. Jones couldn't strike out the image of a meerkat.

"A little, sir."

"I'm all ears."

The meerkat image strengthened.

"Have you had a chance to read the autopsy report yet?"

"I scanned the management summary but haven't had a chance to go through the full version, Jones. In this job"—he waved a hand over the pile of folders—"there's never enough time in the day. Can you give me your thoughts?"

"Of course, sir. Charlie died of sharp force trauma and catastrophic expansion of the abdominal cavity—"

"The injector knife?"

"Yes, sir." Jones shuffled forwards to the edge of his seat. "I asked DI Cryer to search the PNC for murders with similar methods."

"Did he find any?"

Again, the meerkat in Not-Bob Havers emerged.

"None so far. We haven't abandoned that line of enquiry, though. Just put it on the back burner for the time being."

"What about the forensics. Anything from the lab?"

"We found flecks of paint, rust, and dirt under the rug Charlie was lying on. Which is important ...." Havers' questioning look made Jones pause. "We think the killer probably moved the body from the murder scene to the secondary dump site in something like a wheelbarrow, or a garden trailer."

"Wait a minute. Aren't you raising warrants to search two upper-storey flats in the Orchards Estate?"

"Yes, sir. Why?"

"What would a householder in an upper floor of a tower block be doing with a garden wheelbarrow?"

"Good question. There aren't any allotments nearby, if that's what you mean, but there is a park a mile or so away. We're working on the assumption our killer broke into the caretaker's lock-up. There's no evidence of a break-in so far, but we're waiting to talk to someone from the local council. It's an important lead, though."

"Really?"

"Yes. A wheelbarrow would confirm our theory that the actual crime scene is close to the secondary dumping site. Analysis of the dirt under the rug showed a match to the local topsoil."

"And the piece of card found with the dirt?"

"Turns out to be a ticket stub, sir. But the lab can't tell us anything more. The ink was too deteriorated to restore the print, and we can't read any of the information on it. We were lucky it didn't disintegrate when they moved it."

"A ticket stub, like from a train or a bus?"

"Undetermined."

"What about the trace evidence found under DS Pelham's fingernails?"

"Now, that *is* interesting."

Jones pulled out his notebook and flicked it open to a page marked with a rubber band. "It's a white powder, a mixture of silicon dioxide, quartz, and something else. There's a chemical name here that doesn't mean anything to me, but Dr Spence, the new SOCO team leader—"

"Do you mean the *FSI* team leader?" Havers corrected.

Give me strength.

"Yes, sir. The new *FSI* team leader says the powder is an admixture used to waterproof concrete."

"So our killer's in the building game?"

"Quite possibly."

"Excellent, does that narrow the suspect pool for us at all?"

"Not really, the powder is widely used throughout the industry. There's a product code"—he glanced down and read from the notebook—"*BS EN 934-2*. I'll have one of the team look for local builders' suppliers, but there are an awful lot of them in the city. The evidence will probably be more useful when we have something to match it against."

Havers nodded and opened his mouth to speak, but his desk phone chirruped the double warble of an internal call.

"Excuse me a moment, Jones," he said, an apologetic smile on his youthful face, "I need to take this. I'm expecting a call from the Deputy Chief."

Bully for you.

Jones smiled.

Havers picked up the handset and swivelled his chair to face the large window.

"Superintendent Havers," he announced proudly and listened for a moment before ending the brief call with, "Yes, sir. Certainly. I'll organise transport for myself." Without turning away from the window, he stretched out his arm and dropped the handset into its cradle.

"And the blood on the piece of glass taken from the bay window?" he asked, without taking his eyes from the view outside.

"Charlie's, sir. The FSIs think it's secondary transfer."

"From the clothes of the killer?"

"Probably."

Still staring through the window, Havers rested his elbows on the arms of his chair, steepled his fingers, and tapped them against his lips.

"You found a medal, I understand."

"Dr Spence did, sir."

Havers lowered his hands and swivelled his chair to face Jones again.

"Useful?"

"Not so far. A cheap silver St Christopher, found between the rug and the body. Means it wasn't in the room *before* our killer dumped the body. We couldn't find a chain and the medal definitely didn't belong to Charlie. Lydia, his wife, confirmed he didn't wear a medal. We're working on the assumption it belonged to the killer— or the person who dumped the body if they're different people. And we haven't ruled out an accomplice.

"Dr Spence says there were two words engraved on the back, but she could only raise the initial letters, *A* and *S*. We have no idea what it means. It could be a name or a message. Could be any number of things. The size of the medal suggests it was a man's, but since we think our killer's male, it doesn't move us any further along. Ownership won't be easy to establish. The hallmark's readable though, so we might be able to discover where, when, and where it was made. I'll have DC Olganski work on it once we're through searching the two flats tomorrow morning."

Jones checked the time. "DCs Washington and Adeoye are trying to identify the tenants at the moment, but there are almost as many squatters on the Orchard Towers Estate as paying tenants." He paused before adding, "The most important leads we have at the moment are the two hot targets overlooking Orchard Park Lane. Tower 3, Numbers 502 and 110."

"Tell me again why they're such good prospects."

Jones told Havers about the note Ryan found in Charlie's things and about his dalliance with "Dolly Parton".

Havers steepled his fingers again and resumed tapping his lips.

"Dawn raids with Armed Response Units are somewhat resource heavy, Jones. Are you sure you can't narrow the targets further."

Jones ground his teeth together. By "resource heavy" Havers meant "expensive". Surely they hadn't been landed with yet another bean-counter like his predecessor, Duggie Peyton?

"Not a chance, sir. And the raids have to be simultaneous to avoid warning the potential suspects of our interest. After the door-to-door, yesterday, the killer might already have fled."

"Understood, Jones. And the warrants? Do you need my help to expedite matters?"

"DI Cryer's handling that, sir. There won't be any problems. Thanks for the offer, though."

"When do you plan to go in?"

"Oh-four-hundred hours, tomorrow morning. I've tasked Section 14 to keep an eye on the block."

"Section 14?"

"Our covert observation unit, sir. They're based in Division Two. You won't have met them yet. They've been eyeballing the target buildings since lunchtime today and will maintain surveillance until we effect entry. I spoke to the team leader, DS Calvin Stevens, before this meeting. So far, they've seen nothing at all. As far as they can tell, both flats might be empty."

"Can they use infrared cameras?"

"No, sir. The obbo point is too far away for IR cameras. And in any event, the weather's been too hot. There's not enough temperature differentiation. They might see something with the night vision optics after dark, though. I'll check before we force entry. Cal Stevens runs a good team, sir. They won't miss anything."

"I'd love to be there to help, Jones, but I'll be in London this evening for an NPCC meeting. It probably won't break up until gone midnight. That's why the Chief called. I'll need to leave soon."

He glanced at the wall clock—15:13.

Jones grimaced.

He didn't envy Havers' trip to London. He'd heard many horror stories about the National Police Chief's Council meetings lasting well into the night. Politicking of that sort was one of the principal reasons he'd chosen to remain a Chief Inspector. He wanted to fight criminals, not butt heads with bureaucrats and accountants.

"Thanks for the offer, sir, but we'll be ably supported by the ARU."

"Is there anything else?" Havers made a move to stand.

Jones beat him to his feet. "No, sir."

"In that case, good luck."

"Thank you."

"I'll expect a full briefing tomorrow."

"Yes, sir. Of course, sir."

He hurried from the room, happy to leave Not-Bob to prep for his meeting with the NPCC.

Rather you than me, lad.

Chapter Sixteen

TUESDAY 16TH MAY – Afternoon

Police HQ, Holton, Birmingham, England

JONES POPPED into Phil's office on his way down from the meeting with Havers.

"How are those search warrants coming along?"

"Alex delivered them thirty minutes ago."

"Finished already? That was quick."

"They're both pretty much identical apart from the addresses. Simple copy and paste job once I'd written the first one. Alex is standing over the clerk now, but they're struggling to locate an amenable magistrate."

Phil arched his back, stretched out his arms, and groaned.

"Been sitting in this chair for hours. Need some exercise."

"Try climbing the stairs now and again."

Phil broke out one of his boyish grins. "Not a chance."

"Any idea how long before the warrants come through?"

"The clerk says we've made a good case, and the victim was an emergency worker. He's optimistic. Hopefully someone will sign them off by close of play." Phil rubbed his hands together. "Then we can go smash down a couple of doors. It'll save me that trip to the gym."

"Meanwhile there's nothing to do but wait. Oh, while I remember, any luck with the St Christopher?"

Phil sighed. "Nothing so far, boss. I have a pair of uniforms on the phones. They're calling all the jewellers in the city who do engraving. Dozens of them, there are." He smiled ruefully. "Given how old the medal is, I doubt they'll find—"

The mobile on Phil's desk vibrated and interrupted his flow. He snatched it up and accepted the call.

"DI Cryer. ... Okay Alex, that's great news. Get back here as soon as you can." He broke the connection and shot a glance across the desk. "That's it. We're a go for tomorrow morning."

"Excellent. Pull the team together while I call the ARU. Giles and his people are on standby, as are the uniform backup. Briefing room, at four thirty."

AN HOUR LATER, Jones stood next to the whiteboard for the final summary. The screen displayed an architect's drawing of Tower 3— curving plan above, and front elevation below. Three red circles marked the chosen points of entry and the reserve position. Circle A, on the tenth floor to the right of the stairwell, Circle B, on the fifth floor to the left, and Circle C, inside the stairwell on the fourth floor, below the other two.

They'd made the assumption that the interior layout of the flats matched others in the block. The high-rises, built in a post-war frenzy, didn't conform to today's standard layout, and neither Phil nor Holden Bigglesworth had been able to locate detailed floor plans in the council's planning department. They were going in blind, but they planned as best they could.

Jones spoke, slow and loud to reach the back of the room.

"We've had eyes on both flats since thirteen hundred hours this afternoon. There's been no movement into or out of either property, so we can't be sure if anyone's home. We'll proceed on the assumption that both flats will be occupied, and the occupants are dangerous. Giles, if you please."

DI Giles Danforth, stood and took over for him at the board. Tall and broad shouldered with formidable forearms, he wore a dark blue polo shirt with the letters ARU embroidered on the left breast.

"We're going in with three teams of three. One team for each door, and one in reserve on the fourth floor stairwell. When DCI Jones gives the go-ahead, we'll enter each flat at oh-four-hundred exactly. Now, to avoid any confusion, I'll go through this process step-by-step. The lead officer in each attack team will use a 'Persuader' ...."

Giles spoke for five minutes before turning to Jones.

"That all meet with your approval, sir?"

"You're in charge of tactics and weapons, Inspector Danforth. I'm happy to be led by you. Thanks."

Giles nodded and returned to his seat in the front row next to his second-in-command, Sergeant "Bob" Dylan.

Jones took the floor again. "Okay, here's the personnel distribution. Inspector Macklin and Sergeant Dolan, you will deploy your people on the ground out of sight to keep the civilians out of harm's way. We'll also have a pair of paramedics in an ambulance on hand in case anything goes wrong. You know what we're dealing with here, folks. There's no such thing as being too careful.

"As for the rest of you reprobates." He smiled to reduce the insult. "Ben and I will be with Team Alpha, led by DI Danforth. We'll enter Number 110 on the top floor." He pointed to Circle A on the diagram. "Ryan and Alex are with Team Bravo, led by Sergeant Dylan. You'll hit Number 502." He pointed to Circle B in the middle of floor five and slid his finger across and down to Circle C. "Phil will be with the Reserve Unit, who will take up a position in the fourth floor stairwell to cover our rear in case anyone gets past us. But we won't let that happen."

Phil's hand shot up.

"Boss, a word?" he asked, jaw set, face red, anger bubbling close to the surface.

Uh oh.

"Fire away, Philip."

"In private, sir. If you please?" He jumped to his feet and marched to the door.

Jones followed Phil out into the corridor. The moment the door closed behind them, Phil started his attack.

"*I* should be going in with Team Bravo, not Alex."

"Why?"

"Because … I'm second-in-command."

"Which means you need to stay in reserve in case anything goes wrong."

"That's rubbish, and we both know it. Look, if you're worried about my bloody knee—"

"Of course I'm worried about your knee."

"The knee's okay," he said, teeth clenched.

Jones raised a calming hand. It didn't work. Phil seethed in front of him, quivering, taut as a guitar string.

"No, it isn't, Phil. I've seen the way you flinch whenever you have to stand—"

"So Alex takes my place? Do you know how that makes me feel?"

"What? Your male ego's bruised. Is that it?"

"No, of course not, Alex knows her stuff, but … I don't want to be side-lined. I should be in Team Bravo."

"Finished?" he asked when Phil paused for breath.

Phil opened his mouth in preparation to respond, but clearly thought better of it and nodded instead.

"Phil, this is a command decision. You're too important to risk. I'm putting you in the Reserve Unit, and that's an end to it. Am I making myself clear?"

After staring each other down for a few moments, Phil nodded.

"Yes, sir," he said. "I understand. I understand fully."

They re-entered an eerily silent briefing room, and Jones

continued with his roundup. Phil stared at the SmartScreen the whole time, saying nothing. Jones let him simmer. He'd cool down soon enough—once he'd finished mulling things over and seen the logic of the decision.

Ten minutes later, Jones wrapped up with, "Okay people, thanks for your time. Now, straight off home and catch what rest you can. I want you assembled in the car park at two thirty tomorrow morning, bright and fresh. Don't be late or you'll miss the party."

The detectives and uniformed officers dispersed with a clatter of chairs and a murmur of excited voices. On his way out, Giles touched his right index finger to his forehead in salute and left with Dylan in tow. The next time Jones saw either of them, they would be dressed in full paramilitary gear, ready for combat. A fearsome sight. He'd seen both in action a number of times and couldn't have asked for better support.

Finally, he turned to the redhead in the corner. "Thank you for all your hard work, Mr Bigglesworth. You can wipe the board, or whatever you do with it, and head off home now." He almost added, "Its way past your bedtime," but he couldn't be so cruel.

The young civilian worked his keyboard, and the SmartScreen cleared to white. He stood, picked up a leather laptop case from the floor near his feet, and slipped the webbing strap over his head and onto his shoulder. It made him look even more like a student on his way home from school, satchel swinging at his side.

"Good evening, sir," he said. "And good luck for tonight."

Slowly, the room emptied, leaving Jones and Phil alone. He waited for Phil to finish a call before speaking.

"Have you calmed down yet?"

Phil tapped his chin with the phone.

"Guess I have to," he said, reluctance showing in the way he dragged out the answer. "Can't be angry with a dinner guest, eh?" He grinned, back to normal. Almost.

"Sorry?"

Phil held up the mobile. "That was Manda. When I told her we were on a shout early tomorrow, she insisted you come for a meal tonight. She's making a curry."

"Thanks, Phil, but no. I'll head for home early."

"Nah, she insists. Your cottage is miles away, and she's already setting up the spare room."

"Well"—Jones raised both hands in surrender—"I wouldn't want to upset you both in the same day. I'd be delighted, and besides, it'll give me a chance to say goodnight to the little ones."

"And they'll be overjoyed to see their Uncle David." Phil dropped the mobile into his pocket. "I need to fetch my stuff from my office. Want me to grab your jacket?"

"No, it's alright, I'll come with you. I need to collect my grab bag."

They heard the phone in Jones' office ringing from ten doors along the empty corridor.

"Shall we leave it?" Phil asked. "Early start in the morning."

Jones was tempted, but shook his head. "Better answer, could be important."

"I need the loo," Phil said, turning towards the door. "Be right with you."

The phone kept ringing as Jones fumbled with his keys.

"Okay, okay," he said, "I'm coming."

He counted fifteen rings before he could unlock the office door and snatched up the handset.

"Jones," he announced.

"Ah, Jones," Havers said, "glad I caught you. I tried your mobile first. Anything wrong?"

"No, sir. I always power it down when I'm briefing the team."

Saves interruptions.

"Ah, I see," Havers said, his disapproval at being kept waiting evident in his voice. "Makes contacting you rather difficult."

That's the whole point.

In the background a tinny voice announced his train's imminent arrival at Euston Station. Jones raised an eyebrow in surprise. He'd expected Havers to travel by chauffeur-driven car, but the Super no doubt believed that the train should take the strain. A good way to demonstrate his environmental credentials, too.

"How can I can help, sir?"

"Actually it more what I can do for you, Jones. I've just received an interesting snippet of information from the Ministry of Justice via the Home Office. It might be of some value moving forwards."

Moving forwards? Please.

What was wrong with "in future"?

"That would be good, sir."

There has to be a first time for everything.

"WELL, PHILIP," Jones said as they headed towards their cars, the sun fast plummeting towards the western horizon, "this is a turn up."

"What is?"

"Leaving for home in daylight."

"Yeah. So, what did Not-Bob have to say for himself?"

"Apparently, a national standing order issued by the Home Office last week on behalf of the Ministry of Justice could help us 'moving forwards'."

When they reached their vehicles, Jones checked his watch again. "Listen, Phil, thanks for the invite, why don't we do the meal another time?"

"Oh no you don't. Even at this time of day it'll take you forty minutes to reach your place, and we're only down the road. You'll have more sleep if you stay with us, and I can avoid getting back into that bloody Clio 'til tomorrow evening." He glowered at the little car.

"Okay," Jones agreed, "I'll take you home, and you'll give me dinner and a room for the night. Guess who has the better part of that deal."

Phil slid into the soft leather of the Škoda's passenger seat and stretched out, sighing with pleasure.

"Bliss," he said. "Must get myself one of these beauties."

Jones strapped in, engaged drive, and pulled out of the car park.

"So, what's this about the Ministry of Justice?" Phil asked, leaning heavily against the head restraint.

"They've asked us to notify them whenever we bring charges of murder or any serious violent offence. They're specifically interested in men between the ages of eighteen and fifty."

"Why?"

"The MoJ is funding a research project, investigating uncontrolled violent behaviour in men. They're trying to recruit subjects for a scientific trial. But that's not the interesting bit."

"No?"

"No. The scientist leading the study, Dr Andrew Craig, is based at our own University."

Jones flicked Phil another glance and added a double hitch eyebrow lift to his smile.

"And?"

"And," Jones continued, "as part of his research study, Dr Craig runs court-certified DNA tests."

"Ah-ha, that's a bit of luck."

"My thoughts exactly, Philip. I've a feeling that our Dr Craig might come in handy one day. It might be worth chatting him up and keeping him sweet."

"Cool. Want me to contact him tomorrow?"

"When you have a moment, Philip. He's an intellectual. You'll speak his language better than I will. No need to rush, though. It's not as though we have any DNA to test right now."

Chapter Seventeen

WEDNESDAY 17TH MAY – Ryan Washington

Bordesley Green, Birmingham, UK

SILENCE.

Darkness surrounded Ryan Washington, the darkness of the night, the darkness of the back of the Transit van, and the darkness of the excitement bubbling inside him. He was totally buzzing. Couldn't wait to get moving.

The quiet before the storm took its toll, but this was why he loved his job. The middle of the night, waiting to smash down some perp's door. Fantastic. What a rush.

Heart rate in the stratosphere, nerves jumping, sweat pouring. He was pumped about the whole thing. The down side? With the ARU leading the raid, the boss didn't need him to carry a firearm. Bummer. What was the point of being an AFO if he couldn't carry a weapon on a op?

Still, there'd be other times.

When the boss supported his application to become an Authorised Firearms Officer, Ryan couldn't have been more gobsmacked. With Alex and Ben already fully certified, Ryan didn't really expect the boss' support, but he'd received it anyway.

Bloody good man, the boss. A solid gold, twenty-four-carat geezer.

Firearms training? A complete doddle. Well, at least the shooting part.

Having been brought up on a farm, Ryan had been shooting game since growing tall enough and strong enough to hold a shotgun. When he'd first applied for firearms certification, there'd been a freeze on training courses for over a year, and he'd been knocked back. A real bummer, but the boss had earned himself so much clout after the Hollie Jardine business, he'd made a special case for Ryan and they bumped him to the top of the list. He'd made the next course.

Now, there were three fully qualified AFOs in the SCU. It made them the best prepped and best armed detective team in the West Midlands, and Ryan was one of them.

Totally awesome.

Once they'd accepted him onto the course, he'd aced it. No way was he going to fail. He'd never failed anything worthwhile in his life.

The AFO selection process had been gruelling. Even tougher than he'd expected. An unending challenge. Interviews, psychological and physiological tests, medical exams. At each stage, he excelled. Of course he did. Why wouldn't he? He'd been born for it.

The actual mechanical part—firearms handling, tactical awareness and shooting—had been a doddle. He took to it like a natural, passing each practical assessment at or towards the top of the class. Made sharpshooter grade easy. At one stage, he considered applying for a transfer to the ARU, but that would have meant leaving the SCU, leaving the boss.

No way that was happening. None.

He'd nailed his first action as a fully trained and certified AFO, and it still gave him goosebumps whenever he thought about it. He,

Alex, and Ben had raced to London in support of Phil's undercover operation. Yeah, that evening op had been a total blast.

And here he sat, in the back of the van preparing to go in again, guts screwed into a tight ball of anticipation.

Fantastic.

How long now? He checked the time on his watch. Not long before the off.

C'mon. Let's get moving.

Maybe he'd have a chance to make it up to everyone.

The run-in with the boss and Phil had been a real buzzkill. He replayed the verbal arse-kicking in his head. God, what a fuck up. Why hadn't he told them about Charlie and Dolly upfront? As though he could ever hide anything from David Jones?

Fucking Charlie. Always getting him into trouble. Forever asking Ryan to cover for him while he sloped off and played the field. Even dead, the fat fucker was ruining Ryan's life.

Good job he was dead, the useless sod. Best thing that could have happened.

Fuck's sake, Ryan. What are you saying?

The poor bastard's guts exploded out of his belly.

No one deserved to die like that. Not even Charlie Pelham.

God, what a horrible mess. Made everything worse.

And that jibe from the boss about discussing it again during his annual appraisal. What did that mean? A demerit on his permanent record? Removal from the SCU? Losing his AFO accreditation?

Fuck you, Charlie. Fuck you very much.

He glanced across at the gorgeous Alex, whose encouraging return smile made him feel heaps better. It always did. She'd been through so much in the past year—losing her wife to an arsonist. The sadness about her eyes made Ryan want to hug her pain away, but she wouldn't have appreciated that. Not from him.

Bugger it.

If only she felt the same way for him that he felt for her.

Never happen, though. Ryan wasn't her type. Wasn't her gender, either. Shame really.

Man up, will you?

He'd be crying over his unrequited love next, stupid bugger.

That was the trouble with all this waiting. Always made him dwell on the inconsequential bollocks, the stupid stuff, and the adrenaline swirled it all into a great big angry, overblown soup.

Bloody moron.

He breathed deep, held it for a count of twenty, and then released it slow and steady. Repeated twice. An exercise he'd learned during the AFO training course.

As usual, it worked like a dream.

His heart rate and breathing rate returned to near normal.

Ryan tried to copy the way the boss handled things. A true professional. The man had no fear. At least none that showed.

David Jones.

Someone to look up to. Aspire to be like. The boss had been in his element since they'd found Charlie's body. Organising the team. Urging and encouraging but never shouting—except for that one time in his office. But even that time, he'd kept his cool when he could have exploded. Exploded like Charlie's belly.

Not funny, Ryan. Pack it in.

The boss was calm, a leader, someone to follow. Someone to respect, to emulate. Phil, too. The guy had pushed through so much pain to return to work and seemed to be taking things in his stride. How did he do that? How had he come through the knee op? how did he cope so well?

Alex sat beside him, cool and composed, her eyes wide in concentration as she listened to the boss' last-minute safety briefing. She'd tied her long, blonde hair in a ponytail and poked it through the loop in her baseball cap. She radiated Scandinavian strength, efficiency, and calm.

What would he give to be with her?

Anything.

Everything.

Stop it, Ryan.

And then there was Big Ben Adeoye, the SCU's latest recruit. Solid. Strong. Impressive. A former soldier, he'd seen hot action in Afghanistan and Iraq. Won medals for bravery. A solid beat cop, he had the makings of a good detective, too. He sat on the other side of Alex, dwarfing her. Not for height so much, but for width. How long did he spend in the gym to maintain such a toned physique?

Ben had his eyes closed and was smiling. Totally fearless.

Phil, solid and dependable, sat alongside the boss, nodding to each statement. He'd be in the Reserve Unit, out of harm's way.

He'd been livid when the boss first announced he'd be leading the Reserve Unit. Tried to hide it, but anyone who knew him could tell. He and the boss had stepped outside the briefing room for a "quiet" chat, but their voices had been raised. As far as Ryan knew, it had been the first time Phil and the boss had ever fought.

Ryan could understand the decision, though. The boss had the unit's best interests at heart. As the only SCU member with kids, Phil held a special place in the team, and although he'd made a spectacular recovery, the big guy still carried a slight limp, even though he tried desperately to hide it.

Finally, there was the boss, issuing his orders with the quiet air of authority Ryan hoped to develop one day. Unflustered and encouraging, his smooth voice radiated composure. He wore his stab vest securely and, for once, he'd removed his tie. His dark blue SCU baseball cap—mandatory with the ARU in attendance—rested uneasily on his head. His normal dress sense screamed university lecturer, not hard-nosed cop, but now, he looked, well … uncomfortable, but still in command.

They'd been through it all during the afternoon briefing, but the boss reviewed the upcoming raid in minute detail, taking a full fifteen minutes to do it. Drumming in the safety rules. Belt and braces. Nothing could go wrong.

"Time check," the boss said. He raised his wrist and waited. "Oh-three-thirty-two in five, four, three, two … now."

They synchronised their watches.

The boss shifted his weight and craned his neck to see everybody clearly.

"We don't know what we're going to find up there, so be careful. If our man's home, we know what he's capable of doing, so make sure your safety equipment's in order." He paused and studied them. "Simultaneous entries are complicated. Check your earpieces are working, I don't want any miscommunication."

The boss pressed the speaker button on his hand-held unit twice, paused, and repeated the procedure. The four corresponding static clicks in Ryan's earpiece confirmed its operation.

"Anybody *not* hear that?"

No one responded.

"Good. Make sure your stab vests are fitted correctly and the identification marks are visible. You are responsible for each other's safety. Do I make myself clear?"

Alex tapped Ryan on the shoulder and they checked each other's stab vests. She moved so close, her breath cooled his cheek.

Ben and Phil did the same for each other and then Phil checked the boss over.

Ryan smiled inwardly. He had the better part of that deal.

"Final instructions," the boss said, making ready to open the rear doors. "I've said it before, but it's worth repeating. The ARU are in charge until I call the 'All Clear'. Our job is to serve the warrants and arrest any occupants. Right now, let's look lively."

He pushed open the rear doors and climbed out. Phil followed close behind, looking confident.

Ryan closed his eyes to centre himself before the off, but Charlie's bloody and gutless corpse swam onto the screen behind his lids.

Crap.

What must it have felt like to have a knife carve through his belly. Then the freezing gas. What a way to go. Couldn't have happened to a more deserving arsehole, though. Sure enough.

"Ryan?"

He jerked upright, opened his eyes.

"Yes, boss?"

"You alright?" Concern creased the old man's face.

Ryan dropped the smile and nodded.

"Yes, boss. I'm fine."

The others were already out on the pavement, reintroducing themselves to their colleagues from the ARU. Ryan hadn't seen or felt them leave the van.

Bloody hell.

He straightened in his seat.

"Sorry, boss. Just thinking things through. Making sure we've covered all the bases."

"Come up with anything we've missed?"

"Not a one, boss."

"If you're under the weather, you can stay here in the van. We have things under control."

"What?" Ryan slid past him and shot out of the van into the predawn gloom, "and leave you guys to have all the fun?" He turned his back on the boss and waved his hand in a dismissive gesture. "Besides, if I stay here, who's going to look after the rest of the team?"

"Good man," the boss said, patting him on the shoulder.

03:52:33

Ryan breathed steadily as his team climbed towards the fifth floor landing. The stab vest—of questionable protective value against a Hornet injector knife wielded by a madman—made things slightly more uncomfortable, but it beat climbing the stairs in the same body armour the ARU men were wearing.

Ryan knew full well how much the kit weighed and how restrictive it could be. He'd never felt comfortable in the stuff, but by Christ, he wished he wore it now. Wished he was part of the ARU team, armed and ready to break down doors and crack heads together.

He counted every one of the one hundred and thirty steps to the fifth floor landing, concentrating on his breathing and his footing the whole way up. Ahead of him, Alex took the stairs two at a time, maintaining her place behind the third ARU officer with apparent ease. Her breathing rhythm didn't even seem to increase.

Atta girl.

Finally at the fifth floor landing, the ARU team leader—Sergeant "Bob" Dylan—raised his fist to signal a halt. He and his two men fanned out into the opening. Ryan stood on the sixth step down from the head of the stairs, his eyes level with Alex's round, firm backside.

God, if only.

He fought to steady his breathing. Predawn raids always made him antsy.

03:53:27.

Six and a half minutes to go.

They waited.

Chapter Eighteen

Bordesley Green, Birmingham, UK

03:55:15

Jones worried for his team. He hated the idea of going in blind. Two apartments, different floors, entered simultaneously—a recipe for disaster. He'd picked up on Ryan's earlier hesitation and worried for the lad's state of mind. And another thing, placing Phil in the Reserve Team hadn't gone down well, but command decisions had to be made for the benefit of the whole team. Despite the massive progress he'd made, Phil's knee was still a definite liability. Jones had to protect the man from himself. All part of responsibility as a team commander.

He raised his hand to his mouth, and pressed a button on his comms unit. "Team Alpha, in position. Team Bravo, status? Over?"

A burst of static followed, before Alex's subdued response. "*Team*

Bravo in position. All is clear. No, hold … hold! … One of the doors is opening. Over."

"Is it the target? Over."

"Negative. Repeat, negative. It is Number 505. A woman. Hold. Over."

"Jones to all, delay, delay! Await further instructions. Over."

From his position inside the top floor stairwell and behind Giles and the other two ARU officers, Jones was blind. He couldn't see a damned thing.

The silence seemed to stretch out for minutes.

Jones stood in the stairwell with his back against a rough concrete wall. Ahead, an unflinching Giles Danforth awaited his signal. Jones raised his hand, palm open. He sidestepped around the ARU officers and risked a glance at the target flat. Despite the pre-dawn gloom he could see the whole way along the curving walkway to the target door. No movement. No lights. He turned to check the other side. Same thing. All ten doors on the top floor remained closed, the windows dark. He couldn't risk stepping out further to check on the lower floors.

Jones raised the radio to his lips and hit the PTT button.

"Team Bravo? Sitrep, please. Over."

"One second, boss." After another extended delay, Alex continued. *"Okay, the woman has been escorted downstairs to the Reserve Unit. She is not happy, but she is away and safe, sir. We are ready to go. Repeat, ready to go. Over."*

Jones checked the time again. 04:02:15.

"Jones to all. Go. Go. Go!"

Chapter Nineteen

WEDNESDAY 17TH MAY – Phil Cryer

Bordesley Green, Birmingham, UK

04:02:10

Phil watched the neighbour descend the stairs below their position with her uniformed escort, muttering under her breath the whole way. Not a happy camper on her way to work. She'd be less happy at being caught in crossfire, though.

David's, "*Go. Go. Go!*" crackled in his earpiece.

Phil's heart jumped and he focused on the backs of the ARU's Reserve Team. Radio silence would be maintained until the double-entry was complete and any occupants subdued. The muffled sounds of footfalls echoed through the tower, followed by a sharp thump as one of the doors caved under the force of the double-handled battering-ram—the Persuader. Shuffles, grunts, and heavy breathing followed, and then multiple cracks of the second Persuader smashing against a different door, a closer door—

Number 502. This time the entrance proved more resilient. It took another five heavy cracks before the door succumbed and crashed open.

Phil hadn't felt so powerless since lying strapped into his hospital bed with his leg in traction. He could barely constrain himself from bursting past the ARU men and starting the climb. Minutes seemed to pass before Alex's voice on the intercom interrupted his cascading thoughts. *"Team Bravo, all clear. Repeat, all clear. Number 502 is empty and secure. Over."*

Phil brushed past the ARU men and climbed up the final three steps to the landing. He stared into the calm and infuriating eyes of the ARU sub-leader. "Come on, man, Number 502 is secure. We should move up to the next floor. What are you waiting for?"

ARU was still in command and Phil had no authority to order them forwards until the second "All Clear", but he couldn't contain himself. He reached to grab the sergeant's body armour, but the clear-eyed man placed a restraining hand on his forearm, and he held back.

"Team Alpha, all clear. Repeat, Team Alpha, all clear." David couldn't mask the disappointment in his voice. *"Number 110 is empty. Over."*

Phil glared at the ARU officer again and arched a questioning eyebrow. "Well?

The man nodded and signalled his two subordinates to let Phil up to the landing.

Chapter Twenty

WEDNESDAY 17TH MAY – Pre-dawn

Bordesley Green, Birmingham, UK

04:03:16

Jones pressed the PTT button once more. "Rendezvous at Number 502 immediately. Its door was reinforced. Team Alpha, out." Resignation coloured his voice, and he couldn't help it.

Jones and his team marched along the tenth floor walkway towards the stairwell. From his position on the uppermost floor, he had a panoramic view of the opposite side of the curved building. Although nearly a hundred and fifty metres away and five storeys below, he had clear sight of the fifth floor. Phil's Reserve Unit, small in the distance, tramped up from the fourth floor stairwell, turned left, and headed towards the shattered door near the far end of the walkway. A slightly limping Phil and the three ARU men, their Heckler & Koch MP5 automatic rifles pointing up, trudged towards Number

502. The thick air of anti-climax showed in their body language.

A gap formed between Phil and the rest of his team as he turned towards Jones and waved. Even at that distance Jones could see the disappointment scored into his face. Phil's downturned mouth and slumped shoulders told the whole story.

Jones returned his signal.

Ryan and Alex appeared in Number 502's splintered doorway as Phil's team approached. Ryan, head lowered, shoulders sloped even more than normal, headed towards them, leaving Alex to guard the entrance to the flat.

Movement caught his eye.

The door to Number 503 opened inwards.

Phil flinched and pointed to a spot behind Ryan's shoulder. His mouth opened. He called something but the wind carried his words away.

Someone appeared in the open doorway, a blur of dark jeans and a hooded top, hood raised, lower half of the face obscured by a mask. Tallish, slim build. He dropped his shoulder and charged.

"Ryan," Jones screamed. "Look out!"

Ryan spun to face the open door in time to receive Hoodie's shoulder charge. In the middle of turning, his balance compromised, Ryan took the whole of full force of the man's momentum.

He didn't have a chance.

Off-balance, Ryan careened sideways towards the walkway's railings.

Hoodie turned and ducked back inside, and the door to Number 503 slammed shut. The heavy bang echoed throughout the tower.

Ryan collapsed against the safety rails running the whole length of the open walkway. Something gave way.

God, no!

The hairs on the back of Jones' neck prickled and his stomach lurched.

The railings crumpled under Ryan's impact. Decades of weather and disrepair must have taken their toll on the rusty metal.

Ryan's scream cut through the stillness. Eyes wide, mouth open, he scrambled for a hand-hold on the fractured metalwork, his movements frantic, desperate.

Jones could do nothing but stand and stare, breath stalled, heart pounding.

Ryan couldn't find a grip. He toppled out into the cool, early morning air.

"Oh God, no! Ryan!"

Chapter Twenty-One

Bordesley Green, Birmingham, UK

SOMETHING STOPPED Ryan's outward momentum. He hung below the edge. From his position, five floors above and diagonally across from the action, Jones couldn't see what had prevented Ryan's backwards plunge to the courtyard.

Alex dived headlong to the walkway floor and grabbed hold of Ryan's flailing right arm. Microseconds behind Alex, Sergeant Dylan pitched in to help.

Jones grasped the railings in front of him, trying to add his strength to theirs.

Released from his mind-freeze, he screamed, "Hold on to him. For God's sake pull him in!"

Able to move at last, Jones tore loose his iron grip on the railings and darted towards the staircase, following Ben, Giles, and his men.

Why weren't they miles ahead of him? He'd been rooted to the spot for ages, watching Ryan fight for his life, hadn't he?

No, it couldn't have been more than a second or two.

Legs burning, lungs absorbing chilly, damp air, Jones ran. He hit the stairwell and descended three steps at a time in the semi-darkness, oblivious to the risk. Despite his best efforts, Ben and the ARU men easily outdistanced him.

He might as well have been running through treacle. His lungs, arms, and legs burned, cried out for rest, but he drove himself harder.

Bursting into the growing daylight, Jones turned right onto the fifth floor walkway and raced towards Phil, Alex, and the others, some fifty metres away. His vision blurred as his lungs fought for oxygen.

Inexplicably, Ben slowed. Before he had time to react, Jones ran into the back of him. He bounced off a huge, muscled torso and nearly stumbled, but retained his balance and continued the race. He dodged another slowing runner.

Fleeting thoughts barely registered. Why was he passing them?

Closer now, Jones focused his vision on the group of ARU officers at the far end of the concrete walkway.

Why weren't they doing anything?

He skidded to a halt in front of Alex, who sat, legs akimbo, back propped against a concrete support pillar. Phil sat beside her, good leg bent, injured leg straight out in front. Sergeant Dylan stood over them, breathing hard.

Jones sucked in huge gasps of air as relief flooded over him. He smiled as widely as he could while still fighting for air and reached across to Alex's shoulder. As he touched it, she grimaced and squeezed her eyes tight shut.

"Well done, Alex, I thought he was a done for. Bloody wonderful effort, lass. Fantastic. Don't know what else to say."

He glanced around at the officers standing silent above him. "Where is he? Where's Ryan?"

No one answered.

No one looked up from studying the concrete floor at their feet.

Jones turned to Alex who sat and stared at the hands in her lap. The right pinkie finger stuck out at an unnatural angle. Two fingernails on the same hand had been torn off in the rescue. Blood seeped from the nail beds.

"God! They look painful." He touched her shoulder again, this time more gently. "Don't move. We'll fetch the paramedic."

He turned to Phil. "Where's Ryan? Did you take him inside?"

Alex lifted her head and stared at him through huge, tear-filled eyes. "I tried, boss. I tried so hard, but he was too heavy."

"But the others, Sergeant Dylan?"

She opened her mouth to speak but no words came out. She squeezed her eyes closed again and her face crumpled. Tears streamed down her cheeks.

"I tried …" She covered her face with her undamaged hand and wept. One shoulder jerked in time with her sobs, the other, her right didn't move.

Oh God. No.

Jones' knees buckled. A great big chasm opened in the pit of his stomach. With effort, he remained standing. The ARU officers turned away, each in their own private hell.

Phil scrambled to his feet and moved alongside Jones.

"He went so fast, boss. We couldn't …." The breath caught in his throat, choking off the words.

Jones inched towards the edge of the walkway. The damaged iron railings, bent out and away from the building, still vibrated. Something fluttered in the wind, impaled on the sharp end of a snapped, cast iron rod—the unmistakable Velcro strap of a police stab vest. It must have been the thing that arrested Ryan's fall.

The torn strap explained why Ryan hadn't fallen straight away.

Oh God, what am I thinking?

He leaned forwards. Didn't want to look, but forced himself to peer over the edge and down to the courtyard below.

Ryan lay sprawled on the cracked and filthy concrete, his arms splayed wide, his legs buckled and misshapen—broken.

A pool of dark red blood oozed out from beneath his head, and spread over the paving slabs.

Chapter Twenty-Two

WEDNESDAY 17TH MAY – Early Morning

Bordesley Green, Birmingham, UK

04:06

Numb.

Jones felt nothing. It started from his heart, spread throughout his body, and offered a relief, of sorts. The human mechanism protecting itself—at least for the moment.

Experience and training rammed down his emotions, forcing them under the surface to fester. The time to grieve would come later, but now he had to act.

"Ben, get down there! He might still be alive."

Jones turned. Found no sign of Ben. Where had he gone?

"*Sir?*"

A call from below registered in his earpiece. He clung to the nearest concrete support column and poked his head over the edge again.

Ben knelt over Ryan, both hands applied pressure to a leg wound. A second man—one of Giles' ARU officers—stared up, a radio held close to his mouth.

"He's alive, sir! In a bad way and unresponsive, but still breathing. Over."

Still alive? How was that possible?

"Call the ambulance up. Over."

"Already have, sir. Over."

As if to prove it, an engine roared and blue lights flashed. An ambulance rounded a corner and squealed to a halt metres away from the fallen Ryan. Rear doors flew open and two green-clad figures burst out, a man and a woman. The woman, unencumbered, reached Ryan and Ben first. The man, carrying a large bag, arrived moments later.

The woman said something to Ben. He hesitated for a moment before standing and giving her access to Ryan. While the paramedics started their lifesaving work, Ben stood over them, watching, head bowed, arms out from his sides, Ryan's blood dripping from his fingers.

Jones raised his radio.

"Ben, can you hear me? Over."

Ben looked up, held out his blood smeared hands, and pointed to his ear. He nodded.

"How is he? Over."

Ben pinched his lips and waggled his right hand. Not sure.

"Still breathing? Over."

Another nod.

Thank God.

Jones closed his eyes for a moment. Behind him, shouts and crashes barely registered.

"Stay with him, Ben," Jones said. "Give the medics all the help they need. And tell Inspector Macklin to cordon off the area. Those lights are going to wake the neighbours and we don't want a crowd gathering."

Ben shot him a thumbs up. His booming, "Will do, sir," echoed up from the courtyard.

On instruction from his partner, the male paramedic hurried to the back of the ambulance and lowered the tailgate. He appeared moments later, carrying a yellow spinal board and another bag. Ben and the ARU man, both trained first aiders, would help the paramedics load Ryan onto the board and into the ambulance.

He was in good hands.

"Keep in touch, Ben. I want to know how he is the moment you hear anything. Jones, out."

He pushed away from the edge and turned his back on the devastating scene.

"What happened, boss?" Alex's quiet voice broke into his thoughts.

"Didn't you see?"

Alex stared into the middle distance, her eyes unfocussed. She shook her head. "I heard Ryan scream and turned to see him, hanging out over the balcony. His ... his stab vest caught on the railings." Her eyes snapped into focus and she looked at Jones for the first time. "I tried to pull him in, boss. I really did, but he was too heavy for me—for us. *Jag kunde inte hålla honom.* I could not hold him." Tears flowed again.

Jones grasped her undamaged hand. Alex stiffened, startled by his touch at first, but she soon seemed to take comfort from the gesture.

"Didn't you hear, Alex? He's still alive."

Hope brightened her eyes.

"He is?"

She struggled to stand. Jones helped her up and held tight as she leaned over the edge.

"*Tack, Gud.*" The tears returned, this time of relief. "Do you know what happened, boss?"

"A man jumped out of Number 503"—he jerked a thumb over his shoulder—"and barged Ryan into the railings. They collapsed under his weight."

"A man? What man?"

"That's what I'd like to know. Giles?"

He searched the faces on the balcony, but couldn't find the one he wanted. Couldn't see Sergeant Dylan, either.

One of the ARU men stepped forwards.

"They broke in, sir," he said, pointing to the newly smashed door to Number 503. "Inspector Danforth and Sergeant Dylan are inside now, sir. Searching."

Jones stepped forwards, but the ARU man held up a hand. "Sorry, sir. I can't let you go in."

"Step aside, man!"

"Inspector Danforth's orders. Told me not to let you in no matter how much you wanted to."

"I ordered you to step aside."

Jones pushed ahead and walked straight into the man's outstretched and open hand.

The grim-faced man with startling blue eyes shook his head. "Not happening, sir. ARU's in charge until DI Danforth tells me otherwise. Please stand back."

Jones ground his teeth.

"What's your name, son?"

"Kellerman, sir. Pavel Kellerman."

"Do you know who I am?"

"Yes, sir. You're DCI Jones, but you're still not getting past me until DI Danforth says it's safe."

Jones relaxed his jaw muscles. His bluster hadn't worked. Wouldn't work.

"Okay, Kellerman. Okay." He stretched out a hand—a peace offering. "Good man. I'm sorry."

Kellerman nodded and backed away, but not far enough for Jones to burst past him and enter the flat.

Jones gave up. He turned to Alex who didn't look good. She'd collapsed against the column, her face pale and even more drawn than usual.

"Alex, you need treatment."

She straightened, winced, and sucked in a breath of air.

"No, sir. I am okay. Really."

Phil limped closer.

"I'll take her, boss."

"No, Phil, I need you here. You there!"

He signalled to the ARU officer standing beside the blue-eyed Kellerman.

The woman stood to attention.

"Yes, sir?"

"Take DS Olganski downstairs to the ambulance. Make sure she goes with them to the hospital. No arguments." He leaned closer to Alex. "After you've been passed fit by a doctor, you can check on Ryan. That work for you?"

Alex blinked and breathed deeper. A little colour returned to her cheeks.

"Yes, boss. It does. Thank you. Someone will need to contact Ryan's parents. Would you like me to do that?"

"No, Phil knows them as well as anyone. He can call them from here."

Jones glanced at Phil, who nodded and shuffled a few paces along the walkway. He pulled his mobile from a pocket and started dialling.

The ARU officer made safe her rifle, slipped the strap over her head, and pushed it around her back. She approached Alex.

"Ready, Sarge?" she asked, gently.

Alex nodded and allowed the woman to help her up and escort her away. After a few paces, Alex faltered. The ARU officer threw an arm around her and half carried her along the walkway.

A dark form appeared in the doorway to Number 503. Giles Danforth closed on him.

"I don't know what to say, David. It happened so damned fast. Dylan there," he pointed to a stocky ARU man who'd emerged from the flat and looked even more downcast than the others, "said he was a fraction late. There was no time for anyone to react." He grasped Jones' upper arm and squeezed. "I'm so sorry."

Jones tore his arm free, unable to accept any comfort no matter who offered it.

"Ryan's still alive, Giles."

"He is?" Shock and doubt registered in his voice.

"In a bad way, but the paramedics are treating him now."

A beaming smile broke out on Giles' angular face. "Bob" Dylan looked as though he wanted to punch the air and whoop in delight.

Jones faced the building. The door to Number 503, like its neighbour, stood open courtesy of the same Persuader that had given them access to Number 502.

"Did you get him?"

Giles shook his head. "Sorry, David. The place is empty."

"What? How?"

"The bugger was fully prepped. He had a rip line set up. Abseiled down into the ground and legged it."

"Couldn't you follow him?"

"No. The line had a QR system—"

"A what?"

"A quick-release system. The second he hit the pavement, he activated the QR and the line dropped with him. By the time we'd have set up a safe line he'd have been long gone."

Jones shut his eyes, close to snapping at his friend who plainly felt as frustrated as he did.

"Did you see where he went?"

Giles worked his jaw muscles. "Yep. He disappeared into the underground parking area. We radioed his location to the uniforms. There's a full team on the ground now, searching."

Jones took a moment.

"Thanks, Giles. Sorry if I made it sound as though I was—"

Giles shook his head. "You didn't, mate. Both 503 and 502 are clear. I've checked them myself. Is there anything else we can do to help?"

"Yes, there is, but can you give me a moment, please?" He changed the band on his radio to global transmit. "This is DCI Jones to all available units. Officer down. I repeat, officer down." Jones' voice faltered, but he continued. "We're on the Orchard Towers Estate. The suspect is a white male. Approximately five feet ten inches tall, slim build, wearing dark blue jeans and a dark blue or black hooded top." He paused.

What else? Think man.

He released the PTT button and tried picturing the man who

shoulder charged Ryan over the railings. The image blurred in his mind.

"Giles, what did he look like?"

Giles shrugged his broad shoulders. "Only saw the top of his head. I can't help."

"Phil? What about you?"

Phil lowered the phone and covered the mouthpiece with his free hand. "You're bang on, boss. He wore dark gloves and black trainers with white laces. Apart from that, I can't add anything." He removed his hand from the phone and continued his call.

Jones pressed the PTT button again. "Subject was last seen at the rear of Tower 3"—he checked the time—"seven minutes ago."

Bloody hell. Only seven minutes?

"All available units, respond to the Orchard Towers Estate ASAP. I want this man found!"

Jones released the button and stared at the open doorways. Which flat should he tackle first?

"David," Giles said, "what can we do?"

Jones met his friend's eyes and understood his situation. Once the buildings had been secured, the ARU's operational role ended. They should return to their base and sign in their firearms, but Giles obviously didn't want to leave so soon.

Jones handed him a bone.

"Can you find a way of securing the guard rail? Too dangerous to leave it in this condition. But don't touch the metal, and for God's sake be careful. I don't want any more falls."

"Right on it, David." Giles' face brightened at the opportunity to do something practical and constructive. "Kellerman, go fetch a dozen webbing straps from the van."

"Yes, sir."

Kellerman hurried away, at the double.

At the far end of the walkway, the door to Number 500 opened. A greasy-haired, bearded man, hairy belly hanging over a pair of sagging boxers, stepped onto the walkway. He rubbed sleep from his eyes with a pair of massive fists.

"What all fucking noise?"

His hands dropped, and he stood open mouthed, staring at what for him must have been a scene from his worst nightmare.

He raised his hands in surrender and backed slowly into his flat.

"I-I go! I go!"

The door slammed shut, and the letterbox handle rattled against its strike plate.

Another door opened. Number 504. Two small, tousle-haired youngsters' heads poked out, followed by a woman, cigarette dangling from the side of her mouth. Giles dispatched one of his officers to keep back the prying eyes.

Phil ended his call and stepped alongside.

"Done?" Jones asked.

"Yes. Took a while to wake them up."

"How'd they take it?"

Stupid question, Jones.

He was floundering. Couldn't think straight.

"Well enough. Mr Washington's not the demonstrative type. Mrs Washington's in bits, though. They're on their way to Queen Elizabeth's."

"Okay, thanks. You were right there," Jones said, pointing towards Number 504, where the uniformed ARU man stood in front of the youngsters, trying to usher them back inside. The woman with the ciggie had left them to it. "You saw the bugger who pushed him?"

"Profile only. His hood was up, and he wore a mask. Just like you said. Sorry, boss."

"The ARU bodycams might tell us more … *Damn it.*"

Section 14!

"Damn what?"

"Get on to Cal Stevens. Check whether they're still at the obbo point. They might have photos of the bugger."

"Brilliant. Why didn't I think of that?" The mobile reappeared in his hand and he pressed it into action.

Sunlight broke through the thin clouds of morning, holding the promise of another warm summer's day. Jones blinked the haze from his eyes. He removed a clean handkerchief from his pocket and wiped his face and hands. His mobile buzzed. The screen ID showed *Not-Bob, Never-Bob*. Before accepting the call, he closed his eyes and took a deep breath.

Get on with it, Jones.

"Hello?"

"DCI Jones? This is Superintendent Havers," the formality of the words confirmed that the Super was aware of Jones' global announcement. The Emergency Command & Control Centre had swung into action and their conversation was being recorded.

"Yes, sir. This is Jones." The weight of the world pressed in on him, trying to crush him, kill his spirit. He straightened and sucked in a lungful of the cool air. It didn't help.

"I'm at home, Jones. I've just received a call from the station. You have an officer down?"

"It's Ryan ... I mean, DC Washington, sir. He suffered a fall. He's on his way to hospital."

"What?" Havers shouted across the ether. "How ...? No. Hold on. I'm on my way. I'll expect a full briefing when I arrive. Meanwhile, seal off the scene."

"The scene's being cordoned off as we speak, sir. I've launched a local and area-wide search for the suspect, but it's a rabbit warren over here." His voice caught again, and he filled his lungs again. "I could do with some more officers. There's a killer on the loose."

"I'll see what I can do. I'll also organise a forensics unit."

"Get them to send their three best teams, sir. I'll want all three flats swept right now."

"Three flats?"

"I'll explain when you get here, sir. Can you call in the teams?"

"Will do, Jones. And how are you?"

"Nothing wrong with me, sir."

I'm not the one who fell five floors onto a slab of concrete.

"Good, good. But it can't be easy for you. Two men down—"

"Ryan's still alive, sir. And as for DS Pelham, he wasn't my man any longer."

"Of course, of course. We'll discuss things later. I'm on my way."

Jones broke the connection without signing off.

04:18

Waiting for Havers' arrival gave Jones the time he needed to recover some composure. He tried to piece together what had happened.

Being cool in a crisis was an asset Jones took pride in, but Ryan Washington was fighting for his life, for pity's sake. He needed to cut the emotions, drive them back into the pit. Sentiment wouldn't help find Ryan's attacker and Charlie Pelham's killer, who had to be one and the same person. Although coincidences occurred all the time, this situation stretched coincidence beyond breaking point.

He bit back the scream of anguish threatening to erupt from his core, took as deep a breath as his lungs—still raw from his recent sprint—could manage, and exhaled slowly. His legs still shook from the exercise but at least he felt more in control.

Phil ended his call.

"What did Cal have to say?"

Phil frowned and shook his head. "Sorry, boss. They started packing up their equipment as soon as we called the 'All Clear'."

"Are you serious?" Jones barked.

"Afraid so. They have loads of photos and film of the entry, but none of the attack on Ryan. They apologised, but—"

Jones sliced a hand through the air between them and ground his teeth to bite off his next words, at least one of which would have been an expletive.

"How's Alex?" Phil asked, deliberately changing the subject. "I saw Elle Quinton take her away. She didn't look too good."

"Mainly shock, I think. Broken fingers on her right hand, and her shoulder might be dislocated. She'll be going in the ambulance with Ryan."

"Looks like they're off now."

They edged as close to the lip as they dared, keeping to the intact railings on the other side of the support column. Giles kept them well away from the danger area.

A team of three uniformed officers had taped off the area around where Ryan landed to hold back the growing crowd of inquisitive locals. Ben accompanied the paramedics as they wheeled Ryan aboard the stretcher, towards the back of the ambulance. They'd strapped an oxygen mask to Ryan's nose and mouth, which hid most of his face. His eyes were closed, but already an ugly dark bruise covered the left half of his face.

If Jones believed in a God, he'd have prayed his soul out.

"What next, boss?" Phil asked quietly. "Not-Bob's on his way, I suppose."

"He is."

"Coming to take over?"

"Could be."

"What can I do?"

Jones ran his fingers through his sweat-soaked hair, needing time to think.

"Right. Get down there and coordinate the search. I'm taking a look inside. Oh, and Phil?"

"Yes, sir?"

"Send the FSIs up here as soon as they arrive."

Phil headed away and Jones stepped aside to let the ARU team begin the safety work when an idea struck him. Not for the first time in his career, he was about to twist the rules right out of shape.

"Giles?"

"Yes, sir?"

"You can't allow anyone access to this landing until it's *completely* safe. And that goes for the other residents and any visitors that might happen to arrive. And, I'll need you to test all the railings on this side of the stairwell. You understand why?"

Giles frowned in puzzlement for a second until realisation hit. He cracked a thin smile. "I've got your back, sir. Take a good look around." His eyes flicked towards the broken doors. "I'll give you all the time I can." He turned to his fast-moving subordinate, Keller- man, who had his arms full of equipment, and shouted, "Steady on there, Constable. Take it slow. This is a hazardous area. Let do this thing right, shall we? Unfurl that rope and check those carabiners and webbing clamps before we start. Safety first, men. Sergeant Dylan, guard the stairwell. No one's allowed on this side of the landing until we're finished. And I mean *nobody*. Use your weapon if you have to."

Dylan snapped to attention, turned, and marched, double-time, along the walkway to stand guard at the stairwell entrance. Windows and doors opened in the adjacent flats as more neighbours, disturbed by the commotion, craned necks to investigate.

Giles barked at two of his men who'd jumped to help with the ropes. "Digger, Preston, make sure the neighbours stay inside their homes. I don't want any gawkers." The two peeled away from the group and headed back along the walkway.

"Pity," Giles mumbled to Jones, "this means the safety work will take so much longer." He winked and turned back to his team. "No, no, no. That won't do. We'll have to start again. Roll that cable back up and make it right next time."

In the distance, sirens forewarned the approach of reinforcements, amongst them probably Havers and the possible end of Jones' role as SIO on the case. Ryan's fate swayed in the balance. If he didn't survive, the brass would certainly stand Jones down. They'd never allow him to lead an investigation into the death of a direct subordinate. Havers' imminent arrival gave Jones minutes, and he was going to make the most of the opportunity he and Giles had engineered.

He hurried towards the nearest broken doorway. Number 502.

Chapter Twenty-Three

WEDNESDAY 17TH MAY – Dawn

Bordesley Green, Birmingham, UK

WITH TIME RESTRICTED, Jones ignored his normal investigative process and kept the notepad in his pocket. While still outside, he pulled on gloves and booties—there were limits to how lax he was prepared to be.

Number 502's broken front door leaned cockeyed against the inner wall, its heavy lock smashed and the door jamb badly splintered under the Persuader's multiple impacts. He smelled it the moment he stepped over the metal sill and crossed the threshold into the hallway.

Lemon-scented household bleach.

His heart leapt. They'd found the primary!

To minimise his impact on the scene, Jones kept to one side of the hallway. The floor looked spotless—bare, shiny laminate, cleaned recently. Five pairs of shoeprints showed on the otherwise pristine surface—from Ryan, Alex, and the ARU officers when they cleared the building. He reached the first door in the hallway. Again spotless. Dust and fingerprint free. The chrome handle gleamed in the low, early-morning light. With his elbow, he depressed the handle on its outer edge and pushed the door open to reveal a sparsely furnished kitchen.

Jones' early euphoria dipped. If this were the kill site, the murderer would have had six days to sterilise the place, and he certainly hadn't ignored the kitchen.

A small, laminate-topped table with two stools underneath stood against one wall. Its surface clean and bare, save for an inexpensive, plastic condiments set—salt, pepper, mustard on a tin tray.

The opposite wall housed the normal trappings of a small kitchen. In the middle, under a bare window, a stainless steel sink had been sunk into the cheap composite work surface. A small electric cooker to the right of the sink unit looked pristine, unused. To the left, a tall larder cupboard contained non-perishable groceries, including a few tins and dried foodstuffs—all of which were well past their sell-by dates.

A drawer beneath the drainer contained cutlery, neatly arranged. Knives, forks, spoons, and teaspoons, six of each, but nothing to suggest they'd ever been used or that a meal had ever been prepared in the kitchen. No serving spoons, carving knives, or corkscrews. The cupboards underneath the sink, where Jones would expect to find cleaning agents and washing powder, stood empty. A wall cupboard to the left of the window contained a cheap, plain white, six-piece dinner service.

The kitchen had the empty, clinical perfection of a show home or a movie set.

Jones returned to the hall and opened the next door, a bathroom. It had undergone the same cleaning treatment as the kitchen. A mirrored cabinet above the sink reflected a gaunt face—his face. It had dark bags under its eyes Jones hadn't noticed before, and wore an expression close to defeat. He rubbed the face, trying to swipe away the despair.

He peered into the sink and did the same with the shower and the toilet bowl.

With any luck there'd be some trace evidence in the drain traps. *A job for the FSIs. A job for Robyn?*

A commotion outside announced the arrival of newcomers.

Havers' voice rose clear of the others, demanding to be allowed to pass. Time had nearly run out. He wouldn't have a chance to search next door.

Ignoring the commotion as best he could, Jones entered the room across the hall from the kitchen and bathroom. This one was empty. Even the carpet had been removed. Remnants of grey rubberised underlay adhered to the floor, stuck fast with double-sided adhesive tape. Small, it had to be a bedroom. A shoulder-high gallery window allowed the morning light to illuminate the bare walls. No curtains, one slimline, built-in cupboard, no bed. Jones feared the worst. The whole place was going to be devoid of clues, a waste of time.

Damn it.

Why hadn't he started at Number 503? It was the obvious place.

"I'm Superintendent Havers, man. Let me pass!"

"No, sir. It's too dangerous," Bob Dylan announced. "You'll have to stay back until we're satisfied it's all secure."

Dylan and Giles wouldn't be able to hold Havers off for long. Jones had no time to search either of the two bedrooms further.

If the flat conformed to the same layout as the others in the block, the only room left had to be the living room, a lounge-diner.

He backed out of the bedroom and elbowed open the final door which was set into the end of the hallway at ninety degrees to the others. It opened inwards. A large room, it took up the whole width of the flat. Jones stubbed his toe and nearly tripped on the laminate flooring which stood a few millimetres proud of the hallway.

A horizontal picture window cut into the wall opposite the door. To its left, a fully glazed door opened onto a narrow sun balcony. Black safety railings were visible through the glass. The balcony faced west. He marched forwards, staying close to the wall to avoid contaminating what might have been where Charlie had died, and tried the handle. The patio door opened and he stepped out into the cool morning air to be greeted by an aerial view of the Orchard Park Lane.

From here, he could see directly into the front garden of Number 26.

A shiver ran along his spine. A dreadful thought struck a hammer blow to his gut. He should have worked it out earlier. If he'd studied any high-resolution map, he'd have known. Flat Number 110, the one his team had broken into, didn't have as clear a view of Orchard Park Lane as this one. Number 110 faced south-east.

If he'd concentrated the raid's resources on the apartment in which he now stood, Ryan might never have fallen.

Hell!

He'd screwed up and Ryan had suffered as a result, but this wasn't the time for self-recriminations. They would come later.

As with all the other rooms, this one had been recently cleaned. The laminate floor and the sparse furnishings were free of dust. From the balcony door, Jones scanned the room. It had none of the usual clutter he'd expect to find in the living room of a normal home. No magazines, no wall art, no personal items. The only thing of note was the large wooden display cabinet and bookcase that all but filled the right hand wall—the party-wall between this room and next door, Number 503—the apartment from which Hoodie had emerged. As Jones approached the cabinet, something seemed off.

He leaned closer, narrowing his eyes to bring the bookcase into sharper focus.

Surely not?

The commotion outside grew in volume. Giles' voice rose above the others. "I need another couple of minutes, Superintendent Havers. Not long now, sir."

The increase in volume was definitely for Jones' benefit. He didn't have much time left.

The bookcase, wooden and solidly made, had chamfered edge-moulding, rebated shelves, and fielded door panels. Its quality stood out sharply against the inferior standard of the flat's other furnishings.

Why?

He took another pace closer. The lower third of the unit comprised a pair of wide, low cupboards each with double doors. These were separated by a floor-to-ceiling shelf unit containing a few dozen cheap paperback novels. The shelves above the cupboards were bare and dust free.

The unit had been attached to the wall with hidden fixings. There wasn't the slightest movement when Jones pulled at one of the vertical components. He studied the joint where the wooden sides met the wall, but could see no gaps. An expensive, built-in display cabinet? Unusual.

What am I missing?

He returned his attention to the central component, the full-length, floor-to-ceiling bookcase. Definitely something strange about the proportions of the piece.

The shelves were only two-thirds the depth of the cabinets, yet their face edges fitted flush with the fronts of the vertical supports. Jones leaned to the side to gain a different perspective. The back of the bookcase stepped out from the wall. He hadn't noticed earlier since the rear panel had been painted the same colour as the wall. Camouflage.

Jones stepped away and returned his gaze to the unit itself.

There!

A gap. Little more than a crack, visible between the side of the bookcase and the rest of the display unit.

With a fingertip search, he found a small, raised button let into the side rail at shoulder height. So small and well-fitted, he almost missed it.

He pressed. The button clicked, and the leading edge of the bookcase sank two inches into the wall.

Gotcha!

"Chief Inspector Jones? What on earth are you doing in here before the Forensic Scene Investigators have given permission?"

Jones spun.

Havers stood in the doorway, hands on hips, elbows splayed open, feet apart. A deep frown distorted his youthful face.

"Ah, there you are, Superintendent Havers," Jones affected an air of frustration. "I've been waiting for you."

Giles stood in the doorway behind Havers. He shrugged, mouthed the word, "Sorry", and retreated as Havers entered the room, closing the door behind him.

Jones raised a hand to stop him. "Before you come any further, sir, please put on a pair of overshoes. This *is* a crime scene, you know."

His authoritative tone seemed to take the wind out of Havers' sails. The Super stopped, open-mouthed, and stared at his shiny black brogues. Confused, he spread his hands and cast a quizzical look towards Jones, who retraced his steps around the edge of the room and handed over his last pair of booties.

Jones waited while Havers balanced on one foot to don the plastic protectors. He didn't offer a steadying hand. Keeping Havers off-balance might prove useful.

"Before you say anything about my investigating the attack on a member of my own team, sir, take a look at what I've just found."

Havers regained his balance and stood up straight. He adjusted his tie and patted a strand of blonde hair back into place.

"Actually Jones, I was going to say how sorry I am for what happened to DC Washington. He's been with you how long?"

"Three years."

"DI Cryer gave me a quick briefing in the courtyard. From what he told me, there was nothing anyone could have done to prevent it. Out of the blue, he said."

"It was, sir. And thank you."

Jones dipped his head and returned to the bookcase, signalling for the Super to follow.

"Look at this." He pointed to the concealed door.

Havers bent at the waist and peered through the opening.

"Well now. That's interesting. How on earth did you find it?"

"There had to be a reason for the killer to stay in the area after dumping Charlie's body."

Havers arched an eyebrow. "Unless I'm wide of the mark, this looks like the killer's bolt hole into the flat next door."

Give the man a coconut.

"Yes, sir."

Jones pushed the book-lined panel further open and turned sideways to squeeze through the narrow gap.

Havers followed his lead.

The false door opened into a cupboard.

Never comfortable in confined spaces, Jones struggled to control his breathing as he searched for a way into the next flat. He pushed at the wooden panel in front of his face, and relaxed as soon as it opened into a sunlit front room, the mirror image of the one they'd just left.

"Before we go any further, Chief Inspector, I need to have FSI start work next door," Havers said. He hesitated before raising both eyebrows and adding, "Do you agree?

It took Jones a second to realise Havers hadn't intended the question to be rhetorical. The Super was out of his depth, and what's more, he knew it. Maybe Jones wouldn't be side-lined after all. He still had a chance to work the case.

"That's a very good idea, sir."

Jones sucked in the cool air of the open room and tried to relax while Havers spoke into a small comms unit concealed in his right hand.

"You can let the FSI team into Number 502 now." A buzz of static sounded in the cream-coloured earpiece in Havers' ear.

"Do we need to chat, sir?"

"We most certainly do, but I'd like to say something first." Havers reached across to touch Jones' shoulder, but seemed to think better of it and dropped his hand. His eyes took on a steely glint. Jones held his breath. "We both know what the book says."

Here it comes.

Jones gritted his teeth and tried not to clench his fists.

"I have to take over this case," Havers continued, "and you have to step into the backgr—"

"Sir," Jones said, "if I may—"

Havers raised a hand to cut off Jones' interruption. "No, David. Let me finish. Although I have to take titular control, you and I both know that I don't have the experience."

What's this?

"I've never been in charge of a murder inquiry before. You're the expert here."

Jones started breathing again.

"I'm going to need all the help I can get. So, while I'm taking over as SIO, I'll need your support. Can I count on you?"

Relief flooded through Jones but he tried not to show it. "You most certainly can, sir." He took another deep breath. "Would you like the first piece of advice, sir?"

"Please."

"Make sure Dr Spence and her colleagues run the forensics in these two flats. They're analysing the evidence we collected at the secondary site and I'm almost certain 502 is the primary. We need continuity in the chain of evidence. And, in my opinion for what it's worth, her team is the best Racer-Colby has."

"Actually," Havers said, showing him a crooked smile, "she's in the hallway next door at the moment, Chief Inspector. I practically had to clap her in handcuffs to stop her bursting in before we could have our little, er ... chat."

Jones could think of nothing to say and turned to eyeball the room. He'd clearly underestimated the new superintendent.

Seconds later, Robyn arrived and allowed him only the briefest scans of flat Number 503 before excluding him from both places. He had too much respect for the pocket-sized FSI to argue with her and didn't want to hold up progress. Besides, he had something even more difficult to attend to.

Chapter Twenty-Four

WEDNESDAY 17TH MAY – Midday

Queen Elizabeth Hospital, Birmingham, UK

JONES SHUDDERED. Hospitals gave him the willies. Hated the smell, the atmosphere. Hated the memories they provoked, too. He'd spent the worst moments of his life inside their walls. Identified the remains of his beautiful wife, Siân. Watched his impossibly premature son struggle to hang onto life. Held his precious boy in his arms when he took his last breath in a hospital. He'd paced the corridors when Phil Cryer fell through the rotten roof and skewered his leg with a rusty metal rod. And now, he was about to go through the same for Ryan Washington.

When would it end?

He pushed through the double doors and marched along a busy corridor, dodging fast-moving medical staff and slow-moving patients and their families. When he reached the far end, Ben climbed out of his chair.

"Any news?" Jones asked, voice lowered to a whisper.

Ben grimaced.

"Not yet, sir. Mr and Mrs Washington—Bryn and Jackie—are in with the doctor now. I had to step out."

"How've they taken it so far?"

"Bryn's old school, sir. The strong silent type. Jackie's a bit more emotional. She's been crying."

Jones nodded.

"Alex?"

"Downstairs in A&E, sir. She's already been x-rayed. Two broken fingers. Nothing serious. No nerve damage, thank God."

Where's God in this?

"Her shoulder?"

"Dislocated. They're going to pop it back in place soon as they can find an orthopaedic surgeon. After that, she'll have to wait for the medic to discharge her."

"Thanks. Keep me informed."

The door to the consultation room opened and a slim woman in lilac scrubs stepped out. She waited for Jones and Ben to approach.

"Dr Suresh," Ben said, "this is DCI Jones. DC Washington's boss."

The medic—high cheekbones, dark hair cut in a bob, dark skin, dark eyes—had to crane her neck to meet Jones' eye.

"How is he?"

She pursed her lips, no doubt trying to decide how much to tell a non-relative.

"Your colleague has multiple fractures to the limbs, a number of broken ribs, and the distribution of cuts and contusions one would expect from a fall from height. But the ICH is by far the most serious condition."

"ICH?" Jones asked, fearing the worst.

Suresh nodded. "Intracerebral haemorrhage. A bleed within the brain tissue. Think of it as an impact induced stroke, Chief Inspector. Our neurosurgeon, Mr Shepperton, managed to stem the bleeding. Your colleague is currently in a medically induced coma. He will be kept under to give him the best chance of recovery, and we'll be monitoring him closely for the next few days." She forced out a tired smile. "Before you ask, Chief Inspector, we can't give you a prognosis. With trauma of this sort it is impossible to predict outcomes."

Jones' legs buckled for the second time that day. The doctor's words sliced open his heart.

"Where is he?"

"In the post-operative recovery room right now. From there, we'll transfer him to the ICU."

"When can I see him?"

"Not until he's out of the ICU. Medical staff and family only, I'm afraid."

"Understood. Thank you for being so candid, Dr Suresh. Ryan's a first rate officer and a good man. Please do your best for him."

She frowned as though insulted by the implication that she wouldn't do her best for all her patients. "Of course. Now, if you'll excuse me——"

"Are we allowed in there?" Jones glanced at the door to the consultation room.

"Knock first. Mr and Mrs Washington are waiting for someone to take them to the ICU. As you can imagine, they're somewhat upset."

"I understand, Dr Suresh."

He wanted to thank her again, but she'd already turned away, dictating notes into a voice recorder. From the back, she reminded him a little of Robyn Spence. Same body shape. Same rapid, hair-bouncing gait. Similar way she held the voice recorder. Apart from that, Suresh and Robyn couldn't have been more different. Dark brown eyes versus light green. Black hair versus blonde. Nice smile versus ....

Stop hedging, Jones. Get on with it.

"Ben, go keep Alex company while I talk to Bryn and Jackie."

Ben hurried away. Jones hesitated a moment to gather himself before approaching the consultation room and knocking gently.

The deep, Brummie accented, "You can come in," could only

have come from Bryn Washington. Jones would have recognised his voice anywhere.

He pushed through the door into a compact, drab room painted in a particularly unattractive shade of battleship grey. It contained a desk, four hard-backed chairs, and a light box to display x-rays. No expense wasted on unnecessary decoration.

Bryn Washington, an older version of Ryan, down to the coat hanger shoulders, sad brown eyes, and prominent jaw, rounded on Jones before the door had a chance to swing shut.

"What happened, Mr Jones?" he asked, hugging his comfortably built wife.

Jackie Washington dabbed her streaming eyes with a tissue and leaned against her husband, her rock of support.

"Didn't Ben tell you?"

"The lad means well, but he ended up saying very little." Washington took a breath and hugged his wife tight. Any tighter risked a crush injury.

"Ryan fell during a raid. That's all we know."

He eased Jackie into one of the chairs, dropped into the one beside her, and they collapsed against each other.

Jones tried to swallow, but the egg-sized lump in his throat wouldn't allow it. He considered hiding under the cloak of police standard operational bullshit, but couldn't do that to them.

He pulled up a chair, sat, and leaned forwards, resting his elbows on his knees. He told them everything: the investigation into Charlie's murder, the dawn raid, the deliberate shoulder-charge, the weakened railings, and Hoodie's escape using a zipline. Everything. Washington's expression changed from confusion to anger, and from anger to despair. The whole time, he and Jackie held each other tight.

What must it be like to have such support?

The three things they wanted to know—why Ryan lay in a hospital bed, fighting for his life, who pushed him, and what the SCU were going to do next—Jones couldn't tell them. He had no idea.

"You will catch the man, won't you, Chief Inspector?" Jackie asked, her voice quaking.

Oh yes, I'll catch the bastard. If it's the last thing I do, I'll catch him.

"I'll do my best, Jackie. I promise."

"Thank you."

More tears fell, and the tissue worked hard to swipe them away.

"How long before they take you to the ICU?"

"An hour, maybe two," Washington said. "Right now, Ryan's in post op."

"So I understand." Jones eased back in his chair. "Can I get you a drink? There's a vending machine at the other end of the corridor. Can't guarantee what it'll taste like, though." He tried a smile, but it sank like a stone into a pond.

"Do you have the time, Chief Inspector? We wouldn't want to stop you catching the man who did this to Ryan," Jackie said, blinking more tears into the tissue.

"The forensics specialists are working the crime scene, and the whole of the West Midlands Police force is searching for the perpetrator. I can spare a few minutes to drink a cuppa with you. Even if it is from a vending machine. What do you say?"

Washington managed a wan smile. "In that case, two teas, white, no sugar."

Jones stood, happy to have something constructive to do and unable to leave the room quickly enough.

He fed the correct amount of change into the slot, pressed the button, and waited for the "magic" to happen. A plastic cup dropped into the hopper. Seconds later, the machine spurted out a stream of muddy brown liquid, most of which actually ended up in the cup. He added more change and repeated the process.

During the second pour, his mobile phone vibrated. The caller ID showed Ben Adeoye. He scanned the area for "No mobile" signs —found none—and answered.

"Hi, boss. The doctor says Alex can go home. Thought you'd like to know."

Good news at last.

"Excellent. Put her on."

"Can't do that, sir. She's in the loo. Might take her a while with her arm in a sling."

"Okay, tell her I asked after her. Then take her home and settle her in. There's no point in her coming up here. She's better off at home. I'll keep the Washingtons company until they reach the ICU."

"Want me to take over from you after dropping Alex off?"

"No need for that. Report back to Phil. See if he needs your help with the search."

THE VENDING machine tea wasn't as bad as he'd anticipated—it was worse. Much worse. But he suffered it to keep the Washingtons company. To share their purgatory.

"God," Washington said, wrinkling his nose, "this stuff is awful."

"Agreed," Jones said.

"How'd anyone have the brass neck to call this tea?" He lowered the cup to the table and slid it further away.

"I should charge them for breaking the Trades Description Act, 2015."

Washington nodded. Jackie continued sipping. She probably needed to replace the water she'd lost through crying.

An awkward silence developed where Jones and Washington tried to avoid making eye contact. Clearly, neither man could do small talk.

"Not only looks like the coolant from a car's radiator. Tastes like it too. And I should know."

"You've tasted the water from a car's cooling system?"

Another weak smile. "I'm a farmer and a mechanical engineer, Chief Inspector. Accidents happen."

Jones ran his fingertips over the calloses on his palms, the legacy of building stone walls and the interminable renovation of his cottage. He and Bryn Washington had something in common. They knew what practical work entailed.

"Oh," Washington said, raising a hand and pointing to Jones, "don't know if this is the right time to say it, but me and Ryan finished rebuilding the Rover's engine last week. Purring like a big cat, it is. A wonderful sound."

"You have?" Jones asked, the only thing he could think of to say.

When his old Rover 400's engine blew up on the way home from work one night, Jones had thought he'd seen its last gasp. His long-time mechanic had pronounced it DOA and tried to sell him a top-of-the-range BMW. On hearing the sorry tale, Ryan had volunteered to take the old girl home and, in his own words, "See what me and Dad can do."

Ever hopeful, Jones gave father and son the green light to do whatever they saw fit. Within reason, the cost of the rebuild didn't matter. He'd given them carte blanche to go to town. They agreed to "blueprint" the engine, which involved making sure it complied with Rover's original design tolerances. Although expensive, the process promised to increase the engine's operational efficiency significantly. Ryan claimed the new power unit would make Jones' car the best of its type ever built. Better than anything that ever rolled off Rover's production line.

They'd had the venerable car for the best part of a year, and the interminable engine rebuild had become a running joke in the SCU.

"Yes," Bryn Washington said, a proud smile spreading across his face, "that's right. We planned to deliver it to your home last Sunday, unannounced. As a surprise, y'know? But ... DS Pelham's death put paid to that. And now ...." He opened his hands and let them drop into his lap.

Jackie reached across and gripped his right hand in both of hers. "Bryn shouldn't have told you, really. Ryan wanted it to be a surprise," she said. "Please don't tell him you know. When he wakes up, he'll tell you himself. It'll make his day. He's so proud of working with you, Mr Jones. Looks up to you, he does. Never stops talking about how he wants to be as good a detective as you one day." She smiled through her tears.

Jones had no idea how to respond. One of the last times he'd spoken to her son had been to shout at him for hiding the information about "Dolly Parton".

"Ryan's a first rate police officer, Mrs Washington—Jackie. He's well on the way to making an excellent detect—"

The door opened and a nurse entered, saving everyone's blushes.

"Mr and Mrs Washington?"

They stood, Jones included.

"Ryan has been moved to the ICU," the nurse continued, holding the door open. "If you'll follow—"

"How is he?" Jackie asked, her voice faltering.

The nurse glanced at Jones, who stepped back.

"He's stable at the moment, but the surgeon can tell you more. Please ...."

They hurried off, leaving Jones alone in the consulting room. He reached for his mobile and dialled his go-to guy.

"Well, Philip? Did you find him?"

Chapter Twenty-Five

THURSDAY 18TH MAY – Morning

Police HQ, Holton, Birmingham, UK

JONES' office seemed gloomier than usual, and the situation more hopeless. Rarely had he felt so lost. He'd spent the early part of the previous afternoon at the hospital, waiting for news. The rest, he spent with Phil at the OTT, coordinating the search for Ryan's attacker. They'd found nothing of value from a second canvass even though they could include a loose description of the "person of interest". None of the tenants on floors four, five, and six admitted to ever having seen the occupants of Number 502 or Number 503. The suspect might as well have been a ghost, or a vampire.

After calling an end to the search at seven o'clock—Hoodie had long gone—Jones left two officers on guard outside the flats, and set up and staffed a mobile incident room in the courtyard. He'd also broadcast a help line promising anonymity to any who saw fit to call. With the onset of darkness, some of the OTT's more civic-minded occupants might find entering a trailer less daunting than talking to the police out in the open. In his heart, Jones knew they were doing nothing more than going through the motions. No one seriously expected a breakthrough in this manner, least of all Jones.

With nothing else left in his armoury, he sent the team home for a well-earned break and spent another three hours at Queen Elizabeth's ICU waiting room, trying, without success, to comfort the Washingtons.

After a fitful night's sleep, Jones had arrived at work even earlier than usual. He spent the time ahead of the briefing, studying the combined case files. They didn't make good reading.

Two victims, both police officers.

DS Charles Pelham, murdered with an injector knife, body stripped, cleaned, and dumped in a place where his body should be found sooner rather than later. An anonymous call prompting the discovery.

DC Ryan Washington, pushed from a balcony, in full view of a number of police officers, fighting for his life in a hospital bed.

The cases were linked, of course they were, but did it amount to something more sinister? Were police officers being deliberately targeted? His officers? His SCU? It sounded fanciful, paranoid even, but Jones couldn't afford to ignore the possibility.

A gentle, almost timid, knock on the door snapped Jones out of the dark possibilities.

"Come in," he snapped, surprised and a little disappointed at how aggressive he sounded.

The door opened and the dark-haired Sergeant Braxton—one of the uniforms who'd worked the original OTT canvass—popped her head through the opening. Face pale, she seemed worried. Not a good look for an officer of her experience.

"Do you have a moment, sir?"

Jones glanced at the clock hanging on the wall opposite.

"The team briefing starts in an hour," he said, softening his tone a smidgeon. "Can it wait?"

"I'm afraid not, sir. You need to hear this."

"Okay, come in."

She stepped fully into the office and stood aside to allow a constable who'd also been part of the door-to-door team to enter. The constable, who looked even more worried than Braxton, closed the door softly behind him.

Something serious must have happened.

Jones leaned back in his chair, but didn't invite them to sit—that would be taking things too far. They stood to attention in front of his desk, and he looked them over.

The young constable, as pale-faced as Braxton, seemed terrified, close to tears. The youngster also looked as though he might throw up at any moment. Clearly, he'd done something wrong, something related to the case.

Tension rippled through Jones' system, but he forced it down. No point adding to the lad's woes. At least not before Jones learned what he'd done.

"So," he said, keeping his voice calm, "what do you have for me?"

"It's about the door-to-door on the Orchards Estate, sir," Braxton said, staring at a point on the wall behind Jones.

"I'm guessing you two were part of the team who canvassed Tower 3?"

The constable glanced at Braxton who nodded.

"Yes, sir. We did floor five, among others."

"Ah, I see." Jones stared at the constable, who couldn't meet his eye. "You must be Harkness."

The lad gulped, and tears filled his dark eyes. His cleft chin trembled as he felt the force of Jones' deep gaze.

"Y-Yes, sir. You know?"

"I've just finished reading the sheets, lad." He pointed to the neat pile of questionnaires in his out tray. "You knocked 503's door. Mr Jarman."

"Yes, sir. Jarman, sir. Dominic Jarman."

Jones grabbed the questionnaire from the top of the pile and read the top line.

"Dominic?" he asked.

"Sorry, sir. I-I meant Donald … Donald Jarman."

"Relax, Constable. Breathe. You're likely to burst a blood vessel."

Harkness' chest expanded as he took a breath.

"Right. Tell me in your own words. Start at the top."

"Mr Jarman took a while to open his door. I asked him if he saw or heard anything unusual on the night DS Pelham died, but he said he wasn't home."

"Is that it?" Jones asked, holding up the questionnaire and reading the entries.

"Not quite, sir. I could see that Helen, I mean Sergeant Braxton, had no luck with Number 502 and had moved on to 501, so I asked Jarman about his neighbour. He said Number 502 had been empty since he'd moved into the block."

Jones read the questionnaire and confirmed the entry.

"What happened then?"

Another glance at Braxton. "I moved onto Number 500, and drew another blank. The householder, Mr Sikorski, didn't remember seeing or hearing anything on Thursday night or Friday morning. And that was it, fifth floor done. Ten flats, seven answers. Nothing to report."

"Then," Braxton said, "I collected the completed questionnaires and we moved up to the next floor."

"Only," Harkness said, cringing, "that wasn't quite all, sir."

I thought not.

"Go on, Constable."

"When I passed Number 503 again, heading back to the stair-well, the door opened and Jarman hissed at me."

"He hissed at you?"

Harkness nodded. "To draw my attention, sir."

"What did he want?"

Harkness hesitated.

"C'mon, Constable. Spit it out."

"Jarman told me Number 502 used to be a knocking shop, but someone else took the place over when the hooker moved out. A bloke called Alan Smith, no, just a minute." He pulled a notebook out of his breast pocket and flipped through the pages, fingers trembling. "Here it is, sir. Allen Smithee. Jarman took great pains to spell it for me, too."

Jones frowned and held up the questionnaire again. "Why didn't you add this information to the form?"

"Helen had them, sir. I meant to do it when we finished the whole tower, but it … slipped my mind."

"It slipped your mind?" Jones repeated, slowly, trying not to sound angry.

Anger wouldn't help.

Harkness lowered his eyes. "Yes, sir. Sorry, sir."

"And when this Jarman fellow pushed Ryan Washington off that balcony, it didn't tweak your memory at all?" Jones clenched his jaw and struggled to keep his voice under control.

"I've been off duty, sir. Only came back on earlies this morning. Soon as I heard what happened to DC Washington, I told Helen and we went to Inspector Macklin."

Jones relaxed his posture a little. He couldn't take his frustrations out on Harkness. Knowing the name of Number 502's new tenant wouldn't have changed the operation. Would it?

Smithee and Jarman.

Jones tugged his earlobe.

Jarman and Smithee?

Something niggled him. A memory. A tickle in the back of his mind.

C'mon Jones.

What was it? He pondered a moment longer before giving up.

Nope. Nothing.

"Okay, Constable. We'll let it pass. At least you came forwards and didn't try to hide it."

Harkness relaxed his shoulders. A heavy load had lifted.

"Thank you, sir. It won't happen again."

"I hope not, son. Did Jarman tell you why he lied the first time?"

"He said he didn't want to get involved, but got worried about holding out on the police during a murder investigation."

"What did Jarman look like?"

"Didn't see him very well, sir. He stayed in the hallway with the light off and refused to open the door fully. I didn't get much of a look at him, but he didn't raise any red flags. Sorry, sir."

"Basic description?"

"About your build, sir. Taller, though. Closer to six foot."

Jones nodded. Harkness' description matched the glimpse he'd had of the man who shoulder-charged Ryan off the balcony. At least Hoodie had a name now—Donald Jarman.

"Eye colour?"

He closed his eyes to think, but shook his head.

"Sorry, sir. It was too dark."

"Would working with a police artist help?"

Harkness thought for a moment before answering. "I'll try, sir. But like I said, I didn't get a good look at him."

"Arrange a session with the artist after the briefing."

"I am sorry, sir. Did my cockup lead to DC Washington's—"

"No one could have predicted the outcome, Constable."

No one but Donald Jarman.

Jones slid the questionnaire across the desk to the constable.

"Fill in the missing details, son. Sign it and add today's date."

Harkness grabbed the form and turned to leave.

"Do it here, please. Pull up a chair if you need it."

"Yes, sir."

Jones waited while Harkness transcribed the information from his notebook. Three minutes later, the constable handed the form back.

"Is this okay, sir?"

Jones read the addition carefully.

"It'll do, Constable. I'll have someone scan this version into the system. Make a record of this meeting in your shift notes. I'll do the same and that'll be the end of it."

"Yes, sir. Thank you, sir," Harkness said, springing to his feet.

"Okay. Off you go."

Jones waved a hand in dismissal.

"Thank you, sir," Braxton added, practically pushing Harkness through the door.

The wall clock gave him twenty minutes before he had to leave for the briefing. Time enough for a brew.

Jones stood and walked to what he and Phil had laughingly referred to as the "hospitality area"—a filing cabinet whose top housed a kettle and all he needed to make a half-decent cuppa. He checked the water level and flicked the switch on the kettle. Only then did he remember he'd forgotten to pick up a carton of milk from the canteen on the way in.

Hell.

He'd have to make do with cold water. Before he could reach for a bottle, his desk phone warbled the single ring of an external number. He read the caller ID and snatched the phone from its cradle.

"Robyn, how are you?"

"Tired, but happy."

"That sounds promising. What do you have for me?"

"Rather a lot, actually. Do you have time now? I can come to you if you like."

Again, he glanced at the wall clock.

"Well, I'm just about to review the Pelham case with the murder team. How soon can you get here?"

"I'll need an hour to set up my presentation."

"An hour it is. See you in the SCU Briefing Room at nine o'clock."

"I'll be there."

For the first time since Ryan's fall, optimism popped its timid head over the bulwark and waved. Jones left his office, trying not to let his hopes rise too high.

Chapter Twenty-Six

THURSDAY 18TH MAY – Morning

Police HQ, Holton, Birmingham, UK

HOW LONG HAD it been since he'd last entered the briefing room? Jones checked the date on his watch. Only two days? How was that possible?

The image of Ryan hanging by a thread from the railings still haunted him. How close had they come to losing an integral member of the team? It didn't bear thinking about, but he couldn't help himself.

Ryan's visible injuries, a fractured skull, two broken legs, a broken wrist, three crushed ribs, and a battered and bruised face, were bad enough, but they could have been so much worse. If not for Alex's lightning reactions—and Sergeant Dylan's—Ryan would probably have died. As it was, he lay in a coma, fighting for his life, and would do for at least three more days according to the neurosurgeon. Jones had finally managed to buttonhole Dr Suresh again after hanging around the ICU's waiting area until early evening. Jones had convinced her to give him special access to the ICU's monitoring centre—a room next to the ICU filled with medical equipment and staffed by two overworked nurses.

Seeing Ryan in his hospital bed, comatose and hooked up to so many machines, reminded Jones of the first time he saw Phil after the operation that saved his leg. The last thing he wanted was a repeat of that awful day.

Jones shook the horrific image away, dropped his folder on the table, and started pacing. He hated waiting and needed to do something physical or he'd explode. At the far end of one leg of his pacing, he stopped to stare through the window. A low sun tried its best to burn through a thin ribbon of grey cloud. It promised to be a warm day, and if Robyn's results proved as valuable as she'd hinted at, her revelations might be pivotal to the investigation.

The door burst open and Havers bustled into the room. In one hand he carried the inevitable tablet computer. In the other, he gripped a monogrammed glass, three quarters filled with water. He wore a suit—the first time Jones had seen him out of uniform—and exhibited the harried appearance of a college graduate on the way to his final exams.

"Morning, Chief Inspector." Havers' smile appeared forced.

"Sir."

Jones accepted the greeting with a nod and made his way to the table.

"What news of DC Washington?"

"No change, sir. His father called me this morning from the hospital."

"The prognosis?"

"The medics won't be drawn. 'The patient is stable', 'responding well to the treatment', 'too early to tell the outcome', blah, blah. You know what they're like."

"I do indeed. The medical profession has its set responses to questions, as do we." He raised an eyebrow. "'A person of interest', 'the individual is helping us with our enquiries', 'we can't comment on an ongoing investigation'."

Although Havers had a point, his jaunty smile couldn't have been much more inappropriate.

"We'll just have to wait and see, sir. I've sent a Family Liaison Officer to the hospital. He'll let us know the moment there's any change."

"Very good, very good," Havers said, checking his watch. "We must think positively. And we must progress the investigation."

"Yes, sir. I want the attacker found, which is why I called for this review."

"As do we all, Jones. By the way, thank you for arriving early, I wanted a little chat before the briefing started."

"I've been here for two hours, sir." Jones rubbed his scratchy chin. For the first time in ages, he'd forgotten his morning shave. "I wanted to read the files and catch up on the overnight lab results."

"Anything interesting?"

I hope so.

"Dr Spence will be here at nine to walk us through it all."

"Good. Excellent." Havers shifted his weight and pointed to the table and the chairs surrounding it. "Shall we sit?"

Jones frowned as Havers took Jones' normal spot at the head of the table, leaving him with Phil's chair. Reluctantly, he lowered himself into it.

Havers set down his tablet and his glass, and used a manicured finger to ease the collar of his gleaming white shirt. His clip-on safety tie stayed resolutely in place.

"First, I want to repeat how sorry I am for what happened to DC Washington yesterday. We got really lucky there." He sighed and shook his head slowly. "He's not out of the woods, of course, but it could have been so much worse."

"Yes, sir." Jones nodded, glancing away. "I was at the hospital all afternoon and most of the evening."

And there was no sign of you.

"Good, good," Havers said, ignoring Jones' intentional and less than subtle rebuke. "I've read Washington's record again. A fine officer with a good future ahead of him. I certainly hope this doesn't derail his career progression."

Jones frowned. "Why would it?"

"One never knows how such wounds will affect the individual. Injuries of this kind—especially the head trauma—can result in significant physiological and psychological impairment. Memory loss, PTSD—"

"Ryan's a strong lad, sir. He'll recover."

"Of course he will. Of course ... Nonetheless, if—when he regains consciousness, we'll make sure he has the best physiotherapy and counselling available. I've instructed the FMO and HR to map out a structured rehabilitation programme for him. We must look after our people, eh, Jones?"

"Yes, sir."

Jones wondered what leadership manual Havers had been reading. He clamped his jaw tight shut. He didn't need Havers telling him what sort of an officer Ryan was—rubbing salt into open wounds.

"Talking of our people," he said, "I've recommended DS Olganski for a commendation. Sergeant Dylan, too. I trust you'll support that?"

"I will." Havers' smile widened. "Good, good. From what I read in the report, she held onto him longer than anyone could have expected. Slowed his momentum."

"Yes, sir. Without her intervention, Ryan's injuries could have been ...."

Fatal.

"Quite so." Havers pressed his palms together as though in prayer, drawing a metaphorical line under the discussion. "Right, Chief Inspector. Let's move things along, shall we?"

Jones gave him a tight smile and waited.

"I spoke to the DCC last night." He lost the smile. "Whilst DC Washington is still ...." He stopped and started again, but did have the good grace to look embarrassed. "What I mean to say is, given the current situation, the DCC has accepted my recommendation for you to remain involved in the investigation." Havers paused and they locked gazes for a moment before he continued. "I'll handle any media requirements, but you will front all team briefings, set assignments, and lead any interviews. Are you happy with that?"

"Yes, sir."

Jones shuffled in his seat. Phil's chair was uncomfortable but he couldn't tell whether it related to the chair itself, or the reason he'd been forced to sit in it.

At that moment, Phil entered the room and held the door open for Alex, who carried her right arm in a blue hospital sling. Two fingers were splinted and the hand heavily bandaged. Ben followed closely behind.

Jones jumped up and rushed towards her while the others took their usual places. "Alex, how are you? Should you be here?"

"It is nothing, boss. I have had worse playing field hockey." Through a brave smile, her eyes showed the puffy redness of fatigue, pain, and tears. She leaned closer and whispered, "Do not send me home. I need to be here, to help. Please?"

Jones nodded and touched her good arm gently. "Light duties only, lass. You're not to leave the station during the work shift. Do I make myself clear?"

"Yes, boss. I shall keep to paperwork only." She sniffed and managed a thin smile. "This, I promise. Have the FSIs come up with anything?"

Yes, they have. Hopefully.

Jones tried not to smile—he didn't want to raise her expectations, or his own.

"Dr Spence is on her way in."

Jones returned to the table and slid the updated questionnaire for flat Number 503 towards Phil. After flash-reading the new entry, Phil opened his mouth but closed it again when Jones glanced towards Havers and shook his head. They'd discuss it later.

The door opened again and the redheaded civilian hurried in, looking harassed. He smiled awkwardly at Jones then noticed Havers. He stopped and stared, bug-eyed at the Super.

"Come in, Mr Bigglesworth," Jones said. "Glad you could join us at last."

"Sorry, sir. Needed the loo."

A ciggie break, more like.

The young man dipped his head to Havers and scurried off to his stronghold in the corner. The legs of his chair screeched as he dragged it closer to his desk.

"Sorry," he said to the room, flushing bright red.

The door opened again and the rest of the expanded murder team arrived—Vic Dolan and a string of uniformed officers. All had supported them at the raid. Sergeant Braxton and Constable Harkness brought up the rear, avoiding everyone's gaze.

"Hurry along there," Jones barked. "We don't have all morning."

The uniforms took their seats remarkably quietly. Havers' presence must have subdued their normal ebullience.

A few moments later, Barney Featherstone and two young constables pushed through the door. Feathers nodded his apology and hurried his charges to the back row.

While the newcomers settled, Havers sipped some water, set down his glass, and stood in front of the SmartScreen. Jones used the opportunity to reclaim his seat, which was unpleasantly warm. The Super raised a questioning eyebrow, but Jones blanked him.

"Before we start," Havers said, "I'd like to have a moment's silence for a fallen colleague. DS Pelham will be sorely missed."

Not by many.

The Super clasped his hands in front of his waist and bowed his head. The others, including Jones, stood to attention.

He'd better not start praying.

During the minute's enforced and near-silent contemplation, the clouds cleared away from the sun, and golden shafts of brilliant light picked out the motes of dust hanging in the air.

Jones sneered.

If that's a sign from the heavens, where's the man who murdered Charlie and damn near killed Ryan? Show me a sign for that!

Maybe Robyn had some answers. He held out hope.

Havers broke the peace.

"Please sit."

A thin male voice in the back mumbled, "What a load of bollocks". Chairs scraped floor tiles to cover the murmurs of agreement. Havers looked up, searching for the culprit. Jones let the moment pass.

Havers coughed to draw the attention back onto himself.

"As you may know, I've replaced DCI Jones as lead officer in this investigation." Havers raised a calming hand to silence an eruption of muttering. "At least, that's the official line. In actuality, I shall defer to DCI Jones in all investigative matters, and you will all take your instructions directly from him. I'm here for support and liaison purposes only."

The "congregation" relaxed.

Havers continued. "We need to start. So …." He opened his hand to Jones who nodded and stood, but remained by his chair until Havers found an alternative seat. Only then did he take the floor.

"Okay. Take notes and ask questions only if they are pertinent. You all know the drill." He wrung his hands together. "Right, Dr Spence will be along in a while to tell us what the SOCOs—sorry, the FSIs, have found inside the flats. Meanwhile, we'll cover the outside. DI Cryer, what do you have?"

Phil stood and moved towards the SmartScreen. He nodded to Bigglesworth and half a dozen images appeared on the screen.

Phil turned sideways to the SmartScreen and pointed to the top row of images. "These show four external CCTV cameras. They are positioned to cover the courtyard, the staircase, landing five, and the outside walkway. The bast—er, the suspect was following our every bloody move. He saw us coming."

Alex gasped and raised her good hand to her mouth.

Ben balled his massive fists and ground them into his thighs.

Phil's lips stretched out into a thin line. "Using these cameras, he could see us approach. He knew exactly who was outside, and when."

Although he'd discussed the details on the phone with Phil

ahead of the briefing, Jones hadn't seen the pictures before. He hadn't seen the cameras during the raid, either. The fifth floor landing and stairwell had been too dark.

He stood and closed on the screen. "How did our man place cameras way up there?" He enlarged one of the photos and pointed to a pencil-slim rod pointing vertically down from a ceiling inside the stairwell. "How far above the staircase is this one?"

"A fraction over six metres," Phil shot back without having to consult the redundant tablet he'd left on the table. "The FSIs needed an extension ladder to retrieve it."

Jones arched an eyebrow. "So, how did he get it there without being seen? And where are all the cables?"

Phil smiled and double hitched his eyebrows. Anyone unfamiliar with his ways might have considered it condescending, but Jones knew better.

"The images are transmitted straight from the camera into storage servers in Number 503's bedroom."

"Storage servers?" Havers asked from his chair.

"Dr Spence will cover the interior of both flats in her briefing," Jones answered. "Carry on Inspector."

Phil flashed him a crooked smile. Jones scowled.

Will he never give up?

"The signal doesn't have to be strong because the distance is so short. Therefore, no need for cables," Phil said. "As for positioning the cameras, well that's the really neat part." He nodded towards the corner in the back of the room. "Biggles, can you zoom in on the pencil camera—image number four—and enhance the picture quality, please?"

As Bigglesworth worked his keyboard, the fourth photo enlarged and pixilated before sharpening.

"See those triangles on the trailing end either side of the lens?" Phil asked, pointing to the tail of the rod camera. "They're fins. They act the same way as the flights on an arrow. I reckon the suspect used a small crossbow. A full sized bow would have been a little too conspicuous."

"Did he now? Clever beggar, isn't he?" Jones scratched his

stubble again. It had started to itch. First chance he had, he'd put the electric razor in his grab bag to work. "Who manufactures these things?"

Phil waved a hand at the screen. "That's the interesting part, boss. Looks like they're homemade. The lab's working on them now, but I have to say, it's a hell of a piece of engineering. To design a camera with a solid-state transmitter, package it inside such a slim tube, and then make it robust enough to be shot from a bow. Only a bona fide electronics genius could have done this. Assuming our killer built these things himself, it might be a genuine lead. I mean, how many people in the country can create miniaturisation work of this intricacy and quality?"

Phil shot Jones a sideways glance. He raised a hand and patted it in the air. It looked like an act of apology.

"Er ... sorry, boss. I didn't mean to sound like a fan. It's just that the work is extraordinary. Ironically, it's the sort of stuff Ryan would have loved to pull apart. Excuse me a tick."

Phil crossed to the water cooler, filled a plastic cup, and slugged it back in one go. When he returned to the whiteboard, Jones asked the question that had been bothering him.

"Sergeant Braxton, you ran the door-to-door on floor five."

Braxton and Harkness stiffened. Phil shot Jones a sideways glance but kept quiet.

"Yes, sir," Braxton answered, sitting up straighter in her stiff-backed chair.

"Did you see the cameras, Sergeant?"

"No, sir. They weren't there on Monday."

"Are you certain?"

"Positive, sir," Braxton answered. "I looked up at the ceiling in the stairwell on account of all the naff graffiti. Wondered how the taggers could reach so high, sir. And how they could spell so badly."

A couple of the uniforms around her snickered. Beside Braxton, Constable Harkness stared straight ahead, trying to fade into the background.

"And you go along with this, Constable Harkness?"

"Yes, sir," he croaked.

"That's a real shame," Jones said.

"Why?" Havers asked.

Phil answered for Jones. "If the cameras had been in place when Charlie was killed—"

"We might have the murderer on tape?" Havers creased up his face. "I see."

"But it does tell us that Ryan's assailant, a Mr"—Jones picked up the questionnaire and pretended to read—"Donald Jarman, planted the cameras *after* being interviewed by Constable Harkness." He nodded at the young man, who swallowed hard. "Which also tells us a great deal about Jarman's state of mind."

Jones replaced the questionnaire in its folder and lined it up with the edge of the table. He caught sight of the added section and the names stood out fresh.

Smithee and Jarman.

Again, the names tickled something in his memory. What the hell was it?

Jones shook his head, trying to tease out the answer. In a different setting, he'd have started pacing.

Don't force it, Jones. It'll come.

Havers interrupted his musings.

"Apart from the obvious," he said, confusion written large over his face, "that it gave Jarman advanced warning of our raid, what exactly does it tell us about him?"

Jones answered the question with one of his own. With a little encouragement, Havers might be able to work things out for himself.

"After the door-to-door, why didn't Jarman simply cut and run? He had plenty of time."

"Perhaps he thought he was in the clear," Havers suggested.

"Really?" Jones asked.

"More likely," Alex said, "it would have put him on his guard. Made him worried."

"And don't forget," Ben added, talking almost to himself, "we think he dumped Charlie's body in Orchard Park Lane because he *wanted* us to find it."

"The anonymous call?" Alex whispered. "Do you think it was Jarman, boss?"

"Yes," Jones answered her. "I do. In which case, we'll have a recording of his voice."

"And, if Jarman set up the cameras to give him advanced warning," Phil added, "why didn't he scarper the moment he saw us coming? He already had an escape route planned—"

"The zip line," Ben said, nodding.

Jones smiled. Ben had worked it out, too, and Alex's expression showed she'd done the same.

Phil continued. "Jarman could have had it on his toes long before we were anywhere near him."

"Yet he stayed put long enough to attack Ryan and leave him for dead," Jones added.

"You mean he *wanted* us to come?" Havers asked. "He timed his shoulder charge? He targeted DC Washington?"

"Yes, sir."

And the bastard's been playing with us the whole time.

Another rumbled eruption from the group forced Jones to hold up a hand.

"That's enough. If you don't have anything to contribute, keep the noise down."

"Why?" Havers asked Jones when silence returned. "Why did Jarman stay?"

Good question.

Jones' mind flashed back to his rushed search of Numbers 502 and 503, the custom-made furniture, the hidden door, and the slimline wardrobes in the spare bedrooms.

"Because," Jones said, "he had too much invested in the place—"

"What?" Havers demanded, voice raised.

"...and he *wanted* us to come."

"Are you serious?"

"Yes, sir. Deadly."

"But why? Why would Jarman want to draw attention to

himself? Why leave all his equipment—all his evidence lying around?"

Jones glanced at his watch.

"Perhaps Dr Spence will be able to tell us that, sir. She'll be here soon."

Chapter Twenty-Seven

THURSDAY 18TH MAY – Robyn Spence

Police HQ, Holton, Birmingham, UK

ROBYN SMOOTHED non-existent creases from the dark cotton jacket she'd chosen for its professional yet flattering cut. She checked the time on her watch. Although two minutes early, she had a lot to cover and didn't mind appearing keen. With luck, David Jones would be impressed not only with her analysis of the results, but with the deductive leaps she'd made, too.

Time would tell.

She leaned closer to the door and tried to hear what was going on inside, but a small group of uniformed officers passed behind her, chatting loudly. Their noise muffled the sounds coming from inside the briefing room. Her attempt to eavesdrop wasn't helped by the thickness of the office door, either.

She took a deep and settling breath.

Get on with it, Robyn. You can do this.

She rapped on the door and entered.

A sea of faces turned towards her. Most wore uniforms, but those in the front row seated around a table were in plainclothes. She allowed the door to swing closed behind her. It cut off the commotion in the corridor, and the room fell silent.

David Jones and Superintendent Havers, whom she'd met briefly the previous day, stood in front of a large SmartScreen. The picture of the rod camera they'd discovered in the fifth floor stairwell stood out larger than the others. Had David worked out the significance of the surveillance yet? Probably. What about all the other stuff? She'd surprise him with the links she'd made, though. Of that she was certain.

Feet on the ground, Robyn. Don't get ahead of yourself.

"Good morning, Chief Inspector. Sorry if I'm a little late."

That's it. Start with an apology. You idiot.

David threw her his cute, if slightly awkward smile, and closed the gap between them quickly. He had the crumpled, bachelor thing going for him—the salt and pepper hair in need of a trim and a stubbled chin. But those pale, clear eyes seemed to stare right through her.

Oh dear me. Stop it, Robyn.

"Not at all, Dr Spence. Thanks so much for sparing us your valuable time. I realise how busy you are in the lab. We were going over what we have so far, which isn't a great deal."

The quiet, welcoming voice eased her nerves.

Robyn shook his hand—a dry, firm grip—and he showed her to an empty chair. She draped her jacket over the back, and made sure her blouse wasn't too open at the neck. New on today, it had taken her ages to decide on its suitability.

David faced the room.

"For those who haven't met her yet, Dr Spence is the new team leader with the Racer-Colby lab. She's recently joined us after a stellar thirteen-year stint with the Imperial Centre in London."

He'd read her CV?

Of course he had. Hardly a surprise since she'd researched his background, too. For some reason, heat rushed from Robyn's throat to her neck. She prayed it didn't show as a blush.

Robyn cast a quick look around the front row. Searching for familiar faces, allies, she found a smiling Phil, looking impressive and trim in his white shirt and dark tie, his shoes highly polished. She'd met the injured Alex Olganski before and liked her, and recognised the large black man at her side. The man's friends called him "Big Ben", but his enemies would probably call him "Sir". As for the others, she had no idea who they were.

A redhaired young man sat in the corner, part-hidden behind a large monitor, his desk covered in computer equipment. He had to be Mr Bigglesworth, the civilian IT specialist she'd talked to on the phone earlier. She'd transferred her files to the main server and had given him instructions regarding her planned running order.

David himself stood beside Havers who, although a full ten centimetres taller than David, somehow looked smaller, less imposing, and certainly less distinguished.

David glanced at her and continued. "We're lucky to have a forensics expert with such a breadth of experience working with us. Give her your undivided attention."

"Dr Spence," the Super said, "it's good to see you again."

Robyn appraised Superintendent Havers, the new broom whizkid everyone was talking about. Youthful. Bright-eyed. Prizewinning smile. They shook hands and his weak, damp grip made her want to count how many fingers he'd left her with. She took an immediate and inexplicable dislike to the man.

"You too, Superintendent." She pointed at the enlarged image on the screen and turned to David. "You seem to have taken a special interest in the surveillance cameras. Would you like me to start there, or go from the beginning?"

David's eyes narrowed, but his cute little smile widened. "We're in your hands, Dr Spence. Please carry on as you see fit."

So he *did* realise the importance of the surveillance set up. During his unsanctioned search of the flats, had he seen the server room, too? What about the film posters? If he had, it might make the next part less awkward. She took another deep breath. Pity the superintendent had to be there, but if the chain of command meant she had to include him in the request, so be it.

"Superintendent Havers, Chief Inspector," she said, speaking quietly, "before I start, might I have a word with you both. In private?"

"Of course," David said, taking command, not giving Havers time to respond.

The superintendent stared hard at him, but said nothing.

"Follow me. DI Cryer." He signalled for Phil to join their small group.

David led them to a corner of the large room on the far side of the SmartScreen, and they stood in a close circle. Havers' expensive cologne would have been pleasant if he hadn't bathed in the stuff. David and Phil smelled of soap, nothing more.

"Yes, Dr Spence?" Havers asked, impatient to continue.

She spoke directly to David.

"My team and I have discovered some evidence of a highly sensitive and disturbing nature." She glanced at the audience whose focused stares had been drilling into the back of her neck. "I think it might be wise not to share it with the whole station. At least not until you've heard me out."

"Really, Dr Spence?" Havers blustered. "That sounds somewhat melodram—"

"Thank you, Dr Spence," David said, speaking over his boss. "I agree with you entirely. I was about to send the uniformed officers on a short break anyway."

Havers straightened and puffed out his chest. "Jones? Aren't you rather overstepping your—"

On receiving the benefit of David's dark glare, Havers stopped speaking, mid-sentence. At least he knew how to save face.

David turned away.

"Sergeant Dolan?"

A dark-haired, forty-something stood. About the same height as David, but much broader, his handsome face wore an inquisitive and open expression.

"Yes, sir?"

"Do you have all the bodies you need to re-canvass the OTT?"

The sergeant tilted his head to one side and winced. "I could always use more people, sir."

"Superintendent?" David said, glancing at his superior—but only in rank.

Havers pursed his lips, but to give him fair credit, he didn't take long to make his decision.

"Very well, Chief Inspector," he said, eyes glinting. "Sergeant Dolan, tell the watch commander I sanctioned the release of as many officers as can be spared. This investigation takes priority over routine matters. Tell him I will authorise any overtime necessary."

"Thank you, sir," David said, throwing his boss a bone. To Sergeant Dolan, he said, "Revisit every flat in each tower, and the surrounding streets within a half-mile radius of the estate. This time, we have a locus for the search and a general description of the suspect. We also know when and where he was last seen. It should give you more to go on than before."

"Yes, sir." Sergeant Dolan turned to the room, rubbing his hands together. "Okay, you lucky people. Up you get." Seven constables and a female sergeant rose. "Gather in the car park in twenty. Now's your time for a smoke if you need one." He glanced at Robyn and whispered, "Disgusting habit," before heading out with his flock.

Three uniformed officers remained. A grey-bearded and bespectacled sergeant and two extremely young and wide-eyed constables.

"Sergeant Featherstone," David said to the grizzled man, "how far have you got with the CCTV searches?"

The sergeant straightened in his chair.

"There aren't any working cameras on the estate, sir. The bugg —that is, the residents keep lobbing bricks at anything with a lens. There are a few operational cameras on the roads leading into the estate, though. The traffic unit's worked through hours of footage, sir."

"Any trouble with the NADC?" Havers asked, referring to the National ANPR Data Centre in London.

"None, sir. They've been helpful," the sergeant answered.

"I've authorised full ninety-day data access, sir," Phil said.

"Find anything of value?" Havers asked.

Featherstone's mouth turned down at the corners, and he shook his head. "Other than a few uninsured vehicles and a few more with cloned number plates, the ANPR cameras don't show anything useful at the time of the raids, sir. Doesn't look promising, I'm afraid. My eagle-eyed team"—he nodded to the young constables at his side—"and I are about to add our support in the traffic suite."

"Thanks, Feathers," David said, nodding his dismissal.

"Anything we can do, sir," Feathers said, standing. "Ryan's a good lad, and Charlie … well, he was one of us."

Like Sergeant Dolan before him, Sergeant Featherstone led his little brood from the room.

Bigglesworth stood and headed for the door, but Robyn held her hand out to David.

"Mr Bigglesworth and I have already spoken, Chief Inspector," she said. "He's had access to all the data in question, and I'll need his help with my presentation."

"Mr Bigglesworth, you can stay," David said, waving the young man back into his corner.

The young man retraced his steps.

Once he'd settled back into his chair, David said, "Mr Bigglesworth, from now until the end of this case, you're seconded to the Serious Crime Unit on a full-time basis. Superintendent Havers will arrange things with your line manager. Isn't that right, sir?"

Jones glanced at Havers, who nodded his instant agreement.

"Yes, yes. Of course. Best thing all around, I'd say."

"You okay with that, lad?" David asked.

Biggles beamed and sat a couple of centimetres taller. "Yes sir, you can rely on me, sir."

"Good, man," David said. He gave the youngster an encouraging smile and turning to Robyn. "Over to you, Dr Spence."

She took centre stage and launched into it.

Chapter Twenty-Eight

Police HQ, Holton, Birmingham, UK

JONES SETTLED back to watch what he anticipated would be a masterly performance. Robyn started with flat Number 502. She opened with a video walk-through of the flat and moved on to a detailed room-by-room analysis. She shared the preliminary results of every item of interest, which, as Jones had suspected with Number 502, amounted to precious little.

"In summary, what we have here," she waved her hand at the images on the whiteboard, "are, to all intents and purposes, five clean rooms. No fingerprints or shoeprints, except those of the team who gained entry to the flat and cleared the rooms. We also found imprints of your shoes, Mr Havers." She smiled, and he flushed. "As you know, Mr Elliott took everyone's shoeprints for elimination purposes."

Pausing for a moment to allow the information to sink in, she glanced at Jones, who nodded his encouragement. She was doing a fine job.

"In fact," she continued, "the whole flat has been sanitised. Even the drain traps in the sinks and bath had been cleaned with an industrial-strength solvent. There's no trace evidence in any room except the lounge, but I'll cover that in a moment. Generally, it's as though the place has never been lived in. I would say, the flat is little more than a film set." She looked pointedly at Jones, arching a perfect eyebrow.

A film set?

Of course. A film set.

Jarman and Smithee!

What an idiot. Why had it taken him so bloody long to twig?

Rather than smack his forehead with the heel of his hand, Jones smiled at her and nodded.

Robyn had done it. She'd provided the key to unlock the logjam in his head.

Two names and two slimline wardrobes couldn't be a coincidence. They had to be linked. The more he thought about it, the more it made sense. A film set.

Jarman had been playing with them. Directing them.

He and Robyn shared a secret no one else in the room seemed to have worked out yet. He found the concept strangely intimate.

From the first moment he saw her in the house on Orchard Park Lane, Jones knew, he absolutely knew, Dr Robyn Spence would be an impressive and important addition to the team. So far, she hadn't let him down. He glanced at Phil, whose returned gaze was both inquisitive and encouraging.

"What makes you say that?" Havers looked from Robyn to Jones and back as though he'd seen their unspoken exchange.

Robyn paused and picked up the red laser pointer again. "I'm coming to that, Superintendent. We actually found two items of real interest. Mr Bigglesworth, would you put up exhibit photo number twenty-seven, please?" She glanced at her notes. "It's in folder three. Full screen, please."

A colour image of Number 502's lounge-diner materialised and enlarged to fill the whiteboard.

"Once we removed the laminate surface, we discovered the floor of this room is polished, high-density concrete, eight millimetres thick. It piqued our interest because the other rooms are standard, poured and tamped, ready-mixed screed. As are all the other floors in the tower. We conducted a random analysis of the adjacent flats, to confirm this. In fact, from the records, we're as certain as we can be that each of the six towers is constructed from the same material."

"That's why I tripped on the laminate," Jones said, thinking aloud. "I thought it stood a little proud but put it down to bad workmanship."

"Is the concrete the same as the evidence you found under Charlie's fingernails?" Phil asked, picking up on the excitement running between Jones and Robyn.

"Yes, it is," she said. "You already have the full specs and stock number. Have you been able to trace the retailer and the customer?"

"Not yet," Phil said, glancing at Alex, who shook her head.

"We are still working on it," Alex said.

Robyn raised her slender shoulders and continued. "This specialist concrete was developed for large industrial units, shopping malls, and office buildings. It makes the finished surface very nearly impermeable. It won't absorb liquids: blood, lymphatic fluids, urine, nothing. I don't mind telling you, we were rather depressed when we saw it. We didn't think we'd be able to find anything to analyse."

She tapped the black plastic laser pointer against the palm of her left hand and pursed her lips.

"However," she continued, breaking out another smile, "we decided to dig a little deeper. If you take a close look at the image" —she used the pointer to trace a line where the floor joined the walls—"you'll see that we removed that piece of skirting board and chipped away a small section of plaster. The next exhibit, Mr Bigglesworth. Number twenty-eight. Thank you."

The lad superimposed a new picture over the last. It showed the far right hand corner of the same room, but in close up.

"Zoom in even tighter, please," she said. "Thank you. We found small, but significant blood samples near this area. It had been absorbed into the unpainted bottom edge of the skirting board and into the plaster on the wall behind. The killer made a simple mistake. It would appear that he is by no means infallible. And"—she cast another glance toward Jones—"although we've not been able to run the DNA yet, one of the samples is the same blood type as DS Pelham's. In my opinion, there is a high degree of probability that this is the primary crime scene." She paused again before adding, her tone serious, "I'm afraid your colleague met his end in this flat."

Havers started to raise his hand as though he were still at school, but must have thought better of it. The hand changed direction mid-movement, and he ended up smoothing his blond hair back against his scalp.

"You said, 'one of the samples', Dr Spence."

Robyn nodded, and the thin smile on her delicate face faded into frown. "I'm afraid so, Superintendent. So far, we've identified three separate blood types. There may be more, but we have to take extra care during our analysis of the skirting board and the plaster since most of the blood spots are tiny. But there are at least three separate contributors."

Silent until this point, Ben spoke, almost to himself. "It's definitely our murder site?"

Phil and Alex shared a glance, but Havers' focus remained on the photo.

Jones couldn't pull his eyes away from Robyn.

Magnificent.

He could think of no other way to describe her.

"We think so," Robyn answered, "but that's not all. Photo thirty-one please, Mr Bigglesworth."

A close-up shot of the bookcase displaced the one of the flooring. It showed the secret door, fully opened. A white circle had been superimposed on the top, right-hand corner of the image. "Can you zoom in on the highlighted area please?"

"He goes by the name, Biggles, Dr Spence," Phil offered.

The young techie reddened even further, and he buried his head behind his supersized monitor. The photo on the whiteboard enlarged and the image cleared to show a small split in the inside edge of the wooden upright. A tiny piece of material adhered to the cleft.

"This cloth," Robyn said, using the pointer again, "is a mixture of cotton from a shirt or blouse, and human skin. What we have here … might be a piece of our killer." She allowed the nugget to hang in the air, said, "Excuse me one moment," and crossed to the cooler for water.

Havers' drew his attention from the screen. "Is there enough tissue for a DNA analysis?"

Robyn took a delicate sip and nodded, her eyes shining bright.

"Most definitely. You find us a suspect and, if nothing else, we'll be able to place him at the scene. Now, would anybody like to know what we found next door?"

The forensics expert clearly enjoyed presenting her evidence. She might have rubbed her hands together, but the action would have been seen as inappropriate given the serious nature of the investigation. On the other hand, judging by the atmosphere in the room, Robyn's infectious enthusiasm seemed to have transferred to them all.

Since her arrival, Jones felt more optimistic than he had at any time since Ryan's near-fatal plummet.

Chapter Twenty-Nine

Police HQ, Holton, Birmingham, UK

JONES FOLLOWED Robyn's detailed presentation closely, but he didn't need to take notes. Phil would handle that for him.

"And this brings us to what we're calling the 'Comms Room'," Robyn said, using her laser pointer to indicate the full-screen photo of Number 503's master bedroom—a room Jones hadn't entered during his illicit crime scene walkthrough. Robyn and her team had arrived and ejected him and Not-Bob before they had a chance to open the door.

Thirty percent larger than the second bedroom, the master was filled to bursting with electronic equipment: VDUs, CCTV monitor screens, racks of servers, and other computer equipment. All linked by multi-coloured wires of spaghetti.

"Video three please, Biggles."

The new film showed a panning close-up of the equipment, all dead, and with none of the tell-tale green, LED lighting Jones would have expected in an active computer suite.

"A 'kill-switch' isolated the room's power," she said.

The red laser light of her pointer circled a black box on the wall next to the door. "Our suspect is a clever so-and-so. The switch delivered a power surge which had the same effect as running a strong electromagnet over all the servers and the hard drives. We're assuming all the data's been lost. Although it seems likely the suspect backed his data up to the cloud." She aimed an apologetic glance at Jones before continuing. "Since these shots were taken, we've dismantled the whole room and relocated the units to the digital forensics facility in the lab. We're hoping the killer might have left some trace evidence inside the casings." Robyn took another sip of water and tucked a curl of her wavy blonde hair behind her ear. "Our forensic data analysts are working on the hard drives right now, but ...." She shrugged and let the sentence trail off.

"We do know two things, though," she continued. "Firstly, the equipment is all hand-built."

She shared a look with Phil that Jones couldn't quite read. They were, no doubt, impressed by the skills required to build such sophisticated computer equipment from scratch. From Phil's expression, Jones doubted even he—the SCU's technical guru—could manage such a feat.

"My word," Havers said. "Are you sure?"

She glanced at the Super, her expression neutral.

"There are no badges or manufacturers' codes on any of the casings," she answered, returning her attention to the screen, "and only generic serial numbers on the motherboards and data chips. Secondly—and this is true of both flats—we found no usable fingerprints anywhere. All we have are smudges, which indicate the suspect wore gloves the whole time he spent in the place, which in turn, suggests he used the apartments sporadically."

"What makes you say that?" Havers asked, showing his naïvety in matters of deduction.

Phil answered for her. "I wouldn't want to spend my whole life wearing surgical gloves. Would you, sir?"

Havers nodded, his expression one of deep concentration, apparently oblivious to any loss of face. "A fair point, Inspector. So, the suspect lives somewhere else and uses the place as a what, a den?"

"It would appear so, Superintendent," Robyn answered.

"Did the man leave us anything at all to work with?" Jones asked, knowing full well, he had. Robyn's demeanour gave it away.

"Biggles," Robyn said, "can you run film four now? It's in folder five and marked 'Bedroom 2, Flat 503'."

A window materialised in the centre of the board and the white triangle in its centre disappeared, to be replaced by a moving image of the near-empty room. The picture panned up from the floor and inched from right to left. A heavily curtained window, and cream painted, bare walls rolled past. The image stopped at a slimline cabinet, an identical twin to the one Jones had seen in the second bedroom next door.

The cabinet ran from floor to ceiling and covered two-thirds of the wall. Robyn's blue-gloved hand appeared in the movie, grabbed a brushed metal handle, and pulled. The cabinet door opened outwards to reveal a large plastic panel. Behind the panel was a plain white board.

While the video clip ran, Robyn gave a running commentary.

"The cabinet is made of laminated Douglas fir. It's approximately two and a half metres tall, two metres wide, seventy-five centimetres deep and professionally made. By that, I mean there are proper joints all around, rather than nails and screws, or KD fittings."

"KD fittings?" Havers asked.

"Knock-down fittings," Jones answered for her. "They're used in flat pack joinery like kitchen cabinetry. Sorry, Dr Spence. Please continue."

Unfazed, Robyn smiled and carried on from where she'd left off. "The skill required to build this is not inconsiderable. It most certainly is not simple joinery. It might be worth you contacting the local shop-fitters and cabinet makers to find out who could have made these units. There are no manufacturers' marks, but as I suggested, it's probably beyond the scope of all but the most talented hobbyist."

On the screen, Robyn's gloved hand appeared again. The stiff plastic sheet, hinged on the left like the door, swung towards the screen, to reveal another empty sheet behind it and then another.

Robyn continued. "The cabinet has been made to display large posters. I don't know if they still sell them, but I remember seeing units like this in bookshops and newsagents a few years back."

The empty plastic panels continued rotating through the frame. Three, four, five ….

"All told, there are seven empty panels in the cabinet and six full ones. The first of which contained this poster."

The next panel turned to expose a movie poster that sent ice coursing through Jones' veins.

"Oh Lord!" he spoke softly, almost in prayer. He slapped the table in front him with an open hand. "You see what I see, don't you?"

Alex and Ben's sharp intake of breath showed that they certainly understood the relevance of the image. Havers' gasp confirmed that he, too, had grasped its significance.

Phil turned to Jones and shook his head, a look of disbelief on his chiselled face. "It can't be."

On instruction from Robyn, Bigglesworth hit pause. The video froze on a publicity poster for a film directed by Alfred Hitchcock. Grey banner lettering, picked out on a white background read:

The most intense
SUSPENSE ... EXCITEMENT ... EMOTION
ever generated by a motion picture!

BELOW, letters in white on a red background showed the names of the film's lead actors, James Stewart and Kim Novak, together with the director's name and the film's title:

VERTIGO

But the image that stood out and had the others fall into a stunned silence, showed a terrified James Stewart, eyes wide, mouth open in a scream for help. His hands clutched at the edge of the red border in a desperate attempt to prevent himself from falling to his death. The similarity between the image and what had happened to Ryan couldn't have been any clearer.

Phil broke the silence. "We were right. The arsehole planned it in advance."

Robyn's nod and her quiet, "Most definitely," shattered the spell and everyone started talking at once.

"How did he know Ryan would fall through the railings?" Alex asked.

"Did he target Ryan in particular, or was it random?" Ben asked.

"Bastard," Bigglesworth said, and immediately held up his hand in apology.

"The bugger could have had any one of us over!" Phil added.

"That's not all, I'm afraid," Robyn said, and the team fell silent, their stunned expressions fixed on her.

Robyn cleared her throat. "Biggles, the next shots, please. Photos ninety-three and ninety-four in folder six."

All the images on the screen minimised and were replaced by two others. The first, a full-length landscape shot of the fifth floor's curving balcony taken from the head of the staircase. It took in the railings and the webbing straps that Giles' men had erected. The second picture showed a detailed close-up of the broken metalwork. The shiny edge where the metal had parted showed the obvious marks of a hacksaw.

Alex threw her good hand up to her mouth.

Robyn nodded and ran her laser pointer over one of the shiny edges.

"As you can see, the railings were weakened in two important places—the top and bottom rail where they are bolted into the concrete support column. Anyone leaning heavily against them would have ....”

She left the sentence unfinished. Everyone knew the significance of the saw cuts.

Havers' face drained of blood, but he remained silent. His right hand covered his mouth and he stared, unblinking, at the image.

The sabotaged railings proved beyond doubt that Ryan's fall hadn't been an unfortunate by-product of a fugitive's desperate bid to escape capture, but a deliberate, premeditated, act of attempted murder. It made the suspect accountable for at least four serious crimes. Ryan's near-fatality, Charlie's murder and evisceration, and whoever donated the other two blood samples found in Number 502. And what of the other film posters? If they all represented a killing, they'd found themselves neck deep in serial murderer territory. Hell's teeth. The press would go ballistic. It fully justified Robyn's recommendation that they clear the room.

Jones stood and tried to regain control over his raging emotions, but the advertising poster packed a huge punch to his system.

“Dr Spence, would you mind if we pause there for a few minutes? I think we all need time to absorb the enormity of this information.”

“Good idea, Chief Inspector.” She leaned towards the chair she had yet to test, and slipped the laser pointed into the inside pocket of her jacket.

“Mr Bigglesworth, do you need a comfort break?”

The youngster stood.

“Yes, please, sir. I'm gasping.”

He reached in his pocket and pulled out a packet of cigarettes but put them away again when Jones shot the packet a look of disgust.

“Before you go, Mr Bigglesworth,” Jones said, standing to add emphasis to his words. “Not one word of this is to leave the room. Do I make myself clear?”

“Yes, sir. Of course, sir.”

Jones continued. “A dead police officer is bad enough, but if word gets out that DC Washington's fall was a deliberate attempt on his life, and we have a potential serial murderer on our hands ....." He paused for breath before continuing. "Well, it just can't happen. We need to manage the release of information carefully. Is that clear?"

Jones made eye contact with the youngster and each of his team to make sure they understood his orders. He wouldn't normally have considered it necessary to issue such a warning, but Charlie's murder and Ryan's fall resulted in raw nerves and they had to keep things under wraps.

"Alex," Jones said, "you look pale. Are you okay?"

Since the poster reveal, she'd lost colour and a thin sheen of sweat had formed on her brow.

"Yes, sir. It is just that ...." She nodded at the whiteboard. "This is very difficult to take in. We were so close to the monster, but we did not know."

"Do you need some water?" Jones asked, heading for the cooler.

"No thank you, sir. Perhaps something stronger. A coffee?"

Ben stood and held out a hand to help her up. "Sounds like a good idea to me, Sarge. Let's make a canteen run. Tea, sir?"

"A good idea all round," Havers announced. "Drinks for all, and tell the canteen staff to add it to my account. I'll have an espresso, no sugar. Dr Spence?"

"Tea, please. White and strong. No sugar."

Jones made a mental note of her preference, unaccountably delighted she took tea the same way he did.

"Cryer, Jones?" Havers asked.

"I know how they take it, sir," Ben said and left the room after a nod to Jones which said he'd make sure to take care of Alex, who looked in physical as well as emotional distress.

Bigglesworth left behind them.

JONES, Robyn, Phil, and Havers stood in a quiet circle by the water cooler in an otherwise eerily empty room.

Havers filled his monogrammed glass with water and gulped half down in one long swallow.

"Lord, what an awful mess. I don't know what to say."

"Not much *to* say, sir," Jones answered, staring into his plastic cup and wondering why he hadn't thought of buying a monogrammed glass of his own. It would be one way of reducing plastic pollution. He was all for doing his little bit to save the planet.

Hell, Jones. What are you thinking?

With a serial murderer on the loose there were more immediate matters to concern himself with.

Havers carried on. "It seems as though we can attribute one definite and another two possible killings to this man, along with an attempted murder." He turned to Robyn. "He's going to kill again, isn't he?"

"I'm afraid it's probably more than just the three murders, Superintendent," she said quietly.

"Excuse me?" Havers asked.

"Give me a moment."

Carrying her plastic cup, Robyn crossed the room and sat in Bigglesworth's chair. She peered at the monitor for a second before working the keyboard. By the time she'd finished typing, the video window on the whiteboard had disappeared to be replaced by six movie posters. They were displayed in two rows of three. On the bottom right was a small version of the *Vertigo* poster. The one to its immediate left—number five—caught Jones' attention.

"Are these posters displayed in the order you found them in the cabinet?"

Robyn nodded and added a thin smile.

"Do you see the fifth one?" Jones asked Phil who responded with, "Bloody hell!"

Phil understood the ramifications, but Havers hadn't yet twigged. The Super frowned and his gaze flicked from Jones to the poster and back again.

"Well, Jones?" he demanded, scowling. "What am I missing?"

"Dr Spence," Jones said, "would you mind?"

With another key pressed, the fifth poster expanded in front of the others.

The strapline—in white italics—ran along the top of the black border:

The terrifying motion picture
from the terrifying No. 1 best seller.

THE MAIN IMAGE–BLUE and white—showed a swimmer above a great white shark, its mouth open and revealing row upon ragged row of razor-sharp teeth. Above it, the dark red title showed the single word:

JAWS

"DON'T YOU SEE IT, SIR?" Jones asked.

"See what?"

"You see it. Don't you, Philip," Jones said, allowing himself a deep scowl.

"Yes, boss. That poster relates to Charlie's murder," Phil said, barely able to contain his anger.

Over by the techie table, Robyn nodded.

"Will someone tell me what's going on?" Havers demanded. "DS Pelham wasn't attacked by a shark."

"No, sir," Jones said. "He was eviscerated by a Hornet injector knife."

"So?"

"The Hornet knife was originally designed to protect divers from shark attacks," Jones said. "And in the film, the hero blew up the shark with a gas cylinder."

"Oh my God! Of course."

God has bugger all to do with this.

"It gets worse," Robyn said, almost to herself.

Jones had to agree with her. He'd already spotted the relevance of the third poster.

Much worse.

Chapter Thirty

THURSDAY 18TH MAY – Morning

Police HQ, Holton, Birmingham, UK

WITH THE *JAWS* poster still expanded, Alex, Ben, and Bigglesworth returned from their comfort break. Ben carried a tray laden with takeaway drinks and a plate of assorted biscuits. He lowered it to the centre of the table and they gathered around.

Robyn joined them at the table, ceding techie corner back to Bigglesworth, who gratefully accepted the offer.

Alex's colour had recovered slightly but remained miles away from its usual healthy tan. From the stiff way she held her shoulder, it had to be causing her pain. She ignored the biscuits and carried an insulated cup of coffee to her chair.

Jones approached and turned his back to the rest of the team before speaking.

"Feeling any better?" he asked, barely above a whisper.

Alex's smile showed a little of its normal vitality.

"Much better, thank you, boss. Coffee and a breath of fresh air worked well for me."

"Are you sure you're ready for this?"

She straightened. "Yes, sir. I need to work."

"Let me know when you need another break."

"Please, boss. I'm fine." She removed the lid from her cup, blew across the top of the coffee, and sipped. "The *Jaws* poster. It relates to Charlie's murder. The injector knife, yes?"

Jones gave her a grim smile. Despite her injury, there was nothing wrong with Alex's wits.

"Yes. It does." He patted her good shoulder, straightened, and turned to the others. "Okay, everyone. Shall we carry on?"

Like Alex, Ben immediately recognised the significance of the *Jaws* poster, but Jones took a moment to brief the young techie who hadn't been born until something like twenty-five years after the film's initial release. He imagined the poster would mean nothing to the lad.

"Mr Bigglesworth," Jones called, "enlarge the third poster, please."

The *Jaws* poster minimised and the one in question expanded to cover the others.

In poster three, a grey tone dominated the frame. To the top left and sloping upwards, the words:

ONCE UPON A TIME *in Nazi occupied France ...*

TO THE BOTTOM RIGHT:

INGLOURIOUS BASTERDS

THE NEW FILM BY QUENTIN TARANTINO

THE GRAPHIC between the two texts showed a pitted and bloodied Nazi soldier's helmet hanging by its strap from a damaged baseball bat. Blood dripped from the strap of the helmet and blood splatters dotted the image.

Jones had drawn the link immediately, but waited for the penny to drop.

"Anyone?" he asked.

Phil responded first.

"Bloody hell, Sandwell Valley!"

Again, Havers looked nonplussed.

"The dead cyclist?" he asked.

"Yes, sir. The dead cyclist whose face was destroyed with a baseball bat."

"God above!"

Is he?

Havers turned to Jones. "That's in the Smethwick district, isn't it?"

"Yes, sir. DI Jerry Scranton would normally have handled it, but he was in court when they discovered the body. I was called in as the only senior investigating officer available at the time."

"Ah yes, I remember now."

"The next day, we handed the case over to Jerry and his oppo, DS De Villiers."

Another memory scratched away beneath the surface. Another link to the posters.

"Alex?"

She set down her cup and turned stiffly in her chair. "Yes, boss?"

"That hiker we bumped into on the way to the body. What was her name?"

Alex's eyes narrowed in thought, and she shook her head.

"Just one moment, sir."

She reached for her laptop, but it took her a while to find the information.

"Sorry, boss. It is difficult using my wrong hand. … Here it is. Mrs Lean. Annette Lean."

Hell, another one!

Jones clenched his fist.

They were being played. The whole thing was an elaborate setup.

"Boss," Phil said. "You've seen something, haven't you. Care to share?"

Jones shook his head. "Not sure. I'm still working it through. Let's go through the rest of the posters first. I'll tell you when I'm good and ready."

Phil grunted. "You know how annoying you can be at times, boss?"

"DI Cryer!" Havers snapped. "That's no way to speak to a superior officer."

Phil raised his eyebrows and clamped his mouth shut.

Jones leaned closer to Havers and spoke quietly.

"Sir, if you don't mind, I'll reprimand my team as and when I see fit."

Havers sat for a moment, pursing his lips and grinding his teeth, unused to being dressed down in public by a subordinate. In the corner, Bigglesworth gawked. The rest of the team stared at the screen, pretending not to have heard the little sidebar.

"Alex," Jones said, to break the growing tension, "did you confirm Mrs Lean's contact information?"

"No, sir. I uploaded my notes to the system and transferred the case to Smethwick."

"Okay, fair enough. Poor old Jerry isn't going to be too pleased when we take it back from him."

"We are?" Havers asked.

"Yes, sir. Jerry's a good detective, but we need to keep this in-house."

"Seems like a duplication of effort to me, Jones. DI Scranton will have already started his invesig—"

"Sir, if you don't mind, those posters"—Jones pointed to the images on the whiteboard—"tell us there's a serial murderer operating in the area. We need to manage the release of information. The more people who know about this—"

"I understand that, Chief Inspector, but this is too big for one team. How are we going to cope with so few people?"

"We'll manage, sir."

"No, we need more detectives on this. There's too much at stake."

"May I make a suggestion, sir?"

"You may."

"Let's go over the rest of the information first. Then, we'll have a better idea what we're facing. Agreed?"

Havers paused for a moment before nodding.

"Agreed, Jones. I promised to be advised by you on this."

"Thank you, sir. Alex"—he turned to face her—"contact DI Scranton. Find out if they've confirmed the contact details for Mrs Lean."

"Can't DS Olganski just call the woman herself?" Havers asked, plainly lost.

"No, sir. If by some miracle, Jerry's team *has* managed to make contact, Alex's follow-up call would only raise suspicion. If they haven't, we can pay Mrs Lean a visit on our own terms."

"Ah, I see."

"Alex, if you would."

"Certainly, sir." She grabbed her mobile from the table and made her way to the back of the room for some quiet.

"Chief Inspector," Robyn said, raising a hand, "if I may. I've prepared a couple of slides related to the body we found in the Country Park. Would you like me to go through them now?"

Robyn was way ahead of them. She'd made the connection. Of course she had. Why else clear the room of uniforms?

Clever lass. Most impressive.

"Yes please, Dr Spence."

"Biggles," she said, "the first two exhibits in folder ten, please."

The six film posters minimised and slid to the top right corner of the whiteboard to be replaced by two documents large enough for Jones to read the title text only.

The first document was the covering page from the post mortem on the cyclist, who'd been given the name, DB7.

"DB7?" Havers asked.

"It's the seventh unnamed body we've found so far this year, sir," Phil said. "We don't call them John or Jane Doe here."

"Seems a little impersonal, don't you think? Heartless even?"

"We could always call him Eddy, sir," Phil suggested. "For Eddy Merckx."

"Or Sandy, for Sandwell Valley," Ben suggested in a rare flight into humour. "He did have fair hair, too."

"Yes, okay," Jones said. "Sandy will do until we've made the identification. Dr Spence, can you summarise the results please?"

Robyn took centre stage once more and gave a broad brush overview.

"'Sandy', a thirty-something male, fit and healthy at the time of death, died of blunt force trauma—multiple blows—to the head, face, and arms. His face was very nearly obliterated," Robyn continued. "I won't show the autopsy images of the head. They don't make pleasant viewing and won't add anything. There were multiple fractures to the hands and forearms, suggestive of defensive wounds."

"He saw his attacker?" Ben asked.

"It would appear so."

"Do you have an estimated time of death?" Jones asked, having already made an educated guess.

"Judging by the state of decomposition, five to ten days."

"That's before both DS Pelham's murder and the attempt on DC Washington's life," Havers announced, unnecessarily.

"And in the same running order as the posters," Phil noted.

Robyn nodded. "We collected eggs, larvae, and other material from the body. I've asked our forensic entomologist to work on it. Given time, he should be able to narrow down the time of death still further.

"Now, I'll address the murder weapon."

Alex returned from the corner. "I apologise for the interruption, Dr Spence, but I need to speak to the boss."

Robyn held up a hand and smiled. "Please do."

"What do you have, Alex?"

She raised the mobile. "It is on mute. DI Scranton is not happy, sir."

"I bet he isn't," Phil said.

Alex continued. "He would like to speak with you."

Jones sighed. Although he could do without a quarrel with a junior officer, he couldn't think of a way to avoid it. He took the phone from Alex and turned to Robyn.

"Please carry on, Dr Spence. I won't be long."

Robyn expanded the second document on the screen, whose title read, *Northern White Ash (Fraxinus Americana)*. A third of the way down the page, the words *Baseball Bat* were highlighted in yellow.

Jones turned away and started speaking.

"Jerry, how can I help you?"

"David, what the bloody hell's going on here?" Jerry shouted.

Jones had never heard the normally affable DI so agitated.

"Easy, Detective Inspector Scranton. Remember who you're talking to."

Jerry spluttered and took a moment to reply. "Sorry, sir. I'd just like an explanation. Is there something wrong with the way I've handled the investigation so far?"

"Not that I know of, Jerry. In fact, I've no idea where you are on the case."

"So why are you checking up on me?"

"I'm not checking up on you, I'm taking control of the case."

"You're what! Why the fu—"

"Operational reasons, Jerry, Nothing more. It doesn't reflect on your work."

"You're kidding, right? This'll look like a real slap in the—"

"I don't care what it *looks* like, Detective Inspector," Jones said, hating to come across as so officious, "the SCU is taking over the Sandwell Valley case. I'll expect you at my office by two o'clock for a full handover briefing. Is that understood?"

Silence screamed down the phone for a few moments before Jerry answered.

"Yes, sir. Understood perfectly."

Jones could almost hear the man grinding his teeth and crushing his phone in an angry fist.

"Before I let you go," Jones added, "did you contact Annette Lean yet?"

"DS Olganski already asked me that. What's going on here, sir?"

"Answer the question, Jerry."

The put-upon DI grunted. "I put De Villiers on it. Not heard back from him on it yet."

"Where is he now?"

"Out at the Country Park, supervising the search."

"Tell him to carry on with the ground search but he's not to go anywhere near the Lean woman."

"Why not?"

"She's a person of interest in another case," Jones said, cringing inwardly at the use of such a cliché. "Bring him with you this afternoon, and I'll tell you both as much as I can." He paused a moment before adding, "Listen, Jerry, I hate to do this to you, and I'm sorry I couldn't come to tell you in person, but I'm sure you'll understand this afternoon."

"Thanks, David. And I'm sorry for … you know. Running off at the mouth."

"I understand, Jerry. See you later."

He ended the call and handed the phone back to Alex in time to hear the tail end of Robyn's explanation of how they identified the weapon that murdered poor Sandy.

The ME had found a number of wood splinters buried deep within Sandy's skull, face, and jawbone. The lab identified them as northern white ash, hence the contents of the second document.

Jones raised his hand. "How did you identify the wood so quickly?"

"The wide curve on the edge of the largest fragment suggested baseball bat." She looked up from the small screen and glanced at Jones.

"Excellent, thank you. Please carry on."

"The lacquer found on the surface is unique to *Louisville Sluggers*. The good thing for us is that white ash tends to splinter when it comes into contact with hard or sharp objects; like teeth and bone." She winced. "Bill Harrap worked through the night to identify the species for us."

"Why is it always a baseball bat? Does anybody ever use the things to play the flaming game?" Jones halted his tirade when Robyn lifted an eyebrow. "There's something else, isn't there?"

"We found a second blood sample on the largest wood fragment."

Jones' heart flipped. All eyes turned to Robyn. "Could it be the killer's?"

Robyn shook her head and her smile faded. "It's possible but unlikely. We found the sample *underneath* the victim's blood, and it was much older. The bat may have been used before."

"Wouldn't surprise me." Jones could see the complicated threads of the case interweave and tangle in front of his eyes. "I suppose the blood samples are in the queue for a DNA analysis."

"Yes. Along with the tissue from the cyclist, and the tissue and blood samples we found in flat Number 502."

"Don't tell me. There's a three-day wait. Right?"

Robyn held open her hands.

"I'm afraid so, Chief Inspector."

"Do you have anything else on this particular case?"

"That's it, unfortunately. Shall I pack up my things and go?"

"Can you spare us a little more time, Doctor? I've a feeling we're not quite done yet."

She glanced at the clock on the wall above the whiteboard.

"I've signed myself out until lunchtime. I'm happy to stay a little longer if you need me."

"Excellent. Please do. Mr Bigglesworth, next poster, please."

"Which one, sir?" Bigglesworth asked. "We've skipped poster four."

"Ah, yes. Of course, *Sunset Boulevard*. Anyone know it?"

"I do, sir. Billy Wilder's 1950 classic," Ben piped up. "I watched it on the telly a little while back."

"You like old movies?" Phil said.

"Kidding, right? Love the classics, me. Don't make them like that anymore."

"Agreed," Jones said, trying to pull the memory from the vaults. "Haven't see it in years, though. Is there a murder in *Sunset Boulevard*?"

"Yes, sir," Ben announced. "The male lead in the film, played by William Holden, actually narrates the movie *after* he'd been shot dead. His body—lying face-down in a swimming pool—is shown in the opening scene."

"How does that relate to this case?" Havers asked. "Have there been any unsolved swimming pool murders recently?"

"Not that I can think of," Jones answered. "Phil?"

"None," Phil shot back. "A chap drowned in the Moseley Road Baths a couple of months back—"

"Yes, I remember that one," Jones said. "Turned out to be a heart attack, didn't it? Not a drowning."

"That's right." Phil nodded. "Coroner's Inquest put it down as natural causes. We also had that body in the Grand Union Canal last year."

"The partygoer?" Jones suggested.

"That's the one. He had a few too many cocktails and fell in, hit his head. Traffic cams caught the whole incident. Definitely no foul play involved. Death by misadventure, according to the Coroner. Can't think of anything else right now, though. Not locally."

"Sir, when we finish here, I'll search the PNC for any deaths relating to water if you like," Ben offered.

"Thanks, Ben. Okay, we'll shelve *Sunset Boulevard* for now and move on to the next poster. Number two please, Mr Bigglesworth."

The second poster in the gallery showed a scene from the Sergio Leone Spaghetti Western, *Once Upon a Time in the West*.

"Sir?" Alex said. "I apologise for the interruption, but I searched for the contact address Mrs Lean gave me."

"And?"

"It is the Empire Electric Cinema in Rubery."

Another piece slid into place in the puzzle.

Jones nodded, "Used to go there back in the sixties. Didn't think it was still open."

"It isn't, sir," Ben said. "They closed it down a couple of years back. Developers are converting it into upscale apartments. Crying shame, if you ask me. The old Empire was gorgeous. Art Deco. Great atmosphere."

"You really are a movie buff," Phil said.

"Celeste and I love the cinema," Ben answered, "but we can't go as often as we'd like. Too busy these days. Bought ourselves a large screen TV to compensate. You and Manda should come over, make a night of—"

"Poster two," Jones said. "What do you see?"

He'd never seen Ben so animated, and he hated interrupting the arrangements for what might have turned out to be the SCU's social engagement of the year, but they had to crack on.

In the centre of the whiteboard, the image—in yellow and orange with black lettering—contained line drawings of the lead actors at the top. At the bottom, a group of cowboys on horseback —backs to the viewer—watched a man with a noose around his neck standing on the shoulders of another. The noose was tied to a ruined stone arch.

The setup reminded him of something, but he couldn't bring it to mind.

As soon as the image expanded, Phil pointed. "Look, it's the Railway Cuttings suicide. Jerry Scranton's team investigated that case."

"Yes, of course." The memory dribbled back to Jones. As a suicide, he'd only played a peripheral role in the investigation, but he had signed off the report. "Remember what they found in the man's pocket?"

Phil nodded. "A child's toy harmonica."

"Bloody hell," Ben said, his deep voice raised. "I watched that film a couple of months back. I love Ennio Morricone's music. The hero, Charles Bronson, plays the harmonica all the way through the movie. In fact, his character's name *is* Harmonica."

"What happened with the investigation?" Havers asked.

"Jerry wrote it off as a suicide," Jones answered, trying to bleed all emotion from his voice, "and I agreed with him. There was no reason to do otherwise."

Jones tried to bring the case details to mind, but the *Vertigo* poster kept reminding him of Ryan falling from the fifth-floor walkway, frantically grasping at the sabotaged railing.

"Biggles, lose the *Vertigo* poster will you?"

The image disappeared, but somehow, the gap left in the six-pack montage seemed even worse.

Havers pressed a button on his tablet. "Can you remember the name of the suicide?"

Phil responded instantly. "Armin De Silva, forty-eight years old. Died on March 14th." He also cited the case number, to Havers' obvious surprise.

The Super's fingers flashed over his touch-screen.

"Here we are," he said, pointing the tablet at IT corner. "You should have the details now, Mr Bigglesworth. Can you put up the summary report, please?"

They spent the following half hour discussing the case—reopened on Havers' authority. From his desk in the corner of the room, Bigglesworth changed the Railway Cuttings case alphabetic identifier from "C", closed, to "O/U", open-unsolved.

The original conclusions drawn in the case collapsed under the weight of the new evidence. Questions unanswered at the time, took on greater significance. How had Mr De Silva made his way to the railway cuttings? He hadn't used his car—they'd found it parked in the garage at his office. No taxi or cab driver had come forward to admit taking a fare to the cuttings at the time assigned to the De Silva's death. Nor had they found a motive or a suicide note.

Armin De Silva, a middle-ranking civil servant, had no history of depression, and his family hadn't reported any personality changes in the weeks leading up to his apparent suicide. The clincher, the final unanswered question, turned out to be the one that reopened the case. Why did the man have a toy harmonica in his pocket since his son and daughter were fully grown and neither had children of their own?

Now they had their answer.

"Phil, this is another you can add to the list. Send someone downstairs to drag the evidence boxes out of storage. I want a detailed analysis run on the harmonica. Our suspect planted the toy on Mr De Silva, so there might be trace evidence. It's unlikely, but worth a try. I'm sure Dr Spence will put a rush on things for us?"

Robyn nodded, her eyes shone brightly. Evidently, she loved being in the thick of an investigation as much as Jones did.

"Jerry didn't order any tests at the time. Considered it unnecessary," Jones added.

Hindsight is a wonderful thing.

"Dr Spence." Alex sucked a breath between her teeth and cradled her damaged arm with her good hand. "The card stub you found in the topsoil sample at the Orchard Park Lane site, it turned out to be a cinema ticket, yes?"

"Possibly," Robyn nodded, "and before you ask, the cinema flyers we found in the front garden at Orchard Park Lane matched all the posters you see on the screen."

It took a moment for the pieces to twist, shuffle, and lock into position to form a new thought.

"The St Christopher medal," Jones said.

"Yes?"

"Remind me. What were the initials on the engraving?"

"*A* and *S*," she said.

A and S?

Allen Smithee!

Chapter Thirty-One

THURSDAY 18TH MAY – Morning

Police HQ, Holton, Birmingham, UK

"ALLEN SMITHEE! OF COURSE!"

Jones sat back in his chair and slapped an open palm on the table. It landed with a hollow clap, disturbing papers and rippling the water in Havers' fancy glass.

"Who?" Robyn asked.

Jones took a minute to remind them all how the name related to the case, but not its relevance. That enlightenment could come later, when he'd worked it through fully in his own head.

"I'll bet next month's beer money that Jarman planted the St Christopher just like he planted the harmonica and the film posters … and the damned ticket stub. The bugger's taunting us. He's throwing all these clues at us, daring us to link the murders back to him. But the clues don't really tell us anything, do they?"

"Who on earth are we dealing with here?" Havers asked.

Images swirled in Jones' head—medals mixed with harmonicas, Charlie's eviscerated body merged into Sandy's mutilated head, the Washingtons' anguished faces spread and folded into the red pedals of Ryan's blood as it flowed over the dirty concrete courtyard. The only image remaining constant and solid was of Donald Jarman as he barged Ryan through the railings on the fifth-floor walkway.

Jones became aware of a gentle pressure on his shoulder and snapped alert to find Robyn's concerned face less than a foot away from his.

"David? Are you alright?"

He rubbed his face, and tapped his hand on the one she rested on his shoulder. The simple, yet intimate act of touching her hand calmed him in a way he couldn't have expected.

"I'm okay, Robyn. Just wondering what to do about the medal. Can you take another look at it when you test the harmonica? Perhaps somebody missed something and the two items together might … Oh, I don't know, I'm clutching here."

"Of course, David, I'll do the work myself. If there's anything to find, I'll find it."

Jones and Robyn locked eyes. Something intangible passed between them, something intangible and maybe a little troubling.

Havers coughed and the gentle spell dissolved.

"This is all well and good," he said, "but let's concentrate on what we can do now. As I understand it, we have three film images matching three deaths, and a fourth matching DC Washington's fall. They can't be a coincidence. The remaining two posters *must* link with other killings. *Sunset Boulevard* and that last one. Don't you think?"

"Exactly," Jones said and regained his feet, but remained close to Robyn.

They studied the final poster, a scene from the 1969 psychedelic cult movie, *Easy Rider*. Jones had watched the movie in his youth, but scarcely remembered it. The ending involved a motorcycle and an explosion, but he couldn't recall the details. Neither Ben nor anyone else had seen the movie, but Bigglesworth proved his worth once again with a quick internet search. He displayed a synopsis on the SmartScreen.

The end of the film had both leading men killed in a random act of violence, and the film's final shot focused on an exploding motorcycle.

"Any cases spring to mind?" Havers asked Phil, who shook his head.

"Not really. We've had our fair share of RTIs where motorbikes have come off second best to cars and trucks. A couple of hit and runs, but no exploding bikes come to mind."

"Anyone else?" Jones asked, but no one had anything to add.

Jones paused for a moment before taking his place beside Robyn in front of the screen.

"So, to summarise," he said. "We potentially have two more deaths attributable to our suspect, Donald Jarman. A death involving water, and one or two dead bikers and a motorcycle with an exploding petrol tank. Any of these sound familiar?" The blank looks and silence gave him his answer. "Right then. Ben and Biggles, trawl through the PNC and HOLMES II databases for explained or unexplained deaths with more than a passing similarity to these movie scenes. There'll probably be a few, but we'll need to sift through them all.

"Also, plot a timeline between the killings. There might be a pattern."

"That's easy enough," Phil said. "The earliest murder we've identified so far was the Railway Cuttings case."

"Which was?" Haver's asked.

"14th March. This year."

"Yes, that's right," Jones said. "The Sandwell Valley murder took place within the last fortnight or so, and Charlie died last Thursday night or Friday morning. So, if the posters *are* in time order, we should have a death involving water sometime between Charlie and Sandy's murders."

"And we'll probably have an exploding motorbike sometime before 14th March?" Havers suggested.

"However," Jones said, "we can't rely on the killer being neat and tidy and wrapping things in a nice little parcel for us. He may have moved here from a different area, or shuffled some of the posters out of order for the hell of it or to confuse us. Don't limit your search to the Midlands, either. Expand it to the whole country. Scotland and Wales, too." He paused for a sip of tea, which turned out to be cold.

"There is one obvious thing, boss," Phil said.

"What's that?"

"He's speeding up. There were months between the Railway Cuttings and the Sandwell Valley murders, and only days between Charlie and Ryan."

"Yes, I had noticed."

Havers jumped in. "And don't forget to run full background checks on Donald Jarman and Alan or Allen Smithee, however he spells it. I don't for a minute suppose it's their real names, but we can't afford to ignore the possibility."

Jones shook his head. "Scratch that, sir. I think we can say Donald Jarman is *probably* an alias, but Allen Smithee *definitely* is."

"How do you know that?" Havers' frown threatened to bring on premature wrinkles.

"Didn't I tell you?"

"Tell me what?"

"Sorry, sir. We've covered a load of ground today, but it's all about the names. I knew something was wrong as soon as I saw the name Jarman assigned to his neighbour during the door-to-door. Only I didn't work out what it was in time to catch the sod. Our movie sage will tell you about Allen Smithee, won't you Ben?"

"Boss?" Ben shrugged his massive shoulders. "Sorry, but I've never heard that name before."

"Call yourself a film buff?"

"Didn't call myself anything of the sort, sir. Phil did," he said, stretching out an apologetic smile.

"Ah, yes. You have me there, Ben." Jones smiled properly for the first time that day. "Allen Smithee is a pseudonym used by film directors when they don't want to be associated with a turkey of a movie. It's not allowed anymore, but amongst other things, it used to happen when a film has been reedited by a studio against the director's wishes."

"That's impressive, boss," Phil said. "I didn't realise you were a movie aficionado."

"I'm not," he said, shaking his head. "I happened to hear about it on the radio the other night." Jones shrugged, and his eyes were drawn to Robyn when he added, "Sometimes I can't sleep."

Blimey, where did that confession come from?

"What does this mean, Chief Inspector?" Havers demanded. "And why were you so interested in that hiker, Annette Lean?"

"They're all names of film directors."

"What's that?"

"Lean, Jarman, and Smithee, sir," Jones said, reining in his excitement. "They're all film directors. *David* Lean, *Derek* Jarman, and *Allen* Smithee. The killer's recreating movie deaths. Only he's changing the plots, and he's using different director's names for the movies he's recreating."

"To put us off?" Phil asked.

"Possibly. Or to show us he can do it better than the original film versions. Maybe that's why he's included Allen Smithee in the mix."

"But this woman, Annette Lean, can't be our killer," Havers said.

"Why not?" Jones asked.

Havers stood taller. "You saw her yourself. Annette Lean's a woman and the person who pushed DC Washington from that balcony, Donald Jarman, is a man."

"Is he?" Jones asked.

"What?"

"Can we be certain what sex our killer is? After all, we're talking about the performing arts here. Heck, these days, with makeup and prosthetics, people can be made to look like anything they choose."

"Good grief."

A mobile rang. Robyn dived into her handbag. "Excuse me, it's the lab. Hello, Patrick." As she listened, a cloud shadowed her eyes. "Are you certain? … Right, thank you." She ended the call, bit her lower lip, and stepped closer to Jones.

What now?

"Something else?"

"Patrick just finished the analysis on the seven empty plastic panels in the poster cabinet." She hesitated before adding. "Each shows trace evidence of printer's ink. Until very recently, all seven panels contained film posters."

Havers turned to Jones. "You know what that means, Jones," he said.

"I do."

"Donald Jarman has planned at least seven more murders, and he may already have selected the victims."

Jones sighed. Havers might not have been the brightest detective Jones had ever met, but he was well on the way to becoming a master of understatement.

Chapter Thirty-Two

THURSDAY 18TH MAY – Midday

Police HQ, Holton, Birmingham, UK

"WHAT NEXT, CHIEF INSPECTOR?" Havers asked after delivering what he must have thought would be a bombshell.

"We need to put a real name to the cyclist, Sandy."

"Why? What's so important about him?"

Robyn and Phil looked at each other. Jones half expected them to roll their eyes.

"So far, he's the only known victim we haven't identified. Learning who he is might tell us something important."

Havers turned to Robyn.

"No chance of a dental match you say, Dr Spence?"

"Not with what we have, Superintendent."

"And nothing on the fingerprints?"

"There are no fingerprints at all I'm afraid. The body lay half submerged in a fast-flowing stream for the best part of a week.

Advanced skin putrefaction led to the hands and fingers being severely attacked by scavengers. We were unable to obtain any usable prints."

"And there are no hits on the MisPer Database?"

"None, sir," Alex answered.

"So, we're waiting on DNA results and hoping to find a match on the NDNAD, which will take at least three days," Jones said, smiling in apology to Robyn.

"Excuse me, sir," Bigglesworth said, raising his hand.

"Yes, Mr Bigglesworth?" Havers asked, his frown suggesting annoyance.

"Um, I watched a TV documentary on anthropology the other day where the scientists built a Neanderthal woman's face from a skull. Could we use something like that here?"

Havers opened his eyes wide. "That's an idea. Is the skull intact enough, Dr Spence?"

Robyn thought for a moment before answering. "Possibly. I was going to suggest calling in a mortuary artist, but ...."

"Too much damage?" Jones suggested.

She shook her head. "Too subjective. By which I mean, there's too much scope for artistic interpretation. On top of which, it's rather expensive and very time consuming."

"A non-starter, then?"

"Um, not necessarily, sir," Bigglesworth said, pushing a hand in the air. "There's something called 3D CFR." He swallowed hard and stretched his mouth into an embarrassed smile.

"3D what?" Jones asked.

"3D Computerised Facial Reconstruction," Phil answered for the lad. "Of course, why didn't I think of that myself? Nice one, Biggles."

The youngster in the corner smiled, and a flush deepened on his already pink face.

"I know about that particular research, Jones," Havers announced. "In fact, there's a professor at the local university. Llewellyn's the name. I read a few of his papers during my first degree. Fascinating stuff." Excitement shone in the Super's eyes.

"It's amazing what they can do now, with even the most damaged cranial tissue. They use a combination of MRI and PET scans, laser imaging, and 3D printing. Fantastic. They might be able to reconstruct our vic's face."

Jones shuddered at the term.

"It might help us identify the real name of the vic*tim*, sir."

"I sense there's a 'but' coming, Chief Inspector."

"Cost, sir. Any reconstruction of this sort is bound to be highly expensive."

Jones expected Havers to knock the idea on the head right away, but the Super's response surprised him.

"Since we're linking Sandy's murder with that of DS Pelham and all the others, I'm sure I'll be able to convince the DCC to release the funds. Get the details from Professor Llewellyn, and I'll see what I can do about finding the budget."

"Thank you, sir."

"Now," Havers said, reading the time on his Tag Heuer Monaco, "I'm afraid I have a steering committee meeting this afternoon I can't get out of. And I've yet to finish prepping my presentation. Can I leave this with you, Chief Inspector?"

"Of course, sir. And thanks for all your help." Jones tried to make it sound sincere.

After Havers left, everyone in the room seemed to breath more easily, even Bigglesworth.

"Thank goodness for that," Phil said. "Thought he'd never go."

"Easy, Detective Inspector," Jones said, smiling, "that's no way to talk about a superior officer."

"Superior?" Robyn said. "In rank, maybe, but that's all." She raised her shoulders and let them drop again. "Sorry. I shouldn't talk out of turn. However, as for Rhys Llewellyn and his 3D CFR" —she pinched her lips and shook her head—"he may not have all the answers."

"What's that, Dr Spence?" Jones asked.

All eyes turned towards her.

Robyn twisted in her seat, and Jones felt the warmth of her gaze.

"Facial reconstruction is a mandatory module in most forensics courses. I've actually taught a few in my time, and I'm well aware of Professor Llewellyn's work." She paused for a moment. "I attended one of his seminars last year. Hate to say it, but the man's a bit of an old windbag, and he can verge on the overly dramatic. He also has an unfortunate fondness for young, female students."

"But his work, Dr Spence," Jones said, "is it any good?"

As she considered her answer, Robyn tilted her head to one side in a way he'd come to appreciate.

"His methodology seems solid enough. Although, some areas might be improved. He certainly needs to expand his dataset, but I did learn a great deal from the seminar."

The question mark over Llewellyn's work gave Jones reason for doubt.

"I'm not saying his work has no value," Robyn continued, "far from it. His process has reasonable external integrity and validity. What I am saying is that his output depends upon the quality of his input. In computer terminology it's called GIGO, which means—"

"Garbage in, garbage out," Jones said and added, "DI Cryer keeps trying to educate me on the intricacies of the Information Age."

Phil grinned, as did Robyn.

"And with Sandy," she said, "the data might prove overly corrupted. The poor man's face has been completely pulverised. There are very few intact facial bones left in situ."

In the corner, Bigglesworth gagged and threw a hand up to his mouth.

Jones took pity on the lad.

"You can take a break there, Mr Bigglesworth. You've seen and heard enough for one morning. Report back here after lunch, if you can stomach any food."

Still covering his mouth, the youngster jumped out of his chair and hurried from the room.

"Oh dear," Robyn said, "I didn't mean to upset him."

"He'll toughen up. If not, this isn't the place for him," Jones said, hoping not to appear too insensitive. "You were saying, Dr Spence."

"Yes … in the case of Sandy, the quality of the data might not be good enough to produce a reliable reconstruction. I just wanted to introduce a note of caution."

"Your point is well taken."

"Mr Havers seemed rather keen on the idea of a fancy reconstruction," she suggested.

"He did look like a kid in a tuck shop," Phil said, not bothering to keep a straight face. "Can't say I'm happy with the dressing down he gave me, though. I mean, telling me off for saying how annoying you can be! Everyone who's ever worked with you knows that. Come on now, guys. Back me up here."

"Okay, Inspector Cryer. That's quite enough of that. Don't know about you four, but I need some fuel. Dr Spence, do you have time for a spot of lunch in the canteen? Can't promise you cordon bleu, but the cheese and tomato sandwiches are edible and the tea's just about drinkable."

"Is it still on the Super's account, d'you think?" Phil asked, smiling wide and double-hitching his eyebrows.

"I wouldn't push it, Philip. I really wouldn't. As for lunch, I'll pay—"

"Blimey," Phil said, clutching a hand to his chest, "I need a defibrillator."

Jones stared him down long enough for Phil to stop his ridiculous play-acting.

"As I was saying before being so rudely interrupted, I'll pay for our guest, Dr Spence. It's the least I can do for her time and her input."

"How charming," she said. "Unfortunately, I can't accept your kind invitation to lunch, I need to get back to the lab. Pat and Bill won't supervise themselves, and I'll need to prep the equipment for that harmonica. Perhaps another time, Chief Inspector?"

Phil turned to Alex and Ben. "Don't know about you guys, but that sounded like a date to me, eh?"

"DI Cryer!"

Jones waited for Robyn to collect her things, scowling at Phil the whole time. For her part, Robyn took Phil's gentle taunting rather well. In fact, she didn't seem too upset by the idea of a date one little bit.

Get a grip Jones. This is work.

All five of them left the briefing room together and walked to the end of the corridor. Phil hit the button to summon the lift.

Jones turned to Robyn. "Here's where I leave you. Thanks again for all your help, Dr Spence. Ben will collect the harmonica from the evidence lockup immediately after he's finished lunch."

"You don't use lifts?" Robyn asked, glancing at Phil.

"Telling tales out of school again, DI Cryer?" He shot Phil another dark scowl.

"Not me, boss," he said, holding up his hands.

To Robyn, Jones said, "Not if I can avoid them. I prefer the stairs."

The lift arrived and the doors slid back.

"Me too," Robyn said, lightly. "Good for the cardio-vascular system. I don't know about you, Chief Inspector, but these days, I seem to be spending more and more of my time sitting behind a desk."

"My sentiments exactly. Care to join me?"

"What a delightful idea," she said, dismissing Phil with a toss of her head.

"See you in the canteen, Philip," Jones said. "I'll have a pot of tea and a bacon roll."

He opened the staircase door and allowed Robyn through first. She brushed past, leaving a waft of her fresh scent in the air.

"Sorry about all that nonsense, Robyn," he said when certain they were alone in the stairwell. "They're a good team, and I like to give them plenty of latitude, but I'd hate to think they overstepped the mark and upset you."

"They didn't, and don't worry. I enjoyed the banter."

"No," Jones said, adding a headshake. "Philip was getting a little out of hand. I'll have a word with him about it later."

"No need, David. I've known him for years, and I can give as good as I get—especially when I involve Manda." She narrowed her eyes and let out a delightful little chuckle.

"Yes," he said, "on reflection, I rather suspect you can. To be honest—again, on reflection—I almost feel sorry for him. Two against one, you know. Unequal odds." He pointed to the staircase. "Shall we?"

Halfway down the first flight, she glanced up at him.

"Us walking out together like this will probably have the tongues wagging, don't you think?"

He smiled back. "I rather think it might. Do you mind?"

"No, not in the slightest."

Good answer.

"Excellent. And will you answer a question?"

She paused for a moment before saying, "That rather depends upon the question, Chief Inspector."

Another excellent response.

He could grow accustomed to their sparring.

"Do you really prefer walking to using the lift?"

"Yes, I do—when I'm not carrying my metal case, that is."

Robyn Spence was almost too good to be true. The walk down fourteen flights of stairs had never passed so quickly, or in such good company.

IN THE CANTEEN, Phil had nabbed their favourite table in the quietest corner. Jones' lunch, still on its tray, looked inviting.

"Thank you, Philip. Much appreciated."

Jones sat opposite Phil—his back to the wall, facing the room—and poured the tea from its pot. The brown liquid caught the light, its colour perfect.

"I expected you sooner, David. It doesn't normally take you that long to climb down the stairs. Wouldn't be surprised if your tea's gone cold, and as for the roll …" An irritating smile stretched his lips. "Enjoy your private chat with the good doctor?"

"Yes, Philip. I did indeed. She took time to explain Llewellyn's 3D CFR process to me. Fascinating. Really fascinating."

At the next table, Ben and Alex paused their conversation to earwig, and they weren't exactly subtle about it, either.

"Carry on with your lunch, you two. Nothing to learn here."

"Spoilsport," Alex said and tucked into her cottage cheese salad, finding it a challenge to use her left hand only.

Ben bit into his sandwich and they carried on with their conversation.

Jones demolished his bacon roll in silence. It was colder than he'd have liked, but he refused to give Phil the satisfaction of mentioning it.

Roll finished and mouth dabbed with the paper serviette provided, Jones lifted his cup and leaned back in his chair.

"She's impressive, isn't she," Phil announced, after finishing his granola bar and pushing his side plate away.

"Who is?" Jones said, "Alex? Yes, she is. Probably saved Ryan's life even though she blames herself for letting go."

"You know who I mean, David. Robyn's a step up from poor old Ghastly, eh?"

"Yes, Philip. No doubt about that. Her attention to detail is notable. She'll present really well if we ever bring this case to trial."

"And the way she linked the posters to Sandy and put us on the trail of a *serial*"—he mouthed the word—"was inspired," Phil said through another irritating smile.

"Yes," Jones admitted. "She's good. Although, you and I both saw the association as soon as Biggles put the posters on the screen."

"True enough. But you saw the posters in the flat and you didn't twig the *serial* angle. Robyn did."

"Actually, Philip, I didn't see the posters. The SOCOs arrived before I had a chance to search the bedrooms. However, as you say, Robyn's proving to be a real asset."

"She's good looking, too."

"Is she? Hadn't really noticed." Jones tweaked his earlobe.

Phil's eyes bugged. "No, boss. Of course you didn't."

"And in any event, what do her looks have to do with her work?"

"Absolutely nothing."

"Quite right."

Jones finished his cup and poured out the remainder of the tea. It had stewed too long in the pot. Too strong. He pushed the cup away. He checked the time on his watch. He wasn't looking forward to his face-to-face with Scranton and De Villiers, but he still had a few minutes before they were due to arrive.

"I think a private team chat's in order. Alex, Ben, gather round."

He waited for them to join him and Phil at their table.

"Okay, let's start with Charlie. Did you listen to the anonymous tip?" He threw the question at Phil.

"Once or twice." Phil grinned.

"Twice?" Ben asked.

"Okay, once."

"What did you make of it? Digitally modified?" Jones asked.

"Definitely. We won't be able to use it for a voice ident."

"Agreed. You didn't find anything strange about the message or the words he—or is it, she—used?"

"Want me to play it for you? As a reminder." Phil held up his mobile.

Jones glanced around the rapidly filling canteen and shook his head. "Not here."

"You can use my earbuds if you like."

Jones grimaced. "If you don't mind, I'd rather not."

The idea of using someone else's earpieces turned his stomach, even if they were Phil's.

"Okay, understood. I'll lower the volume and you can listen up close. Fair enough?"

"Okay."

The team understood Jones' eccentricities and didn't take offence with the refusal as others might. For a few moments, Phil ran his fingertips over the mobile's screen.

"Ah, here it is." He handed Jones the phone. "Hit the triangle and you're good to go."

"Thank you, Philip. I have learned how to play sound files, you know."

"Sorry, boss."

Jones tapped the play button, lifted the phone to his ear, and listened to the brief emergency conversation.

POLICE OPERATOR: *"WHAT'S YOUR EMERGENCY?"*

Caller: *"There's a body at number 26, Orchard Park Lane, Bordesley Green. Hurry!"*

Police Operator: *"A body?"*

Caller: *"A dead man. At least I think he's dead."*

Police Operator: "Is the man breathing?"

Caller: *"Don't know."*

Police Operator: *"Caller, can you check his breathing?"*

Caller: No response.

Police Operator: *"Caller, I need you to check his breathing. I can help if you need it."*

Caller: No response.

"THE CALLER'S VOICE," Jones said after replaying the voice file, "flat and emotionless. Computer generated, you think?"

"It's a good bet," Phil answered, retrieving his mobile.

"No help there."

"Not a lot."

Phil swiped the screen clear and lowered it to the Formica surface.

"So," Jones said, "Jarman killed Charlie and dumped his body in Orchard Park Lane—a place where he expected it to be found quickly, right?"

"That's the assumption."

"And in the meantime, Jarman has plenty of time to disappear if he wants to, but he doesn't. Instead, he scrubs the crime scene clinically clean and hangs around, waiting for the police to call."

"Then he sets up the CCTV cameras," Ben said, "but he only does that *after* the first door-to-door. After he's primed the pump."

"What do you mean by 'primed the pump'?" Alex asked.

262

"When Jarman gave Constable Harkness Allen Smithee's name," Ben said, "maybe he was hoping for a police raid?"

"Ah," she said, "I see. But why?"

"That, Alex, is something we'll need to work out. Or we can ask Jarman when we find him." Jones checked his watch again. "We'll discuss the Sandwell Valley case after I've had my little chat with Jerry Scranton. Which will be in five minutes."

"What next, boss?" Phil asked.

Jones stood and turned to Alex. "You and Ben can head to the evidence locker and sign out the boxes for the Railway Cuttings case. Take a couple of uniforms with you for the heavy lifting."

"And me?" Phil asked.

"Contact that professor chappie and arrange a university visit ASAP."

"Will do, boss. I'm actually quite keen to learn more about the 3D CFR stuff. Always loved sci-fi, me."

"After that, you and Mr Bigglesworth over there"—he pointed to a distant table, where the young redhead sat with a bunch of other civilians, all heads down, eyes glued to their mobile phone screens—"can search for cases related to the other posters, *Sunset Boulevard* and *Easy Rider*."

They stood and made their way through the canteen to the exit, collecting Biggles on the way. The lad seemed less keen to re-join them than he had been to skedaddle from the briefing room less than an hour earlier.

Jones let the others go on ahead while he hung back a little and eased alongside the young man.

"Feeling any better, Mr Bigglesworth?"

The lad couldn't hide an uncomfortable smile.

"Sorry about that, sir. I-I felt a little queasy. Couldn't help it."

"That's alright, lad. Happens to us all."

"Even you, sir?"

They pushed through the canteen doors together and stopped.

"Mr Bigglesworth," Jones said, hiding his mouth behind his hand, "the first time I saw a picture of a bloated dead body, I threw up over my best pair of shoes."

"You did, sir?"

"Wasn't much older than you at the time, but let's keep this between you and me, eh?"

"Between us, sir," he said. "Yes, sir."

This time, his smile seemed less forced and much more natural.

"By the way, exactly how old are you?"

"Twenty-six, sir. Although people tell me I look much younger."

"They do?" Jones said, straight-faced.

"Yes, sir."

"People used to say the same thing about me."

"They did, sir?"

"Yep, but don't worry, lad. It won't last."

Never does.

Chapter Thirty-Three

THURSDAY 18TH MAY – Afternoon

Police HQ, Holton, Birmingham, UK

WHILE BIGGLESWORTH AND the rest of the team headed for the bank of lifts at the far end of the entrance hall, Jones waited for the West Bromwich contingent.

The sergeant staffing the reception desk—a man Jones once had reason to dress down and who definitely held a grudge—picked up the telephone as he approached and turned away.

Jones ignored the intentional slight, strolled towards the exit, and pushed through the doors. While he waited, a breath of air— even the grubby city centre air—might blow away some of the cobwebs.

As he stood at the top of the atrium, sucking in the gritty atmosphere, two large white trucks, satellite dishes and aerials sprouting from their roofs, pulled to a stop in the car park. One of the trucks had BBC Local News decals stuck to its side panels, the other sported the Sky News logo. Five SUVs followed close behind. Within seconds, a miscellaneous collection of individuals poured out of the vehicles. Some busied themselves with equipment—cameras, microphones, cables, and tripods. Others—business-suited, front-of-camera types—stood groomed and preparing for action. Within seconds, a gabbling crowd had gathered in front of the entrance steps. Camera flashes pricked Jones' eyes and a hot flash of anger stabbed his heart.

He cursed under his breath, darted back inside, and rushed to the reception counter.

"Sergeant Ogilvy, what's the press doing here? As far as I know, we've nothing in the schedule."

Ogilvy cradled his phone and gave Jones a blank stare.

"No idea, sir. First I've heard of it."

"Phone the press officer. Tell her the media's just arrived. A whole posse of them."

Ogilvy stretched his neck to peer through the glass-fronted atrium before slowly reaching for the phone. He dialled, held the phone to his ear for thirty seconds, and shook his head.

"No answer," he said, returning his focus to the commotion outside.

"Try Superintendent Havers."

"He's in a steering meeting, sir. Told me he wasn't to be disturbed."

Jones glared at Ogilvy long enough for him to pull his eyes from the windows and pick up the message. He dialled again. This time, someone answered. The desk sergeant spoke briefly and handed the phone across.

"Jones?" Havers asked, sounding harassed. "What's going on?"

Jones turned his back on the earwigging Ogilvy and stepped away from the desk. "The media's arrived and the nationals are in on the act. This is going to get ugly. Someone must have talked about the case."

"Who would do such a thing?"

"No idea, sir."

Jones wanted to say more but clamped his mouth shut tight in case he said something he'd later regret.

"When I find out, I'll have their job," Havers grumbled. "Don't move, I'll be right there."

Jones returned the handset.

"Trouble, sir?" Ogilvy asked, eyes shining, revelling in Jones' discomfort.

"Only for the person who called in the vultures, Ogilvy. Definitely not you?"

Offended, the man sat back in his chair, bristling.

"Why would I call in that bloody shower? I guess this is about DS Pelham, huh?"

Jones leaned against the counter.

"What do you know about it, Sergeant?"

"Don't know nothing, sir. Only that Charlie Chuckles was found, dead, on the OTT. And that he'd been gutted. That's all."

"Charlie Chuckles?"

"That's what everyone called him, sir. Behind his back, like."

"Have some respect, man. He was a fellow officer."

Although not much of one.

"Yes, sir. Sorry, sir."

Ogilvy's insipid delivery and his blank expression didn't exactly scream sincerity.

"Don't let any of them inside."

"'Course not."

Jones left him to his gloating and approached the lifts. A few inquisitive officers had gathered in the foyer. They stood in small groups, gawking at the melee in the carpark.

"If you don't have anything better to do, I can find you something," Jones snapped, barely managing to keep from shouting.

The uniforms hurried away, no doubt to find a less public vantage point.

An electronic *ding* drew Jones' attention to the bank of lifts. One of the lights above the lift doors lit up, the brushed metal doors slid opened, and Havers rushed out. He signalled for Jones to accompany him to the glass atrium, but made sure they kept out of sight of the horde.

"What should I do?" Havers whispered, looking less assured than Jones had ever seen him.

"You could always send them away. I mean, we didn't call a press conference, did we?"

"Well, I certainly didn't."

"Superintendent Havers?" Ogilvy called from behind his desk. "I think you should see this, sir." He pointed to his computer screen.

Havers rushed to the desk, and Jones followed a little more sedately.

"I took the liberty of searching the news feeds, sir," Ogilvy said, being ever so ingratiating.

He angled the screen towards Havers and Jones. The tickertape notice running along the bottom of the Sky News bulletin read:

BREAKING NEWS: Birmingham cop murdered! Hacked to pieces with a knife. West Midlands Police call press conference for two o'clock this afternoon.

"FOR PITY'S SAKE. Who's responsible for that?" Havers demanded, almost shouting.

"Not me." Ogilvy shrugged and glanced at Jones. His wince could have been mistaken for a mischievous smile.

Havers dragged a mobile from his jacket pocket and dialled a number, but no one answered the call.

"Where's the press officer when you need her?"

"Where indeed?" Jones answered what he imagined was, in fact, a rhetorical question. "She wouldn't call a press conference off her own bat. There are rules in place. Sir, might I have a word?"

Jones moved away, fighting the desire to drag Havers away from the desk by his arm.

"Someone's set this up," Jones whispered, fully aware of Ogilvy's tendency to earwig. "It has to be Jarman."

"What?" Havers gasped. "I mean, what makes you think that?"

"Who else would it be? Jarman's a serial murderer who thinks he's a film director. He's been directing this whole thing from the start."

"Dear Lord."

"Maybe he's angry at the lack of recognition. He might want the world to know what he's doing."

"Ah, yes." Havers placed a finger to his lips and paused for a moment's thought. "It's well known that some serial murderers actually enjoy their celebrity status. Many delight in the media attention. Do you think Jarman's the same?"

"Wouldn't surprise me, sir."

Havers nodded. "Makes sense though. There were months between the first few killings, but he's stepped up the pace recently. He's clearly developed a taste for it, and now he wants the world to know what he's doing. He wants to spread terror. Bloody hell."

"I'd like to know how he did it."

"What do you mean?"

"A random civilian can't just ring Sky or the BBC and call a police conference. There are protocols in place. At the very least, the researchers would call back to confirm it wasn't a hoax. And look outside"—Jones pointed to the car park—"there are dozens of reporters from different outlets. To arrange this so quickly, he'll have had to promise them a real scoop."

"Good Lord, What am I going to do?"

"You could tell them it's a hoax and they can all bugger off, I suppose."

"Wouldn't that make us appear like idiots? And wouldn't it increase press speculation?"

A very good point.

"And it might provoke Jarman into even more radical action."

"Indeed." Havers nibbled on a manicured fingernail. "I think someone should face them, don't you?"

"Not my decision, sir."

That's it, Jones. Pass the buck.

Havers tugged the creases from his uniform jacket. "I'm really not looking forward to this, Jones. I'm usually better prepared when I face the media. It's starting to look like a rugby scrum out there. Any advice?"

"I'd play it with a straight bat, and tell them nothing important."

"Right. Okay. Will you face them with me?"

No bloody chance.

"Don't think that's a good idea, sir. Do you?"

"No, of course not, what was I thinking?"

Jones peered through the windows and the hot flush of anger rose again. What the hell had Jarman told them? What did the media expect to hear?

"I'm sure you'll be fine without me, sir."

Havers ran his fingers through his hair.

"Darn it, I don't have my hat."

"You look fine, sir. Imposing."

"I do?"

"Yes, sir. Definitely."

Havers stood taller, took a breath to collect himself, and strode out to brave the massed ranks of the Fourth Estate. The barrage of questions started before he reached the hastily erected bank of microphones.

"What can you tell us about the Orchard Park Butcher?"

"Do you have any suspects?"

"Did Detective Constable Washington fall or was he pushed?"

"Are the cases linked?"

"Is this drug related?"

"How did DS Pelham die? Why are you keeping the details from us?"

"Knife crime on the OTT is out of control. Is the OTT a no-go area for the police?"

The final question came from a woman Jones recognised from the BBC local news.

Thankfully, none of the questions included the phrase, "Serial Killer".

Jones relaxed a little. Maybe the full extent of the case remained between the police and Jarman.

"COME IN, JONES. COME IN," Havers called in answer to Jones' knock.

"You wanted to see me, sir?"

"Yes indeed. Please, sit."

Jones lowered himself into the visitor's chair opposite Havers, who seemed pleased with his performance in front of the press.

"Went rather well, don't you think, Jones?"

"Sorry, sir. I only saw the start."

"Really?" Disappointment showed on the impossibly youthful face.

Jones stared at the Super. How he'd love to play a few hands of poker with the man.

"Afraid so, sir. Jerry Scranton and his oppo arrived while you were making your opening statement. Which was very good, by the way. Professional and polished, I thought."

No harm buttering up the youngster. It might help in the longer term.

If his relieved smile was anything to go by, Havers seemed to appreciate Jones' praise.

"At least none of them asked about the Sandwell Valley murder. It seems that Jarman or Smithee, or whatever he prefers to call himself, didn't want that getting out. How did it go with DI Scranton?"

"As well as can be expected."

"Have they made any progress?"

"Not really. They're still searching the country park for evidence and interviewing hikers. They've made the usual appeals for information. I told them to finish the ground search and send anything they find to the lab and copy any witness statements directly to me. I informed them about Professor Llewellyn's 3D thing and promised to bring them in on the wider investigation the moment I could."

"Seems like a good way of keeping them onside, Jones."

I thought so.

"Changing the subject, sir. Did you find out who called the press conference?"

Havers dropped his smile and turned it into a frown.

"That's just it, Jones. The notification came directly from our inhouse press feed. It had all the correct assignment codes, too. There was a follow-up confirmatory email from the press officer herself."

"What does Ronnie say about it?"

"Ronnie?"

"Veronica Poole, the press officer. We call her Ronnie."

"Ah, I didn't know her nickname."

And why would you?

Havers continued. "It turns out she's on emergency leave and has been for over a week. Her mother took ill suddenly. Serious chest pains. Ms Poole had to return to the family home. Her deputy, Richard Connors, assures me that he didn't call the press conference. He also claims not to have access to Ms Poole's personal email account."

Jones gritted his teeth. "Must have been Jarman. How did he get into our system?"

Havers leaned forwards and steepled his fingers, his signature move when about to deliver an important point. "No firewall is completely impenetrable, Jones. Given the time and the correct motivation, any talented hacker would be able to break through ours. And the hardware we found in the flat Number 503 shows us Jarman's capabilities on that front."

"Why not contact us directly and force us to make a public announcement. Why do it through Ronnie's email account?"

"You're asking me to guess what's going on in the mind of a serial killer, Jones. I can't possibly fathom—"

It struck Jones in a blinding flash.

Ronnie Poole. Swimming pool.

"Oh God. No!"

He jumped to his feet, plucked the mobile from his jacket, and dialled Phil's number.

"What's that, Jones?" Havers stood and planted both fists on the desk. "You've thought of something?"

"Boss?" Phil said, answering the call on the third ring.

"Where are you?"

"In my office. Just finished talking to Professor Llewell—"

"Do you know Ronnie Poole's home address?"

"Yes, it's—"

"Meet me in the car park right away. Bring Ben with you, but not Alex."

Ben would come in handy if they needed to smash through any heavy doors.

Jones ended the call.

Havers left the protection of his desk and stepped into the centre of the room. "Jones. Explain yourself."

"Ronnie Poole," Jones said, heading for the door. "*Sunset Boulevard*. She's the body in the swimming pool!"

"Oh dear God. I'm coming with you."

Chapter Thirty-Four

THURSDAY 18TH MAY – Evening

City Centre, Birmingham, UK

SHIVERING AND DEFLATED, Jones re-entered the hall outside Ronnie's home—an expensive top-floor apartment in a city centre block a million miles away from the OTT. He had to pick his way through the door that had taken Ben two powerful shoulder charges to crash through. Jones leaned against one of the magnolia-coloured walls and closed his eyes. Slowly, by feel alone, he peeled off the crime scene gloves and removed the paper overshoes.

"Well?" Havers demanded.

He'd evidently been pacing the landing while Jones and Phil entered the apartment, calling out to Ronnie the whole time.

"Did you find her?" Havers added.

The man obviously couldn't read body language. Maybe he should enrol on another bloody course. A course that explained human behaviour.

Bloody useless individual.

"She's in the bath."

"Dead?"

"Of course she's bloody dead! You didn't hear her scream when we burst in on her, did you?"

Havers straightened. "Chief Inspector, there's no need to take that tone with me!"

Jones held up a hand in apology and scrubbed his face, trying to wipe away the image of Ronnie Poole in the bath with a carving knife driven through the centre of her chest. At least Jarman had left her fully clothed, protecting her dignity even as he'd ended her too-short life. What was she, thirty-four, thirty-five?

God help us.

"I've known Ronnie Poole for years. Give me a moment, will you ... sir?"

"Very well," Havers said, having the good grace to look upset with himself. "I'm sorry for your loss, Jones."

"Thank you, sir."

At least the man remembered the module in the police handbook on how to deal with victims of loss.

"Bastard," Phil muttered. "The fucking evil bastard." He turned to Jones. "Why the hell?"

"When we find the bugger, we'll make sure to ask him," Jones muttered, half to himself.

"He's taunting us. Killing people in the service," Havers said. "Making it personal."

"But how does the cyclist, Sandy, fit in with that theory?" Phil asked.

By way of an answer, Havers raised his eyebrows and sighed.

"This idle speculation doesn't get us any closer to finding the bugger," Jones said.

"How long, do you think?" Havers asked, directing the question at both Jones and Phil.

"Rigor's long past. Same as Charlie," Phil said. "She's been gone at least thirty-six hours. But the aircon's running full blast.

Bloody freezing in there. Might be difficult to determine an accurate time of death."

Jones ran a hand over his stubble. Should he grow a beard? It would make his life easier. Hell, what was he thinking with Ronnie lying dead and cold in her own bath? He hugged some warmth back into himself.

"Longer," Jones said. "Judging by the decomp, I'd put it at a week. Lividity suggests she died in the bath where we found her, but the ME will confirm it. Phil, can you call Tim Scobie?"

Phil nodded, pulled out his mobile, and turned away to make the call.

"The timeline fits with the posters," Havers said. "*Sunset Boulevard.*"

Jones looked up at Havers and nodded. "Ronnie died to make a point."

"What point?"

Jones allowed his shoulders to sag. He couldn't muster the strength to pull them back. "He's telling us no one's safe, and he can do what the hell he likes. Hell, the bugger can tap into the police IT systems and ... Oh, I don't know."

Blue flashing lights through the south-facing window announced the arrival of the uniformed support and hopefully, the FSIs.

"Ben," Jones said, "help the uniforms set up a perimeter and organise the initial canvass."

Ben nodded and took the stairs, ignoring the lift. A man after Jones' own heart.

Phil lowered his mobile and turned his back to the sunny window.

"The prof's on his way in, boss. Won't be long."

"Thanks," Jones said, finally warming up enough to stop shivering. "Can you find out if that's of any use?" He pointed to the CCTV camera on the ceiling above the lift doors. "It'll have a perfect view of Ronnie's front door. Any luck, they'll retain the recordings longer than a few days."

Phil started dialling again.

"You can't possibly know who operates the surveillance in these apartments, can you?" Havers asked Phil, but glanced at Jones.

"Didn't you see the notice in the lobby and the other one in the hall inside Ronnie's apartment, sir?" Phil asked, then held up a finger as the call connected. "Hello? Hockley Security Systems? ... Good, I'm Detective Inspector Cryer, West Midlands Police. I understand you operate the security systems for the Crystal Villa Apartments on Clement Rise? ... Ah, excellent. I wonder if you can help me ..." Once again, Phil turned to face the window to continue his call.

"What notices?" Havers asked, lowering his voice.

"The ones telling the residents who to contact in case of an emergency. I read it, but darned if I can tell you the phone number. I'd have to enter the flat and risk contaminating the crime scene further. Either that, or traipse all the way downstairs to the lobby."

"But DI Cryer read the notice once and remembered the number? That's incredible."

Certainly is.

"Won't do us any good though," Jones said, fighting the anger and despair that had settled over him since finding Ronnie's corpse. She didn't deserve to die so young and in such a manner. No one did.

"What do you mean?"

"Jarman's too smart to let himself be caught on camera. He'll have messed with the feed or destroyed the recordings somehow. DI Cryer knows it, too. He's just following standard operating procedure."

"Thank you, Mr Ventnor," Phil said, turning to face them, his expression grim. "Ring me on this number if you have any luck."

He ended the call and dropped the mobile back into his pocket.

"Don't tell me," Jones said, "there's a gap in their recordings. And it's never happened before?"

Phil up-nodded. "How did you guess?"

"Didn't you know? I'm clairvoyant."

"Claire who?"

Jones waved away the pun.

"What did Hockley Security Systems have to say for themselves?"

Phil pinched his lips together. "They had a nationwide computer glitch last week. Lost all their recordings from midnight on Sunday through to one o'clock Tuesday morning, that's between the 8th to the 9th of May. Their computer department can't find a cause, and they're still trying to retrieve the missing data. They'll call us if they manage to do so, but—"

"Don't hold our breath?"

"Exactly."

Jones glanced at Havers but held off saying, "Told you so."

"There's your window of opportunity," Havers said, stating the blindingly obvious yet again.

"When did Ronnie call in sick?" Jones asked Phil.

"The evening of Monday the 8th."

"How did she do that, by the way? Email or phone?" Jones asked.

"Email."

"Of course she did. And didn't HR confirm her absence with a phone call?"

"Not with Ronnie, boss. She lived for the job. Never took a day's sick leave since joining us. And anyway, we're allowed five days' self-certification nowadays, didn't you know?"

"Of course I know. Why didn't HR call to check up on her last Monday, when her time was up?"

Phil lifted a shoulder. "The day after we found Charlie's body? I imagine they had their hands pretty full."

Jones turned his head to stare through the window. The setting sun had started throwing long shadows.

"Jarman's been a busy boy," he muttered to himself.

"What was that, Chief Inspector?"

Havers might not have been the brightest spark in terms of detection, but Jones couldn't fault his hearing.

"DI Scranton received the autopsy on Sandy—the cyclist from Sandwell Valley Country Park—yesterday. His team hasn't scanned it into the system yet. They didn't have time."

"What about it?" Havers asked.

"It estimates Sandy's time of death as the weekend of the 6th and 7th. The ME can't narrow it down any further. The lab is waiting for results from the entomologist."

"Bloody hell," Phil said. "Jarman killed Sandy on the 6th or the 7th, Ronnie on the 8th, and Charlie on or around the 11th. And he had a go at Wash on the 17th. The bugger *has* been busy."

"What's pushing his buttons?" Jones asked.

"Maybe he's developed a taste for killing," Phil offered.

"He killed Armin De Silva way back in March."

"March 14th," Phil added, ever the details man.

Jones nodded. "Right, March 14th. So what's happened between then and now to light his fire?"

Phil rubbed the back of his neck. "We still haven't found a murder for the *Easy Rider* poster—"

"Which was probably the first killing," Havers suggested.

"As far as we know," Jones said, unable to push away the mounting gloom.

"And we still haven't identified Sandy," Phil said.

"Right, and that might hold the key."

"In what way?" Havers asked.

God alive, we've already been through this. What's wrong with you?

Jones stared through the window at the blue flashing lights. The uniforms should have turned them off by now.

"We know who all the other victims are," he said, almost to himself. "Jarman made the anonymous call to point us to Charlie, and he left the tattoo intact to ease the identification. He made sure we could identify everyone but Sandy. Why?"

"Makes tomorrow's meeting with Professor Llewellyn even more important, eh?" Phil said, his jaw stiff.

"Ah, excellent," Havers said. "I'll clear my calendar and join you."

"Wonderful, sir," Jones said, unable to match Havers' excited smile—or Phil's wicked grin.

A call from below and footsteps on the staircase announced Ben's return. Jones met him at the half-landing between floors.

Havers crowded in behind, but Phil stayed in the top floor hallway, knowing better than to leave a crime scene unattended.

"Sir," Ben said, "you need to come and see this."

He turned and retraced his steps. Jones and Havers followed.

"What did you find?" Jones asked.

"Mr Nugent on the ground floor—the chap who let us in, sir. Turns out he's an agoraphobic. Hasn't left his flat in years."

"And?" Havers asked, pushing close to Jones.

Too damned close.

He almost breathed down Jones' neck. Jones stiffened and hiked his shoulders.

"Although he doesn't leave his apartment, he likes to know what's going on outside. He's fixed private surveillance cameras to every window in his flat and on his door entry system. He might have caught a shot of the killer. He's running through the footage now."

They reached the ground floor in a hurry, bunched up. Ben held up a hand.

"Sorry, sir," he said to Havers. "Mr Nugent's a real nervous type. Took me ages to persuade him to let me into his flat. He doesn't like crowds."

Who does?

Jones glanced at Havers. "Mind if I take this, sir?"

"Be my guest, Chief Inspector. I'll check what's happening outside. I'll also inform the Chief Constable. He'll need to know about Ms Poole. God what an unholy mess."

Not much fun for Ronnie, either.

"Thank you, sir."

Havers headed for the exit, head lowered. He stopped at the double doors to tug at his jacket, before pressing the unlock button and pushing through the doors.

Using his mobile, Jones called Phil, who answered instantly.

"Yes, boss?"

"Find out an ETA for the SOCOs, will you? And give the hospital a call. I want to know what's happening with Ryan."

"Right on it, boss."

"Meanwhile, I'll send a uniform up to guard the crime scene."

Jones ended the call and nodded to Ben, who pressed the intercom button on Nugent's front door.

"Mr Nugent, it's me, Detective Constable Adeoye."

The front door opened a crack to reveal half a face. Pale skin, long light brown hair, and one pale blue eye. "I can see it's you, Constable. That's the whole point of the video entrance system. Who's that?" A long index finger poked through the gap, nail trimmed short, and aimed at Jones like a gun.

Jones fished his ID from his pocket and held it up to the single eye.

"DCI Jones, sir. May I come in?"

The eye scrutinised the warrant card for ages, reading every word, and then compared Jones' face with the image.

The door closed, a chain rattled, and the door opened again, this time wide enough for Jones to see the whole of the thin face, including both eyes. A handsome, if gaunt face in desperate need of some sunshine.

"Please wipe your feet," Nugent said and backed into the hallway. "Only you, Mr Jones. Please stay outside, Constable Adeoye."

Jones wiped his feet on the unwelcome mat sunk into the floor on the other side of the doorway and followed his host into a pristine, open plan apartment. Pure white walls glared back at him. Even the windows were made opaque with a pale white film. Nothing out of place, and very little personality. It looked like the inside of an empty white cube.

Jones liked things neat and tidy, but Nugent's home took minimalism to a whole new level.

Nugent crossed the quartz-tiled floor and pressed a hand into the wall. A door-sized panel opened outwards, and the slim man entered what turned out to be his viewing gallery. He summoned Jones inside but didn't offer him a seat. With only one chair in the room—positioned in front of a bank of TV screens—he didn't have a spare to offer.

"I'm not a voyeur, Mr Jones," Nugent said, lowering himself into a chair that wouldn't have looked out of place in a Bond film, or on the bridge of a battleship, "this is how I earn my living."

He pressed a button on the arm of his captain's chair. A tray with a built-in keyboard slid out from one arm and joined the other to form a table.

"If you don't mind my asking, what do you do?"

Nugent swivelled the chair to face Jones. Disappointingly, he used his feet, not an electric motor.

"I am a 'social media influencer', Mr Jones. Do you know what that is?" he asked, making it clear that he considered Jones too old to understand the concept.

"Vaguely, Mr Nugent. Companies pay you to flog stuff on the internet."

Nugent frowned briefly, then laughed.

"Actually, in a nutshell, you're bang on. Would you like to know what I'll be 'flogging' next week?"

Not really. I'm hunting a serial murderer.

"Surprise me, Mr Nugent," Jones answered, showing interest to humour the man.

"Would you believe, tickets on the first private space flights?" He laughed again. "And me a confirmed agoraphobic."

"The world's a strange place, sir." Jones made sure Nugent saw him check the time on his watch.

"Okay, Mr Jones. I take your point. What timeframe are you looking for?"

He gave Nugent the dates of the Hockley Security Systems' outage.

"What dates did you say? 7th to the 9th, yes?"

"Actually, we've narrowed the time of interest to Monday 8th, sir?"

Nugent nodded. "Reckon I can definitely help you there, my man." He swivelled the chair to face front and started tapping on his keyboard, his fingers a blur. The largest screen in the centre of the cluster powered up and showed the small square outside the front of the apartment block, currently filled with police vehicles and uniformed police officers. Havers stood to one side speaking into his mobile, back straight, almost standing to attention. No doubt reporting to the Chief.

"I remembered this, because Ms Poole rarely had visitors and never accepted courier deliveries at night."

The picture changed to a night-time scene with the square lit by orange streetlights. The timestamp running along the top right of the recording confirmed the date and time as 21:03:57, Monday the 8th of May. After a few seconds, a large motorbike, headlights glaring, pulled up outside the front. The biker kicked out the side stand and dismounted. Tall and slim, clad head to toe in black leathers and wearing a black full-face helmet with a darkened visor, the biker strode straight up to the front doors as though he knew exactly where he was heading.

"Ever seen this chap before or since, Mr Nugent?"

"Nope."

"What made you remember him?"

"Watch."

Nugent hit another series of keys and the view on the screen changed to an overhead and outside shot of the entrance hallway. The biker flipped up his visor, pressed the top button on the panel, and leaned in close to speak. His face remained hidden from shot.

"Can we hear what's being said?"

"No way, Mr Jones. I told you I wasn't a voyeur. I'm not an eavesdropper either."

Pity.

On the screen, the biker pushed open the front door and stepped inside.

"She let him in?"

Nugent nodded.

"Must have. There's no other way those doors could have opened."

"No one else in the block could have released the lock?"

"Uh-uh. Apartment two is empty. Has been for months now, and the Al-Jabbars in apartment three are in Jordan visiting family. Don't look so surprised, Mr Jones. I might not go outside these days, but I am quite sociable within the confines of this building. The neighbours are always dropping in for a coffee. Even poor Ronnie. What's happened to her exactly?"

"How long did the biker stay inside?"

"About an hour, maybe a little longer. Would you like to see more?"

Jones nodded. "Yes please."

More quickfire typing delivered another camera angle, this one from Nugent's front door camera. It showed the biker enter the building and turn sharp right heading for the staircase. A flash of white lettering on the front of the leather jacket caught Jones' eye.

"There," Jones said, pointing at the screen. "Can you stop and rewind it?"

"Of course."

Nugent worked the keyboard again and the image reversed in slow motion. The biker turned to face the camera.

"Back. A little more. There, stop!"

The white lettering became clear. A single word, *TRIUMPH*. The lower arm of the "R" extended in a curve and formed the central bar of the "H".

"A 'eureka' moment, Chief Inspector?" Nugent asked, expression hopeful.

"Afraid not. Just a bike manufacturer's logo. I was hoping for something like a courier's name. He stayed an hour, you say?"

"About that. Here he is again."

The next few minutes of screen time, seventy-three minutes later, closely followed the first, only in reverse. At no stage did the biker remove his helmet or look directly at any of the cameras in the block. Once outside, he strode along the path and climbed onto the bike, a Triumph Bonneville according to Nugent, who admitted to having been a bike enthusiast in his misspent youth. Considering Nugent couldn't have been much more than Ronnie's age, Jones wondered how long ago the misspent youth could have been, and how long it could have lasted.

Nugent stopped the replay when the bike disappeared from the screen.

"Weren't you worried when Ms Poole didn't leave for work the next morning? Or when you didn't see her for over a week?"

Nugent swivelled away from the viewing wall and faced him again. An embarrassed wince crossed his face.

"That Tuesday, the 9th, I had an … episode, Mr Jones. Some people call them panic attacks, only mine are worse. Much worse. I couldn't force myself out of bed all morning. So bad, I had to call my counsellor. We had a full hour's therapy session via video. We did, honest." Nugent started panting and flattened a hand to his chest. "You can call her if you like. Anna McDermott, from the Chapel Road Practice in Edgbaston. She'll confirm it. Really, she will."

Jones stretched out a hand. "Easy, Mr Nugent. Nobody's accusing you of anything. I know all about panic attacks."

"You do?"

"Yes, sir."

Personally.

The man's breathing slowed and his skin tone returned to its normal shade—a pallid and sickly grey.

"Sorry, Mr Jones. This is all very worrying. Poor Ronnie. He killed her, didn't he? The motorcyclist killed her. Why else would a Chief Inspector be interrogating me?" His lower lip trembled.

"Mr Nugent, this is a witness interview. You're helping us, that's all. You're not under any suspicion. However, this is an ongoing police investigation and I would like you to keep all this information to yourself."

"Of course." He blinked tight, squeezing tears from his eyes. "Who am I going to tell?"

Your counsellor? Your social media followers?

"Mr Nugent, I'm sorry to press you on this, but why weren't you worried when you didn't see Ms Poole after the biker's visit?"

Nugent swiped away the tears with his fingertips.

"Didn't I say?" He shook his head, clearing the cobwebs. "She sent me an email telling me she was going to visit her mother for a week or two. Funny though."

"In what way?"

"She'd never mentioned her mother before. I always had the idea that she'd passed away a long time ago."

"Thanks for all your help, Mr Nugent. Could you forward that email to me and all the film you have of the biker."

"Film, Mr Jones? It's not film," Nugent said, breathing deeply and returning to his former techie self. "This is the digital age, you know? I can send you the MP4 file. That's MPEG-4, Part 14—a digital multimedia container format commonly used to store video and audio—"

"Thank you, Mr Nugent. You sound like my Inspector. If you'd send me the email and the ... MP4 file, I'd appreciate it. Our data forensics staff might be able to enhance the images."

"Of course, Mr Jones. I'll do that right away."

Jones pulled a card from his wallet and handed it across. Nugent pinched the card between finger and thumb and placed it carefully on the left arm of his chair, lining it up with the chair's leading edge. He retracted the bridge and climbed to his bare feet.

"I'll show you out."

He rushed through the main room—almost running—and into the hallway and, without actually touching him, practically pushed Jones through the front door.

Nugent slammed the door on Jones', "We really do appreciate all your help, Mr Nugent."

Phil stood in the hallway, waiting.

"That was a bit rude," he said, looking at Nugent's front door, which might still have been vibrating from the slam.

"Go easy on him, Phil. He has his demons."

Jones shuddered.

There but for the grace of God ....

"What do you have for me?"

"Tim Scobie's deputy has been and gone."

"Already?"

"Yep. She was passing by on her way home. Confirmed death and gave the provisional cause as 'sharp force trauma to the chest'."

"*Quelle surprise.*"

"Didn't know you spoke Spanish, boss." Phil stretched out a small grin.

"Ha, ha."

"Anyway, she wouldn't hazard a guess as to time of death, but we've already narrowed it down to—"

"Between nine and ten fifteen on the evening of Monday the 8th," Jones announced with a slight head bow.

"Blimey, that's precise enough."

Jones told Phil what he'd learned from the housebound Nugent, and asked him to confirm the man's medical condition—and his alibi for the day after Ronnie's death—with his counsellor as soon as possible.

"A bloke on a Triumph?" Phil said, squeezing his eyes part closed as though in pain. "Doesn't narrow it down much, eh?"

"Not to Jarman's identity, but we've reduced the time of death to a sixty-minute window. What more do you want?"

"Jarman's photo—"

"It's on the MP4 file heading to my email address," Jones interrupted, without apology.

"—and his address and current location," Phil added, raising an eyebrow.

"That, I can't help with. The coroner's body-snatchers?"

"Unable to collect her for at least three hours."

Jones clicked his teeth. "Hasn't she been up there long enough?"

"She'd probably prefer the bath to where she's going next, boss."

The autopsy table.

Jones shuddered. This time, it had nothing to do with the temperature.

"Good point, Philip. And the SOCOs? Sorry, I mean the 'FSIs'?"

He really did have to keep up with the times.

"Be here in five minutes. Afraid it's the second or third stringers. The first team—and Robyn—are off shift." He dropped the raised eyebrow and exchanged it for a wink.

Jones groaned internally.

"Will you ever let that go?"

KERRY J DONOVAN

"Not until it gets old, boss." He rubbed his hands together. "Five, maybe ten years?"

"What about the hospital?"

Phil dropped his stupid grin.

"No change, I'm afraid. They're still keeping Wash under."

"I'll pop in on my way home. See if Bryn and Jackie need anything."

"Meanwhile?"

Jones sucked in a deep breath and let it out in a long sigh.

"Meanwhile, you head off home. I'll stay until the 'second stringers' arrive. No point hanging around until afterwards, though. They'll be here hours. You and I can search the apartment in the morning."

"Sorry, boss. That won't work. We're due at the university tomorrow morning. Nine o'clock sharp."

"We are? Ah yes, Professor Llewellyn and his 3D magic. Almost forgot. Can we push that back until the afternoon?"

"Afraid not," Phil answered, shaking his head. "He's lecturing all afternoon, and his next free slot isn't until Monday morning. Academics don't do weekends—not unless they're under contract, which he isn't. At least not yet." Another small smile.

"Monday? We can't wait that long. We need to give Sandy a face. It could hold the key."

Phil held up an index finger. "Why don't I wait here for the SOCOs so you can head straight to the hospital. If we get access to Ronnie's flat before, say, eight o'clock this evening, I'll call you back and we can have a rummage around tonight. If not, I'll get here first thing in the morning and search the place with Ben. Sound good?"

"And leave me to interview the professor alone?"

"Not alone, boss," Phil said, smiling again. "You'll have Not-Bob for company, remember?"

Jones groaned aloud. This time, he didn't mind Phil hearing it.

"A morning with a wide-eyed technophile and a nutty professor? That's all I need."

"Look on the bright side, boss."

"What bright side?"

"While Not-Bob's soaking up all the techie details, you might have a chance to slope off and schmoose Dr Craig."

"Dr Craig?" Jones frowned.

"Yep, Andrew Craig." Phil nodded. "The bloke with all those handy and court-certified DNA blood analysers."

"Ah, *that* Andrew Craig."

Jones smiled. Maybe there was a bright side after all.

Chapter Thirty-Five

FRIDAY 19TH MAY – Morning

University of Birmingham, Edgbaston, Birmingham, UK

AT 08:47, Jones and Havers showed their warrant cards to a grey-haired jobsworth at the university's main security barrier and waited ten minutes for the blithering idiot to confirm their appointment.

Jones parked his Škoda in a visitor's spot seven minutes' fast march from the University's Human Biological Sciences building—a structure that defied architectural classification. Red brick and crenelated towers on the outside, and linoleum floors, steel and glass staircases, and chrome everywhere inside, it looked like an elderly person with a very bad facelift.

The Human Biological Sciences receptionist, a cheerful, bubble-haired youngster pointed to a corridor and gave them directions.

She finished with, "If you lose your way, follow the signs to the CRL, the Cranial Research Laboratory." She smiled brightly at Havers and all but ignored Jones. Havers smiled back. Jones didn't.

Lit by rows of power-hungry fluorescent tubes, the corridor seemed to stretch out forever. Their footsteps, amplified by glass-fronted display cases lining the spaces between the doors, bounced off the walls and echoed around them. The cases housed an eclectic mixture of articles and artefacts, ranging from human bones to odd-looking mechanical devices. It reminded Jones of his most recent visit to the Natural History Museum—way back in the '80s.

"Place smells like a cross between a library and a hospital."

"You never went to college, did you, Jones?"

Jones craned his head to gauge the Super's expression, not condescending but matter-of-fact. "Not many of us did in the '70s, sir. I joined before 'fast-tracking'. Back then, the brass didn't value academic qualifications as much as they do now. Practical experience won over book-learning."

"Unlike like me, you mean?" Havers said, still smiling.

"Times change."

Jones pointed to a sign hanging from wires above their heads, directing them left down another long corridor. "There you go, the 'Cranial Research Lab'."

They made the turn and carried on walking.

"You went to university, sir. Perhaps you can answer a question for me?"

"Happy to, Jones. Fire away."

"Where are all the students? This place is a mausoleum."

"Ah, yes. These days, a great deal of tutoring happens online, not face-to-face. You have lectures, seminars, and practical sessions of course, but much of the sessions are packaged for online access."

"Like the Open University, you mean?"

Havers waggled an open hand. "The OU is a good model, highly egalitarian, but limited. Most of the benefits of a university education comes from personal interaction within the student body."

"The parties, you mean?"

A frowning Havers shot Jones a sideways glance and shook his head. "No, Jones. I mean the intellectual stimulation, and the sharing and development of ideas. The atmosphere can be electric."

"Of course, sir."

I'll take your word for it.

Halfway along the second corridor, the contents of a display unit signposted the door they were looking for—it contained academic posters depicting a number of facial reconstructions and damaged skeletal remains. Taking the lead, Havers knocked and they entered a small but brightly lit office.

The right hand wall of floor-to-ceiling glass, allowed views to a small and beautifully manicured courtyard garden. A water feature in the centre of a patch of grass—a medicine-ball sized sphere on a plinth—dribbled a constant flow of water into a trough. Jones could imagine how peaceful it must be to sit out there in the warm sun, listening to the fountain, and playing academic mind games. Perhaps he shouldn't have been so sniffy about university life.

A door in the wall opposite the glass opened, and a large man entered. Jones assumed it to be the academic in question.

If Jones could draw and he'd been asked to produce a sketch of an archetypical university professor, Rhys Llewellyn would have been close to the top of the list of life models he'd have chosen.

A man with a large girth, Llewellyn sported a Father Christmas beard, and had tied his long white hair in a loose ponytail. His crumpled fawn jacket had brown leather patches sewn into the elbows. Llewellyn wore a white t-shirt, denim jeans, and open sandals without socks. Jones had to double-check to make sure he hadn't imagined the sandals. To complete the look, the academic wore a pair of glasses on top of his head as though he needed to read something on the ceiling. Jones flashed his warrant card as the academic approached.

"Ah, Chief Inspector Jones," he said, holding out his hand, "I've been expecting you. Welcome."

Despite the Welsh name, Llewellyn spoke with a slight Midlands twang.

They shook hands.

Llewellyn turned and offered his hand to Havers. "You must be Inspector Cryer. I've been looking forward to meeting you after our telephone chats."

"My name's Havers, Professor. Superintendent Havers. I've been looking forward to meeting you and learning more about your work."

Llewellyn stepped back.

"My, my," he said, "a Superintendent and a Chief Inspector. This is a very high level delegation. I *am* honoured."

The door Llewellyn used opened again to reveal a slim young man in a white lab coat. A smile barely creased his face when he dipped his head to acknowledge their presence. "Can I have a quick word please, Professor?" He spoke quietly, his voice soft and delicate.

"Excuse me, gentlemen. I won't be but a second." Llewellyn disappeared through the door, but left it ajar and returned moments later. "The presentation is ready. If you would come through to the lab, we can begin."

They entered and stood at the base of one arm of a large L-shaped room, each arm about the same width, but twice as long as a squash court. Strip lighting, in multiple paired rows, threw a harsh white light into the laboratory. The glass inner walls of the "L", like the outer office, overlooked the patio garden. Bright sun augmented the glare from the artificial illumination.

The left-hand wall groaned with shelving sagging under the weight of books and periodicals. Jones had seen less well-stocked libraries. The bookshelves must have been at least fifteen metres wide and three tall, with hardly a gap in sight. Half way along the wall, a reading desk and chair stood below one of the half-dozen skylights. The desk's surface lay hidden beneath a huge computer screen, a keyboard, and piles of reading material.

They followed the professor into the other arm of the "L", less cluttered than its twin, but just as brightly lit. It contained work-benches, rack after rack of computer equipment, and half a dozen glass-boxed machines Jones didn't recognise. On the far wall, a whiteboard, twice the size of the one in the SCU briefing room, displayed a computer window.

"When you're ready, Kurt," Llewellyn said and pointed them towards the whiteboard.

An image in the window slowly rotated clockwise—the familiar multi-coloured double helix of a strand of DNA.

Slowly, the single strand of DNA divided and grew into a mesh cubic matrix, constructed from more and more strands of DNA. They transformed from a cube into the stylised outline of a human skull. The matrix skull then appeared to "grow" human tissue—bones, muscles, skin, eyes, hair, and teeth. Increasing speed, the image changed from pale white to colour, added skin tone and shadow, and finally, changed from male to female. Jones stood transfixed as, in a final act of bravura, the face on screen smiled and winked at him.

Llewellyn laughed and clapped Jones on the shoulder. "This little demo often impresses our guests. It demonstrates how a single strand of DNA forms the fundamental building block of every human being." The professor beckoned them to follow him to a desk in the far corner. "Please take a seat, gentlemen, and I'll begin."

Chapter Thirty-Six

University of Birmingham, Edgbaston, Birmingham, UK

"INSPECTOR CRYER TOLD me you're having trouble identifying the body of a man in his middle thirties," Llewellyn said.

"We considered mortuary art but ruled that out," Jones said. "The face was too badly damaged."

"I see," Llewellyn said, nodding amiably. "Do you have any photos, scans, or x-rays of the unfortunate man's head?"

Havers held up a memory stick. "This is an encrypted USB. Have you a secure system I can access?"

"Certainly, Superintendent. We have a standalone computer loaded with government-level security. As you know, our work is part-funded by the Home Office, as is the work of our colleagues next door." He waved a hand in the general direction of the glass wall. "You and Kurt can work at that station." He pointed to his assistant who sat in front of the large computer monitor with his back to them. Wires from a pair of earbuds trailed down his back and disappeared into the pocket of his lab coat.

Llewellyn crossed the gap and tapped Kurt on the shoulder. The slim man jumped and spun his seat around to face the group. He removed the earbuds and the tinny sound of driving music hissed until he slid the buds into his coat pocket.

"Kurt, would you mind helping the superintendent with these files, please?"

Without speaking, Kurt reached for the memory stick and swivelled his chair back around again. Havers wheeled a chair to Kurt's station, and Jones returned his attention to the professor. "You mentioned your colleagues next door, Professor."

"Hmmm?"

"One of them wouldn't be a Dr Andrew Craig, by any chance?"

The professor nodded and beamed. "Young Andrew? It most certainly is. Why?"

"I understand his work deals with violent offenders."

A light shone behind the professor's dark brown eyes. "Quite so. He's made a real breakthrough in the field of genetics and aberrant behaviour. I'm surprised your paths haven't crossed before now."

"Really?"

"Oh yes, his research involves interviewing and assessing violent offenders, often beginning at the pre-charging stage. As I understand it, he visits police stations throughout the UK. A few months ago, he finally gained access to the prison population. Dr Craig is one of this university's brightest stars. He's almost as gifted as me." He winked and showed his uneven teeth in a wide grin.

"Would you be able to introduce us after our meeting? I'd love to find out more about his work."

And gain access to his DNA analysers.

"Will do, Chief Inspector, will do. Assuming he's around. Now, shall we return to the matter in hand?"

Llewellyn led them back to his desk, took his seat, and indicated that Jones should use one of the chairs opposite. After he'd settled, the professor clasped his palms together and clamped them between his legs. He leaned forwards and spoke quietly. "How much do you know about our work?"

"Superintendent Havers gave me a briefing on the way here. I think I have a handle on the basics."

Llewellyn's mouth turned down in disappointment, "I was going to tell you about the origins of our project, but I see that isn't necessary. Perhaps we should wait until Kurt has uploaded the images of your man."

Jones nodded and pointed to the screen showing the transforming head. "An impressive display, Professor."

"Thank you. One aspect of our project uses computer algorithms to transform laser-scanned 3D images of skulls into faces. We've found our results to be significantly more accurate than sculpted restorations." Llewellyn turned to face the rotating, winking head. "We've also managed to speed up the process and make it more reliable. Kurt is an absolute genius when it comes to building and programming our test equipment. Since starting with me, he's developed his own version of a virtual reality modelling language. I really couldn't do without him."

Jones scratched an earlobe and turned to look at Havers, who was deep in quiet conversation with Kurt. The two men evidently spoke the same language—geek. Or it could have been Greek.

Llewellyn called to his assistant. "Kurt, are you ready over there?"

"Ready when you are, Professor," he answered, giving a double thumbs up.

Havers stood and rolled his chair to join Jones and Llewellyn at the main desk.

The revolving image on the screen disappeared to be replaced by multiple autopsy images of Sandy's destroyed head. Jones found the grotesque images difficult to stomach, but the others seemed to take them in their stride. Even Havers looked on with keen interest; the academic distance must have anaesthetised him to the horror.

Kurt swivelled his chair to face the screen and placed the keyboard on his lap.

After a minute's deep reflection, Llewellyn began, while Kurt manipulated the position and size of the images depending upon which part of the face and head Llewellyn discussed.

"In the case of your victim, we have more information than the basic skull. For example we know his hair colour and shape of his hairline …"

The image with the best view of Sandy's fair hair expanded to fill the screen.

"…colour of eyes …"

A close-up of Sandy's single intact eye slid over the first photo.

"…and the overall condition of his body."

The body, lying naked on the stainless-steel mortuary table appeared over the second image.

Llewellyn continued without pausing. "We know, for example, your man was lean and well-muscled. So we can be reasonably certain as to the disposition of adipose tissue on his face. We also know his approximate age. These data points will add significant accuracy to our completed model.

"On the negative side, your skull is very badly damaged. So we'll have to create a 3D model of each fragment of the skull and rebuild it like a virtual jigsaw puzzle. We can use any undamaged pieces and flip them to match the bilateral structures that are beyond repair."

Jones interrupted. "Bilateral structures? Sorry, Professor, I'm afraid you've lost me."

A benign smile stretched the professor's beard—a smile that made Jones grind his teeth rather than slap it from the academic's round face. But Llewellyn was simply doing what they'd asked of him—lecturing an ignorant student.

"Well now, Chief Inspector. The human face is largely bilateral in structure. Two eyes, two ears, two cheeks, and so on. What I'm saying is, where we have an intact feature, say part of a *left* cheekbone, we can duplicate and reverse the image to stand in for the missing *right* cheek. Now this doesn't always work, of course—no human face is perfectly symmetrical—but we can use it as a starting point."

"So, the more intact features you can find, the more accurate the reconstruction?"

"Precisely."

Jones studied one particular image—a close-up of Sandy's left cheek. "The post-mortem report said that most of the blows, seventeen in all, landed on the left side of the head and face. "Looking at photo eight"—a right-profile shot, filled the screen—"thank you, Kurt. That's the least damaged area we have. So you might be able to use that and build out from there. Is that right?"

"Exactly so." Llewellyn beamed. "I don't suppose there's any chance of us gaining access to the actual skull, is there?"

Havers answered for Jones. "If necessary, a visit to the mortuary can be arranged, Professor."

Again, Llewellyn clasped his hands together. "Excellent. Really excellent. Direct physical measurements are always more accurate than ones taken from photographs and x-rays. Using them, we'll be able to produce something closely approximate, but I must give you this warning." He paused and raised a finger. "It is important to remember that the actual human face bears only a moderate resemblance to the underlying bone structure. What we do here is inherently inaccurate and certainly couldn't be used as a proof of identification in a court of law."

"We wouldn't expect to use it in court," Jones said.

"Not at all," Havers jumped in, eyes alight with excitement, "we're simply looking for help with the initial identification. Once we know who the unfortunate man is, we'll be able to use other methods to confirm the identity in court."

"DNA, for example," Jones suggested.

Llewellyn beamed.

"Good, good. Because what I'm saying is, facial reconstructions are scientifically informed artistic restorations." The professor punctuated each word with a stab of his half-clenched right hand, a conductor waving a baton. "I prefer to call the resulting model a 'facial approximation'. It's a best-fit effort built from all the data we can garner. Despite our best scientific rigour, we can only provide an interpretation. However, a forensic facial reconstruction will often allow you to rule people *out* of your enquiries. It may also act as an *aide memoir* for potential witnesses if you wish to bring in the media.

"Of course, we will have to prepare the remains of the head before we can make accurate measurements and scans of the bone fragments."

"What sort of preparation?" Jones asked.

Llewellyn pinched his face and sucked in a breath between his teeth before answering.

"That part's a little delicate, Chief Inspector. Do you actually need the … details?"

Jones arched an eyebrow. "The coroner might."

"Ah, yes. It sounds rather baric, but we shall have to … er … boil the head and bone shards in a beaker. Unpleasant, I know, but it really is the only way to clean the … fragments with any degree of success."

"Of course," Jones said, trying to hide his distaste.

"There is one other issue, gentlemen." Llewellyn stopped and dropped his shoulders. He pursed his lips, and the big grey beard folded in on itself.

Havers leaned forwards in his chair. "Which is, Professor?"

Llewellyn's pained smile returned.

"This is rather, er … sensitive, Superintendent. You have to understand, the processes we have discussed here take time, and whereas I am more than happy to volunteer my services gratis, the university would insist that our overheads are covered at the very least." Llewellyn spread his hands, palms up in apology.

Havers nodded slowly, his expression a study in professional gravitas. "I'm sure we can agree to releasing some funds for this, but we'll need to have an idea of what the cost is likely to be."

"Excellent," Llewellyn said. "I think you'll find our costs minimal compared with the private sector."

God save us from the bean counters.

Jones pressed his hands into his knees and stood.

"Sir, if you don't mind," he said, speaking to Havers, "I'll leave you to discuss the details. In the meantime, Professor, would you mind telling me where I might find Dr Craig's office?"

"Simplicity itself, Chief Inspector." Llewellyn turned in his chair and pointed through the picture window. "Do you see that fellow in

300

the courtyard wearing the rather dapper cravat?" Jones projected a line from the tip of the professor's finger to a figure on the far side of the water feature. "That young man is Dr Jeremy Armstrong, Dr Craig's associate and collaborator. Turn left at the outer office where we met. Access to the courtyard is the second door on the left." He paused, before adding, "Oh, and don't take our Jem at face value. He's a brilliant mathematician, but prone to, er … well, let's call it hyperbole, shall we?"

"Thank you, Professor. This"—he waved a hand at the big screen on the wall—"has been most enlightening."

Jones and the professor shook hands and he made a telephone sign to Havers with his thumb and little finger as he headed for the exit door. When he passed Kurt, he paused to thank him, but the slightly built, slim-shouldered young man had replaced his earbuds and turned his back to the room once again.

Chapter Thirty-Seven

FRIDAY 19TH MAY – Morning

University of Birmingham, Edgbaston, Birmingham, UK

SHADING his eyes from the brilliance of the late-morning sun, Jones stepped through the open doorway and out into the courtyard. Protected on all sides, it proved to be a suntrap. Sweat formed under his arms and down the middle of his back. He mopped his brow with a handkerchief and draped the jacket over his arm.

The journey from Professor Llewellyn's lab had taken less than a minute and during that time, he'd been able to study Dr Jeremy Armstrong through the panoramic windows most of the way. The man lit one black cigarette from the butt of another and sucked in the blue-black fug as though worried the next drag would be his last. A heavy textbook rested open on his lap, but he'd thrown back his head and creased his eyes tight shut to absorb the sun's warmth.

"Dr Armstrong?"

The man jumped and squinted as Jones rounded the bubbling

water feature. He shielded his eyes with the hand holding the cigarette.

"Bloody hell, *mun*. You almost gave me an 'eart attack, you did."

Jones flashed his warrant card at the startled academic. "DCI Jones, West Midlands Police. Might I have a word, sir?"

The little man struggled to his feet with the speed and agility of a cold blancmange and deposited his cigarette in a smokers' bin next to the bench. He then threw both hands in the air.

"Don't shoot, Officer," he cried. "I'll come quiet, like."

"Very good, sir. That's a new one."

Unlike Llewellyn, Armstrong had a strong Welsh accent, musical and lilting. It took Jones back nearly forty-five long years.

"Sorry, Chief Inspector, couldn't 'elp mesself. Been dying to say that for years, mun." He pushed out a pudgy hand. "Jeremy Armstrong at your service, but people call me 'Jem'. Not on account of my name, mind. It's 'cause I'm a real jewel, see. What you might call a diamond geezer." He beamed. "Now, 'ow can I assist the West Midlands Police Service?"

"I understand you work with Dr Craig?"

Armstrong stiffened. "Yes, is there anything wrong? What's occurred?"

"Nothing, as far as I'm aware, sir. Why? Are you worried about him?"

"No, not really. It's just that when the police call and start asking after a mate you 'aven't spoke to for the best part of a fortnight, it tends to put the wind up you a little."

"Is Dr Craig missing, sir?" Jones' heartbeat spiked.

"No, not that I know of." Armstrong frowned and shook his head. "Shall we start over, Inspector? What's this all about?"

"When did you last speak to Dr Craig?" Jones felt close to an answer and couldn't let it go.

"Couple of weeks back, before 'e left on sabbatical." He scratched his head and looked to the pale blue sky for inspiration. "Can't remember the exact day. First weekend in May. Thursday? No, Friday evening, I think." He nodded. "Yeah, Friday evening. About, oh, I dunno. Six, six-thirty?"

"Would that be Friday the 6th, sir?"

Armstrong scrunched up his face and nodded.

"Yeah, sounds about right, mun."

Jones jotted the date in his notebook.

"And you've not heard from him since then?"

Armstrong shook his head and shot a lingering glance at the cigarette butt that still smouldered in the tray.

"Is that unusual, sir? Dr Craig dropping off-grid like this?"

"Not at all, mun. Once or twice a year per'aps. Usually 'appens when we're between trials and Andy needs to go off and write 'is reports or schmooze for some research funding, see."

"A sabbatical, you say. Just to write?" Jones couldn't hide his surprise. "I have to write my reports *while* I'm at work."

Armstrong held up a nicotine-stained hand.

"Just 'ang one a minute there, Chief Inspector," he huffed. "Andy's worked non-stop on Phase 2 for the past five months. Works most weekends, too. So, if the bloke needs peace and quiet to write 'is reports, the guy should damn well get it, in my opinion. Right?"

Jones had to give the Welshman credit for defending his colleague and nodded.

"Have you any idea where Dr Craig is at the moment, Dr Armstrong?"

The little Welshman's shoulders twitched in a shrug.

"'Fraid not, mun. When Andy's working from 'ome, 'e often powers down 'is mobile and unplugs the landline. Sometimes goes away to a B&B. One time, couple of years back, 'e rented a cottage for a fortnight." He grinned. "They call it *purdah* if you're the Chancellor of the Exchequer."

"So they're regular occurrences then? His disappearances, I mean."

"No, Inspector. Once or twice a year, not regular at all."

Jones tried not to let his frustrations show in his voice or on his face. "Have you tried contacting him at home recently?"

"No, Inspector. Have you?"

"Dr Armstrong, where is Dr Craig right now?"

"No idea, mun. But there's no need to worry, Andy'll be back Monday, I expect."

Finally, an answer.

"Why, are you looking for 'im, Chief Inspector?"

Jones frowned and tilted his head. "Yes. I wouldn't be asking for him otherwise."

The Welshman paused for a moment and looked confused. "No, no, what I mean to say is, why … do … you … want … to … speak … to … Andy?" Armstrong spoke slowly, as though chatting with a moron.

Jones nearly brained the man. "I understand you analyse blood samples for DNA analysis."

"Yes, Inspector. We're certified and licenced by the Ministry of Justice. We got all the equipment we need to analyse individual samples right 'ere in the lab." He pointed to the windows running parallel to Llewellyn's lab.

Hallelujah!

"Should the need ever arise, would it be possible to use your lab to run DNA samples in an emergency? During times when our labs are swamped?" He held his breath.

Armstrong's eyes narrowed. "Tissue or blood samples?"

"Both."

The Welshman stuck out his lower lip.

"Nah, we can only deal with blood. Don't got the equipment or the need to analyse tissue."

Why ask about skin samples, then?

Jones forced himself to remain calm

"Okay, blood samples only then. But it's possible?"

Another tiny shrug.

"I suppose so, but Andy's the only one who can authorise a test run, and it depends on the availability of the equipment. For court authentication, 'e needs to run the tests personally, you see. Mind you, 'e might 'ave finished his report by now. Would you like me to contact 'im for you?"

Jones closed his eyes and started to count to ten, but only made it to four. "Yes please, Dr Armstrong. Yes please."

He tried to relax his jaw but that didn't work either.

"Why didn't you say so, mun? You only had to ask."

Armstrong reached into his trouser pocket and drew out a mobile and began dialling when Jones' own mobile vibrated. *Not-Bob, Never-Bob* flashed up on the display. He hit the connect button.

"Jones," he said.

"Jones, you need to get back here right now!" Havers' voice screamed in a stage whisper, his excitement barely contained. "I've found him. Jarman, I mean. I found him!"

Jones turned his back on Armstrong and lowered his voice.

"Excuse me, sir?"

"It's Kurt! I'm certain of it," Havers hissed.

Really?

"I'll be right there. Don't do anything 'til I arrive."

He ended the call and turned to face the little Welshman.

"Excuse me, Dr Armstrong." He attempted to keep his voice calm and emotionless, but his heart raced. "I need to pop over to Professor Llewellyn's lab for a moment."

"No bother, mun," Armstrong said, the mobile phone attached to his ear. "Gasping for a fag, me. You take your time."

Jones darted towards the glass door, retraced his steps, and barged through the outer office and into the 3D CFR lab. He beckoned to Havers from the library alcove.

"Exactly what do you have, sir?" He spoke quietly, trying to calm the Super, whose eyes gleamed and opened wide with excitement.

"It's Kurt, Jones," Havers whispered. "Kurt."

"What makes you think—"

"His surname, it's *Lang*."

"Lang?"

"Like the silent-era, German film director, Fritz Lang. It all makes perfect sense—the hand-built computer equipment, the strange way he looked at us when we arrived."

"He might have been nervous, sir. It sometimes happens when people meet police officers."

Havers threw up a hand.

"I know that Jones, but it's him, I tell you. Kurt Lang!"

Llewellyn looked up from his seat near the computer display and nodded a smile.

"Steady, sir. Not so loud. Llewellyn might be part of this. Where's Lang right now?"

"He took off for an 'early lunch' just after you left the lab. Couldn't get away fast enough. I'm going to raise the alarm, get a search started. He might still be on campus!"

"Hold on a moment. Before you do anything, let's think this through."

Havers grabbed Jones' forearm so tight he had to prise the man's fingers loose for fear of losing feeling in his hand.

"Lang *is* Jarman," Havers hissed, white spittle flying and making Jones grimace. "I'm certain of it. Everything fits."

"Steady, sir. Let's take a moment before we close the case and put our feet up."

Jones had been too long in the game, and had seen too many false dawns, to be carried away by the thrill of the chase. He walked across to where Llewellyn sat staring at them from his desk. "Where does Kurt normally eat lunch, Professor?"

"Kurt? Why?"

"Answer the question please."

Llewellyn shot a questioning look at Havers before answering.

"Normally, he munches on a sandwich over there." Llewellyn pointed to one of the empty seats by the wall of books and periodicals. "I can't remember the last time he ate out. He doesn't even visit our tranquil courtyard. Says is gets too hot when the sun shines and too cold when it doesn't. What's this about, Inspector, and what does Fritz Lang have to do with anything?"

Llewellyn undoubtedly heard the Super's outburst.

"A lead we're working on, sir. How long has Kurt worked for you?"

"Um … let me think." Llewellyn frowned and scratched his chin through the beard. "I'd say it's been a little under nine months."

Around the same time Jarman and Smithee rented the flats in

the OTT. Jones and Havers shared a look. Havers recognised the timeline, too.

"How did you end up employing him?"

"He applied for the job through the normal channels. My last assistant left without notice. She always was a bit … flighty." Llewellyn's eyes flickered at the memory. "We advertised for a replacement. I interviewed Kurt with a member of our HR Department. What exactly is the problem, here? Why the sudden interest in my assistant?"

"Did he supply the correct details, references, home address, and bank account?"

"Well, he must have, mustn't he? Otherwise HR wouldn't have called him up for interview. As for the bank account, how else would we be able to pay him?"

"Salary is paid by bank transfer," Jones said, thinking aloud.

"Of course. We're a university, not a backstreet garage. The payroll department doesn't exactly go round on Friday afternoons doling out little brown envelopes stuffed with cash."

"Hmm. Do you have his personal details here in the lab?"

"No. Of course not. You'll have to ask HR for that information." Llewellyn rose from his chair and loomed over Jones. "Really, Chief Inspector, I must insist you tell me why you're asking about Kurt?"

Jones considered having Llewellyn call Lang, but didn't want the technician warned, just in case.

Havers circled behind Llewellyn and surreptitiously searched the desk Kurt had recently vacated.

"Does Kurt drive a car?" Jones asked.

"I have no idea."

"How well do you know him, Professor?"

Llewellyn scratched his beard again, his brow furrowed. It took him a few seconds to reply. "I really can't say. Kurt's not an easy person to get close to. Keeps himself to himself. He's so quiet, I sometimes forget he's here."

"What about outside the lab, sir? Do you ever socialise? Drinks? Meals out with wives or partners? Anything like that?"

"Kurt doesn't drink alcohol. At least, I've never seen him drink any. I've never had a meal out with him and his partner. In fact, I have no idea what his preferences are in that department—boys or girls. Not that it matters, mind you. At least, not to me." He added the last two sentences more quickly than strictly necessary. "I haven't a clue where he lives. How extraordinary!" Llewellyn's left hand reached up and flattened against his breastbone. "We've worked side-by-side for all this time, and I don't even know where he lives."

So far, Lang did fit the loner profile Jones had constructed for Donald Jarman. Judging by equipment in the lab, Lang was certainly skilful enough to build the apparatus they'd recovered from Number 503 and the pencil camera retrieved from the stairwell. He also had a peculiar ability to fade out of view and become invisible; but did he have the strength or the anger to kill with a baseball bat or a Hornet injector knife? A bullet in the chest, possibly, but a baseball bat?

Jones tried to superimpose Kurt Lang into his memory of when Jarman shoulder-charged Ryan into the railings. They were of similar height and build, but could he be sure they were one and the same person?

No, not at all.

"What can you tell us about Lang?"

While Jones asked his questions, Havers continued searching, taking care Llewellyn didn't see him. Jones shifted to the left to turn the professor further away from Lang's desk.

"Not a great deal, Chief Inspector. He's conscientious, brilliant at what he does, hard-working and … quiet. Very quiet. That's about all I can say." Llewellyn's mouth formed an "O" and he clicked his fingers. "Wait a moment. I've just told you a lie, Chief Inspector."

Jones stiffened. Havers stopped rifling through the drawers and lent an ear.

"Professor?"

"I *have* had a meal with Kurt. Of course I have. What was I thinking. He's a vegetarian, no, it's more than that—a vegan. That's it! Only eats veggies. It's no wonder he's as thin as a pole." Llewellyn shook his head and patted his ample belly. "I don't understand how he manages. I wouldn't be able to survive without my fair share of meat, cream, and butter."

"And where was this, Professor?" If the meal had been in a restaurant and the two men paid separately, they might have access to credit card records.

"Last week, in Lyon, the Rhone-Alps. Spectacular place. Have you ever been, Chief Inspector?"

"France?" Jones' balloon of excitement began to deflate. "The two of you were in France last week? Together?"

"Not in the Biblical sense, Chief Inspector. I'm a happily married man."

In Jones' experience, any man who professed to be happily married usually wasn't, but he let the uncharitable thought pass.

"I presented a paper and chaired three seminars on facial reconstruction at Interpol HQ."

Now the million pound question.

"When was this, sir? Exactly when were you and Mr Lang in France?" Jones held his breath and mentally crossed his fingers.

"It was a four-day conference. Wednesday afternoon to Saturday evening, but we couldn't book a flight home 'til Sunday afternoon, so I had a lovely time visiting the Interpol archives. You should see the evidence they have in their archives, Chief Inspector. Some of it would curl your toes."

"And Mr Lang was with you the whole time?"

"He was with me during my lectures and seminars. But it sounds as though Kurt needs an alibi, Chief Inspector. Yes?"

When Jones didn't answer, Llewellyn crossed his arms and lowered his head. "Well, as I said, we didn't share a room, but we did stay at the same hotel. If you're asking whether Kurt had time to travel to England, commit a crime, and then return to the conference without us noticing? I would say definitely not. Unless he had his own private jet, and the university certainly doesn't pay him enough for that." The professor chuckled. "We did have the whole of Sunday morning off, though."

The timeline put Lang in the clear for Charlie's murder, but not the attempt on Ryan's life, and they still hadn't totally ruled out the possibility of an accomplice. Theoretically, Lang and Jarman could still be the same person.

"Kurt caused quite a stir at the pre-closing banquet on Friday evening," Llewellyn said, his smile wide. "For all their claims of leading the world in terms of cuisine, the French aren't that familiar with catering for vegans. And he was definitely with me when I made the closing address at the conference on Saturday afternoon."

In France from Wednesday to Sunday, including the whole period they'd assigned to Charlie's murder and body dump.

Havers used the back of his thigh to close the drawer and raised his shoulders in apology. His expression was a mixture of disappointment at losing a red-hot suspect and relief that he'd been spared the embarrassment of launching a massive, city-wide search for an innocent man. Career-threatening embarrassment had been averted.

A few seconds after the drawer closed with a whisper, the door behind Jones opened and Jeremy Armstrong breezed into the lab. Kurt Lang followed two paces behind, carrying a transparent grocery bag containing two carrots, a tomato, and an apple.

Chapter Thirty-Eight

FRIDAY 19TH MAY – Morning

University of Birmingham, Edgbaston, Birmingham, UK

JONES COULDN'T HELP STARING at the approaching technician who stopped mid-stride. His eyes opened wide, and his chin started trembling.

"Wh-What's wrong?" Lang's quiet, high-pitched voice cracked.

Jones spoke first. "Sorry, Mr Lang, we thought you were on your lunch break."

Lang swallowed and raised the plastic bag. "W-We ran out of bread this morning, and the refectory doesn't really cater for vegans."

Jones took the opportunity to study the young man for the first time. Without his white lab coat, it became obvious Kurt Lang couldn't be Donald Jarman. Not in a million years.

Although similar in height to the killer he'd seen on the balcony, Lang didn't have the build or body-mass for the job. One look at the skinny arms sticking out of the oversized polo shirt, would tell any decent investigator the man couldn't have barged Ryan over the balcony or carried the heavyweight Charlie Pelham down ten flights of stairs. Nor could he have placed the body in a wheelbarrow, pushed it half a mile, and dumped it in the house on Orchard Park Lane. Not without help—and, although they hadn't totally ruled it out, they had no evidence that Jarman had a partner-in-crime.

Damn.

In fact, the young man didn't look as though he had the strength to *lift* a baseball bat, let alone swing one with enough force to do the damage seen on Sandy's head and face.

"Do you mind telling me where you were last Wednesday morning, around four o'clock?"

"Y-you mean when the policeman f-fell off that balcony?" Lang stammered. He took a step back, swayed, and looked as though he might fall. Jones prepared to leap forwards and catch him. Armstrong looked on in amusement.

"Not to worry, Mr Lang. We're simply ruling you out of our enquiries. Where were you?"

Lang looked from Llewellyn to Armstrong and back again, took a deep breath, and the words tumbled out. "I was at home, asleep. With my partner, if you must know. And there's nothing wrong with that, is there? We're consenting adults, and we were doing nothing illegal." He stood tall, for once, puffed out his frail chest, and clenched his hands into fists.

Two sounds invaded the silence of the lab—the rustling as Kurt crushed the plastic bag in his hand, and the water trickling in the courtyard fountain.

Jeremy Armstrong threw a knowing glance at Llewellyn. "Told you, Rhys. That's a fiver you owe me."

"Inappropriate timing, Jeremy," Llewellyn scolded.

Jones raised his hands to calm the young technician, whose face had flushed beet red. A vein distended on his left temple. "We're not concerned with your sleeping arrangements, sir. We're investigating a serious attack on a police officer. These are standard questions that we ask everyone we come into contact with. I assume your partner will verify where you were?"

"She'd better, or she's in trouble!" Lang relaxed his hands and took a deeper breath.

"She?" Armstrong asked, eyes wide.

"Yes, she," Lang snapped. "Vanessa! And you lose the fiver, Dr Armstrong. As it happens, Vanessa and I plan to marry next year. What of it?"

Armstrong shrugged. "My mistake. I'd love to meet your Vanessa. She sounds like a wonderful woman."

"She is. She really is!"

Keen to bring the conversation back to the point, Jones broke into their conversation.

"Mr Lang," he said, "could you give me your address and Vanessa's full name and contact details, please?"

"Of course, Chief Inspector. Happy to. But can you be discreet? She hasn't told her family about the wedding yet." Lang flicked a nervous glance in Llewellyn's direction and bit his thumbnail. "You couldn't talk to her at her work, could you?"

"I'll try to accommodate your request sir, but I can make no promises."

Lang pressed his lips together tightly, flounced to his desk, and opened a thin leather satchel. He returned carrying a beige business card. The words *Vanessa Étage – Yoga Instructor and Personal Trainer*, together with her contact details, were embossed in silver. The lower right-hand corner of the card held a line drawing, in red ink, of Leonardo da Vinci's *Vitruvian Man*, only the figure inside the circle and the square showed the obvious curves of a woman.

"Interesting name," Jones said, sliding the card into his wallet. "Vanessa Étage."

Lang's face lit up as he spoke, the adoration for his girlfriend evident. "Vanessa's French. She has private clients all over the city and offers one-to-one fitness sessions." Jones couldn't avoid looking at Lang's puny arms. The technician flushed again and spoke through clenched teeth. "She likes me as I am, Chief Inspector. I'm an intellectual, not one of her flabby or musclebound clients."

314

"I apologise, Mr Lang, I didn't mean to upset you, but I do have one more thing to ask."

Lang blinked twice. His jaw muscles bunched again. "Yes?"

"Your surname, German is it?"

"Yes, Chief Inspector, my paternal grandfather immigrated as a child in 1935 before the worst of the … well, you know … the bad stuff. Our original family name was Langergraber. Grandfather shortened it to Lang to make it easier for the English to pronounce. Why, is it important?"

Jones shook his head. "Not at all, sir, I'm interested in anthroponomastics—the study of personal names. It's a hobby of mine."

Lang edged away. "I see. If you've quite finished, Chief Inspector, I need to eat. My blood sugar level is plummeting, and I'm feeling a little lightheaded."

"Yes, sir. That's all, for now. And thank you for your assistance."

Lang spun and dived for the safety of his work station, showing them his skinny, hunched back. Jones rubbed his chin and turned his attention to the round man in the gaudy cravat. "I apologise for the interruption to our conversation, Dr Armstrong. Did you manage to contact Dr Craig?"

"Nah. Call went straight to 'is messaging service. I tried 'is land line too, but no joy, I'm afraid. I left messages for 'im to contact you though, if that's any use."

"It is, sir, thank you. Can I trouble you for his contact details? When I have a little time, I'd like to call him for a chat relating to that matter we discussed."

"No worries, Chief Inspector. Just a sec." Armstrong snatched a pad from Lang's desk, scribbled the details, and handed the note to Jones. Lang didn't look too pleased about the invasion of his private space, but said nothing.

"That's 'is address and both phone numbers." He tapped his temple. "Got a good memory for numbers, me. It's my job."

"Thank you, Dr Armstrong." Jones glanced at Havers. "Do you have anything else, sir?"

"No thank you, Chief Inspector. I have all I need."

They headed for the door.

"Anthroponomastics?" Havers asked quietly. "A hobby? Really?"

"Yep. It's been my hobby for exactly one day. Nice word, though. I found it during a Google search last night."

Havers held the door open for Jones, who stepped through into the darkened corridor.

"By the way," Havers said after closing the door on the academics, "thanks for saving my blushes back there. It would have been so embarrassing to call a city-wide search for a man with a cast-iron alibi. I'd never have lived it down."

"Not a problem, sir. And who said Lang's alibi is cast iron?" Jones asked, adding a knowing smile. "We still have to check it out. At least, one of the team does. I'll put Ben onto it."

Chapter Thirty-Nine

Police HQ, Holton, Birmingham, UK

JONES LOOKED up from his umpteenth reading of the joint case file and checked the time.

Hell.

The wall clock hung off square. Why had he taken so long to notice it? He stood and nudged it straight before flopping back down and dropping his head in his hands.

Waiting had always been the worst part of any investigation. Waiting for others to complete their assigned duties, waiting for tedious processes to be waded through, and waiting for evidence to be extracted and sifted. He'd tasked the team and they worked industriously, but they had no other immediate lines of enquiry. So he waited.

On Friday afternoon, Ben had visited Vanessa Étage at work, and she had supported Lang's alibi for the time of the raid—they'd been in bed asleep. She'd also confirmed her own whereabouts when Charlie had met his end. While Lang worked in France, she'd taken the opportunity to visit her parents in Reims. Alex, the team's polyglot, called Vanessa's mother who verified the visit. She also double-checked the return flight Vanessa took to and from Birmingham International. As far as could be determined, both Kurt Lang and Vanessa Étage were in the clear for Charlie's murder and the attack on Ryan, as Jones suspected.

Ben and Phil's search of Ronnie Poole's apartment turned up precisely nothing. No tell-tale calendar entries explaining why she'd allowed access to her killer—the biker in the Triumph leathers. In fact, the apartment had been conspicuously devoid of calendars whether traditional or electronic. There had been no sign of a laptop or desktop computer either, which aroused suspicion in itself.

In all the time Jones had known Ronnie Poole, he'd rarely seen her without a smartphone pressed to her ear or a laptop bag hanging by a strap from her shoulder. Jones' assumptions? Triumph Biker had taken the phone and the laptop. Ronnie hadn't owned a desktop.

More suspicion.

As for the academic strand of the investigation, Llewellyn and Lang had been at the morgue since eight o'clock that morning. Jones had introduced them to Tim Scobie. Jones and Ben had helped them carry their equipment from their van into the morgue, and he'd watched them set it up. When they'd started boiling the pieces of poor Sandy's head, Jones had taken his leave. He'd used the pretext that since he hated people standing over him at work, it seemed only fair for him to offer the academic and his sidekick the same courtesy. In fact, the stench of boiled ham bubbling out from the large glass beaker atop the electric hob turned his stomach inside out.

As Jones waited for Llewellyn's call, he considered chewing his nails or taking up smoking for the first time in his life—anything to take away his mounting tension. He paced the office, drank more tea than normal, and pored over reams of paper, but nothing took his mind off the wait.

For want of something better to do, he called both Dr Craig's personal numbers, and his lab at the University repeatedly, but the scientist had apparently moved off planet.

Where the bloody hell was he? Jones even contemplated passing some time by driving to Craig's home and banging on his door, but decided against it. Interrupting the academic's sabbatical wouldn't exactly endear Jones to him, and since Jones was about to ask a personal favour, he didn't want to start the relationship off on a sour note.

That morning, he'd sent PC Kelly, a responsible, level-headed young woman, to the AV suite to study each of Jarman's chosen films. She was in the process of duplicating every murder scene in each movie and taking note of any murder even mentioned in dialogue. Jones joined her for half an hour, but took his leave when they reached the psychedelic scene towards the end of *Easy Rider*. He'd been bored stiff the first time he'd watched it back in the '60s and refused to sit through it again, even if it did relate to the hunt for Charlie's killer. He could only take so much.

He'd given Phil and Alex the day off—for family reasons in Phil's case and for recuperation in Alex's. Currently, Ben, ably assisted by the industrious and extremely capable Holden Bigglesworth, sifted through the local and national archives. So far, they'd come up with no cases they could associate with the *Easy Rider* poster.

Nothing. Not a bloody thing.

AFTER A HURRIED AND UNFULFILLING LUNCH, Jones returned to his office and tried to catch up on his ancillary paperwork. He glared at the clock again. Was it still off-kilter? He stood to pay another visit to PC Kelly in the AV suite when the shrill ring of his desk phone nearly made him drop his mug. He snatched the handset from the cradle and paced the office.

"Jones here."

"DCI Jones? Er … this is Rhys Llewellyn," the normally enthusiastic and annoyingly verbose professor sounded wary, defensive. "I need you to come to the mortuary straight away."

Jones stopped mid-stride. His heart leapt. "Are you finished, Professor?"

"Er, we have something, but there might be a problem with our dataset. I've asked Jeremy Armstrong to come along, but we need a police officer, too, and right away."

Bloody technology.

Jones resumed pacing. "What sort of problem?"

"I'd rather not say over the telephone. It's serious though. And urgent."

What the hell?

"I'll be there as soon as I can."

Jones dropped the handset into its cradle and grabbed his jacket on the way through the door. He considered collecting Ben from the briefing room, but experience had shown that Ben's techie skillset didn't extend much further than Jones' own. Holden Bigglesworth might prove useful, but Jones couldn't expose the young civilian to the horrors of the autopsy suite. Bigglesworth's union rep would never approve, and the lad's earlier reaction to the crime scene photos had been bad enough. Lord knew how he'd respond to the lingering aroma of a boiled human head. No, the civilian could stay where he was, earning a good day's overtime to help pay down his student loans in the relative comfort of the briefing room.

Jones thought a moment longer before smiling and reaching for the phone again.

BY THE TIME he arrived at the car park of the Racer-Colby crime lab, Robyn was waiting at the entrance, clutching an elegant leather handbag, which made a nice change from the big metal evidence kit. The jacket draped over her arm—despite the oppressive heat of the day—showed an awareness of their destination. He appreciated her forethought, as would she later.

The warm smile she sent him and the sparkle in her eyes lifted his spirits. He returned her greeting.

He leaned across the passenger seat and pushed the door open. She climbed in beside him, bringing in a waft of the same light and floral perfume he'd smelled earlier.

"Thanks for dropping everything, Dr Spence. I know how busy you are."

"Your call intrigued me, DCI Jones," she said in mock severity.

She rested the handbag on her lap, and Jones wished he'd made time to clean the inside of the car. "Nice car, Chief Inspector, but Manda told me you drove a Rover 400."

"It's currently off the road."

The mention of his old Rover bought with it the image of a bruised and battered Ryan hooked up to so many medical devices. A pang of guilt clenched Jones' stomach.

"That's a pity. Is it terminal?"

"The engine blew up. Literally."

"Ah, I see. That really is a shame."

"Ryan Washington and his father were rebuilding it for me, but …." Jones winced. "Damn … I have no idea what to say to Bryn, Ryan's dad. When I think of the lad lying in that bed—"

"He'll recover, David."

"Will he?"

She smiled. "While waiting for you, I called the hospital and spoke to his doctor."

Jones turned to face her. "You spoke to Dr Suresh? What did she say?"

"The prognosis is … encouraging. The cranial swelling is receding, they've removed the ventilator, and he's breathing on his own. The neurologist, Mr Shepperton, plans to reduce his anaesthesia slowly. He'll hopefully wake from the coma tomorrow or the next day. No one can be certain of the prognosis, but they are hopeful."

Jones closed his eyes.

"Thanks, Robyn. I spent four hours at Queen Elizabeth's yesterday and nobody would tell me a thing."

"One of the benefits of my job and my title is being able to batter down the NHS firewalls."

"How bad is it really? He looked an unholy mess when they let me into the ICU monitoring room."

"Multiple fractures. Right leg. Left wrist. Three broken ribs. One of which punctured a lung and caused a tension pneumothorax—that's a collapsed lung. All are serious but Ryan's young and they'll heal. The cranial trauma, though." She bit her lower lip. "There's no telling how much functional impact that will have until he wakes."

Jones ground his teeth. Jarman had so much to answer for.

"As you said, Robyn. Ryan's young. He *will* recover." Jones tried to make it sound more confident than he actually felt. "Ready?"

She fastened her seatbelt.

"Whenever you are, Chief Inspector."

Jones exited the car park and pulled the Škoda into High Street South. For once, they made steady progress in light traffic. Jones tried desperately to find something to say that wasn't work related, but came up with nothing. He certainly wasn't about to mention the weather.

After five minutes' steady progress, Robyn broke the slightly awkward silence.

"Škoda's are pretty good these days, but I really love Rovers," she said. "Solid old cars. My father had one. A little thirsty on the petrol, but dependable, just like my dad."

Oh hell, she thinks I'm her dad.

She laughed and brushed Jones' knee with the side of her hand. "Don't look so mortified, David. I'm kidding. These days, my father drives a classic Lotus Elise. A mid-life crisis thing." The afterglow from her touch lingered. Jones swallowed and concentrated on passing a slow-moving van.

He needed to change the subject. Move to firmer ground.

"I'm glad you're aware of Llewellyn's work. A lot of what he told me flew right over my head."

She fixed him with a piercing stare.

"We'll have none of that, David Jones. From what I've seen of you, I doubt that very much."

He flushed and managed to avoid rear-ending a dawdling Mini. He flashed his lights at the unfortunate driver and shot past her in an aggressive overtake.

"You hide your light, don't you? You want people to think you're a dinosaur, a plodder, but I've seen how you work. You're methodical, you miss very little, and your mind's a razor." She faced the front again and Jones relaxed his grip on the wheel. Her presence made him uncomfortable, but in a good way.

"I don't know what you have against technology," she continued, "but it's certainly not that you can't understand it, or that you minimise its value."

Jones couldn't explain it, but he needed to let her into his life, into his mind. He paused for a beat and then dived in.

"Since you asked, I hate the way people have come to depend on technology. They've come to use IT as a crutch rather than rely on their eyes and ears, and their brains. When I see people walking down the street with their eyes glued to their smartphones, ignoring the world around them, it makes me sad rather than angry. Also, the 'gruff, grumpy old man' thing is a bit of an act. Inside, I'm actually a real softie." He glanced at her and winked.

"I knew that from the first second we met."

Over Charlie's corpse?

"Really?"

"Really," she said, "despite the location and the circumstances."

"Hmm."

They lapsed into another silence for a few minutes until he felt the need to break it.

"Can I let you in on a secret?"

"Ooh, I love secrets," she said, twisting at the waist to face him fully, her eyes alive and glittering.

"A few months ago, I signed up to an online IT course, bought my own laptop and everything. Don't tell anyone, especially Phil, but I've even had broadband installed in the cottage."

She faked a gasp.

"Believe it or not, this old codger"—he released his grip on the wheel long enough to jab a thumb into his chest—"has become part of the Information Age."

"Ha, a closet techie? I knew it! Never fear, David. Your secret's safe with me." She slapped his thigh again and added, "And don't you ever call yourself an old codger in front of me. You aren't that old."

"Thank you, Dr Spence."

He hadn't told her everything, though. Not by a long chalk. The identity of his IT tutor had to remain a secret. Corky—a world-class hacker—would be seriously miffed if he learned that Jones had blabbed about their late-night internet sessions. And Lord knew what the information would do to Jones' hard-won reputation as an honest broker if the information escaped into the wider police community.

"David, for a man of your ... experience, there's really no need to be nervous around me. I don't bite."

Pity.

He smiled. "I didn't think anything of the—"

"Unless I'm hungry," she added, smiling again.

He matched her smile and relaxed his grip on the wheel a little more.

"That's enough, Dr Spence. We'll discuss your dietary needs at a later date—"

"A date?" she said, placing the tips of her fingers on her chest. "You're asking me out on a date?"

"No, I—"

"But we've only just met, Chief Inspector. What kind of a girl do you think I am?"

He tutted and shook his head.

"Be serious for a moment, please. We're heading to a mortuary."

"I'm sorry, David. But you can be a bit of a stuffed shirt sometimes."

"I can. And I know it, but ... let's stay on topic for now, shall we? When you met Professor Llewellyn that time, did you happen to meet his sidekick, Kurt Lang?"

"No, I didn't. He's the one Superintendent Havers thought might be Donald Jarman, but he has an alibi, right?"

"You've been talking with Phil?"

"As part of the team working the case, I think I'm entitled to ask a few questions."

"You are indeed." Jones eased off the accelerator long enough to negotiate a mini-roundabout before building up the speed again —not that he wanted to shorten his alone time with Robyn.

"So, Lang's alibi. Is it solid?"

Jones nodded. "Certainly seems to be. Llewellyn gives him a solid alibi for the time of Charlie's murder, and his fiancée says they were together when Ryan was attacked."

"I know. Phil told me about Ben's meeting with Vanessa Étage. Apparently, she's quite the physical specimen. Tall and strong, but a little on the masculine side for our Ben. According to Phil, Ben found her a little intimidating."

"Ben? Intimidated?" Jones scoffed. "I doubt that. It would surprise me if anything could intimidate Ben Adeoye. That's not exactly the way he described her to me. He actually called Vanessa Étage, 'An Amazon who could eat Lang whole for dinner and still have room for pudding'. He also thought she could beat Phil in an arm wrestle."

"And your response?"

"I told him it takes all sorts to make a world."

She nodded.

"So, as far as you're concerned, Kurt Lang is no longer a suspect?" Robyn asked, clearly determined to pull out every last morsel of information.

"It certainly looks that way," Jones said, as noncommittal as ever and trying to keep his options open. "Ah, here we are."

He turned left into Stillhouse Lane, made an immediate right into Newton Street, and parked in one of the spots designated for official visitors.

Chapter Forty

SATURDAY 20TH MAY – Morning

Coroner's Court Buildings, City Centre, Birmingham, UK

JONES HELD the main mortuary door open for Robyn and led the way to the autopsy suites. Kept at a constant five degrees Celsius, the suites were commonly called meat lockers—but not by Jones.

As they walked along the short corridor together, Jones became acutely aware of Robyn's lack of stature. Around one metre sixty—five feet two in old money—she made him feel tall and protective.

Weird.

They stopped outside the door marked *Autopsy Suite 3*.

"Do you mind?" she asked, holding out her tan leather shoulder bag–Versace, according to the embossed "V" on the front flap.

Jones recognised the designer from a case of insurance fraud he'd worked a few years earlier. The investigation concerned a fake burglary where the householders claimed to have lost a fortune in jewellery and designer accessories. The woman of the

326

house included a Versace handbag to the list of stolen items. Jones
had nearly fallen over when she revealed the retail price of the
item.

"Not at all."

He took it, surprised by its weight. What did she carry in the
thing? House bricks?

"Cold in here," she said, pulling on the grey jacket and fastening
the buttons.

"Wouldn't want it any other way," Jones said, handing back
the bag.

"Quite right." She draped the strap over her shoulder and took
a deep breath. "Ready when you are."

They entered AS3, a large room with a low ceiling. Sometime in
the distant past, the room's bare brick walls had been painted white
to amplify the light emitted by the fluorescent tubes and operating-
theatre spotlights. But the dead weren't considered as valuable as the
living, and they didn't warrant much of a redecoration budget.
Scuff marks from the rubber-sided trolleys and the discoloured paint
combined to produce a dreary backdrop, which suited the room's
function. Thankfully, the air conditioning units had dispelled the
aroma of "poached Sandy".

Stop it, Jones.

A stainless-steel examination table took centre stage. Jones half
expected to be greeted by Sandy's discoloured and disfigured
corpse, but mercifully the table stood empty and spotless.

"Ah, there you are Chief Inspector," Llewellyn said, with forced
bonhomie, "and, do I recognise your companion from somewhere?
Wait, don't tell me." His eyes darted up and to the left. "The lovely
Dr, er, Spencer, isn't it?" He reached for her hand.

"Spence," she corrected. "I'm surprised you remember me from
last year, Professor."

"Oh, I never forget a pretty face, my dear." He turned from her
to Jones, and his expression became serious. "Thank you for coming
so promptly, Chief Inspector." He pointed to a corner, where Kurt
Lang assumed his usual position, facing a computer terminal with
his back to the room. Shoulders hunched, he wore a heavy woollen

sweater under his white lab coat and seemed to blend into his surroundings—a human chameleon.

"We've tried a number of approaches," Llewellyn continued, "but I'm afraid we might be having a problem with our transcription algorithm."

Jones lifted his chin. "In what way, Professor?"

Llewellyn hesitated a second before ushering them towards Lang. "Come and look for yourselves."

The verbose and supremely confident Llewellyn of the previous day had disappeared. The new professor seemed hesitant, uncertain. His usual mobile, open face had become fixed and serious. "I did warn you that the results might prove open to interpretation, didn't I?"

"You did, Professor. But what's the problem?"

"A number of skull fragments were highly distorted and difficult to measure. So, we've run the program using five different baseline metrics. The trouble is, we keep producing very similar results. Kurt is completing the final merge algorithm now. The aim is to produce a best-fit facsimile from the five reconstructions."

"Surely that's a good thing, Professor? If your results are constant, doesn't that mean they are likely to be accurate?"

Robyn answered for the professor. "Consistency doesn't necessarily demonstrate accuracy, Chief Inspector. It simply means the results are reproducible. If you start with poor data, you'll end up with poor results."

"GIGO," Jones said.

"Quite so, Chief Inspector," Llewellyn butted in, his smile as ingratiating as it was annoying. "Kurt, are you ready with the final rendering?"

"Just about, Professor." Lang's quiet voice barely carried above the incessant hum of air conditioning. He continued tapping until the white characters on a grey background disappeared, and were replaced by a man's face.

The image rotated anti-clockwise and showed a rugged, angular face. Fair, wavy hair—long and shaggy—covered the ears and receded into a gently described widow's peak. A small, but distinct scar ran upwards from the outer edge of his left eyebrow. Thread-like crow's feet set his age at mid-to-late-thirties. Uncomfortably, Sandy's pale blue, almost grey, eyes looked down and to his right, as though avoiding eye contact with the room. Three days' worth of stubble and a slight frown made the face look pensive, scholarly. His lips were thin without being cruel.

"That's spectacular, Professor. Wonderful detail." Jones couldn't help being impressed, stunned even.

The face on the screen was handsome, but was it an accurate representation of the real Sandy?

The image stirred memories but not enough for Jones to bring them to the surface. His jaw muscles clenched, and he bit back the renewed anger he felt for Donald Jarman.

He shot a sideways glance at Robyn who stood tense and still, studying the image through narrowed eyes. She pursed her lips and said nothing, but kept her full focus on the screen.

"I think I recognise him from somewhere," Jones said. "How confident are you in the results?"

Llewellyn frowned and stared at his assistant who for once, faced the room, showed his palms, and shrugged. "I've triple-checked the programme and the raw data, Professor. It keeps producing the same output. It's as precise an image as we can produce, given the condition of the skull and the facial fragments. I'm sorry." He hung his head in disappointment and mumbled, "I don't know what else I can do."

Llewellyn's shoulders sagged. "I hope to God we've made an error somewhere. Maybe Jem will find something wrong with the algorithm." His flat delivery and dejected expression showed a defeated man.

"He won't," Kurt said, his tone defiant.

Realisation dawned on Jones. "You recognise him, don't you?"

Before Llewellyn could answer, the door flew open and a breath-less Jeremy Armstrong rushed into the room. He wore motorcycle leathers and a full-face helmet dangled against his thigh, its chin-strap gripped in Armstrong's right hand. Last thing Jones expected was for the squat Welshman to be a biker. He checked for a

Triumph logo, but couldn't find one. In any event, Armstrong's rounded, squat build couldn't have been more different to the person Jones had witnessed attacking Ryan on the balcony.

"Got 'ere as soon as I could. Now what's the emergency?" Armstrong drew level with the screen. "Fucking 'ell!"

He stopped mid-stride. The helmet crashed to the floor, and the colour drained from his chubby face. He raised a fist and pointed at the screen.

"What the fuck are you playing at Rhys? That's Andy Craig!"

Chapter Forty-One

Coroner's Court Buildings, City Centre, Birmingham, UK

JONES FINALLY UNDERSTOOD why the face was so familiar. He'd seen it when reviewing the university's online prospectus. But there was still something that didn't make sense, something he wasn't able to reconcile. The niggling doubt returned.

Armstrong broke the spell.

"You're wrong!" he screamed, voice pitched high. "You've got to be."

He rushed forwards and dragged a reluctant Lang from his chair, dropped into the vacated seat, and started tapping at the keyboard.

Dr Craig's face disappeared from the monitor and a horizontal line split the screen in half. A mesh cube, similar to the one Jones had seen in Llewellyn's lab, appeared in the top half. In the lower section, white text on a black background scrolled up the panel as Armstrong typed an expanding series of hieroglyphs.

The new matrix deformed, squeezed, stretched, and dimpled into a fresh human skull. All the time he typed, Armstrong chanted, "Be wrong. Please be fucking wrong."

The louder his fingers crashed on the keys, the more solid the image became. Teeth, muscles, connective tissue, eyes, and skin grew inside the matrix. It reminded Jones of a time-lapse film of a plant growing in seconds, from seedling to flowering.

Robyn stood beside Jones while Armstrong worked. She leaned against him and shivered, with what … cold, excitement? Jones forced himself to breathe normally. For a reason he couldn't explain, he had more faith in the Welsh statistician than the wraith-like Kurt Lang.

Llewellyn stood back, chewing his fingernails. He was supposed to be in charge, but the man looked old, shrivelled, and uncertain— an afterthought in his own project.

Jones took a pace to the side of Armstrong and studied him in profile. During the fifteen-minute process, the Welsh statistician concentrated on the lower segment of the screen and the keyboard. His eyes rarely flicked to the top half.

Time stood still and the only noises in the room came from Armstrong's typing, the hum of the air-conditioner, and a damned ticking wall-clock. Why did the dead need to know the time?

As the reconstruction neared its conclusion, Jones backed away from the computer. He fished in his pocket for his mobile and called Havers.

"Jones? Where are you?"

"I'm at the mortuary, sir." He lowered his voice to avoid disturbing the increasingly frenetic Armstrong. "I think you'd better get over here. The reconstruction is just about ready. It's not good."

"No! Jesus, no!" Armstrong turned to Llewellyn, his eyes glistening. "This can't be? Did you check the scanners for calibration errors?"

"Twice," Llewellyn said, resting his meaty hand on Armstrong's shoulder.

Jones studied the upper half of the large monitor and whispered, "Damn it." Apart from remaining in a fixed position instead of rotating, the only significant differences between Armstrong's image and the one created by Kurt Lang were the eyes.

From the screen, Dr Andrew Craig's face seemed to stare out and look straight at him in accusation.

WITHIN HALF AN HOUR OF JONES' phone call, Havers and Ben arrived, along with a uniformed constable, who stayed in the background on a watching brief.

"Bloody hell!" Ben said after taking one look at Craig's image on the screen. "Excuse me, Dr Spence. I didn't see you there. I haven't seen one of these reconstructions before. Impressive." He paused and studied the face again. "So, that's Sandy?"

Armstrong's head snapped up, his eyes red and tearful. "Who?"

Jones ignored the question, closed on Ben, and spoke quietly. "The face on the screen belongs to a colleague of theirs."

"Sorry, sir. But that reconstruction. It's uncanny. So lifelike."

"It is." Jones nodded.

Havers grabbed Jones' upper arm and pulled him to one side. "I don't want to upset the academics, but this is fantastic news." His eyes shone, and he spoke more quickly than normal. "It's a crying shame for Dr Craig and his friends, of course it is, but least we've finally identified the body. We'll have something to show the press now, eh?"

"No, sir, I disagree. We're finally getting close to Jarman, the last thing we should do is show our hand."

Havers yanked his arm away from Jones and raised the hand to his chest. "I don't know, Jones. I'm inclined to distribute Craig's photo to the media right away. If we hurry, we'll be able to make the ten o'clock news bulletin."

Jones' defence mechanism clicked into action again, the warning bell tolled loud. He couldn't ignore it any longer.

"Sorry to sound the note of caution, but I'm not convinced. I've a feeling the reconstruction's wrong, but I can't explain why." Jones glanced at the monitor. The eyes of the image seemed to have followed him to his new position in the corner of the room. "I'm sorry to put a dampener on your plans, sir, but I recommend we hold off on the media blitz." Havers stiffened and dropped his hand, but Jones continued. "At the very least, we need to search Dr Craig's home first. He might have a day planner or a diary. Heck, for all we know, he might be tucked up safely in a cosy B&B in the Cotswolds writing his end-of-study report."

Havers took a half-pace back and straightened his tunic. His eyes had turned from open pale blue, to closed steel grey. He leaned close and hissed, "Pity's sake, Chief Inspector, what is it with you and technology? This reconstruction was your team's idea, remember? I realise you only approached me to humour DI Cryer"—Jones ground his teeth—"but as soon as we catch a break on this case, you pull this Doubting Thomas, Luddite nonsense on me."

No, don't say it.

"I'm sorry, Jones, but it's dinosaurs like you that have always held back progress in the service."

Dinosaurs!

Havers continued with voice low, lips barely moving. "We have the UK's leader in facial reconstruction in the room and, by all accounts, one of the country's best statisticians in Dr Armstrong. They ran the analysis multiple times, produced a similar image on each occasion, and still you don't agree. What wrong, Jones? Gut instinct? Honestly!"

Jones managed to bite back his immediate response. He took a breath and forced himself to be calm. "Instinct, experience, call it what you will, but I'm advising caution, Superintendent Havers. I'd hate for us to move too early on this. Let's wait until after we've searched Craig's home, shall we? We should hold off the media announcement until tomorrow morning. After all, who watches the news on a Saturday evening anyway?"

"And what happens if Jarman gets away because we've been sitting on our hands? Or worse still, kills again?"

"Jarman's had plenty of time to run or plan his next attack. If we're wrong, an announcement of this sort might make him angry. It may even force his hand. Do you want that on your conscience?"

Havers flicked a glance over Jones' shoulder to the computer screen and scratched his chin—still stubble free so late in the day. The man might actually have shaved on his way to the morgue.

Havers' eyes cleared, and he tugged his tunic straight, decision made. "I'm sorry, Jones. It was absolutely unforgivable of me to call you a dinosaur."

"Yes, it was," Jones said, not caring how it sounded, petulant or otherwise.

"DS Pelham was one of my men, and DC Washington still is," Havers said, "I want Jarman as badly as you do."

No you don't.

Jones still seethed at Havers' insult.

"Let's hold off letting Jarman know we've identified Sandy until we're absolutely certain, *okay?*" He sensed the struggle behind Havers' eyes. Caution fought his confidence in the reliability of technology. "I hate to remind you, sir, but you did promise to let me handle the investigation." Jones played his final card. "And I was right about holding off on the search for Kurt Lang." He nodded towards the frail technician.

Five seconds ticked by with the speed of setting concrete.

Jones scanned the room. Llewellyn tried to console Armstrong, while Kurt Lang stood in the opposite corner to Jones. He hadn't moved or spoken since being jerked out of his chair, but stood glowering at Armstrong, his expression set to full-blown hate.

Robyn had said little since the initial reveal, but the eyes under her furrowed brows remained glued to the computer screen as if mesmerised by the 3D CFR "approximation".

Finally, Havers broke the tension.

"Okay, DCI Jones. You win. I'll give you until midday tomorrow."

Caution's won. Praise be.

"I'll arrange a press conference at the station. If you haven't found him by then, you'll stand beside me when I announce the search for Dr Andrew Craig. Agreed?" Havers arched an eyebrow.

"It doesn't give me long, sir, but it'll have to do."

Havers dipped his head and turned towards the work station.

"Sir?" Jones called.

"Yes?"

"Thank you."

Jones approached the distraught little Welshman, who sat with his elbows on his knees and his face buried in his hands. Jones touched the man's shoulder and Armstrong's head snapped up as though he'd been tasered.

"I understand how you must feel, sir," Jones said. "I really do, but I wonder whether you would help us?"

"Huh?" Armstrong's reddened eyes stared up at Jones and his lower lip quivered. "What can I do? What's 'appened? Is Andy really dead? I don't know nothing. Leave me alone."

Jones raised his hands. "Try to stay calm, Dr Armstrong. You said it yourself, facial reconstruction isn't infallible. We're not certain of anything yet."

"Jem," he said, "my name's Jem."

He rubbed his face with both hands and pushed up and out of his chair.

"I understand, Jem. Will you help us?"

Armstrong took a handkerchief out of his jacket pocket and blew his nose. Jones looked away as the Welshman returned the soiled cotton to the pocket. "What can I do, Chief Inspector?"

"Have you ever been to Dr Craig's apartment?"

He frowned and pulled in his chin. "Yeah. We'd fetch a carry-out and share a few beers at 'is place after work. Couple of times a month. Why?"

"I'd like you to come with us to Dr Craig's flat and tell us whether anything's missing."

"You're looking for an appointment book or day planner?"

"That's right."

"There's a calendar on the wall by 'is landline. Uses it to make notes, and I can let you in, too. I've got a spare set of keys to 'is flat in the top box of my motorbike."

"Excellent. If you have his keys, we won't need a warrant."
Jones turned to Havers. "Sir?"

"Chief Inspector?"

"Dr Armstrong has tacit approval to enter Dr Craig's home."

"Well, what are we waiting for?" Havers gathered himself. "Professor Llewellyn, Mr Lang, I must thank you for all your efforts today. I'll make sure the university's invoice is paid promptly."

Kurt shot Havers an expression Jones couldn't interpret. It could have been anything from embarrassment to rage.

"I realise how distressing today must have been for you, so I—we—appreciate you continuing to work under such circumstances and hope you'll keep all details to yourselves," Havers continued and raised the printout of the image Llewellyn had provided. "If you could email me a copy of the JPEG? Please wait here and I'll have my officer help you with your equipment."

He turned to the constable in the doorway and wafted a hand in the general direction of the computer screens. The uniformed officer stepped forwards, apparently eager to help.

AFTER TAKING their leave of the two academics, Jones, Robyn, Armstrong, Ben, and Havers exited AS3 and walked in silence along the extended corridor towards the exit.

"David," Robyn touched his arm, and he slowed his pace to match hers. She waited until the others had pulled well ahead, her voice little more than a whisper. "There's something wrong."

"Wrong with what?"

She'd seen it too!

"The reconstruction." She stopped and they turned to face each other in the empty hallway. "It doesn't look, no, it doesn't *feel* right to me."

Jones' heartbeat increased as Robyn's eyes locked on his. "In what way?" He kept his voice as low as hers.

"I can't tell you how I know it." Her lips thinned and she shook her head slowly but didn't break the eye contact. "You'll think I'm nuts."

"Try me."

"It's difficult to explain, but when I first arrive at a crime scene and study a body, especially a damaged one, I always try to imagine what the person looked like, standing and smiling—living. It helps me focus on my work. Gives it meaning." She shrugged. "I know it doesn't make sense, but the image on the screen back there didn't match my mental picture of Sandy." She squeezed his arm. "Am I making any sense at all?"

Despite the situation and their location, Jones smiled. Couldn't help himself.

She pulled back, eyes wide. "David? Are you okay?"

"Yes, I'm fine, Robyn. And I felt exactly the same thing. There's something wrong with that reconstruction, but I don't know how we can prove it."

Robyn beamed, rose up on tiptoes, and pecked him on the cheek. Jones nearly fell over. "I might have a way."

"Go on."

"Ever since I took Prof Llewellyn's seminar, I've been working on a simplified facial reconstruction system for my own work. It's not as advanced as Lang's, and doesn't have all those bells and whistles and rotating smiling faces, but I've had some success."

"Why didn't you tell me this earlier?"

Her eyes flicked away. "I wasn't sure you'd listen. And it's only a hobby project, in the development stage. Superintendent Havers placed a great deal of faith in Llewellyn's work and I didn't want to rock the boat." She fixed her eyes on his again, and he picked up on her desperate need to be taken seriously. "But I couldn't stand by and say nothing. I think the basic shape of the face is wrong—it's too narrow, and there was no evidence of old scar tissue on Sandy's face, not that I could see. So where did the scar over his eyebrow come from? But I can't produce an alternative without taking my own direct metrics of Sandy's head and facial bones."

"You don't want to use the measurements Llewellyn and Lang have already taken?"

"No. Remember what I said about GIGO?"

"Do you want to take the new measurements now?"

Robyn's gaze flitted over Jones' shoulder, towards the room they'd recently left. She leaned closer and lowered her voice further. "I'd prefer to wait until they're gone. The little guy gives me the creeps."

Jones couldn't believe how closely her thought processes aligned with his. He held her by the arms and was within a heartbeat of pulling her into a hug. "Can you wait until later this evening when I'll join you?"

"Certainly, I'd prefer not to be here on my own, anyway." She shuddered. "Pick me up at home. I'll be waiting." She smiled.

"I don't know where you live."

"Hand me your phone and I'll add my contact details."

He passed the device to her and waited while she worked the screen.

"Okay, I'll be as quick as I can. Are you sure it'll be okay? Not too late? You have a young son, don't you? Zach?"

"Now then, DCI Jones, you've been checking up on me." Her smile widened. Jones blinked and lowered his eyes. "I'm flattered, but Zach's not an issue. I live with my mother. She's my live-in childminder."

"So, it's a date, then. Um, I mean, I'll call for you when we've finished searching Dr Craig's apartment."

Jones turned away to hide his embarrassment and called to Ben.

The others had reached the foyer and started the process of signing out of the building. Ben turned. "Yes, sir?"

"Take Dr Spence back to the lab and head back to Holton. See if Mr Bigglesworth has come up with anything on the posters."

"Yes, sir," Ben said, unable to hide his disappointment at being side-lined.

As for Jones, the memory of Robyn's kiss on his cheek stayed with him all the way to his car.

Chapter Forty-Two

SATURDAY 20TH MAY – Evening

Dr Craig's House, Harborne, Birmingham, UK

UPON ENTERING Andy Craig's disappointingly empty flat, Jones headed straight for the landline in the hall and pressed the redial button. He copied the number displayed on the handset into his notepad and showed it to Armstrong.

The Welshman, who'd followed the police convoy on his bright red Honda VFR, shrugged and shook his head.

"Never seen it, mun."

It took eighteen rings for the call to be answered by a bored-sounding woman with a slow, West Bromwich accent, "Second City Taxis."

Yes!

The last time Craig used the phone he'd called a cab.

It took Jones a full five minutes to explain who he was and what he wanted. The suspicious dispatcher took Jones' details and rang off to confirm his identity with police headquarters.

Jones sent a willing Havers to interview the immediate neighbours and spent another age searching the hall while he waited. The calendar on the wall above the phone held no entries for the preceding three weeks and none for the next two. No help there.

When the taxi firm's dispatcher finally called him back on Craig's landline, he cajoled the required information out of her.

"Yes, we *do* keep records of *all* our bookings, Chief Inspector Jones," she answered as though none of her drivers would ever *dream* of working off-book for cash. "Dr Craig is one of our Premium Account holders, actually. Uses our service at least once a week. One minute while I check our records. ... Ah yes, Hassan, one of our regular drivers picked him up that Friday evening."

"Is Hassan working tonight?"

Could they be that lucky?

"No. He's not due in again 'til tomorrow morning."

Oh brilliant.

"I need to speak to him. Can you give me his phone number? It's a matter of some urgency."

The woman paused before saying, "Absolutely not. I can't give out the contact details of our drivers. It's completely out of the question."

Why is everybody such a bloody jobsworth?

"However, what I *can* do," she continued, "is call Hassan and ask him to ring you. Will that do, sir?"

Jones took back his unspoken insult. "Yes please. That would be most helpful."

"We always try to help the police, Chief Inspector."

Of course you do.

He gave the dispatcher his mobile number and ended the call, hoping that Hassan spoke decent English and had at least a modicum of civic responsibility.

He took Armstrong with him to scour the open-plan kitchen and living area.

"Anything missing, Dr Armstrong—sorry ... Jem? Please don't touch anything, though."

Without moving from the hallway, Armstrong examined the room with the desperation of hope. "Er ... I don't think so. Andy keeps this place so neat and tidy, I'd definitely notice something obvious."

Jones took in the kitchen and the lounge in one continuous sweep. If Armstrong considered Craig's flat neat and tidy, he was glad they weren't searching the Welshman's place.

"Does the apartment usually look like this? Please take your time."

Jem scanned the room again.

"It's a touch less tidy than usual, I suppose. I mean, Andy normally puts 'is dishes in the dishwasher. But it isn't too bad."

"What about the sink, Jem. What do you see?"

"Cereal bowls, side plates, cutlery, and two coffee mugs." Armstrong smiled but his eyes remained sad. "Breakfast, I'd say."

"*Two* mugs and there's lipstick on one of them."

They moved closer to the sink.

"Bloody 'ell, so there is. How did you spot that from all the way over there?"

"Do you recognise the colour?"

"Don't be ridiculous. How would I recognise one lipstick from another?"

"Are you colour blind, sir?"

"Not at all, mun. I don't spend my time trying to remember shades of lipstick, is all. Could be EJ's I suppose."

"EJ?"

"EJ Bennett. *Doctor* EJ Bennett. A visiting lecturer. Gorgeous, she is. And they liked each other, too. A blind man could tell that. I ain't seen Andy look at a woman that way for years. Far as I'm aware, last time 'e went on a date since was before 'is wife died." The words tumbled out of Armstrong as though he thought talking about Craig would make him walk through the front door.

"Dr Craig's a widower?"

"Yeah. Rhiannon was mugged in the street, six years ago now.

Fell and banged 'er 'ead. The evil drunk bastard got away with thirty-five quid and some loose change. Fucking terrible, it was. Pardon my language. Knocked Andy sideways."

"I can imagine," Jones said. "I'm afraid I don't remember the case."

"Not surprising really. Occurred in Cardiff, see. That's where Andy and I met."

"Did we, I mean, did the police catch the mugger?"

"Sort of. Arsehole turned 'imself in the next day after sobering up. Mortified, 'e was. Repentant, you know? Didn't do nothin' for Rhiannon, of course. But it did give Andy a focus for 'is research. The effects of alcohol on the anger gene."

"Yes, I read the briefing notes from the Ministry of Justice. Most interesting. I'm sorry but can we carry on, Jem?"

Armstrong wiped his eyes and nodded.

"Yeah, sure."

They moved through to the lounge and took their time, but found nothing worth noting.

"Sorry, Chief Inspector. Far as I know, Andy keeps 'is contact information and 'is calendar in 'is mobile phone scheduler, and there's no sign of that anywhere."

Havers returned from interviewing the neighbours. A woman in the flat below confirmed Craig had been with a woman matching Armstrong's description of EJ Bennett on the morning of Saturday the 6th, the day after Armstrong had last seen Craig. She hadn't seen him since.

"We might return in the morning and canvass the rest of the estate," Jones said, "but I'm not sure what good it'll do. Does Dr Craig have a garage?"

"No. There's a carport, and 'is TR6 is still there. I saw it when we arrived. Battery's dead. Been off the road for months."

Jones asked Havers to search the bedroom while he rifled through the area Craig had set aside in the living room as his office.

A couple of minutes later, Havers popped his head out of the bedroom. "Dr Armstrong? Can you check out his closet and tell me if there are any clothes missing?"

Armstrong practically bounced from the room.

Jones' mobile buzzed. He didn't recognise the number.

"DCI Jones here."

"Chief Inspector Jones?" The cultured Home Counties voice, sounded tired. "I'm Hassan Hussein. I understand you've been trying to contact me?"

The man spoke perfect English and might have made a BBC news reporter.

So much for stereotyping. Shame on you, Jones.

"How can I help you?" Hussein asked.

"You collected Dr Craig from his home last Friday week. That's the 5th. Is that correct?"

"Yes, that's right. I took him to *Chez Gerard's* on the High Street."

"Was he with anybody?"

"No, but he was dressed for a date, and I happen to know he had a meal with a woman."

"Did you see him with her?"

"No, sir. I didn't, but one of the other drivers took Dr Craig and his date home later that night. Turns out they were very friendly."

"How do you remember this from over a fortnight ago, Mr Hussein?"

"Don't let my part-time job fool you, Chief Inspector. I'm studying genetics at the university. Dr Craig is one of my lecturers. Rather good he is, too. Interesting and entertaining, unlike most of the boring old farts. I always make a point to drive him if I can. Is he in any trouble? If he needs a character witness, I'd be happy to provide one." The taxi-driving undergraduate laughed.

"That won't be necessary, Mr Hussein."

Jones thanked the man and rang off.

Havers and Armstrong returned from the bedroom.

"Any joy?"

"Can't tell," Armstrong answered. "Never had the need to look in 'is wardrobe before. There are some empty 'angers, and the sock drawers aren't exactly full to overflowing, but I dunno. Might have packed for a trip. Can I?" Armstrong pointed to a dining chair.

Jones nodded and the academic lowered himself into it. The chair and his bike leathers squeaked.

"Have you tried contacting Dr Bennett?" Havers asked.

"Yeah, I called 'er when Mr Jones asked me to contact Andy. She didn't pick up." He paused a moment before continuing. "She were supposed to be heading to New York last week for a conference, but planned to be back in London tomorrow."

"Might Dr Craig have gone with her to New York?" Jones asked, clutching.

"Nah." Armstrong shook his head firmly. "Not a chance. Missed a conference in Germany last month 'cause 'is passport's out of date. Forgot to renew it. Needs a full-time PA, but there ain't no funds in the budget, see."

The next question came from Havers. "Did Dr Craig ever meet any of his more dangerous subjects out of hours, or in their own homes?"

"Don't be daft, mun. Andy only deals with convicted criminals or remand prisoners. Dangerous arseholes, the lot of them. Potentially, anyway. Only ever interviewed them in prison or in the nick. It was part of the trial's protocol."

Havers' lips thinned. He couldn't hide his disappointment.

"Did Dr Craig own a laptop?" he asked.

"Yes. Carries it in 'is backpack. Goes everywhere with it. Except when 'e were cycling. A sports nut is our Andy, did I say?"

Havers shot a look at Jones, an "I told you so" glint in his eye.

"A keen cyclist, you say?" Havers asked.

"Yeah," Armstrong answered. "Off on 'is bloody mountain bike whenever 'e's got a spare moment. Bloody nutcase. I mean, what's wrong with a motorbike?"

"I haven't seen a backpack here," Havers said, his excitement growing, "or a cycle come to think of it. Where does he store it?"

"In the lab. Cleans the mud off it with a jet-washer. No room for it in 'ere."

"Is it still there?" Jones asked.

"No, but 'e would have taken it with 'im."

"How?" Havers demanded. "He didn't have a car."

"Could've 'ired himself an SUV. Done that before now."

"Who from?"

Armstrong shrugged. "Dunno, mun. Some place on the internet. One of them firms that delivers the car to your door, I imagine."

"Where does he do his off-roading?" Havers asked, leaning closer, practically bouncing on his toes.

He could sense a breakthrough, but Jones was still less than certain.

"No idea. Never been out with 'im on a bike. Andy's the sports freak, not me. The mad bugger even jogs into work most days. "

"How far is it to the university from here?" Havers asked.

"Couple of miles," Jones told him.

"Andy goes the long way round," Armstrong butted in, "unless 'e's short for time. Most days, 'e takes in a loop of the golf course, too. Bloody mad for it 'e is. Fit though. Unlike me." The Welshman patted his pudgy stomach. "Likes me food and me beer too much."

Not to mention the cheroots.

Jones offered his hand to Armstrong. "Right. That's it for now. Thanks for all your time this evening, Jem. *Diolch yn fawr.*"

Armstrong's eyes bulged. He rolled to his feet.

"*Rydych chi'n siarad Cymraeg?* You speak Welsh?"

"*Ychydig.* A little. Thanks again, Jem. Your information has been invaluable. We won't need you any more tonight, though."

The academic's face fell. "Are you sure? I'll stay if you need me. Don't fancy sitting at 'ome on my own, see."

"No, we're just about done here now. And you should go home. Dr Craig might try to contact you." Jones shot a look at Havers who rolled his eyes and didn't look best pleased.

"You've left messages for him, haven't you?" Jones continued. "So, you should be there in case he calls."

Armstrong's expression brightened. "You're right, Chief Inspector. I need to check my phone messages and my emails." Half way to the corridor and while cramming his head into the motorcycle helmet, he added. "I'll call you if I hear anything."

"Ride safely, sir."

"What do think?" Havers asked after the Welshman had hurried from the building.

He closed on Jones who stood in the centre of the lounge.

"All my instincts tell me he's taken a 'sabbatical' with this EJ Bennett."

Havers' face reddened and he looked ready to burst.

"What the hell is wrong with you, Jones?" The sinews stood out on his neck and he appeared to be having difficulty controlling his breathing. "Craig's a keen cyclist. Nobody's seen or heard from him in a fortnight. And we have the facial reconstruction. Sandy *is* Dr Craig. It's so obvious! Two weeks ago, he headed out for an early-morning ride and Jarman killed him. It's a random attack, pure and simple. Craig was unlucky. Wrong place, wrong time." He took a breath. "Jarman simply wanted a victim to fit with the film poster. Anyone would have done. Any random stranger."

"I don't see it that way, sir. Nothing Jarman's done so far is random—except maybe killing Charlie. The way I see it, Jarman's pretty much planned everything down to the last detail."

Havers clenched his fists. "You're giving the man too much credit. I'm beginning to think I was wrong in not calling the press conference for tonight. I shouldn't have let you talk me out of it."

"Really, sir?"

"Yes. We need to get out in front of this, be more proactive."

Jones nodded and took a moment.

"Mind if I say one thing, sir?"

Havers released a long breath. "If you must."

"Let's say you're right and Sandy *is* Craig, and he was nothing more than a random victim."

"Go on."

"What would we learn from releasing his picture tonight? If anybody'd witnessed the attack they'd already have come forwards, wouldn't they?"

"You don't understand, Jones. Pressure is building on this investigation. If we can demonstrate at least some progress, it will do a great deal to improve public perception of—"

"Propaganda? Is that it? You want a nice soundbite for the evening news? Give me strength."

Havers stepped back and stood taller. "Chief Inspector Jones, we are a public-facing organisation, funded out of the public purse. We need to justify our—"

"And what if we're wrong? What if we have to issue a retraction later? How will that make us look? What would the 'public perception' be then?"

"Why can't you admit you're wrong? It's obvious to me that Sandy and Dr Craig are one and the same person."

"Is it? Why?"

"Okay." He held out his hands. "I've explained my take on the clear evidence already. You're turn. What's your read on the situation, Jones? And I don't want any of that 'gut instinct' nonsense. Give me facts and logic. Evidence, if you have any."

Jones waved a hand around the room.

"What I see here," he said, speaking through clenched teeth, "is *evidence* of a man packing up and leaving on a trip with his girlfriend. Nothing more. For all we know, Andrew Craig is in a hotel somewhere having a wonderful time with this EJ Bennett person."

He paused, giving Havers time to take in his words.

"What's the harm in waiting another few hours? I'd hate to give Jarman the satisfaction of thinking he'd fooled us. I'd much rather try to keep him off-balance. He may start making mistakes. The man's been pretty near faultless so far."

Havers puffed out his cheeks and blew out air in a silent whistle.

"I'm afraid I disagree with you, Jones. But … I'm a man of my word. You still have until midday tomorrow to find me evidence that Llewellyn's reconstruction is wrong or that Dr Craig is alive. When I hold the conference, I will be circulating Craig's description and asking for public assistance in his disappearance. You have"—he checked the time and ran the calculation—"a little over fourteen hours to change my mind. But I'm going to contact the Deputy Press Officer, Richard Connors, now and have him prepare a statement."

"Thank you, sir. Can I leave you to secure the apartment? I have a few things to do."

"At this time of the evening?"

"Yes, sir. A detective's day never ends."

"Where will you be if I need you?"

"Searching for Dr Craig. As you say, I only have fourteen hours."

"Slightly less now," Havers said, smiling.

Jones turned and left Havers to it. Confirmation of Sandy's identity now rested on Robyn's homegrown program, and he'd promised to do all he could to help.

Chapter Forty-Three

SUNDAY 21ST MAY – Morning

Police HQ, Holton, Birmingham, UK

OVERNIGHT, the nine-day heat wave broke to be replaced by a thin sheet of cloud and a light drizzle. Jones and Havers headed to the canteen—the only space on the ground floor large enough to accommodate a full-blown press conference. The weather matched Jones' mood precisely.

"You're still not convinced, are you, Jones?"

"No, sir. I'm not."

"I really don't understand why you can't accept Llewellyn's reconstruction. I can't believe it's just because you don't trust the tech—"

Jones reached his arm across Havers' chest and they stopped, face-to-face, in the middle of the empty corridor.

"Excuse the interruption, sir." Jones chose his words with care. "I haven't told you this yet, but Dr Spence agrees with me. Neither of us thinks the reconstruction is accurate."

Havers studied the ceiling before returning Jones' steady gaze. "For God's sake, Chief Inspector, what on earth does Dr Spence have to do with this?"

"Listen for a minute, will you," Jones snapped, and his aggressive tone seemed to stun Havers into silence. "If you remember, both Robyn, er, Dr Spence and I spent quite some time studying the body at Sandwell Valley last Monday afternoon."

"What of it?" Havers eyes narrowed and he took a guarded pace backwards.

Havers obviously didn't appreciate Jones' tone, so he dialled the belligerence back a few notches. "I'm sorry, sir. But I can't explain it. Llewellyn's reconstruction doesn't fit our image of what Sandy *should* look like."

"So, we're back to your gut feeling again, are we?"

"It's not only that, sir." It was Jones' turn to take a deep breath. "After leaving Dr Craig's flat last night, Dr Spence and I returned to the mortuary—"

"You did what? Who gave you permission—"

"Professor Scobie, sir. As I was saying, I accompanied Dr Spence to the mortuary to help her take her own measurements of the remains of Sandy's head and face. She's in the lab running her own analysis right now. Dr Armstrong's helping her with the numbers and the programming. They've been working on it since about three o'clock this morning. I expect to hear from them any moment now."

Havers closed his mouth. His lips thinned.

"Can you delay the conference while I call to find out how long they're going to be?"

"Not a chance, Jones. The media's already here. With me, now."

Havers turned and hurried towards the canteen, heels squeaking on the tiled floor.

Camera motors whirred, shutters clicked, and lights flashed as Havers arrived in the canteen doorway, resplendent in his freshly pressed dress uniform and peaked cap. Jones hung back a couple of paces—the Super's reluctant support act.

Havers marched through the crowd and stood behind a bank of

microphones and tapped the podium. Feedback screeched and squealed around the canteen until the sound technician cut the feed, reduced the volume, and powered up again.

As agreed the day before, Jones stood behind Havers to lend an air of mature authority. He still had no idea what Havers intended to say.

"I have prepared a statement for general release."

The cameras flashed again as Havers waved a sheaf of papers, one of which held a print of Llewellyn's reconstruction. A number of the journalists, hoping to steal a march on their colleagues, fired off questions in quick succession.

"Is this about the Orchard Park Butcher?"

"Do you have any suspects in custody?"

"How many others are going to die before you catch him?"

"Did the Butcher attack DC Washington?"

Havers held up his hand for silence. "Things will go a lot faster if you hold off your questions until *after* I've made my statement."

A tall redheaded women in a tight-fitting business suit called out, "Chief Inspector Jones, how did you feel when DC Washington fell? Did you feel responsible? Were you to blame?" The two journalists either side of her stared aghast and shuffled away. It took a lot to silence a hard-bitten media crew, and in her fervour the redhead had overstepped the bounds.

Jones marked her down for a quiet word once the furore had settled.

Havers stared them down for an extended moment and shot a glance over his shoulder at Jones. He frowned again, glanced at his sheaf of papers, and bunched his lips. Decision made, his forehead smoothed and he leaned towards the microphone. "I've recently received new information. If you bear with me for a few more moments, I shall be right back. Please help yourself to refreshments." He turned his back and signalled for Jones to follow him to the lobby. As he passed Jones he whispered, "Your Dr Spence better turn up with something soon."

Jones could barely hear him over the howls from the media pack behind them.

UP in the blessed sanctuary of Jones' office, Havers sank into a spare chair.

"Thank you for that, sir. What made you change your mind?"

"After that women's outrageous outburst, I thought I'd give you more time to explain your reservations. I'd prefer to incur the wrath of the local media than upset my best and most senior detective. Come on, Jones. Out with it."

He leaned forwards, rested his elbows on the table, clasped his hands, and fixed Jones with a piercing stare.

As Jones opened his mouth to begin an under-prepared explanation and risk Havers believing him a raving lunatic, the phone on his desk trilled the single ring of an internal call. He snatched at the handset, nearly dropping it in his haste. "Hello, Robyn?"

"No, sir, it's Sergeant Ogilvy from reception." The desk sergeant's uninspiring voice killed Jones' burgeoning hopes.

"What is it, Sergeant?"

"Sorry to disturb you, Chief Inspector, but you need to come to reception right away."

Ogilvy broke the connection before Jones had the chance to ask any questions.

"Trouble?" Havers asked, eyebrow arched.

"Could be. I'm needed at the front desk. Something's happened."

"Carry on, Jones. Let me know if it's anything important. I'll be in my office, revising my statement to the press. I can't hold them off for long. Maybe half an hour, forty-five minutes?"

"Thank you, sir."

Jones rushed along the corridor and descended the stairs two at a time, only to be obstructed on a landing by a trio of chin-wagging constables.

One of them gave forth a loud, "European Union, be damned. We should have left years ago. Allowing free entry to all them foreigners is a bloody—"

"Don't you three have anything better to do than stand around gossiping?" Jones called as he shoved past them.

When he finally reached the lobby, Jones couldn't see a reason for the summons until he rounded the side of the reception desk.

Two people, a tall man and a slim woman, dressed casually, stood in front of the desk, talking to Ogilvy. As Jones stepped towards them, Ogilvy said, "Here's DCI Jones now, sir."

The couple turned to face him.

"DCI Jones? I understand you've been looking for me."

"Dr Craig?" Jones asked, hardly daring to believe his eyes. "Dr Andrew Craig?"

The man nodded.

Jones didn't know whether to be delighted Craig was still alive and he'd been proven right, or disappointed to be back at the beginning, again. He chose delight and smiled in welcome.

Jones and Craig shook hands.

Chapter Forty-Four

SUNDAY 21ST MAY – Midday

Police HQ, Holton, Birmingham, UK

THE FOLLOWING few minutes passed in a blur.

Andrew Craig introduced Jones to his companion, Dr Eleanor Josephine "EJ" Bennett, PhD. Her smile lit up the lobby and Jones found it difficult to imagine a more attractive looking couple. They were the kind he'd expect to find gracing the cover of a glossy magazine, not that he'd ever read such a rag.

One minute after Craig's miraculous resurrection, Robyn and Jeremy Armstrong rushed into the lobby. The Welshman's reaction when he spotted Craig was one of pure joy. He did a classic open-jawed double-take, yelled, "Andy!" and brushed past Robyn, knocking the folder she carried out of her hand, which fell to the floor in a cascade of floating papers. He ran towards Craig and practically jumped into the unprepared man's arms.

Craig's understated, "Bloody hell, Jem, I've only been away a couple of weeks. Didn't think you cared," made Jones grin.

"Where've you been, mun?" Armstrong demanded, joyful tears squeezing from his dark eyes.

"We rented a cottage in the Cotswolds. Lovely this time of the year, isn't it, EJ?"

"Beautiful," she said, nodding and clearly confused by all the fuss.

"When did you leave Birmingham?" Jones asked.

"Saturday morning. The 6th, wasn't it?" Craig turned to his friend, who nodded. "Bloody hell, was it really only sixteen days ago? We've packed a hell of a lot in since then, eh love?"

EJ Bennett blushed through an embarrassed smile. "Certainly have. DCI Jones, what's this all about?"

"I'll explain as best I can, Dr Bennett," Jones said, "but we'll need somewhere quieter."

"Excuse me, Chief Inspector," Robyn said, squatting to collect the fallen papers, her eyes sparkling in triumph tempered with fatigue, "but you really need to see this."

She stood and raised a buff-coloured folder.

"Dr Craig, Dr Bennett," Jones said, "please bear with me. I'll be back in a moment."

He and Robyn stepped to a quiet corner of the foyer and she opened the folder to reveal a 2D representation of a man who looked a little like Craig, but not enough to matter.

Both Craig and Sandy had fair hair, blue eyes, and square chins, but Robyn's reconstruction showed a man with a slightly receding hairline and more rounded cheeks. In general, he wasn't as lean as Craig. Familiar, though. Strangely familiar. But Jones couldn't put a name to the face.

"How accurate would you say it is?" Jones asked, studying the image more closely.

He'd seen the man before, but where?

"Jem and I worked on the data through the night," she said, hiding a yawn behind her hand. "We think it's pretty good. It certainly 'feels' closer. What do you think?"

Jones studied the image more closely. After a few moments, he smiled.

"It's is absolutely brilliant. Just the way I imagined him. Bang on, in fact."

"Chief Inspector," Craig said, closing in on them with Dr Bennett at his side, "EJ and I have been travelling all morning. Will this take long?" He caught sight of Robyn's rendering and dipped a head towards it. "Oh hell. Tommo isn't in trouble again, is he?"

"Who?" Jones asked, excitement flipping his heart rate into overdrive.

"Tommo." Craig said. "Thomas Tomlinson."

"Bloody 'ell," Armstrong said, "Thought 'e looked familiar, but I only met 'im the once."

"Tomlinson?" Jones said, holding up the sheet again. "Of course! I *knew* I'd seen him somewhere before."

Robyn tugged at his arm. "Thomas Tomlinson?"

"The guard from Long Marston prison."

"Who? … Oh, of course. I remember now. He's the one accused of encouraging a prisoner to hang himself?"

Not just any prisoner.

"Yes, he's the one."

"He got off, didn't he?" Robyn asked. "Cleared of all charges?"

Jones took in the reconstruction once again and nodded. "Yes, but it would appear that someone didn't agree with the results of the internal review." He turned to Craig. "Are you sure it's Tomlinson?"

Craig peered at the sheet. "As certain as I can be. That image makes him look younger, but not by much. Is that one of Rhys Llewellyn's reconstructions? Tommo isn't dead is he?"

"Sorry, sir, but I'm not at liberty—"

"Don't give me that bull, Chief Inspector. Tommo's a friend of mine, and we've given up our time this morning to come here for reasons you've yet to tell us. Is Tommo dead?"

"Please doctors," Jones said, speaking quietly, "if you would follow me." He opened his arms and ushered them all—Armstrong

357

included—towards the lifts, forcing himself to enter the tiny metal box. Robyn at his side helped quell his nerves.

Once in the privacy of the lift, Craig rounded on Jones.

"Chief Inspector," he said, "that"—he tapped the sheet of paper Jones now carried—"might not be accurate. I'm afraid you can't rely on anything that comes out of Llewellyn's CFR lab. I hate talking down a colleague like this, but it's true. The old chap's relying on past glory, I'm afraid. He hasn't published a peer-assessed paper in nearly a decade. In fact, he's in the academic wilderness."

Jones gave Robyn a sideways glance. She acknowledged it with a knowing smile.

"Really, sir? Professor Llewellyn speaks very highly of you."

"He does? That's interesting. He's been rather jealous of my growing profile in the criminal research community."

"Nah," Armstrong said, still beaming. "That rendering's got bugger all to do with Rhys, mun. Me and Dr Spence created that one. She's developed a brilliant process. Elegant, it is. Clean. I 'elped with the maths and the processing."

Jones' stomach lurched as the lift slowed to a stop. The warning bell dinged and the doors parted. He led the party into his office and invited them all to settle.

"If you'd wait there for a second, I'll be right back."

He popped along the corridor to collect Phil, Alex, and Ben from the main office. When they re-entered his office, Craig, Bennett, and Robyn were seated on the visitors' side of his desk, and Armstrong stood behind Craig as though frightened to let him out of his sight.

Jones sat behind the desk, while Phil and Ben stood alongside Armstrong. Alex took the remaining spare chair. The room had become a little overcrowded, but Jones couldn't exactly invite the civilians into the main office where they'd catch sight of the crime scene photos and the film posters.

"Okay, from the top," Jones said, looking at Craig. "Tell me how you know Supervising Officer Tomlinson."

Craig released his hold on EJ's hand and leaned against the back of his chair.

"If I do," he said, "will you tell me what's going on?"

"I'll let you know what I can, sir. Now, please." Jones lowered the rendered image to the desk, turned it to face Craig, and held open his hands, waiting.

"How much do you know about my work, Chief Inspector?"

"I read the Ministry of Justice's briefing document and your university bio. You're working on the so-called 'anger gene'."

"That's right," Craig answered. "The monoamine-oxidase A gene, or the MAO-A. It's one of two neighbouring genes responsible for encoding mitochondrial enzymes, which catalyse—"

"Excuse me, Dr Craig," Jones interrupted, "I'm not a neuroscientist. Words of one syllable would be preferable."

Sitting slightly apart from the academics, Robyn frowned at him, but he shook his head at her.

"My apologies, Chief Inspector. This is my baby and I tend to get a little carried away. I'll tone down the science as best I can." He took a breath and glanced at EJ Bennett as though in apology, then returned his attention to Jones. "Numerous studies have shown that men—and it's only men, I'm afraid—with a low-functioning version of the MAO-A gene are prone to violence, particularly if they were exposed to childhood abuse."

Childhood abuse.

There it was. The words chilled Jones' blood, but the connections started to make sense and the clues began tumbling into place. He finally understood Jarman's motivation. Whether the understanding brought him any closer to the man's identity, only time would tell.

"Jem and I," Craig continued, "have discovered a link between MAO-A and a transcription error in another gene that codes for 5-hydroxy—"

"Andy," EJ said, taking his hand in hers and squeezing it hard, "the Chief Inspector's eyes are glazing over."

"Ah, sorry again, Chief Inspector. Okay, put simply, Jem and I have developed a potential amelioration strategy ... I mean, treatment therapy. In time, we hope to reduce the instances of violence in men with the faulty MAO-A gene. To test our hypothesis the

Ministry of Justice has funded an extensive research programme. They have allowed us access to violent offenders in the West Midlands region. In short, we are recruiting criminals with the faulty gene into a drug trial."

"And for that you need their DNA profiles?" Robyn asked.

"Exactly, Dr Spence."

Jones smiled. The pattern fit.

"HMP Long Marston, a Category A prison, happened to be one of the custodial institutions on our list. Tommo, I mean, SO Tomlinson, was my primary contact in Long Marston. He could see the benefits of our research. As I'm sure you can imagine Chief Inspector, not all prison officers are that supportive. In fact, Tommo and I got on really well."

As he took at Robyn's reconstruction again, sadness crept into his eyes.

"Tell me, Dr Craig," Jones said, "I don't suppose you recruited a prisoner called Arthur Buckeridge for your trial, did you?"

"Buckeridge?" Robyn gasped. "The Hollie Jardine case? He's the one responsible for killing all those girls in France?"

Jones nodded.

Phil ground his teeth and his hands formed fists. He'd made the same deductive leap as Jones. They'd reached the same conclusion.

"Actually, no," Craig answered, shaking his head. "We interviewed Buckeridge, but he didn't fit the criteria."

"He didn't have the faulty gene?"

"No, Chief Inspector. Nor did he suffer abuse as a child."

No, he was the abuser, not the abused.

"I see," Jones said, still nodding. "Can you tell us anything else that might be relevant?"

"Only that when I interviewed Arthur Buckeridge, I saw a man totally convinced of his right to do anything he damn well pleased with whomever he chose. Furthermore, I saw no risk of a potential suicide, and I added that to my report. As for the accusations against Tommo, they were totally spurious. SO Tomlinson would no more encourage Arthur Buckeridge to hang himself than he would help smuggle drugs into prison. He's one of the most scrupulous individuals I've ever known.

"No, Chief Inspector," Craig said, adding emphasis to the "No", "Arthur Buckeridge was a victim of his own delusions. He refused to be placed in secure lockup and insisted he should remain part of the general prison population. The man was absolutely convinced that he could bend even the worst of the Category A prisoners to his will. Completely deranged. I'm convinced—as was Tommo's review board—that Buckeridge was killed by his fellow prisoners, and they tried to make it look like a suicide. It had nothing to do with Tommo. Absolutely nothing."

"When exactly did Buckeridge die?" Robyn asked.

"Thursday, the 9th of February," Phil said without needing time to think. "Just over a month before Armin de Silva."

"Bloody hell," Ben said, which shocked everyone who knew him.

At work, Big Ben Adeoye swore about as often as Jones did— which was never.

"Armin De Silva," Craig asked. "Who's he?"

"Another case, sir," Phil said.

"Another apparent suicide by hanging?" Craig asked, one eyebrow raised into an arch.

Smart as a whip was Andrew Craig.

Jones held up a hand. "I'm afraid I'm not—"

"At liberty to say?" Craig grumbled.

"Exactly, sir. But," Jones said, "as soon as I am, I promise to tell you all I can. Now." He stood and glanced at Ben. "If you wouldn't mind accompanying DC Adeoye to an interview room."

"What for?"

"We'll need a statement for our records. You and Dr Bennett can go together."

"Is that really necessary?"

Jones shrugged. "Not at all, sir. You can give your statements separately if you so choose."

"That's not what I meant, Chief Inspector. I mean do you need the statement today?" He read the time on the wall clock. "We've already been here ages."

"It would save you having to come back in, sir. Ben, if you please."

Ben stepped a little closer and waited. His powerful and looming presence encouraged the two academics to stand.

"You too, Dr Armstrong," Jones said. "But before you go, I must thank you for all your help and ask that you keep what you've learned here to yourselves."

"But you've told us nothing, man," Craig said, finally losing his academic cool.

"In that case, I must ask you to keep your speculations to yourselves. We're reaching the end of a highly sensitive and complicated case, and if any information were to leak out, it might compromise the investigation. Do I make myself clear?"

"Perfectly clear, Chief Inspector," Craig said, eyes narrowed. "But I'm holding you to your promise. I, we"—he waved a hand to encompass EJ Bennett and Jem Armstrong—"will expect a full explanation the moment you are free to give one."

"Rest assured, Dr Craig, I always keep my promises," Jones answered, pleasantly.

Especially to a man with court-certified DNA analysers.

Jones remained standing until the door had closed behind Ben and the three doctors.

"What did you think of him?" Jones asked the room.

"Craig?" Phil asked.

"Yep."

"A bit arrogant, but he seemed sound enough. You?"

"The same."

"I thought he was rather nice," Robyn said, eyes wide. "Highly intelligent. Jem Armstrong's a little darling, too."

Jones sighed and hoped she was messing with him.

Phil's cheeky grin reinforced Jones' hope.

"By the way," Phil said, "when you said we were 'reaching the end of a highly sensitive and complicated case', did you mean it?"

Jones smiled. Trust Phil to pick up on that.

"In fact, I did. That somewhat pompous—but rather nice—academic has just broken the case wide open."

"He has?" Robyn asked, incredulity in her tone.

"I think so. Alex," Jones said, "did you and Ben bring up all the evidence boxes from the Railway Cuttings case?"

"You asked us to, sir, but …" Alex looked pained, "I am afraid the evidence has gone missing, including the harmonica."

"What! Why didn't you tell me?"

"You were busy, and I hoped—"

"Who signed it out?"

"Nobody, sir. The evidence boxes have been transferred to the secure archive facility in Dudley. I ordered the archives officer to recall the boxes, but he has yet to locate them. I am sorry, sir."

"We closed that case less than three months ago. Why were the boxes transferred so soon?"

"The Holton evidence locker is too small. They have to transfer the boxes much more quickly than normal."

"But three months? They were supposed to have enough room for six. Who okayed the transfer?"

"It is a standing order issued from the top floor, sir," Alex answered, her eyes still downcast.

Jones turned to Phil. "Suspicious or coincidental?"

"Impossible to say."

"Okay, Phil. Give the minions in Dudley the hurry-up. I want that evidence found, damn it."

"I am on it, boss," Alex said, leaning forwards to stand.

"Alex," Jones said, "this isn't your fault. Do what you can."

At his side, Robyn tried to hide a yawn with her hand.

"Robyn, what am I thinking? You've been up all night. You must be exhausted. Phil, arrange a driver to take Dr Spence home."

She held up a hand. "No, no. It's fine really. I don't live that far away."

"Dr Spence," he said, scowling at another of Phil's grins, "I insist. We will keep in touch, though. I promise."

Her shoulders sagged in agreement.

"Well, if you insist, I'll have to accept. It would be good to see Zach before he forgets who I am. Thank you, Chief Inspector."

"No, Dr Spence, thank you for all your sterling efforts."

Bloody hell.

Why did everything he say to her sound so bloody trite?

Phil escorted Robyn through the door, leaving Jones and a smiling Alex alone, and the room quiet.

"Why the grin, Detective Sergeant?" he asked in mock severity.

"You like her, yes?"

"Of course, I do. She is an excellent forensics officer."

"It is more than that, boss." Alex's smile widened.

"Give the idiots in the evidence locker a chivvy up, will you?"

Her smile faded, but not by much.

"Yes, boss. I will go down in person," she said, climbing to her feet. "They need a rocket up their backsides, yes?"

"Make sure they know how urgent it is. Tell them I'm not a happy bunny."

Alone in his office, Jones slumped back into his seat. He spent ten minutes reviewing the new information before remembering the call he had to make. He picked up the nearest desk phone and gave Havers the news. To give him his due, Havers' magnanimity was instant.

"Well," he said, "I'm glad I listened to you in the end. What should I say to the media? According to the desk sergeant, they're screaming blue murder down there."

Which probably had something to do with the canteen not serving alcohol.

"I suggest you issue a bland statement and ad lib the answers to their moronic questions. They aren't going to be too happy about it, but I'm sure you'll cope. This afternoon, I'll pull together what we know about SO Tomlinson and we'll take it from there. We'll want to search his home at some stage."

"Yes, quite. I owe you a great deal for this, David. That's twice you've saved my blushes now. I won't forget in a hurry. What are you going to do?"

"It's Sunday, it's getting late, and we need to regroup. I'll pull everyone in tomorrow first thing and we'll thrash things through."

He almost said he needed to sleep on it, but he'd rattled off enough clichés for one telephone conversation.

"Good luck with the press, sir."

"Thank you, Jones."

Havers rang off and left Jones alone with his thoughts. The idea of taking time off when in the middle of a serious investigation simply because it happened to be a Sunday had never entered his head. Swerving Havers' potential interference certainly had.

Chapter Forty-Five

SUNDAY 21ST MAY – Early Afternoon

Police HQ, Holton, Birmingham, UK

"PHIL," Jones said, speaking into his mobile, "are you going to be long?"

"Nope. Just fetching drinks and some munchies. Where are you?"

"In the briefing room, and I need you to help me with the SmartScreen."

"You can't call Biggles?" Phil laughed.

"On a Sunday? His union rep would have kittens."

"As would his mother, I expect. Be there in five. I'm having a chicken salad baguette, you?"

"Cheese and tomato, please."

"On my way."

While he waited, and since no one else could see, he moved to Bigglesworth's IT corner and hit the enter key. The screen awoke to display the blue oval of the West Midlands Police logo. He entered his ID and password and typed Armin De Silva into the name field.

The details of the Railway Cuttings Case flooded onto the screen, and he started reading to refresh his memory. By the time the door opened to admit Phil and Alex, he'd worked through the first few dozen pages. Phil carried a tray full of food and drinks, leaving Alex to hold open the door.

"Blimey, Alex. Look," Phil said, making a point to nod in Jones' direction. "My blood sugar must be running low. I'm hallucinating."

Alex shook her head slowly.

"That's more than enough cheek from you, Inspector Cryer. Hand over the food and be quick about it." Jones grinned.

Phil lowered the tray to the table, approached IT corner, and read from the screen.

"You want us to start with the Railway Cuttings case? I thought we'd be cracking on with SO Tomlinson's murder now we know who Sandy really is."

"No, I want to work chronologically. According to the posters, De Silva was the first murder. Seems like a good place to open this case review."

"Okay, that makes sense," Phil said, biting into his baguette and chewing furiously.

"What did they say in the crypt, Alex?" Jones asked.

"A team is scouring the Annex, but they have had no luck so far."

"Right. Leave that with me."

He gave up the techie's seat to Phil and headed to the table. Before unwrapping his baguette and tucking into his Sunday lunch, he pulled out his mobile, dialled the Evidence Annex at Dudley, and chewed the ear off the duty officer—a sergeant he'd never heard of before.

"How many people do you have on the search, Brennan?"

"Two, sir."

"Two? Is that all?"

"It is a Sunday, sir."

"I know what day of the week it is, Sergeant! We requested

those box files days ago. This is a murder case, man. I want them found."

"Our records show it as *Closed-no further action*, sir."

"Well, it's been changed to *Open-Unsolved, and Pull Your Finger Out*, Brennan. Draft in as many officers as you need to find that evidence, and do it now!"

"Er … yes, sir. Right away, sir."

Jones hit the red button to end the call—when he would much rather have slammed a real phone into its cradle—and removed the lid from his takeaway cup. The tea steamed and tasted of nothing but hot water. The cheese had enough flavour to make it edible, but no more. At least the baguette was fresh.

"Did we ever find out what Armin De Silva did for a living?"

"A mid-level civil servant, it says in the summary report," Phil answered.

"What branch?"

"The Prisons and Probation Ombudsman, based in London."

"Didn't that sound any alarm bells to Jerry Scranton's team?"

"Apparently not. De Silva wasn't an investigator and had no involvement in any high-profile prison deaths. Definitely not the Buckeridge suicide or Jerry would have brought us in."

"What does it say in the case file? Did Jerry interview De Silva's line manager in the PPO?"

"His oppo did."

"Your mate, De Villiers?"

"Yep. Just a sec." Phil scrolled down the screen, reading at a speed Jones could only dream of matching. "Here we are. De Silva was the PPO's Regional Press Officer."

"A press officer!" Alex gasped.

Phil shook his head. "Not in the same way as Ronnie Poole. He didn't front any media briefings. The PPO likes to keep as low a profile as possible. De Silva's role was more like a copy editor, making sure the PPO's reports made grammatical sense. But his name did appear on the PPO's latest annual report, and that's in the public domain."

"Which is how Jarman identified and targeted him," Jones said, making it a statement not a question.

Phil's answering smile could have been a grimace. "I doubt it would be too difficult for anyone with a basic grasp of IT to find Armin De Silva. He was probably on Facebook. Hang on." He opened a web browser and ran a search. "Yep, here he is. Armin De Silva, location, date of birth, favourite restaurants, family members. All the information Jarman would need to locate him. And the Facebook page is still active. His family hasn't even announced his death."

"What makes people bare all to the world?"

"It's what they do, boss," Alex said, shrugging her good shoulder.

"So," Phil said, "we have a definitive link between the murders of Armin De Silva and our own Ronnie Poole. Donald Jarman is targeting press officers—"

"And police officers," Alex interrupted.

"And prison officers," Phil agreed. "People in authority."

"And all with at least a peripheral association with Arthur Buckeridge," Jones said.

"How so?" Phil asked. "As far as we know, Ronnie never even met Buckeridge."

"But she did prepare the police statement when we charged him. And she did stand on the podium with the Chief Constable when he read out the statement she prepared after Buckeridge's conviction. As I remember, the statement was particularly scathing of the man."

Phil smiled, this time with real warmth. "Agreed. Ronnie was pretty vitriolic, using phrases like 'despicable acts of violence' and 'untold depravity' and 'perhaps the worst criminal the West Midlands has ever brought to justice thanks to the sterling efforts of our highly dedicated investigative officers, led by DCI David Jones'. I could recite the whole speech, or I could play the recording. It's on the media page of our website. Makes good viewing. I can go fetch some popcorn, if you like."

Jones shot Phil a disgusted look. "That won't be necessary, thank you, Detective Inspector."

"Why didn't Jarman target the Chief, or you, for that matter?" Alex asked. Free of her sling, she gently massaged her injured shoulder.

Jones gave her question serious consideration and took a moment to answer. "The chief constable is too high a profile target, and he has a full-time protection detail. More difficult to access. On the other hand, Ronnie is—was—a softer target. As for me, that's just it, I *am* being targeted. First with Ronnie, whom I liked, then with Charlie and Ryan. Jarman is getting closer to me with every kill."

"Making it personal," Phil said.

"As Buckeridge did when he goaded me and when he"—Jones glanced at Alex and changed tack—"did the other stuff."

"It is okay, boss," Alex said, jutting out her jaw. "You can say it. When Buckeridge paid an arsonist to burn down my house and killed Julie instead of me."

"Sorry, Alex. I didn't mean to open old wounds."

"They're not old wounds, boss. They are still fresh."

"I know." He held out a hand. "I know."

"Okay," Phil said, "what's our next move?"

"We've been on the back foot since the start, and I've had enough. I'd love to go on the attack. Draw the bugger out."

Phil held up a hand. "Last time you did that you ended up being shot in the chest."

Jones rubbed the area where Buckeridge's bullet smashed into his sternum which, from time to time, still ached. Without the light-weight ceramic vest Giles Danforth made him wear, he'd have died that day in Buckeridge's derelict boy's home.

"Point taken, Philip. I actually meant, 'I *would* love to go on the attack', but we need more ammunition first."

Before he could say anything more, the door opened and Ben strolled into the room.

"All done with the three doctors?" Phil asked.

"Yes, sir. When I escorted them to the exit, the little one, Jem

Armstrong, was dancing around the other two like an excitable puppy. Never seen a grown man so worked up."

"In his defence," Jones said, "Armstrong spent most of the past twenty-four hours thinking his best mate had been clubbed to death with a baseball bat."

"And," Phil added, smiling, "he did stay up all night working on that reconstruction with Robyn Spence."

Jones waited for the inevitable wink or snide comment, but this time, Phil resisted the urge.

"When he first caught sight of Dr Craig," Jones said, "it was like that scene in the original series of Star Trek."

Ben, Alex, and Phil looked at him, faces blank.

"You know," Jones continued, "the episode when Spock thinks he's killed Captain Kirk and then discovers he's still alive."

Nothing. No reaction.

"Don't tell me you've never seen it?"

"Yes, boss," Phil answered, "but we're all stunned you've ever watched TV."

Ben and Phil grinned like idiots. Alex remained straight-faced.

"Yes, yes. Highly amusing. Are you quite finished?"

Ben stopped chuckling first, and Phil soon followed.

"Yes, boss," Phil said.

"Good. Tomorrow, Philip, you and Ben can visit Llewellyn's lab and find out what went wrong. Haul Kurt Lang over the coals, too. The way I see it, Lang had more input into the reconstruction than Rhys Llewellyn, who looked like a passenger in the process. I'd like to know if Craig's face appearing on the board was a genuine mistake or intentional. And if it *was* intentional, you can tell them we might consider bringing charges against them for wasting police time."

"We have their home addresses. Want me to send a couple of patrol cars and bring them in today?"

"No, let's leave them to stew for a while. In the morgue, when Armstrong pulled Lang out of his chair and took over, Lang looked like he was going to burst into tears. A few hours pondering the error of his ways might loosen his tongue a little."

"Sounds like a plan to me," Phil said.

"Right," Jones said, slicing his hand through the air to end the topic. "Let's get back to work, shall we? Next case. What vital piece of information did we learn today?"

"Sandy's identity," Ben said after a moment's pause for thought.

"And that he was a supervising officer on Arthur Buckeridge's wing in Long Marston prison," Phil added.

Ben and Alex nodded their agreement.

"And," Jones said, holding up an index finger, "that he was accused—at the very least—of turning a blind eye when Buckeridge was found hanging in his cell."

Phil nodded. "The PPO—our specific link with the De Silva murder—received a number of emails accusing Tomlinson of leaving the cell door open for the prisoners to help Buckeridge tie the knot and slip the noose over his head."

"They did?"

"And there were a few high-profile tweets from the Prison Reform League screaming about corruption in the prison service."

"That's hardly news. They always cry 'foul'," Jones muttered.

"But Tomlinson was fully exonerated in an internal investigation by the PPO. However," Phil said, flash-reading from Bigglesworth's largest monitor, "it says here that the PPO received a petition from the PRL, complaining about the way they investigated the case. In particular the unreasonable speed of Tomlinson's exoneration." He continued reading. "In fact, the PRL organised a demonstration outside the PPO building in London three days after they published their report into the Tomlinson review. Not much of a demo though. Only a few dozen placard-waving diehards turned up. They didn't even slow traffic in the area."

"What date was that?" Jones asked, struggling to read the screen from distance.

"The report hit the PPO website on Tuesday, 25th April, and the PRL protest rally took place on Canary Wharf, the following Friday, April 28th."

"And Jarman murdered Tomlinson what, a week later?"

"Eight days," Phil said, "May 6th."

"And since then, Jarman has killed Ronnie, Charlie, and he's left Ryan for dead."

Phil opened his eyes wider and pursed his lips. "A busy boy."

"Do you have any pictures of that PRL demo?"

"You don't think—"

"Looks like Jarman's a Buckeridge acolyte, to me. You never know, he might have attended the protest."

"Could we get that lucky?" Ben asked.

Phil tilted his head. "I'll try the Met Police database. It's standard operating procedure for them to film demonstrations even if they remain peaceful. Give me a second to sign in."

Phil's fingers rattled the keys. It took him longer to find than he promised. Jones counted to forty-three before the moving images darkened his screen.

"Here you go, boss. Let's see who the Met's cameras picked up, shall we?"

He hit another key and the SmartScreen flickered into life, showing a video window with the controls running along the bottom of the frame.

They watched five minutes of razor-sharp surveillance images, shot from above the protestors, no doubt using local traffic or ANPR cameras. Jones counted seventeen placard-wielding protesters in all, dressed in wet-weather gear to protect them against the squally April showers blowing in from the river.

"Call that a protest?" Ben scoffed.

Alex smiled. "Some might have been put off by the weather."

"Fairweather protesters," Jones said, "not like in my day."

Alex jerked upright. "You were a protestor, boss?"

"Nope, I was one of the poor sods holding back the coal miners on the picket lines. Now they were men and women who knew how to protest. Wait … stop there!"

The film stopped rolling and focused on a small bunch of people at the outer edge of the small crowd.

"Can you reverse the film slowly?"

"Only by jumping back a few seconds at a time." Phil hit the back arrow on his keyboard and the image jerked backwards by five seconds. The faces, soaked and miserable, slid towards the right of the screen, bringing the edge of another protestor into shot.

"Again," Jones instructed.

Another picture jolt revealed a group of five, three in front and two behind, their faces partially concealed by placards.

"Once more."

The group moved to the right again, and the two in front seemed to look directly into the camera.

Phil pointed to the protestors in the front row. "Look, boss. That's Kurt Lang, and I'm guessing the tall woman beside him is Vanessa Étage."

"Yep," Ben said, "that's her. I'd recognise the woman anywhere. See the way she towers over Lang, protecting him? It's like she's his minder."

"Boss," Alex said, "do you recognise her?"

Jones nodded. "I do."

"It is Annette Lean!" Alex announced.

"The hiker from Sandwell Valley?" Ben asked.

"Bloody hell," Phil burst. "They're all working together."

"Looks like it," Jones agreed, but his attention had been drawn to the man in the back row whose face was part-hidden by Lang's hand-written placard which read, "*Protect Our Prisoners.*"

"Look there in the background." Jones jumped up, closed on the screen, and jabbed a finger on the paused video. "Who's that standing between them?"

"*Herregud!*"

Ben's eyes popped open.

"Bloody hell," Phil said. "It can't be."

His fingers attacked the keyboard once again, manipulating the image. As Holden Bigglesworth had done days ago, the picture enlarged, pixilated, and sharpened again.

"It *is* him."

"The bastard!" Phil said, voicing Jones' thoughts precisely.

In an instant, everything became crystal clear. Everything.

Chapter Forty-Six

Police HQ, Holton, Birmingham, UK

JONES GLOWERED at the photo of the murdering turncoat standing out clear on the SmartScreen. Innocent blue eyes stared out of an overly youthful face.

Butter wouldn't bloody melt.

Jarman had been working amongst them the whole bloody time. No wonder he knew their every move.

"Anyone know where he lives?" Jones asked.

"It'll be in his personnel record," Phil said. He settled back in his chair and resumed typing.

Jones crossed to Bigglesworth's corner and stood, looking over Phil's shoulder while he accessed the West Midlands Police's HR portal. A few keystrokes later, the man's dossier emerged on the screen.

"Here we go," Phil said, his shoulders tense. "229 Triumph Way.

It's in Water Orton. Ben, get to the armoury and draw a weapon on my authorisation. No, not you Alex, you're grounded, remember. Boss, are we going to call in the ARU?"

Jones sighed. Jarman had messed with them again.

"Don't bother, Phil. That's a dead end."

"What do you mean?"

"It was way before your time. 229 Triumph Way burned down just after the millennium. 2003, I think. No, 2004. The fire destroyed the houses on other side, too. The council never rebuilt them. After what they called 'due consultation', they ended up knocking down the whole row to make way for a shopping centre."

"I remember it from before I joined the police," Ben said. "Arson wasn't it?"

"That's right. Two died. A husband and wife, Robert and Linda Anderson. I was a DI at the time. Ran the investigation. Sad story. Their son did it."

"Their son?" Alex asked, turning her eyes to the image on the screen, her expression shocked.

"Yes, Jack. A kid who liked playing with his dad's cigarette lighter. Had no idea what he was doing. Or so he claimed when we interviewed him under caution and in the presence of an appropriate adult. But I knew better, and so did the jury in the end. The evil little toerag knew exactly what he was doing. Showed no remorse either."

"Anderson," Ben mused. "Lindsay Anderson. Another British film director."

Jones sighed. "I hadn't missed the connection, Ben."

"Don't tell me," Phil said, almost groaning, "little Jack Anderson was found guilty of parricide, arson and ended up in Derby Borstal, under the care of one Arthur Michael Buckeridge?"

Jones nodded. He couldn't think of anything more to say.

"You didn't recognise him, boss?" Alex asked.

Jones found his voice again. "He's changed a fair bit since I interviewed him, and Jarman clearly knows how to change his appearance, blend into the background." He couldn't prevent his eyes from being drawn back to the image on the SmartScreen. "Hell, no wonder Ronnie let him into her flat. She knew him."

Phil nodded. "She posted an article on our website when the new tech arrived. There's a photo, too. Not-Bob looked like he'd been given the keys to the local sweetshop. Ronnie interviewed members of the IT Department and even included a quote from Biggles. Want me to throw up the article, boss?"

"Don't bother, Phil. It won't tell us anything we don't already know. Did anyone ever see him on a motorbike? Damn it, the motorbike leathers!" Jones slammed the side of his fist into the table. "The bugger was taunting us all the time. Triumph motorbikes, Triumph Way. Why didn't I see it?"

"You can't blame yourself, boss."

"It's not me I blame, Alex," Jones said, jabbing a finger towards the SmartScreen. "It's that bastard I blame. Him and Arthur Buckeridge. Evil bloody—"

The shrill ring of the office phone cut off the rest of Jones' invective. Being the closest, he snatched the handset from its cradle.

"Jones here."

"It's Sergeant Lilly in the operations room, sir. I have a Professor Llewellyn on the line."

That's all I need.

"Tell him to go boil his head."

Alex's jaw dropped.

"Sorry, sir?" Lilly said.

"I'm busy—"

"He says it's urgent, sir. He sounds really upset."

"Oh, he does, does he?"

"Yes, sir. Shall I put him through?"

Jones sighed and allowed his shoulders to droop a little.

"Go on then. If you must."

The line clicked and heavy breathing filled Jones' earpiece.

"Professor Llewellyn?"

"DCI Jones? Oh my goodness, is it you? I-I didn't know who else to call. I-I thought about dialling 9-9-9, but then I saw your card on my desk and thought it would be quicker to call you directly. You know what to do, don't you? You're experienced at—"

"Professor Llewellyn, slow down. You're babbling."

Jones hit the speaker button—he already had the team's full attention.

Llewellyn's heavy breathing continued for a moment, then slowed.

"Where are you, Professor?"

"Here, in the lab. University security called me in from home. Everything's gone. Everything I've built. My whole life's work. It's gone."

"You've been robbed? You call me in the middle of a murder investigation to tell me you've been burgled?"

"No, no, it's worse than that. Much worse. He's destroyed everything. All of it. All my equipment, my files, the data. Everything. The little swine has wiped it all."

"Who has?"

"Kurt. Kurt Lang."

"How do you know it was—"

"Apart from me, he's the only one with access to the files and the equipment, Chief Inspector. They caught him on the security cameras, smiling the whole time. Why? Why would he do such a terrible thing?"

"I have no idea, sir," Jones said, not the least bit bothered about lying to the distraught man, "but I will send a team as soon as I can. In the meantime, please don't touch anything before they arrive."

"How long will they take?"

"They'll be as quick as they can, sir."

"And Kurt, will you be looking for him?"

"Oh yes, Professor. You can bet your life on that. We'll certainly be looking for him. Goodbye, sir. I'm sorry for your loss."

He lowered the phone into its cradle.

"Well, that's answered one question," Phil said. "Kurt's false reconstruction was definitely deliberate."

Jones pointed to the image on the SmartScreen. "There was never any doubt about that, Philip."

"I know. Just wanted to state the obvious."

"Well, don't. Your name isn't Not-Bob Havers."

The same phone rang again.

"Bloody hell," Phil said. "What now?"

Jones snatched up the phone once more. "Is that you again, Lilly?"

"Hello? Hello?" a man called, his voice hurried. "Is that Chief Inspector Jones?" Wailing alarms in the background made him shout.

"It is." Jones frowned and glanced around the room. "Who's this?"

"Constable McIntyre, sir. I'm the FLO with Mr and Mrs Washington at the Queen Elizabeth. There's been an … incident, sir."

A hole opened up in Jones' stomach.

"What sort on an incident? Is Ryan okay?"

"Um, it's difficult to explain, sir. You need to get here right away."

"Answer me, McIntyre. What's going on there?"

"It's one of the doctors. I think he's gone mad."

"Explain yourself, Constable."

"The doctor, sir. He's barricaded himself into the ICU with all the patients. He's demanding to speak to you in person."

"Asked for me by name, has he?"

"Yes, sir."

"Are you still in contact with him?"

"Yes, sir. He's shouting through the door. Saying he's going to burn everyone alive if you don't come right away. He's waving something through the window. Something shiny. I think it's a cigarette lighter. All the oxygen in there—"

"I understand the threat, Constable. Try to stay calm."

"I'm trying, sir."

"What does this doctor look like?"

"Didn't get much of a look at him, sir. He's wearing scrubs and a facemask. Tallish and slim."

"Okay, I've got it. Evacuate the immediate area."

Ben rushed past, his right hand forming the shape of a gun. Jones nodded him on his way to the armoury.

"I've already done that, sir," McIntyre shouted down the phone line. "Hospital security is clearing the wing now, but Mr and Mrs Washington refuse to leave, and I can't make them. I'm on my own here, sir."

"Okay, McIntyre, I understand. The emergency responders will get there soon. Meanwhile, tell Jarman I'll be there in thirty minutes."

"Jarman? You know this nutcase, sir?"

"Yes, Constable. I do. Can you tell him I'll be right there?"

"I'll try, sir."

"Excellent. I'm going to hang up now, McIntyre. If you need me, call my mobile."

"I don't know your number, sir."

Neither do I.

"Just call me through the switchboard, Constable."

Jones cradled the phone, blinked hard, and stood. He cast a lingering look around the office, finally ending at Phil and Alex. He fought back the fleeting realisation that he might never see them again. And what of Robyn? He'd have liked the opportunity to get to know her better.

Damn it, Jones. Don't go there.

Chapter Forty-Seven

SUNDAY 21ST MAY - "DONALD JARMAN"

Queen Elizabeth Hospital, Edgbaston, Birmingham, UK

DONALD JARMAN SAT astride his Triumph Bonneville T100, the engine thrumming between his legs, and studied the hospital's main entrance.

Jarman, yeah.

He thought of himself as Donald Jarman more and more these days, and never as Anderson. The Jarman identity gave him power. The power to make cuts and changes to life and death. Especially death. Everything had come down to this. All his planning, practically his whole adult life, had come down to this one moment, and he wasn't about to stuff it up.

Everything would end in a blaze of glory. The fiery light of death. And Jones would die, too. Along with any of his cronies who tagged along in his wake. He'd show them. Yeah, he'd show them all. All the world would tremble in his wake.

"Made it, Ma, Pa. Top of the world!" he muttered inside the full-face helmet, where no one could see or hear him.

He smirked at the modified quote from *White Heat*. 1949, yeah. They didn't make films like that anymore. How could they? Real actors like James Cagney didn't exist these days. Real actors who *lived* their roles. Actors who suffered for their craft.

Yeah, well Jarman showed them how to act, how to die. And there were more to come.

A blaze of glory.

Finishing off DC Washington—the lucky pig bastard—in the middle of a busy ICU, and in broad daylight—would take some balls, but no one ever accused Jarman of lacking courage. Not anymore. Not since he'd done for the miserable toady, De Silva.

Things had gone pretty near perfect since that night at the Railway Cuttings. What did they say about never forgetting your first kill? Yep, his, no, *their* first kill—he shouldn't forget the "hired help"—turned out to be everything they all wanted. Everything they all hoped.

Such a buzz. But it didn't last.

Working as a team was okay at first, but it deflected the glory away from the main man. Jarman had to be at the centre of the movie, in glorious closeup. That's why he wrote Kurt and Vanessa out of the plot. They had to go. Especially after Kurt's ridiculous piece of improvisation. Making the reconstruction look like someone recognisable. What a stupid move. Unforgivable.

Unforgiven!

But he'd paid for it. Kurt and his partner in lunacy. They wouldn't be improvising anymore. No chance of that. Not now. Not ever.

Ha! What a blast.

Since De Silva, everything had gone pretty much according to plan. And what a plan. As intricate and exciting as the best screenplay ever penned. Only this wasn't a screenplay. This wasn't fiction. This was real life.

Life as he, *Donald* Jarman, directed it.

Even when Charlie Pelham turned up unexpectedly, pretending

he was raiding the old tart's flat, even that had worked out right in the end. He'd made it fit perfectly. It required a change to the screenplay, but that was okay. Not even the best of screenplays were set in concrete. They could be adapted and modified according to the way the director interpreted the action.

Seeing the fat fucker's belly explode in front of his eyes had been a total blast—literally, a blast. Never expected it to happen so fast. And the look on the greasy bugger's face the moment he realised he was already dead ... what a buzz. Orgasmic. But not literally. Jarman wasn't a sick pervert like some he'd met in the boy's home.

No. Not a pervert. An artist. An artistic director.

It had taken courage and a plan, and everything had gone well, but Washington ... a loose end. An unfinished scene in need of a tight edit. A dangling thread.

Jarman couldn't hold back a chuckle at the unintentional pun.

The newly rewritten ending would work out even better than the original.

White Heat!

Why hadn't he thought of it in the first place?

God, what a dream ending. And what a list of names to add to the final credits.

De Silva, Tomlinson, Poole, Pelham, Lang, and Étage. An impressive list which would grow that very afternoon.

Yep, he'd add Washington and Jones, and anyone else who happened to be close enough to end up as collateral damage. Every blockbuster had them. The uncredited extras who died for the greater glory of the film itself. The ultimate sacrifice for their art.

His snort boomed inside the crash helmet.

Jarman looked up at the cloud-dotted sky and the pale orange sun. After a squally start, it had turned into a beautiful day. A beautiful day to kill people. A whole load of people.

A beautiful day to die.

The list would expand today. The film of Jarman's life would end on a high.

"Top of the world, Ma, Pa," he repeated.

The ending would have been different if Jones had only been

smart enough to make the connection. It would have been more intimate. An Art House indie rather than a Summer Blockbuster, but so be it. The *White Heat* ending would work well enough, so long as he had the chance to make Jones squirm a little first. Jones needed to know *why* he had to die, *why* he had to suffer.

The end would come, but only on Jarman's terms.

Why hadn't the old fool worked it out yet? What was taking him so bloody long? Jarman had given him enough damn clues. The Triumph logo on the leather jacket should have nailed it, but no. The famous detective had forgotten all about it. Forgotten all about Triumph Way.

Typical.

Close the case and move on, that was Jones' MO. But not everyone had the chance to move on. Some ended up in a boys home at the mercy of thieves, rapists, and killers. Were it not for Arthur, little Jack Anderson wouldn't have survived the very first night.

Okay, so he may have been kidding himself. Not everything had gone to plan. Kurt's fuckup had thrown a spanner in the gearbox. Stupid arsehole. All he had to do was change a few zeros and ones and alter the reconstruction a little, but he had to play silly buggers. What the hell was he thinking of, making it look like someone so familiar? Andrew Craig, one of the university's most recognisable researchers? Almost anyone else would have done, but no, Kurt couldn't help himself. The dumpy Welshman, Armstrong, had wound him up from the moment he'd taken the job with Llewellyn, questioned his programming skills, not to mention his maths. So Kurt deliberately messed with Armstrong's head by making him think Craig was a goner.

Kurt may have found it funny watching the Welshman writhe, but Jarman didn't find it the least bit amusing. No effing way. Kurt's stupidity ended up pointing the finger right back at him. It meant Kurt had to go. And go he did. Both Kurt and his tart, Vanessa. Okay, so their deaths hadn't exactly been original. Jarman didn't have time to plan, so he'd returned to a trusted favourite, the one he'd used on Charlie Pelham. He'd reprised the John Hurt dining table scene from *Alien* and gutted the buggers. In the end, it had turned out okay with guts exploding from their bellies rather than an ugly baby alien.

In the trade, they called it the *money shot.*

The poster's strapline, "In space no one can hear you scream," appeared on the screen in his head. It was close, but should have read, "In a canal boat in the middle of nowhere, no one can hear you scream!"

Ha!

Pithy. Apt. Would anyone make the connection? Jones wouldn't. He'd be dead before anyone found the canal boat and its gory cargo. Long dead.

Good job Jarman had been there to record the kills in all their magnificence. His film would be a classic that nobody would ever see. Recorded, not on film or video or MP4, but in his memory. Indelible, even if short-lived.

Jarman sighed. As with all good things, it had to end.

Still, it had been a good life in the main. He's accomplished all he'd set out to do. Ending it in a blaze of glory would be fitting.

It would be a suitable tribute to Arthur, the man Jarman loved more deeply than his own father.

Arthur, yes. Dear, loving Arthur.

Ultimately, Jarman owed everything to him. His technical and directorial skills, his money, and his life. Everything.

Arthur had created his special movies for a highly selected audience—an audience who paid so very well—but Jarman wouldn't charge for his work. No, he'd give away his art for free. His final scene would reach a TV news audience of millions.

What a way to end it all, and he'd dedicate his last blockbuster to Arthur.

The world would finally know Arthur's true worth. A wonderful person who deserved the highest praise, not an unmarked grave in a prison plot.

Jarman sniffled back a tear.

He turned the key in the ignition and killed the Triumph's big brute of an engine. He locked the handlebars in place and set the alarm. Not that it mattered. With the *White Heat* ending, he didn't need a getaway vehicle, now, did he? Nope, not today.

Not ever.

Jarman removed the bike gloves, unclipped the chinstrap, and tugged the helmet from his head. The fresh air cooled the skin on his face. It felt so good. Invigorating. He raked his fingers through his hair, cut short at the back, left long on top, and dyed black especially for the scene. No one would mistake him for Jimmy Cagney, but that didn't matter. After all, how many people remembered *White Heat* anyway?

Philistines.

Jarman climbed from the bike, stowed the gloves inside the helmet, and the helmet inside the top box. He unzipped the leather jacket and draped it over the saddle. Wouldn't be needing it anymore. The green scrubs were creased and sweaty, but that was the point, right? He looked the part—that of the hard-worked junior doctor nearing the end of a thirty-six-hour weekend shift. The laminated identity pass hanging from the lanyard around his neck gave him All Areas Access to the hospital, including its "secure" Intensive Care Unit.

Secure?

Pathetic.

Insecure more like. Queen Elizabeth Hospital happened to run the weakest IT security system he'd ever had the desire to hack.

Okay. Time to call "action".

With tension mounting—the tension of excitement, not fear— he headed towards the rounded glass entrance and its wide automatic doors. Although he'd never been inside the hospital before, he knew exactly which way to go. The hospital's online emergency evacuation plan had been child's play to access and simple to navigate.

Smiling, he strode forwards, humming the harmonica theme from *Once Upon a Time in the West* in his head. He didn't hum it out loud in case he drew attention to himself.

Oh no, that would never do.

Not yet.

Chapter Forty-Eight

Queen Elizabeth Hospital, Edgbaston, Birmingham, UK

BY THE TIME JONES, Ben, and Phil reached the hospital, the carpark resembled a warzone, its main entrance blocked by emergency vehicles—most with blue lights flashing—their first-responder occupants already disgorged and carrying out their various designated roles.

A man wearing a fluorescent yellow tabard stood in the middle of the entrance, directing people out of the building. Nurses and porters were busy rolling patients in wheelchairs and beds to other entrances within the hospital grounds. Visitors and medical staff were being pointed towards the designated fire assembly areas. It looked chaotic, but it could have been worse. At least it had stopped raining.

Jones barged his way against the flow of foot traffic and towards the conductor, holding up his warrant card.

"DCI Jones, West Midlands Police," he said. "And you are?"

"Chief Officer Hughes, head of hospital security," the man answered, his expression stern. "Are you the one the madman's been screaming for?"

"I am." Jones pointed at Phil and the armed Ben, both of whom wore ballistic vests and baseball caps. "These two are with me. We know where we're going."

"Glad somebody does," Hughes said, giving them a stiff smile and waving them through. "Good luck."

"Thanks," Phil said.

On the way to the lifts, Jones' mobile buzzed. The caller ID showed *Not-Bob, Never-Bob*. He powered down the phone and returned it to his pocket.

"Shocking reception here," he said to Phil and Ben.

For the second time in as many weeks, Jones raced towards danger.

"YOU MUST BE MCINTYRE," Jones said to the only uniformed officer in the outer corridor leading to the surgical ICU. He kept his voice down.

The young man tried to appear calm, but he breathed hard and fast and kept looking towards the exit doors as though desperate to dive through them and make his way to safety.

"Yes, sir. I've evacuated everyone from the area except the doctor and Mr and Mrs Washington. They still refuse to leave."

"Okay, lad. Take it easy. I'm here now. How many patients are left in the ICU?"

"Including DC Washington, four. Dr Suresh begged him—Jarman, I mean—to let her take the other patients out, but he told her to … well, go forth and multiply." His lips stretched into a thin and apologetic smile.

"Dr Suresh, where is she now?"

"In the ICU monitoring room, sir, keeping an eye on the

patients. It's along the corridor, third door on the right, just ahead of the ICU."

"I know, son. Been here before. Mr and Mrs Washington?"

"Family waiting room, sir. Climbing the walls."

"Good. I'll take over from here. Report to Inspector Macklin in the car park. He could probably make use of another safe pair of hands."

"Yes, sir." McIntyre turned away, relieved.

"Well done, Constable," Jones called. "You did well here."

McIntyre stopped long enough to transform his frown into a tentative smile.

"Thank you, sir," he said and hurried away.

The exit doors squeaked closed behind McIntyre, leaving the wing empty and eerily quiet.

"At least someone's killed the bloody alarms," Phil said, standing with hands on hips and taking in the scene, but making sure to stay out of sight of the doors to the ICU.

"Did you have to use the word 'kill', sir?" Ben asked.

Phil winced and held out his hands. "Oops, my bad. What's your plan, boss?"

"I'll think of something," Jones said, trying to make it sound more confident than he felt.

Jones poked his head around the corner and took in the corridor leading to the ICU and the nurses' station that guarded it.

The windowless door to the monitoring room stood closed. He tried to remember its internal layout. Two chairs, a control desk with switches and dials, and a double bank of monitors—a pair for each bed. It also included a large window that looked into the six-bed ICU. It had been set-up so that anyone inside the monitoring room could see the whole of the ICU without craning their necks. On the downside, anyone inside the ICU would be able to see who was sitting inside the monitoring room, too. It wouldn't be a good idea for him to enter. On the other hand, Dr Suresh wasn't exactly tied to the monitoring desk.

Switches and dials.

Jones scratched his chin and read the time on the clock above the nurses' station. They didn't have long, minutes only.

"I've seen that look before," Phil whispered. "You've thought of something, right?"

"Might have."

"Care to clue me in?"

"No time. Jarman's expecting me any moment. Before I say hello, I need a quick word with Dr Suresh. Ben, you're with me."

"Anything I can do?" Phil asked, jaw tense, undoubtedly annoyed at being kept in the dark, again.

"Try talking Bryn and Jackie Washington into leaving."

"And if they won't?"

"You're bigger than both of them combined, Philip. Drag them out to the evac area kicking and screaming if you have to."

"Will do," he growled, anger burning in his eyes.

"And stay out there with them."

"What? And leave you and Ben in here having all the fun? Kidding, right?"

"That's an order, Detective Inspector Cryer," Jones snapped. "Don't you even think about breaking it. Am I clear?"

Phil hesitated for a moment before answering.

"Yes, sir," he said. "If you insist." He wanted to say something else but held off.

"I do, Philip. Now, go work your magic on the Washingtons."

Still reining in his anger, Phil turned away, heading for the waiting room four doors up from the nurses' station.

Jones took his turn to move.

Hugging the near wall to keep out of sight of the ICU doors, with Ben close behind, Jones made his way to the monitoring room. He knocked and waited. Nothing. He knocked again.

"Who's that?" Dr Suresh asked, her voice muffled by the heavy door.

He opened the door a crack and, keeping out of sight, whispered, "Dr Suresh, this is DCI Jones. We met the other day. Can you spare me a moment?"

Jones backed away.

The feet of a chair scraped on floor tiles. Moments later, the door opened fully and Dr Suresh appeared in the opening, worry etched on her tired face. She looked even more worn and haggard than the first time he'd seen her, but an underlying core of steel showed through the fatigue. A strength she would need.

"DCI Jones?" she asked. "He's been screaming for you."

"Well, I'm here now. What's he been doing?"

"He's opened the valves on all the backup oxygen cylinders. He's flooding the room with O2."

"Creating a firebomb?"

"Yes. I've isolated the main O2 feed into the ICU, and told maintenance to disconnect the main supply, but … I'm not sure what good it will do. There's enough O2 in the room to—"

"Where's Jarman now?"

She turned and glanced into the room.

"Standing over Mr Washington's bed, playing with his cigarette lighter. He's been rambling, talking to someone who isn't in the room. I'm not a psychiatrist, but I'd say he would appear to be in a dissociative state. I've seen something similar in patients suffering with PTSD. To be completely honest with you, Chief Inspector, the poor man might not even know where he is right now."

"Oh, he knows where he is alright. And don't waste your sympathy on him, Dr Suresh. That 'poor man' is responsible for at least six murders, and he fully expects to add us all to that list."

Suresh straightened her shoulders. "He is still worthy of our sympathy, Chief Inspector. He also mentioned someone called Arthur, saying how you murdered him. Is that true?"

Jones shook his head. "Not a bit of it. I'll tell you all I can when this is over. In the meantime, I wonder if you'd could do something for me?"

She frowned and tilted her head towards the room. The light from the monitors bathed her pallid face in grey.

"I don't … What can *I* do?"

He told her and she blanched.

"No, that's too dangerous. The patients—"

"I'm open to alternative suggestions, Dr Suresh. If you have any."

After a moment's hesitation, she shook her head.

"Your patients are relying on you," Jones said. "Don't let them down."

"I won't." Her words seemed confident, but they didn't match her doubtful expression.

"Dr Suresh," Jones said, holding up a hand, "need I remind you that the man in the ICU has murdered at least six people? He wants me dead and is prepared to take as many of those patients with him as he can. I can only think of one way to stop him. Will you help?"

She hesitated again before nodding.

"I-I'll do it. I hope you know what you're doing."

Me too.

Dr Suresh backed into the monitoring room. Jones pulled the door closed behind her.

"Did you hear all that, Ben?"

A man of few words, Ben nodded. He de-cocked the Glock 17, making it safe before returning it to its holster and buttoning the retaining strap.

"Good luck, sir," he whispered. "I'll be ready."

"Remember," Jones said, speaking slowly and as clearly as possible, "the doors to the ICU open *outwards*, not inwards. Pull, don't push."

In a different situation, Jones might have interpreted Ben's answering look as insolence. But he deserved the benefit of any doubt.

"Take care, sir."

"Always."

Chapter Forty-Nine

Queen Elizabeth Hospital, Edgbaston, Birmingham, UK

JONES CLOSED HIS EYES. An image floated into his head, an image of Ryan, lying in his hospital bed, fighting for his life, mere inches away from a serial killer.

Hang in there, lad. I want my Rover back. And I want you to hand it over in person.

He glanced behind him. Ben, standing with his back flat against the wall, gave him the thumbs up. At least one of them would be ready. God only knew if Jones would be.

Jones turned to Ben. "Is your phone on silent?"

Ben frowned. "Yes, sir."

Jones pulled the mobile from his pocket, powered it up, and dialled Ben's number. Ben accepted the call.

"Put it on mute," Jones whispered. "I'll keep him talking as long as possible. You never know, we might be able to draw a confession

393

out of the mad sod." Jones dropped the mobile into his breast pocket. "Can you still hear me?"

Ben pressed his phone against his ear and blocked his other ear with the flat of his hand. "Repeat that, sir."

"Can you still hear me?"

Ben dipped his head, but said nothing.

"Okay, I'm going in."

Jones closed his eyes and took a breath.

Get on with it, man.

He swallowed hard and rapped on the ICU door.

"Who's that?" Jarman yelled.

"It's me, DCI Jones. Can I come in?"

"Are you alone?"

"Yes."

"The limping blond prick with the fancy memory out there?"

"No, I promise."

"What about Ben, your guard dog?"

"He's at the far end of the hall, making sure we're not disturbed."

"And you," he called, slightly calmer, "are you armed?"

"No," Jones lied.

"Not carrying that telescopic truncheon of yours? The one you used to kill Ellis Flynn?"

"I didn't kill Ellis Flynn."

He told the truth. Hollie Jardine stabbed the paedophile— another of Buckeridge's disciples—in the back with his own knife, but Jones wasn't about to tell Jarman that.

"Liar! Arthur saw you!" Jarman screeched. "He saw you!"

"Jarman, wait. Look!"

Jones dipped a hand into his jacket pocket and removed the baton. He pulled open the left hand door with one hand and waved it in the gap.

"Listen."

He tossed the baton, underhand, behind his back. It clattered on the floor tiles and rattled until clanking to a stop against the leg of a trolly twenty metres down the corridor.

"Hear that, Jarman? I threw it away."

"Yeah, yeah. I heard," he answered, slightly more under control.

"Can I come in?"

"Yeah, come in, but do it slowly."

Jones pulled the door fully open.

"I'm coming. Easy does it."

A smiling, glassy-eyed Jarman stood over Ryan's bed, the severed tube of an oxygen cylinder in one hand, pointing at Ryan's face. He held a cigarette lighter in the other, flipping the lid open and closed, open and closed.

"Come in, Chief Inspector Jones," Jarman said, a beatific smile on his youthful face. "But keep your distance." He flicked open the lid of the lighter and rested his thumb on the flint wheel.

Jones stopped short of the first bed, its occupant, eyes closed, blissfully unaware of his proximity to death.

"What now, Jarman? Or would you prefer Biggles?"

The killer chuckled. "Actually, I prefer Jarman these days. You finally worked it out. How?"

"You shouldn't have attended that demonstration in Canary Wharf last month."

The manic chuckle stalled and turned into a sigh. "Ah, London. Surveillance capital of the world. Can't move a muscle without it being filmed by someone." He raised the lighter, used it to scratch the back of his ear, and returned it to the end of the tube, giving Jones no time to strike.

"Looking back," Jarman continued, "I can see how that might have been a mistake. Still, no use crying over—"

"We have pictures of you with your two friends, Kurt and Vanessa." Jones inched past the first bed and stopped at the second, this one empty. Not far. A few metres away, no more. But far enough.

Jarman's detached smile showed a complete lack of concern. He was in control, but barely.

"Was it really necessary for Kurt to destroy Llewellyn's life's work?"

Jarman shrugged. "Ah, dear Kurt. Always has been a bit difficult to read. No telling what he was going to do from one minute to the next. I mean that nonsense with the facial reconstruction. Of all the people he could have chosen, the idiot had to make it look like Dr Craig. What a doofus."

"He wanted to annoy Dr Armstrong?"

"Ah, you spotted that. Good. Very good. Armstrong could see right through Kurt's act. I mean, Kurt could no more design and build a new motherboard than you can type with more than two fingers."

"You built all the kit in the CFR lab?"

"'Course, I did. And I taught Kurt how to program the reconstruction algorithm. He was a quick study, but had no real skills in terms of innovation."

"What was Vanessa's role?"

"Ah, Vanessa," Jarman said, a sad smile forming, "poor confused Vanessa, who started life as Vincent"—he pronounced it in the French way, with the 't' silent—"but ended it as … Transgenders, I never could understand them, either. Anyway, 'Vanessa' was the muscle. Wiry strong, she was. Way stronger than Kurt and me. She always wanted to be a woman, and I promised to pay for her transition. The poor girl lapped it up. She'd have done anything for me, and even more for Kurt. Potty over him, she was. Fuck knows why. A mother hen thing, I imagine."

"You have the money?"

Jarman frowned. "'Course I do. Whatever you think of me, I'm no liar. Before Tomlinson let the inmates kill Arthur, the dear man gave me the access numbers to all his offshore accounts. Millions, there are. I'm a very rich man. Could have retired and lived the rest of my life in comfort."

"Why didn't you?" Jones asked, stealing another couple of feet.

Jarman scowled. "And how would that have helped Arthur's legacy? I wanted to provide an epitaph worthy of such a great man."

"Arthur Buckeridge was a paedophile and a serial killer," Jones said, leaving all emotion out of the statement.

Jarman's shoulders stiffened and his chin trembled. "Arthur was a wonderful, wonderful human being. He took care of his boys, especially his chosen ones. Boys like me and Ellis and Kurt. He protected us all. Loved us. Without him, the bigger boys would have—"

"Kurt and Venessa won't get away, you know. We will find them."

"Of course you will," Jarman said, the sly smile returning. "In fact, you'll find poor Kurt and Vanessa in a boat under a bridge on the Grand Union Canal, just outside Saltley. No rush though, they aren't going anywhere."

"You killed them?"

The madman's smile broadened.

"Oh, you are quick, Mr Jones. I'll give you that. I've been speaking about them in the past tense. Didn't you notice?"

Yes, I noticed.

Jones took another step.

"That's far enough!" Jarman shrieked. He moved the lighter closer to the hissing tube pointing at Ryan's face. The skin on Jarman's thumb compressed as he added more pressure to the flint wheel. "I've got a cigarette lighter, and I'm not afraid to use it!"

"I can see that, Jarman," Jones said, holding up his hands in surrender. "But before you do, can I ask a question?"

Jarman showed a petulant scowl and shook his head.

"Just the one, I promise."

The thumb pressure eased a fraction.

"Go on then," Jarman muttered, "I'll give you a few more seconds of life. But listen. If Inspector Danforth or any of his ARU goons try storming the ICU with their flash-bangs, this place will go up like a firework display on Bonfire Night." Another manic chuckle cut through the quiet.

"I know that, Jarman. No one's going to burst in on us, I promise. They wouldn't be rash … and dangerous."

"Yeah, we'll see. So, what's your question?"

Arms still raised, Jones stole another foot.

"Why did you make those modifications to the flats on the OTT? What was the point in that special concrete floor?"

"That's two questions, Mr Jones," Jarman said, through a gleeful smile, "but I'll give you a pass. It's simple, really. I'm a certified germophobe, didn't you know? Can't stand dirt and grime. When I took them over, they were filthy." He shuddered. "Couldn't have that. I needed them clean for my work. Spotless. You can't make true art in squalor.

"I intended for those flats to be my long term base of operations —and my recording studio—until the council finally pulled the towers down, but Arthur's murder changed all my plans."

Jones inched closer.

"Stop!" Jarman raised his arm. The cigarette lighter glinted. "I warned you, Mr Jones!"

"Don't do it, Jarman," Jones said, "or would you prefer *Jack?*"

"What?" Jarman stiffened. His thumb lifted from the flint wheel.

"*Jack Anderson!*" Jones shouted.

The emergency alarms screamed.

Jones dived forwards, arms outstretched.

Behind him, the doors opened outwards. Ben raced though, CO_2 fire extinguisher raised, discharge horn extended, already hissing and belching a cloud of white gas. Ice cold steam froze the back of Jones' head as he grappled with a squealing, howling madman.

The extinguisher clanged to the floor. Ben grabbed Jarman's right wrist and twisted. Jarman's animal screech drowned out the alarms.

Jones butted the bridge of Jarman's nose. The cigarette lighter dropped to the floor. The madman's eyes rolled up, his lids closed, and his head thumped to the floor. Resistance ended.

Moments later, the alarms cut off, and tinnitus rang loud in Jones' ears.

"Wha' … What's … goin' on?"

Above Jones, a bed creaked, an arm movement drew his attention.

Ryan? It can't be.

"You got this, Ben?" Jones asked above the buzz still affecting his hearing.

"Yes, sir," Ben said, unclipping a pair of handcuffs from his belt. "Jarman's going nowhere."

Jones pushed away from the prisoner and scrambled to his feet. He stood over the bed.

"Ryan?"

Swollen eyes flickered open in a bruised and bandaged face.

"Ryan?" Jones repeated. "Did you say something?"

"Hi, boss," Ryan said, lids drooping, face slack. "Bloody ... c-cold in ... here. And who's ... Jack Anderson?"

Chapter Fifty

SUNDAY 28TH MAY – Early Evening

Bromford, Birmingham, UK

JONES PULLED the Škoda to a stop as near to the Cryers' semi-detached house in the residential area of Bromford as he could—a two-minute fast walk. His usual spot had been taken by a pearl white Toyota C-HR Hybrid. Nice, if you liked that kind of thing. He'd barely grown accustomed to the Škoda and definitely wasn't in the market for a Japanese SUV. He studied the slate-grey sky through the windscreen. The clouds hid the sun and a gentle breeze shook the leaves in the copper beech trees lining the road.

Jones yawned long and hard and, being alone, revelled in the luxury of a private, back-arching stretch. He didn't even bother to cover his mouth. The previous week had been a non-stop carousel ride of prisoner interviews, taking witness statements, attending briefings with the brass, making media presentations, report writing, and more bloody paperwork than he could handle. It only ended when they delivered a report to the CPS which actually passed their infamous "full code test". On Friday morning at 11:37, they finally charged Jonathan "Jack" Anderson, aka Donald Jarman, aka Holden Bigglesworth, with multiple counts of murder, one count of attempted murder, and numerous other offences, including domestic terrorism.

They had been long, long days with precious few breaks and many hours of lost sleep. He could barely keep his eyes open. For a fleeting moment, he toyed with the idea of calling to cancel, firing up the car, and heading for home, but that wasn't an option. The last thing in the world he wanted to do was upset Manda who would have spent the best part of the weekend prepping a wonderful meal. Apart from that, he hadn't seen Jamie or little Paulie for a while and his usual carefully chosen "Uncle David presents" rested in the carrier bag on the passenger seat, alongside two bottles of a rather nice claret.

He slapped his cheeks awake, pushed open the car door, and accepted the auditory assault of the traffic rumbling from the nearby Spaghetti Junction—an integral part of the city's raucous and incessant symphony.

The Škoda's door opened with its usual vacuumed pop. Jones climbed out and returned the nods of the elderly couple walking a pair of sausage dogs.

"Evening," he said, pushing his bonhomie to its limit.

He locked the car, turned towards the setting sun, and started walking.

THE GARDEN GATE closed easily on well-oiled and correctly fitted hinges. Jones smiled. Phil—the world's least adept DIYer—must have hired a carpenter. Spending his inspector's salary wisely. He picked his careful way along the path, stepping around the discarded plastic toys. The front door looked smart with its crisp coat of green paint and new chrome furniture. Jones pressed the bell and the door opened instantly to a pair of bright-eyed, smiling children.

"Uncle David!" they squealed in unison.

Jamie stood back, giving way to Paul, who held up both arms for a carry. Jones obliged and soon had the little lad wriggling and giggling in his tickling embrace.

Manda appeared in the hallway behind them, her smile only slightly less brilliant than those of her offspring.

Jones held up the carrier bag and nodded to Paul.

"Hi, Manda. I'd give you a hug, but ...."

"I can take that for you, Uncle David," Jamie said, offering her hands.

"It's quite heavy, lass."

"It's okay. I'm really strong. Feel." She held up her right arm, flexed her elbow, and bunched her little biceps.

"Let me check."

Jones handed the bag to Manda, reached out, and tickled her ribs. Her giggles made Paul chuckle and ask for the same. They also made Jones smile, his fatigue pressed into the background.

"Come through," Manda said, "Phil's out back struggling with the barbeque."

"I'm not struggling with anything," Phil called from the back garden. "This thing's working a treat. Come on out, David."

"A barbie?" Jones said, trying to maintain the smile. "How wonderful."

"Don't worry, David," Manda said, moving close enough to whisper and still be heard above the children's infectious laughter, "I'll be supervising. No raw burgers with charcoal crusts in this house."

"Thank heavens for that." He winked.

In the hall, Manda stopped and peeked into the bag.

"David," she said, "you don't have to bring these little monsters presents every time you pop over."

"I'm not an 'ickle monster," Paul said, sticking out his lower lip.

"Neither am I, Uncle David," Jamie added, using her serious face, the one that made her look even more like her mother..

"Aren't you?" Jones scratched his chin. "And what's wrong with giving my favourite little monsters tiny gifts? There are a couple of bottles in the bag for the grownups. Or should I take them back, too?"

"Okay, David. Point taken." Manda lowered the carrier to the kitchen surface and pointed him through the French doors and onto the patio. "Go on through. Our other guests are looking forward to seeing you."

Inwardly, Jones groaned.

"Other guests?"

The well-meaning Manda Cryer had been trying to match him up with her single girlfriends for years, and every time it had been a disaster.

"Don't look so horrified, David. It's Robyn and Zach. And Robyn's mother."

"Ah," he said, mouth already drying. "I see."

Jones kissed the top of Paul's head, lowered him to the floor, and he raced towards his mother, arms up again.

Fickle things, children.

"You should have told me. If I'd known, I'd have—"

"Phoned to cancel?"

Possibly.

"Not at all. Wouldn't dream of it. I'd have picked up another bottle of wine and maybe something for the lad."

And he'd have put on a dress shirt rather than the polo shirt he currently wore. At least he'd made time for a proper shave before leaving his cottage.

He raked his fingers through his overlong hair. It needed a trim. Maybe next week.

"Do I look respectable enough?" he whispered.

Manda's eyes sparkled.

"David, you darling."

He tried to swallow, but a dry throat wouldn't cooperate.

"Sorry?"

"You've never asked that before. You like Robyn, don't you."

"She's a colleague and I wouldn't want to embarrass you in front of your guests by turning up looking like a vagrant."

She reached out and touched his upper arm. "You've never been scruffy in your life."

You never saw me in the bad days.

"Thank you, Manda, but what do you think? Am I okay?" He waved his hands in front of his body.

Manda leaned forwards and kissed his cheek. "You look great. Now, out you go. Your audience awaits."

ROBYN, a picture in a knee-length summer dress and low sandals, sat next to Jones, sipping her second glass of tonic water and lemon —no alcohol since she was driving. The youngsters were in bed, delighted by the books Jones had brought, and even more so when he'd tucked them in and read them the opening chapter of *The Wind in the Willows*. Robyn allowed Zach, a quiet and introspective twelve-year-old racing towards his teens—to stay up a little later.

With Manda's help, Phil made a first class job of the barbie. Everyone had eaten their fill, Jones had tossed a healthy green salad, and they'd emptied both bottles of claret.

At nine-thirty, Robyn's mother, Glenys, stood. "And now, I'm afraid, it's time to leave."

"Do we have to?" Zach asked.

"Yes, dear. You have school tomorrow."

For the first time that evening, the lad scowled. "But it's just getting to the interesting part."

Jones tried to hide his disappointment. He glanced at Robyn, who made no effort to stand.

"What interesting part?" Glenys asked.

"The part where the grownups start discussing the Poster Boy case."

"Zachary Spence," Robyn scolded—she all but wagged an index finger at him, "have you been on the internet again? Remember what I said about boundaries?"

"No, Mum. The boys in school were saying how the police

arrested the Poster Boy serial killer, and since you're an FSI and Mr Jones and Mr Cryer are detectives, I thought—"

"That's enough, Zachary," Glenys said. "It's close to your bedtime. Say goodnight to everyone."

"Are you staying, Mum?"

"Only for a little while. I want to discuss the Poster Boy case, too." She grinned at the lad.

"Oh, Mu-um!"

After a desultory round of "Goodnights", Zach finished by kissing his mother's cheek and stopping in front of Jones. "It was very nice to meet you, sir." He held out his hand.

Jones stood and they shook like grownups.

"Nice meeting you too, Zach."

Glenys took her grandson by the hand and led him away.

"A well-behaved young chap," Jones said to Robyn. "You must be very proud of him."

She grinned. "He has his moments. As for that last part, Mum and I have been coaching him to say that all day. It's earned him an extra hour on the Xbox next weekend."

"Bribery and corruption? Not sure I can condone that sort of behaviour."

"He deserves it, poor lad."

"Did you come in two cars?"

"No, just the one. We have the Toyota."

"The white one outside?"

"Yes, the C-HR."

"Lovely car," he said, only part-lying. "How are you getting home?"

"I'll take a taxi. It's not far."

"Wouldn't hear of it. I'll drive you … if you like."

Judging by her raised eyebrows, his spontaneous offer took them both by surprise.

"Thank you, that would be lovely."

Jones caught Phil and Manda exchanging knowing and delighted looks, but at least they had the good sense to keep their thoughts to themselves.

"Talking of cars," Phil said, "why didn't you come in the Rover?"

"I don't have it yet."

"Why not? First thing Ryan said when they let us visit, was that he and his dad had finished the rebuild."

"Yes. He said the same to me the moment Ben dragged Jarman out of the ICU. Wouldn't stop talking. I almost asked Dr Suresh to put him back into the coma."

"David!" Manda admonished. "That's a horrible thing to say."

"I'm kidding. The only reason I didn't give the lad a bearhug was that I didn't want to hurt him."

Jones didn't tell them he nearly burst into tears at Ryan's near-miraculous recovery. Too much information of that sort might make him look weak. He didn't want to appear like a wimp in front of Robyn, nor did he want to give Phil any more ammunition for his ridiculous jibes.

"So, why *haven't* you picked up the Rover?" Manda asked.

Jones scratched at the itch on his earlobe.

"I told Ryan to hold onto it until he could drive it to me himself."

"That's a bit harsh," Phil said.

Although he owned a brain with the processing and memory power of a small planet, he didn't always use the thing to its optimal level.

"Is it?"

"Phil," Manda said, slapping the back of his hand. "You can be really thick, sometimes."

"Sometimes?" Jones asked.

"An incentive," Robyn announced. "You wanted to give him an incentive to get better."

Jones nodded. She understood him so well.

"I did. Assuming he needed one. He has an awful lot of rehab ahead of him."

"Don't envy him that," Phil said, rubbing his knee. "Not one bit."

Manda squeezed the hand. "But it's worth it, right?"

"It is."

Robyn raised her glass and grimaced. "I've been on this stuff all evening, but since I don't have to drive home, might I have a nightcap?"

Phil jumped to his feet. "What can I get you?"

"A small red wine would be lovely."

"Coming right up." Phil hurried into the kitchen to do the honours.

Jones took his final sip. Two small glasses was his limit since he had to drive precious cargo home.

"Mind if I have a cuppa, Phil?" he called.

Phil popped his head through the open kitchen window. "Won't be long. Manda?"

"Coffee please."

"On its way."

While their host filled the kettle and rattled dishes in the kitchen, Jones fell silent and forced himself not to cast sideways glances at the lovely woman sitting to his left. It wasn't easy. He gazed up at the moonless sky. Light pollution in the city killed any chance of seeing stars this early in the evening. Not even Sirius, the Dog Star, could make it through the haze—and the broken cloud cover.

"David?" Robyn said, making him jump.

"Yes?"

"Mind if I ask you a question about the case?"

"What case?" he asked, pretending ignorance.

"David!" Manda said, in full scolding mode.

"Sorry. Answering a question with another question's a bad habit of mine. Please ask away."

"How did you get Biggles to confess?"

"His real name's Jack Anderson, but he prefers to go by Jarman these days. And I didn't do anything much."

"But I heard he started by screaming police brutality."

Jones rubbed the spot above his left eye where his headbutt connected with Jarman's nose. The swelling had reduced to the size of a garden pea.

"He soon calmed down when I walked him through our case

and played him the phone recording Ben made. It didn't take him long to start talking. And when he did, his solicitor couldn't get him to stop. He ranted on about how Arthur Buckeridge looked after him as a youngster when he first arrived in the boys' home. Took him under his wing. Jarman actually considers Buckeridge to be one of the best film directors never to have won an Oscar."

"Even though the paedo only shot snuff films," Phil said, carrying a tray full of drinks from the kitchen. "The guy's a total loon."

"Who, Jarman or Buckeridge?" Manda asked.

"Both," Jones answered for Phil. "It's difficult to tell who was worse. Buckeridge tortured and chopped up young girls for money, and Jarman killed people in tribute to his mentor. No one was safe, not even his partners."

"Kurt and Vanessa, you mean?" Robyn asked.

"I do."

"You didn't work the canal boat, did you?" Manda asked Robyn, who shook her head.

"Nope," Phil said, "the second stringers had that dubious pleasure."

Robyn showed another of her captivating smiles. "My team were concentrating on the evidence from the flats on the OTT. One of the blood samples turned out to be from a prostitute and another from a drug—"

"Whose names have yet to be released," Phil said, wagging a finger at Robyn.

They discussed the case and its ramifications for another two hours. The whole time Jones tried, and failed, to think of a way to wrap the evening up early. Not due to fatigue, but because he couldn't wait to drive Robyn home. It would be their first real time alone.

At least, it would be their first real time alone, without having to share the space with a slowly rotting corpse.

The END

DCI Jones Series

Please Leave a Review

PLEASE LEAVE A REVIEW

If you enjoyed Perfect Record, it would mean a lot to Kerry if you were able to leave a review. Reviews are an important way for books to find new readers. Thank you.

About Kerry J Donovan

ABOUT KERRY J DONOVAN

#1 International Best-seller with *Ryan Kaine: On the Run*, Kerry was born in Dublin. He currently lives in a cottage in the heart of rural Brittany. He has three children and four grandchildren, all of whom live in England. As an absentee granddad, Kerry is hugely thankful for the advent of video calling.

Kerry earned a first class honours degree in Human Biology, and has a PhD in Sport and Exercise Sciences. A former scientific advisor to The Office of the Deputy Prime Minister, he helped UK emergency first-responders prepare for chemical attacks in the wake of 9/11. He is also a former furniture designer/maker.

Printed in Great Britain
by Amazon

28414103R00236